CLUB RIO BRAVA

CONTROLLED BY *Love*

ANN JACOBS

Ellora's Cave
Romantica Publishing

What the critics are saying...

ജ

4 1/2 Hearts "The author does a wonderful job of building each scene, taking her time and vividly describing in detail the characters, the plot, the scenery, and the situations that create the fast pace of this red hot plot. The love scenes are a cross between heart pounding, burn up the sheets sexy hot and an enchanting, emotionally riveting feast of spiritual delight that enhances the reading pleasure of this tale. If you are looking for a delicious treat to spice up your reading pleasure look no further than this wonderful story." ~ *The Romance Studio*

4 1/2 Hearts "The sexual adventures are deliciously scorching hot and the edgy BDSM play emphasizes the enjoyment that both the hero and heroine get from sex that includes a whole lot of kink and major fun! This book is a true delight to read that has a great deal of heart and sensitivity to it and lots and lots of thrills. I am anxiously awaiting book three in this wonderfully entertaining series." ~ *The Romance Studio*

4 Hearts "Ann Jacobs is a master at crafting memorably erotic stories brimming over with tender touches, smoking hot characters, and sizzling seduction that play with women's fantasies. I can't wait to see what's next for this amazing author." ~ *The Romance Studio*

5/5 Rating "This book brings home the fact that where there's love and a will; a couple can make a go of their life together despite the outside influences which include work and children. This series is a keeper! Don't miss any of them." ~ *Romance Junkies Reviews*

An Ellora's Cave Romantica Publication

www.ellorascave.com

Controlled by Love

ISBN 9781419959394

Edited by Sue-Ellen Gower.
Cover art by Syneca.

This book printed in the U.S.A. by Jasmine-Jade Enterprises, LLC.

Trade paperback Publication September 2009

CONTROLLED BY LOVE

LOVING CONTROL

ഇ

Trademarks Acknowledgement

ഇ

The author acknowledges the trademarked status and trademark owners of the following wordmarks mentioned in this work of fiction:

Dr. Phil: Peteski Productions, Inc.

JAMA: American Medical Association

Oprah: Harpo, Inc.

Velcro: Velcro Industries B.V. LTD

Prologue

ꙮ

Trauma surgeon Elijah Calhoun squelched the need that nearly took his breath away when he walked Margaret back to University Hospital's physicians' lot, kissed her briefly, helped her into her car and watched her drive away. As much as he'd like to, he wasn't about to get off on the wrong foot by putting the moves on third-year resident Margaret Berman even though the ache in his cock almost made him reconsider.

Up until now he'd kept their relationship professional, as an attending's should always be with the residents on his service. But they'd both needed to unwind after the long, dicey surgery, and now it was three a.m. A haunting melody floated from the nearby lounge where they'd just shared a drink and danced, its frankly sexual lyrics firing his libido even more. Holding her, feeling her warmth beneath his hands, imagining he was caressing smooth skin and not a set of scratchy scrubs, had felt good. Right. Damn, it scared him how having her in his arms had fed his libido in a way not even the most experienced subs at his club outside San Antonio had been able to do lately.

The chilly night breeze, typical of fall in south central Texas, made Eli shiver. It had been a hell of a night for him, too. He should have sent Margaret straight home when they'd finished the case but she'd looked so drained. Unusually vulnerable, as if the tight control she maintained at work had suddenly snapped and she needed a friend to hold her. He told himself that was why he'd asked her to dance and why, when she'd tilted her head back and smiled up at him, he'd kissed her.

The heady taste, the softness of her lips, had left their marks on his mind. It had started out innocently, a brief meeting of lips as they swayed to the tune of something mellow, slow and sexy. But she'd responded as though she was starving. As though she needed a man, wanted *him*. He'd managed to keep the kiss practically platonic until she ran her tongue along the seam of his lips, tangling it with his as soon as he opened up and let her in.

He'd been shocked at the instant sexual tension that crackled between them when she tangled their tongues with an enthusiasm he'd never have expected, never have dared to initiate. He'd gone instantly hard, was still painfully aroused.

You should have followed her home. If you had, you wouldn't be hurting now. As he climbed into his own car and started the engine, he regretted momentarily that he hadn't. But then he thought about his lifestyle and tried in vain to imagine Margaret as the submissive of his wildest fantasies. It didn't compute. She was too competent, too controlled. For all he knew, she might be a Domme. She certainly hadn't been shy about initiating that French kiss.

If he wasn't mistaken, and he didn't think he was, he'd felt something on her tongue. Not a ring or anything he would definitely have noticed if she wore one at work, but rather a small plastic disk resting on her tongue. A tongue piercing retainer? Seemed damned out of character for Margaret to have one, but he'd felt it again when they kissed goodnight beside her car.

Could he have read Margaret wrong all this time? Eli doubted that. Although he hadn't seen much of her outside the hospital setting, she sure as hell gave everybody there the impression that she never let go, never let emotions override reason. Still…none of the vanilla dates he'd kissed had ever had a pierced tongue.

Get Margaret Berman out of your head. Eli sat for a few minutes, listening to the hum of the engine and trying to quit picturing Margaret going all soft and submissive, responding to his orders in the bedroom the way she did when he stood behind her in the OR and instructed her on a new technique for reinflating a collapsed lung.

Damn. It was too late to go home. He'd no more than get there before having to come back here again. He'd catch a few hours' sleep on the couch in his office. He turned off the car and got out, hit once more by the hot, dry August air. Letting out a breath, consciously pushing Margaret from his mind, he crossed the street to a glass-and-chrome building. Gleaming, contemporary and imposing, the place represented professional and financial success. Something Eli noticed after having spent the past six years working out of the house staff's offices at a series of military hospitals.

He glanced up at the prominent but tasteful logo that had been set into the chrome just last week. *Blackstone, Silverman, Calhoun and Associates, P.A. Trauma Surgery and Rehabilitation.* Eli had worked too damn long and hard to get this far in his profession. He'd repaid the Air Force for having put him through medical school and had earned a partnership in one of the best-known trauma associations in Texas. There was no way he'd risk his future to make a pass at a resident assigned to his service. Not unless he knew for a fact she wanted the same thing he did.

Not for the first time, Eli envied his senior partners Kurt Silverman and Mark Blackstone for having gorgeous, loving wives and a handful of kids between them.

Chapter One

A month later

ꟹ

The fates must have known she'd be covering the thoracic surgery service tonight, alone except for two green first-year residents. All the post-op patients seemed to be resting well, and that was what third-year resident Margaret Berman was about to do. She stationed the junior residents to keep watch over their sleeping patients, grabbed a blanket from the warming cabinet in Recovery and headed to the residents' sleeping lounge to get what she hoped would be a few hours' uninterrupted sleep.

She sank onto a narrow cot, enjoyed the quiet as she took off her shoes and massaged tired feet. The pillow beckoned. Just how long had it been since she had any sleep? Unfolding the warmed blanket, she wrapped it around her and lay down, her eyelids heavy.

The sound of a siren in the distance penetrated the thick concrete walls of the hospital suite, resounded in her ears. Margaret slid further under her blanket, prayed the impending emergency wouldn't be for her. Told herself serious chest traumas couldn't possibly happen twice in the same twenty-four hours. And she'd scrubbed in just before noon with senior attending, Eli Calhoun, on what had been a fatal gunshot wound.

They'd lost the burly SWAT team leader despite making every effort to save him. She'd managed to hold on to her emotions, follow Eli's lead. She'd even gotten a tight hold on her feelings and gone through the rest of her day, hopefully without anyone noticing the slight tremor in her hands, the sheen of unshed tears that blurred her vision. Maybe someday she'd be able to handle losing a patient better, so long as she knew the team had done its best.

Eli Calhoun was definitely the best when it came to chest traumas. The burly surgeon never hesitated, went straight to the problem, faster and more painstakingly than she'd have believed anybody with his huge hands could manage. She remembered that night a month or so ago when he'd comforted her after another case, his incredible control, the hard heat of his big body when they'd danced at a nearby club.

The kiss she'd wished would go on forever but known mustn't happen again.

He must have felt that way, too, because he'd kept their conversations strictly business, the physical contact limited to a steadying hand on her shoulder, his hands on hers as he'd shown her how to tie off an artery that had kept slipping away from her.

Stop it, now. The last thing you need to do is lose sleep over a man you can't have. No matter how masterful he seemed when he'd known she needed company to hold on to her sanity that night.

She'd just buried her head under the covers and quieted the sense of foreboding when a strident voice boomed over her pager. "Dr. Berman. Emergency Room. Stat."

Instantly awake, Margaret shoved her feet in her shoes and sprinted for the elevator, running her fingers through her mussed curls as she went.

So much for the fates.

Tim Case, the orthopedic resident on call, was already there, barking orders to nurses. A man lay on a gurney, desperately pale even though a nurse was pushing whole blood. Margaret could see his femur was shattered, the leg bent at a grotesque angle. "'Bout time you got here, sleepyhead. We've got to get this guy to surgery quick, or he'll bleed out. Bullet nicked the femoral artery."

She stepped closer, saw what looked like an entry wound high on the patient's chest. Blood seeped out, obscenely red against the pallor of his skin. "X-rays?"

A nurse snapped two films into readers. Not even a first-year med student could have missed a flattened bullet lodged in the pericardium, or the one that had turned his leg into a shattered mess. Margaret assessed her choices. There weren't any. If this patient was to have any chance at all, they had to get him to surgery right away, stop the bleeding in his leg and get that bullet out of his chest. "Get him to surgery, and put in a call for a senior attending. Tim?"

"Dr. Silverman's on his way," the ER charge nurse said when she poked her head through the door.

Lucky Tim. Maggie turned to her. "Try to reach Dr. Calhoun." If there was a God, Eli would be somewhere close by, like in his office across the street. Fat chance. He'd told her after the case this afternoon that he was off call for the first time in weeks. He'd mentioned something about chilling at his cabin, catching some fish. Why had Jerry, the fellow in thoracic surgery who'd ordinarily get summoned for a case like this, picked this week to go interview for a new job in Hawaii? "We'd better go scrub."

The elevator seemed to take forever, its low groan punctuating the panic building in her gut. *You can do it.* Maggie repeated that in her head, a mantra. Or was it a case of false bravado? *You've cracked chests before.*

But not when five minutes' time might mean the difference between life and death.

When the elevator finally ground to a halt, she took a deep breath, settled down. She'd manage. She had to. The motions long ago memorized, she switched out of her clothes and hurried into OR Three where several nurses and the anesthesiologist were prepping their patient. "Please try to contact Dr. Calhoun again," she told the circulating nurse as she started to scrub her hands and arms.

When she looked down, she realized she'd scrubbed them nearly hard enough to draw blood. No matter. Holding out her arms for gloves, and letting a circulating nurse tie on her gown, she shoved aside her trepidations and stepped up to the table.

"He's out," the anesthesiologist said.

None too soon. This was her show now. Hers and the orthopedic surgeon's who had already opened the leg wound. She drew on the remoteness, the self-control she'd learned to rely on early, when she'd been trying to please her demanding parents.

"Scalpel," she said, holding out her hand and feeling the satisfying smack of the small instrument when it hit her palm. And so it began, the small line of blood marking the spot for the cut, the whir of the bone saw, its heaviness in her hands reminding her how a big man—Eli—was far more suited for this particular job than she. Finally, she had the patient's chest cracked, barely registering the anesthesiologist's voice when he told a scrub nurse to hang another unit of blood. It had only been a few minutes, but it seemed like hours since she'd made that first, tentative cut.

* * * * *

Eli wasn't with it tonight. Not really. As badly as he needed to pour out his frustration into the dark-haired sub he'd chosen when he walked into the cool, dark atmosphere of Club Rio Brava, it wasn't working.

Six months ago, when he was still in the Air Force, he would have relished this very private BDSM playroom a radiologist had built years ago on some rural property he'd inherited. But he wouldn't have been able to afford belonging to it then, had to satisfy himself by doing mask and leather at a club in a town as far away as possible from the base, and hope no one ever saw him coming or going.

Now that he'd gotten a good start in private practice, Eli had jumped on the chance of joining a BDSM club where he could show his face and have no fear that any of the other members might out him. Each member had as much need for privacy as the next, similar professional reputations to protect. Nobody had to worry, either, about being seen coming or going because the place was in the country near Riomedina, close enough to get back to San Antonio in a half-hour or less but isolated by acres of land owned by the club and sold in parcels to members who wanted to build a weekend home. He'd bought his own place down the road, where he often went to relax and fish in the river.

Tonight, though, he was having a hard time immersing himself in sensation, letting go of the other Eli who'd just lost a battle of a different kind to a warrior more powerful than he. He hated losing control, and he'd lost it big time in the OR. SWAT team leader Elton Gaskins shouldn't have died. His supposedly bulletproof vest should have kept that steel-tipped bullet from penetrating his chest. But it hadn't, and Gaskins had died twenty minutes into the desperate surgery meant to find and plug the bullet hole. Ever since facing Gaskins' sobbing widow a few minutes later and telling her Elton hadn't made it, Eli hadn't been able to shake an unfamiliar feeling of inadequacy. Half of him was back at the hospital, going over the OR report, trying to see if they could have done anything different to save the man's life.

Strong men don't cry.

Eli hadn't. Not then. He'd managed to hold his emotions in check, feign strength in the face of the widow's tears. Later he'd sequestered himself in a shower stall in the surgeons' lounge and tried to pretend the hot, salty trickle of fluid down his cheeks was nothing more than errant spray from the shower head.

After seeing patients in his office and doing a workout at the gym that should have left him drained, he'd come directly here and chosen his sub from a handful of unattached women.

He hadn't even bothered to change into one of the leather costumes he kept in his locker here. No need to bother. He was in no mood tonight for complex scenes or ménages. He'd immediately brought his partner to pleasure with his hands and mouth. No toys, no restraints. Just raw sensation. The giving of satisfaction to another human being, the same physical release she now was trying to bring him. Eli closed his eyes, trying hard to concentrate on the arousing heat of the woman's mouth on his cock, the tickle of her damp breath against his groin, the softness of her fingertips when she rolled his testicles between them.

It wasn't working. Not that his partner wasn't trying, because she was on her knees before him, her slender fingers digging into his ass, her mouth working his cock with practiced skill. He sank his fingers into the silky mass of her hair, watched another couple—married to each other, if their matching wedding bands meant anything—playing out a scene that had started with the guy doing some damn competent work with a cat o' nine. It was winding up now, her husband and another Dom fucking her cunt and ass while she lay suspended in a rope contraption that left her open for the double onslaught.

What he was seeing and feeling should have had him ready to go off. Hell, he should have come by now from nothing more than the blowjob that was getting more intense with every passing minute.

But he wasn't. Not at all. When he looked at his enthusiastic partner, he thought of Margaret Berman, imagined her pierced tongue running along the pulsating blood vessels on his cock, wondered if she was having a quiet night on call. When he imagined himself losing his cool, crawling into her narrow cot in the residents' sleeping room and mastering her there, his cock finally came to full attention.

"More," he growled, tangling his hands in the silky strands of the sub's hair and encouraging her to deep-throat him. Her increasing ardor sluggishly raised his own. He might actually come and manage not to shame himself by rewarding her efforts. "That's it. Suck me hard. Make me come."

The beeper he'd set on a nearby window ledge suddenly went off. Its rattler-like vibration against the well-seasoned wood immediately turned his mind away from the faceless woman giving him head. "Stop, sweetheart. Duty calls."

Just as well. His heart wasn't in the game. Not only because he couldn't stop dwelling on that crumpled, brittle widow and her four fatherless kids. Or hearing the echoes of her wails or seeing the stark pain in eyes glistening with tears.

It wasn't just that. He hadn't been "on" with his sex partners for a while.

Maybe it had more to do with wanting a particular woman he dared not take. When Eli thought about it, he was pretty sure his sexual paralysis had happened that day when Margaret Berman kissed him and awakened fantasies that would never come to fruition.

Eli pulled up his pants, hurried to his SUV, started the powerful engine and merged into light freeway traffic. Damn, for early fall, it was unusual to encounter this all-encompassing fog. He stepped on the gas, figuring the best he could do was cut the usual forty-minute drive to thirty, even though from what the ER charge nurse had said, he guessed the patient might not make it until he got into the OR.

And Margaret was on call. She was the one up to her elbows with no backup in sight, hiding her fear behind a veneer of iron control.

Even though he knew Margaret was a competent surgeon and that she'd maintain her cool no matter what. Only the sweat on her brow would hint she wasn't fully confident, fully in control. He'd be sweating too. Gunning the engine, Eli held on to the wheel, watched the speedometer creep up to a hundred m.p.h., then backed off to eighty-five. He wouldn't do Margaret or the patient any good if he killed his crazy self.

"Call surgery," he said as he pulled off the outer loop and headed for the hospital.

"This is Dr. Calhoun. I'll be at the hospital in less than five minutes," he said when the OR night supervisor came on the line.

* * * * *

Margaret could do this. She had to. Where was Eli? The OR supervisor had sent word that he was on his way. And where was the circulating nurse? Margaret blinked. "Wipe!" she snapped as sweat rolled off her forehead into her eyes. "I need more retraction." She could barely see the tear in the pericardium for the rapidly darkening pool of blood obscuring the operative field, couldn't tell how far the bullet had been sucked into the victim's heart. It didn't help her concentration, listening to Chief of Orthopedic Surgery Kurt Silverman fire instructions to his resident who was desperately trying to help staunch bleeding from the patient's shattered femoral artery.

"Cardiac arrest!" The anesthesiologist's voice carried the usual controlled terror that accompanied such unplanned crises in surgery.

Both OR teams stepped back from the table. Margaret reached for the defibrillator paddles as Eli stepped up, paddles in hand. "Easy there. I've got it. Stand clear!" Once, twice, three times, he shocked the patient's heart. Nothing.

He'd come. She'd known somehow that he would. His take-charge presence served to slow the racing of her pulse, although her breathing became as erratic as the read-out on the cardiac monitor had been before the patient arrested. She stared down at the dying man, watched his body shudder with each jolt of electricity. *I've killed him. As surely as if I were the one who'd put that bullet through his chest wall.*

She wondered if her fellow resident felt the same overwhelming guilt that flowed through her. Probably not. After all, Tim was male and about to finish his orthopedics residency. Besides, he was busy holding a tourniquet on the patient's thigh while she was standing back, doing nothing but taking in the tragic scene.

"Blood flow's slowing down," Dr. Silverman said, his tone serious.

"I know." Eli shook his head, stepping back from the table. "He's gone." A defeated scowl on his ruggedly handsome face, he followed Dr. Silverman out of the suite, leaving Margaret to suture the gaping chest wound while Tim closed up the leg. No need for finesse now. This corpse, victim of a drive-by shooting, was headed to the autopsy table.

"Time of death, eleven-forty-one p.m.," the anesthesiologist said, his gaze on the pristine white clock hanging on one pale green tile wall. "Sorry 'bout that. Shit happens, but everybody did their best."

Numb, Margaret followed Tim from the OR, leaving the nursing staff to finish readying the body for the morgue.

Mechanically, she stripped off her bloody scrubs, showered and dressed. She started to shrug into a fresh lab coat but changed her mind. Rounds could wait until morning. For tonight at least, she'd had enough of hospitals and death and dying.

Come on, Margaret. You did your best.

Her best hadn't been good enough. "You could have saved him if you'd been here from the first," she told Eli when they practically collided a few minutes later in the surgeons' lounge. "Not that I resent you having a night off now and then." The last thing she wanted was to hang a guilt trip on him when it was all her fault.

"I doubt it. You did nothing wrong. He was too far gone. Come on. I arranged coverage for you and signed you out. I'll buy you a drink. You look as though you need one." Eli turned to Dr. Silverman. "Kurt, do you want to join us?"

"Thanks, but I've got to get home. For some reason Shelly expects me to do diaper duty every now and then." That didn't surprise Margaret. Everyone at the hospital knew the story of how the renowned workaholic had reformed once he married his long-time buddy, Shelly Ware, a physical therapist who'd resigned a few years ago to play full-time mom to his son, their twin toddlers and the baby girl who'd been born last month.

Margaret needed more than a drink. She needed... "All right." While she had no desire to rehash the events in the OR, she could seriously use a drink and some down time with Eli. Even though he was technically her boss, he also was a friend. Not to mention a hot male animal who fired her blood the way nobody had done for ages, since Dale her old master had moved his construction company headquarters down to Houston. Since that kiss a month ago, she hadn't thought a lot about Dale. It was Eli's face she saw in her dreams, the taste of his lips that lingered on hers.

She still went hot and weak when she recalled that kiss, the strength and vitality of his big, heavily muscled body. Unlike most of the men she'd dated since breaking up with Dale a year earlier, Eli might be able to make her come. Excitement built in her as she relived that kiss, imagining a repeat of it—and more. Of course, she might just be fooling herself because of the stress and post-adrenaline flow of the surgery. How many times did she have to be disappointed to realize once and for all that she needed a Dom for full release?

Still, she couldn't stop the excitement from building in her when she watched Eli sign them out for the night, saw the stubborn set of his jaw, the massive shoulders she imagined could carry not only his burdens but her own.

* * * * *

He'd take her back to the lounge down the street from the hospital, with its fuck-me music. Same place where she'd kissed him. They'd dance again, and if he got lucky she'd kiss him again the way she had before. This time maybe he'd invite her home, tamp down his compulsion to control and enjoy...

But damn it, he wanted to control her. Why shouldn't he give her what he really was, see if she could handle it?

He knew why. Because for the first time in a long time, this mattered. Margaret meant something to his heart as well as his libido. He'd take it slow, even if it killed him. "Leave your car here. I'll drive us to the lounge, and afterward I'll take you home."

"All right."

She didn't seem worried about how she'd get to work in the morning. Instead, she smiled up at him after settling on the passenger seat of his SUV, which he took as silent assent to his seduction plan. "You need some peace and quiet after a day from hell, don't you?" He remembered the first time he'd had to crack a patient's chest without the comforting feeling that there was a chief resident or attending thoracic surgeon backing him up. Margaret had to have been at least as terrified as he'd been back then. "Cat got your tongue?"

She turned to him, her lips turned up in a semblance of a smile. "I guess so. That poor man. I still say you'd have cracked his chest faster. So would Jerry. Either of you could have saved his life."

"Doubt it. What you're feeling now is aftershock from being called in to start a serious emergency case because your chief resident's on vacation and I wasn't close enough to get there right away. Go easy on yourself. You're good. Good enough that I'd trust you to operate on my mom."

"Thanks. I think." He loved her soft, sure voice, a blend of budding confidence and femininity. Not even the baggy sweats she had on managed to mask the fact that she was a supremely female woman. As he pulled into the parking lot behind the lounge, he found himself imagining her in silk and lace. In nothing. He tried to conjure up a mental image of her in a black leather bustier like those he associated with the Dommes he occasionally played with at the Club. The image didn't fit, other than the piercing she kept open with the unobtrusive disk that hinted she might have flirted at some time with the BDSM lifestyle. Not that a lot of vanilla chicks these days didn't pierce body parts other than their ears, but Margaret didn't seem the type to have ever gone for the Goth look.

Once he'd helped her out of the car, Eli laid a hand on the small of Margaret's slender back, felt the tension there. She'd always hidden that tension under a tightly controlled, unflappable exterior. And pushing down his leaping desire, he thought about how many women in demanding careers nurtured the souls of desperate submissives in the bedroom. He had a feeling Margaret might be one of those driven women who needed to relinquish control in their private lives to achieve balance with the tight leash they had to keep on their emotions to succeed in their careers. If he was right, then Maggie might be the sub of his dreams. She might not even know her sexual mindset, but maybe he could be the one who would open her up to it. A sub beyond his wildest fantasies, lust that went hand in hand with liking, professional respect.

Under his touch, he felt her sigh, heard the ragged sound of her breathing. "Relax, Maggie," he murmured. "If you don't, you'll crumble."

"I know." Her voice was small, needy.

"Leave Dr. Berman at the hospital and just be Maggie." The mellow sounds of jazz coming from a live piano player embraced them when Eli opened the door and waited for her to go inside.

* * * * *

Eli's big, steady hand felt warm, protective as they crossed the dance floor toward a table for two in the corner of the lounge. Some feminine sixth sense told Margaret he wouldn't be a dud in bed, the way her latest lover had been. Unfortunately, the successful tort attorney had pretty much convinced her she needed more than just any attractive man to find satisfaction. He hadn't satisfied her in bed, either, but then he hadn't cared.

Frigid. Ice queen. His parting words reverberated in her head, silent warning that she'd be letting herself in for the same sort of frustration and rejection if she started up a relationship with another vanilla hero.

She'd wanted at the time to tell the guy he was wrong, taunt him with stories of how she'd gone wild with hard-edged Doms, lovers she could hardly have dragged with her to hospital social functions.

It would have done no good. The lawyer wouldn't have understood why she needed him to take control of her body yet allow her the freedom to exert control over her own professional life. Besides, he hadn't been a dominant man. If she'd voiced her needs to him, he'd have labeled her some sort of pervert.

Would Eli? When they first met she'd fantasized about the big, muscular surgeon being a Dom, but he'd never given her any overt signs. Finally she'd decided her hunch had been wrong. Eli was a mentor and friend, nothing more. Still, when he laid a hand on her thigh, she couldn't help imagining…

Him, stripping her naked in the surgery lounge. Using some sterile gauze dressing rolls to bind her arms…her breasts. Rendering her helpless to his sensual onslaught. Her nipples tingling as he bent his dark head to one straining peak.

God, just thinking of him making her give in to his will and her own desires made her juices start to flow. Eli Calhoun was a good man, one she could so easily love—if he proved half as commanding in the bedroom as he was in surgery.

"Come on, Maggie," he said, his expression fierce. "You've got to learn to trust that you did all you could. Otherwise, you'll drive yourself crazy. I know."

Margaret blinked, hoped her cheeks weren't as flushed as they felt. "I'm okay. I was just thinking."

"Are you still worried about the case? Don't. No one could have saved him. Not with him having a bullet lodged in his heart and another one that wrecked his femoral artery. It was a miracle he lasted long enough to make it onto the operating table." Eli tilted her head back, looked her in the eye. "You're well on your way to becoming one of the best thoracic trauma surgeons around here. Don't doubt that for a minute."

If only. If only she'd been thinking about business and not about the way his big, long-fingered hands would feel skimming over her neediest places…or how he'd make her let go of inhibitions so strong that they needed force to overcome them. He'd release the pent-up need that gripped her. "I'll try not to. I wasn't rehashing the case just now, though," she said, forcing a smile and lifting the frozen margarita the waiter had just slid in front of her, removing the empty at the same time.

While she finished her drink, Eli sipped his half-full Scotch on the rocks. "Shall we dance?"

Margaret's stomach, already assaulted by those margaritas, rebelled at the thought of swaying to the beat of the incredibly sensuous piece the pianist had just begun. "I don't think I want to dance, but I could use some…" She dared not tell him what she really needed. "Coffee."

"What you need is to let go of all that frustration. I see it in your face, in the tight set of your shoulders. Come on now. Loosen up for me." Was she imagining things, or had his voice taken on the tone of command?

Her skin grew warm, and her pussy contracted at the thought of Eli taking over, making her submit. It had been a long time. Too long. Ever since the kiss they'd shared, he'd hinted now and then—very subtly, so subtly she'd told herself she was only imagining his intent—that he'd like to fuck her. She drew a deep breath, gathered her courage. "Do you have any ideas about how I might accomplish loosening up?" She met his gaze, hanging on that precipice, wondering if he'd know, if he had what she needed. If he did, he'd pick up that gauntlet.

"In bed." He spoke in a husky whisper and took her hand, laying it over the bulge of his half-hard cock and grinning. "With me." He couldn't have gotten more specific than that. Without a moment's hesitation, he'd picked up the gauntlet, and it was as if she were watching him take it to his nose, inhaling her scent as a tracker would when he knew he'd trapped his quarry.

Holy God, it was possible. Eli might be a Dom, whether he practiced his sexual mastery in a dungeon or in the privacy of a bedroom, behind closed doors. She saw it, even under his wrinkled scrubs, in the broad, muscular shoulders and narrow waist and in the huge, pulsing sex beneath her fingers.

Margaret couldn't help imagining those straight, white teeth nibbling her nipples, the rasp his short mustache and goatee would make against her tender skin. When she met his compelling gaze, she saw promise—promise she prayed he could deliver on. Mastery.

She wanted to submit to him. At least at this moment, she was too aroused at the prospect to think clearly. So she closed her hand, tightening it around his throbbing cock. Fantasizing about what he'd look like naked, she decided he had everything she needed to turn her into a helpless lump of erotic submission.

Why hadn't she paid closer attention when he'd introduced himself to her early last summer, his first day in the OR as her senior attending? If she had, she realized now, she'd have seen all the signs of a Dom. The aura of supreme self-confidence, of his taste for benevolent control, had hung on his shoulders like a mantle. She should have known, instead of reading him as sure of himself as most surgeons were, maybe a bit more so because of his impressive size.

His retaliatory squeeze on her upper thigh and the challenging look in his eyes assured her that he knew what she wanted. And that he was more than ready to deliver it. If she was lucky, she might have found a true Dom looking for a new sub. When Margaret imagined Eli pinning her to the mattress with his strong, capable arms, making her take his hot male flesh in her mouth, she creamed her panties. He'd fuck her until she begged for mercy. And then he'd fuck her some more.

From the feel of it through his pants, his cock was long and thick. Her whole body tingled at the thought of him coming in her mouth, the thick, slick fluid sliding down her throat. He'd let go of his reserve, shout out his satisfaction. He wouldn't be content with coming once. He'd make her come. She knew it. He'd take what he wanted, and in doing it he'd bring her to pleasure.

Yes. Eli could satisfy her. She was confident of that. But if he was truly the Dom she'd been seeking, would he steal the self-control she'd worked so hard for and take over her mind as well as her body? Every sub knew that danger, that the need to be dominated could easily destroy her whole life if her partner proved unworthy of trust. It was part of the knife edge, the craving that was too strong to be called a preference. But Eli had always been her mentor, the center of her support network at the hospital. And frankly, at the moment, whether or not it was the stress of her day impairing her judgment, she just didn't care. Not when every cell in her body urged her to reach out and grab for that elusive brass ring of satisfaction.

But she hadn't entirely lost her mind. The cloak of self-containment she'd fashioned for her image as a respected surgeon had been too hard won. She'd take him home for tonight, see if he could deliver beyond that one knee-weakening, panty-dampening command. Then she'd see if he was worth risking her heart again.

"Let's do it," she said, giving his cock a squeeze that was almost playful, challenging him as she put her shields in place again. *Do your worst, Eli. Impress me. God, please impress me.*

Chapter Two

ഇ

Eli could hardly believe his luck. While he'd never have risked a sexual harassment claim by propositioning a coworker, he had no qualms about taking her up on her blatant offer. Not when it was what he wanted as much as she did.

He wasn't about to ask what had come over her. No way would he turn down her brazen invitation, not when his entire body ached to claim her. She'd been quiet on the way home—to her own place, not his. She'd insisted on that.

She was trying to withdraw behind that cool façade again. He could tell. So when he got to her door, he silently held out his hand for her key, waiting to see if she'd give it to him, give him that sense of control. She did, her fingers whispering on his, a swallow almost hidden in the shadows making him tighten his hand on hers a minute before he turned, put the key into her door and stood back so she could go inside first.

It shocked him that she'd apparently done nothing to personalize her surroundings, that this place bore no hint as to who and what she was. The beige and black furnishings might have easily been found in a generically decorated three-star hotel room or one of the hospital's lounges or waiting rooms. He'd bet even the few photos in their plain black wood frames had come with the place. Nothing reflected Margaret's taste as he knew it. The apartment felt damn cold. And too organized to get comfortable in .

Like Margaret herself. Or like he'd thought she was before that kiss…

Eli had an inexplicable urge to trash the place, just as he wanted to break down the reserve Margaret had always shown him before that night when she kissed him on the dance floor. Heat her up and destroy that cool, collected persona.

But there hadn't been anything remotely cool or collected about the way she'd stroked his cock under the table at the bar tonight. She'd shown him glimpses of the sensual creature he suspected lay below the brittle, controlled surface he was damned well going to shatter.

"This place reminds me of the surgery lounge. How do you stand it?" he asked, mentally contrasting the place with his own condo that he'd decorated in vivid colors, with an eye toward comfort. He'd lived in bachelor officers' quarters too long not to have wanted some creature comforts in his life once he had a choice.

She shrugged. "This is the way it came when I rented it. Certain slave drivers at the hospital keep their residents too busy to worry much about their surroundings during the few hours they have at home. Come on. The bedroom's more inviting."

It was, but only because she was in it. Her deliberate movement as she peeled off her sweatshirt called his attention to hard little nipples outlined against the pale green silk of her bra, and when she stepped out of the pants he caught a glimpse of a dark shadow at the apex of her thighs, beneath a matching lacy thong.

He noticed a slight tremor in her usually steady hands when she hooked her thumbs into that hot-looking underwear. "You're beautiful. Don't be shy." Her poise seemingly restored, she unhooked the bra and let it dangle between her fingers after stepping out of the thong.

Stripping down for sex. She'd done it methodically, with a singular lack of passion that disturbed Eli. Was she trying to tell him she wanted to come but didn't plan to risk her emotions in the process?

Usually he didn't care. But usually his feelings for his sex partners were purely physical. With Maggie, the lust was all mixed up with friendship and respect for the caring doctor and human being she was. Damn it, he wouldn't let her withdraw emotionally. She wasn't just another fuck, and he wasn't about to let her use him just to scratch the itch between her legs. He wanted more. Much more. And he wasn't about to let her deny him. "Look at me, Maggie."

When she did, he read hesitation, maybe even a little fear in her expression. Desire shone in her eyes though. "Is it me you want, or will any hard cock do?"

"I want you. Please." It was there. She had it strangled behind a low, even tone, but he sensed it. He couldn't have read her wrong. He'd been doing this too long, although in some ways she was a first. He couldn't recall ever having wanted a woman as much as he wanted her, or needing to make this work they way he sensed they both needed it to. Should he risk it? Was he reading it right that she wanted him to Master her?

His balls were about to burst. Her breasts were ripe and full enough to fill his hands. The way the nipples puckered with arousal made Eli's mouth go dry with the need to taste them. God, but she took his breath away. Blood slammed into his cock so fast it left him breathless.

He couldn't help imagining her firm, slender thighs cradling his cheeks while he gorged himself on the moist, warm haven of her neatly trimmed pussy. She had to be aware of the erotic picture she made, but she still stood there. Still but for a tiny tremor in her hands, the nibbling on her lower lip. She wasn't as calm and collected as she apparently wanted him to think, but she was obviously determined to wait and let him make the first move.

He'd break through that reserve. He'd dig his fingers into her auburn curls, muss up her tidy coiffure. He'd take her mouth and tongue-fuck her until she begged for mercy, then fist his hands in her hair and drag her full, inviting mouth down on his aching cock.

God, she was a beauty, a naked goddess he had to admire from head to toe. If his mom hadn't taught him a man had to act a gentleman around a lady he'd have grabbed her, forced her then and there to give over that control, accede to his mastery. Emotionally as well as physically.

She had delicate-looking eyebrows above big, cat-green eyes. A modest pug nose, the result of a damned good rhinoplasty unless he missed his guess. If she had on any makeup, he couldn't tell. The column of her throat seemed made for kissing—and collaring. He liked her body, slim and athletic but with surprisingly full, firm breasts. Her pale, creamy skin that had a few barely discernable freckles dotting her shoulders and arms made his fingers itch to stroke it.

He liked his pussies shaved, and hers wasn't. The neatly trimmed mahogany curls attracted his gaze, though, because they looked so soft. His cock twitched when he imagined her locking his face to her pussy, holding him captive there while he nibbled at her clit. His balls tightened almost painfully.

Still she didn't move. That unnerved him. Damn it, he *would* find a way to defeat that scary self-control of hers. Make her let go. He'd make her come not once but over and over, and he'd storm the defenses he sensed she'd deliberately erected around her feelings.

"Do you like what you see?" she asked, her tone conveying cool amusement.

Damn. He'd been staring at her cunt like a guy who'd been locked away for years. "Yeah. I like it a lot. Is it my turn now?" He visually raked her naked body once more before beginning to strip off his own clothes, tossing the lab coat and scrub shirt carelessly to the floor. Teasing her, watching her eyes glow with anticipation as he bared himself to her gaze, he made an unnecessarily complex production out of untying the knot in his scrub pants and letting them drift down to his feet.

"Want to see the rest?" Briefly he worried that his piercing might put her off.

"Don't be shy now." She met his gaze, her own full of challenge.

Margaret let out a little yelp when he shoved his boxers down around his ankles. Her eyes widened and her mouth dropped open, but she didn't say a word.

"Well, doctor. I never imagined the sight of a naked man who isn't strapped to a gurney would trigger such a shocked reaction. If I'd known, I'd have stripped for you a long time ago."

"Maybe you should have." Margaret couldn't tear her gaze off him. The man was beautiful, broad-shouldered and lean hipped, his well developed muscles a reminder that she'd heard he was an avid bodybuilder. Her gaze settled on a shiny, hefty-looking gold barbell peeking from either side of the head of his long, thick penis. A fully aroused penis, its plumlike pierced head glistening against his taut, bronzed belly. The piercing was an Ampellang, said to enhance the sexual experience better even than the more common Prince Albert.

She wanted to taste the drop of lubrication gathered in the slit at the tip of his cock head and fondle the large testicles drawn taut in their sac against his body. She wanted to sample every inch of him, run her hands over his hard torso. She liked that he didn't have much body hair to mar his deeply tanned body, except for the silky dark growth on his head, brows and eyelashes, his neatly trimmed mustache and goatee—and the soft, dark nest that cushioned his sex. Just looking at him had her pussy steaming.

At the lounge when he'd taken control, put her hand on his cock and given her that even look, she'd been sure she was dealing with a Dom. But her heart had sunk a little as she'd stripped off her clothes, feeling her usual shielding settling into place. He'd just stared at her, as though he wasn't sure what to do about her sudden remoteness.

Tear it down. Make me yours. If he was a true Dom, he should have been able to see how she was trapped inside herself. He should have known she needed his control to break free, let herself go. No, she wasn't being fair or rational, not these days when Oprah and Dr. Phil said a woman had to talk about her feelings *ad nauseum*. But it was what she was. What she needed. She wanted him to connect with her on a primal level far below such civilized turnoffs and *know* what she wanted without her saying a word.

Then he brought her hope back to life with such a rush that she swayed, her knees suddenly going weak. "Sit on the edge of the bed." His stern tone was an order, not a request.

Omigod. He *was* a Dom. A closet one, maybe, but still a Dom. She should be thrilled. Part of her was. She should also be terrified that he'd want to extend his dominance much farther than the bedroom. Thrilled would do for the moment, though. Listening to the clear tone of command in his voice and looking at his impressive sex left her speechless with anticipation for the pleasure she sensed he'd deliver. Her flesh grew hot, and moisture pooled between her legs. Her nipples tightened and tingled.

"I said 'sit'. I want to make you feel good," he repeated, stepping closer, as though her hesitation was testing his patience.

Margaret knew he'd force her to relinquish the control she fought so hard for. She couldn't stop him. Truth was, she didn't want to stop him. Yes she did. She didn't dare give in. But he left her no choice because her body screamed for his touch, his mastery. She sat on the edge of her king-size bed, not bothering to turn back the duvet with its quilted cover.

"Lie back." Not waiting for her response, he knelt and pulled her legs over his shoulders.

"Yes, Master." There must have been some part of her perverse enough to want to let him know he'd found a secret sub in the body of a take-charge sort of woman. That was the only explanation she could come up with for the words that had just escaped her mouth.

His expression toughened, as if the significance of what she'd just called him was sinking in. Then he smiled, his face a feral mask not unlike a big cat stalking his mate. "That's a good slave," he said, sliding his big hands up her torso, cupping her breasts and running his thumbs over the distended nipples before sliding his hands back down between her legs.

Her cunt was weeping for him to take her. Mold her to his will. His hot, wet breath on her pussy honed her anticipation to a fever pitch, and when he used his thumbs to open her labia and touched his tongue to her swollen clit, she became his willing sex slave.

He tasted her honey, making long, lazy strokes of his tongue along her slit, driving her mad to come. Then he opened his mouth over her throbbing clit and sucked it in, nipping at the rigid bud with his teeth when she threaded her fingers through his hair, holding him captive there. His groan reverberated against her flesh, the sensation incredibly arousing. Almost as arousing as the musky smell of sex that surrounded them.

Encouraged when he sank two fingers into her sopping cunt, she pressed harder on his perfectly shaped head, tunneling her fingers into his short, brown curls, so smooth compared with the sandpapery texture of his cheeks as they brushed against her swollen labia. But he only flayed her clit with his tongue and sucked her deeper into his mouth. Then he blew on her clit once more—and laughed at her when she whimpered at the delicious feelings that were building inside her.

"You like that, don't you?" The rumble of his words bounced off her sensitized flesh. Delicious tension built up in her belly, her nipples, her swollen cunt.

"Oh, yes. Thank you."

He looked at up her, a frown on his rugged face. He wanted her to say it. If she'd had doubts about him being a true Dom, he'd just chased them away.

"Thank you, Master." At the moment she wanted—no, she needed—to be Eli's sex toy.

"You're welcome." His hot gaze locked on hers, he licked her essence off his lips and chin. It was the most sensuous act she'd ever witnessed. Then, still focusing on her face, he ran his hand along her slit, dipping a finger into her cunt then lower, rimming her anus. "I'm going to fuck you here, too."

His cock was too big. It would split her apart. "No."

He slipped his finger inside, just far enough to rest against her tight anal sphincter. "I'll be ever-so careful, baby. Relax. You'll love it." Getting up, he positioned himself over her on the bed. "Taste yourself on my mouth."

Then he kissed her, filling her senses with the slick, salty essence and heady smell of her own arousal. Oh God. Remembering the delicious sensation of him kneeling between her legs, tonguing her, sucking her clit and exploring all the orifices he'd soon fuck had her incredibly needy. She was frantic—horny in a way she hadn't been since she'd said goodbye to her former master.

Was it crazy for her to think that in a matter of moments, Eli had realized the only way she could come was when her lover made her helpless in fact as well as powerless to resist his command? But it hadn't been just a sudden realization. He'd been working with her for months, and apparently he'd studied everything about her, picked up things she'd never known she'd revealed. Now, as if proving it, he met another need when he tangled his tongue with hers, taking her breath. He lowered his body onto hers, pressing her into the mattress, showing he could control her with nothing more than his superior size and strength. Her nipples throbbed at the contact with his hard, muscular chest.

Damn it. He seemed content to toy with her, make her so hot she'd beg. She needed his big cock in her cunt now. She longed for him to make her submit to pleasure. Stretching out one arm, she opened the drawer of her nightstand.

She wrenched her lips away from his. "Please. Use whatever you want to." When he turned and perused her selection of toys, Margaret trembled with anticipation. Although some of the toys worked well when she had to satisfy herself, others had been bought to please her former master.

Turning away from the drawer, Eli got up and dragged her to her feet at the edge of the bed. "On your knees. You can suck me off while I choose what I'm going to use on you." Eager to please him and even more eager to taste the pierced head of his massive cock, she wasted no time complying with his order. Kneeling, she ran her tongue around his cock head, tasted the salty, slick lubrication at its tip. Tangling her fingers in his pubic hair, she tightened her fingers around the thick base and squeezed. Curious, she licked the length of him then used the tip of her tongue to nudge the ball-shaped tip of his cock jewelry. "Roll the barbell around with your tongue. Mmmm. Keep it up. You give great head. Go on. Squeeze my balls, too. Easy. Don't want to make me come too soon. And close your eyes. I want to surprise you with my choice of toys."

She closed them. Anticipating the toys he'd choose, she sank further onto his cock. Deep-throated him. Drowned herself in the senses that suddenly grew stronger now that she was deprived of sight. He felt smooth, silky against her tongue, a vein pulsating, his testicles tightening in their sac when she played with them and used her tongue to explore his piercing, her teeth to grasp the round, warm ball and twist it. That elicited a throaty growl.

Would he want to restrain her hands, or would he rather have her free to fondle him the way she was doing now? Her cheeks grew hot when she thought about the selection of dildos she'd collected, and an ornate pair of clamps that made her nipples tingle at the mere thought he might want to use them. She'd know soon enough because the drawer closed with a thud, and she felt the mattress shake a bit when he tossed some items onto it.

He was close to coming. She could tell by the slick, salty lubrication that oozed from the slit in his cock. She pulled almost off him, slowly. Then she took a deep breath and took his cock as far down her throat as she could. God, but she wanted him to come. She wanted to serve his pleasure, take her own by enhancing his. When he lifted her onto her feet, she wished she dared to protest.

"I like your choice of playthings. Crawl onto the bed and lie down on your pretty belly. Your safe word is 'armadillo'."

His touch was gentle, soothing yet ever so arousing when he lifted her and stuffed a pillow beneath her hips. "Give me your hands now," he said, and when she did he wrapped Velcro restraints around each wrist and secured the other ends to the headboard. "That's right. Now, your ankles." With practiced ease he caught one ankle at a time and tethered her, spread-eagled, to the footboard of her antique iron bed.

Yes, she thought with a mixture of relief and dread. He was a good Dom, one who knew how to take his time and build her desire to a fever pitch, overriding her own sense of urgency, not allowing her to set the pace. After securing the rope on her right ankle, he licked and kissed and nipped his way up her leg to her sopping cunt. She lay, squirming, on the brink of coming, her cunt and anus exposed to his gaze, his hands, his mouth.

She felt totally, deliciously helpless when Eli knelt between her legs and rubbed his cock against her sopping slit. "What do you want, Maggie?"

"Want?"

"Do you want me to take you this way? With you bound and unable to resist?"

"Please, Master. Fuck me. Fuck me however it gives you pleasure." Everywhere he touched her, her skin tingled. With every brush of his hard cock against her swollen pussy, she wanted to cry out for him to take her and end the longing that was stealing her sanity.

She relinquished that sanity willingly, eager to experience the sensations of seduction—his hot, moist breath on her cheek, her neck, the tickling torment of him nibbling his way down her back. His late-night beard stubble grazed her skin, reminded her of his maleness, the control he exerted over her every emotion, every sensation. The sensations took her breath away, got her hotter with every playful bite, each swipe of his tongue as he moved to her buttocks, his long surgeon's fingers exploring as they followed the trail he'd laid out with his mouth.

"Oh yes, Master." She loved his touch, gentle yet unquestionably in control. For a moment when her nipples protested their isolation she regretted he'd bound her this way, with them inaccessible to his hands and mouth while he half sat, half lay between her outstretched thighs.

He rose up and rubbed the head of his rock-hard cock along her swollen slit. As he leaned forward so his breath caressed her spine, the growl in his words alone had her shuddering. "No one would ever know you were a sub, Maggie, except the man meant to master you. I've been hoping and wanting this for months. I damn near took you the night I felt the piercing in your tongue."

"Do you mind?"

He laughed out loud. "Hardly. You're perfect for me. I'm considering taking you to my private dungeon and letting you see what being my slave is really like." When she whimpered, her hips rising to brush against his hard belly, he teased her with the tip of his tongue. "You like this idea, don't you? Now, relax and enjoy the ride." Shifting to one side, he left her pussy bare.

But just for a moment. Something cold and wet and rigid slid along where his cock had been, coming to rest at her rear entrance. She shuddered, straining against her bonds when she realized what he had in mind.

"Easy now. I'm going to take your ass, but not yet. Not until we get you stretched out enough so I won't hurt you. My cock will feel like this, but so much better."

Her anal sphincter clenched, then gave way to the unrelenting pressure of a gel butt plug. From the feel of it, it must be the smallest of the three she had. Still, it had been a long time since she'd engaged in anal play. The pain radiated, yet as she'd learned long ago, it gave way quickly to a sense of fullness, and a heat that radiated to her cunt, her womb. "That hurts so much. Feels so good. Please don't stop." She was close, so close.

He withdrew the plug and inserted a larger one in its place. "I don't intend to stop. Not until you've come for me. Your cunt's already hot and wet and swollen. After I fuck you I'm going to lick up every drop of that sweet honey."

His cock throbbed against her thigh. God, but she wanted him to fuck her cunt. Her ass. Any place that gave him pleasure would take the jagged edges off her arousal. "Please," she begged, hating herself for whining yet needing him now. Him, not the toy embedded in her ass. Her clit throbbed and her cunt gushed with lubrication. She'd never needed a man's cock so very much.

He must have realized she was hurting with need because he worked the largest plug into her anus until its flared edge lay flush against her body. Then he shifted, stretching out over her prone body. His cock head throbbed against the entrance to her swollen cunt.

She tried to move, couldn't. "Please, Master. Fuck me now."

"Ask nicely, tell me how much you want my cock in your tight, wet cunt." When he found her clit and pinched it between two fingers, she let out a little whimper. "Ask me."

"Please put your cock in my cunt. Please fuck me. God, it's been so long." If only she could move, she'd suck him inside her, end this longing that had her practically mindless. She couldn't, though, and she loved it. Loved him taking control. Total control over her.

"Just a second. Let me get on this condom." Raising himself up on one elbow, he put it on. Then he grasped her hips and entered her, inch by delicious inch, until she felt him pressing against her cervix. His big cock throbbed against her vaginal walls, hot and slick with her juices and his, She'd never felt so full.

Slowly, so slowly, he began to move as she stretched to accept his full length, inch by delicious inch. He was so big and so hard, and he knew just how to move to bring her the greatest pleasure. Pressure built in her cunt, her belly. She was about to come, but she didn't want the feelings to end. Not yet. "Oh, yes. Fuck me harder. Please, Master."

"Yes indeed." His breathing turned ragged as he pumped into her, deeper with every thrust. His cock pressed against the opening to her womb, and his heavy testicles bounced against her clit with each inward motion. It felt so good. So full, as if he surrounded her the way her cunt surrounded his cock.

His chest felt hot and silky against her back when he leaned over her and at last reached down to squeeze her aching, needy breasts. At first gentle, he kneaded them harder when she begged for more. Knowing what she needed, he rolled her nipples between his fingers until they ached.

Pleasure and pain. A heady combination. The sensations of fullness in her cunt and ass spread, igniting flames in every nerve cell, carrying her inexorably toward the release she hadn't found with a man since…

Her cunt began to milk his cock, a spontaneous reaction to his touch, his nearness. It felt good. So good. Bells rang in her ears. Oh, God… "Don't stop. Please."

"I won't stop. Ever. That's it. Let go. Damn, but you're tight. That's it, squeeze me. Come for me. Make me come." His gruff order set her free, free to take the release he offered. Just when her cunt began twitching and delicious sensations started radiating through her body, he bit the sensitive nape of her neck and sent her hurtling over the edge to the best orgasm she'd had since…

For longer than she could remember. Maybe forever.

She hadn't come down yet when she felt his muscles tense, heard his shout of triumph as he came. The staccato bursts of semen, even caught inside the condom as they were, nudged her to yet another climax, this one softer, more mellow than the first explosive burst of sensation.

She'd done it. She'd found the man she wanted for her Master, one who made her body sing. At least in the bedroom. But she pushed that niggling worry away as she realized he planned to make her sing again. Because he didn't loosen her bonds…

Instead he paused long enough to discard the condom before untying her and flipping her onto her back.

"I'm leaving this in," he said, wiggling the butt plug's base and setting off another mild wave of sensation. "And adding this." Her large vibrating dildo slid into her cunt.

Then he stretched out beside her, ran his hands over her as if learning every inch of her. She loved it, the connection that went beyond fucking, that seemed as if it touched her soul. They lay here for what seemed like hours, not moving except for his stroking hands, enjoying the afterplay so many men considered an unnecessary waste of effort.

"Forging a bond," Eli said after a while. "Do you feel it?"

"Yes, Master."

"Good." Sitting up, then turning and straddling her face backward, he fed her his cock. "Suck me. I've dreamed about having your pretty lips around me this way. Licking and sucking my cock. Yeah, baby. Like that."

He was so big he stretched her lips, filled her so fully that it was hard for her to stroke him with her tongue. But she loved that he was velvety smooth. So smooth and hot she wanted to consume him. She concentrated, taking his cock a little deeper with each breath until his scrotum lay heavily against her nose. When she caught one end of the barbell with her tongue and wiggled it, he groaned then stretched out above her until he could flail her clit with his tongue. His mustache and goatee abraded the insides of her swollen pussy lips while his silky hair tickled her inner thighs.

There wasn't an unstuffed orifice on her body. He possessed her completely, as a Master should. Incredibly arousing, she thought, this total possession she'd only experienced before when her old Master had shared her with other Doms in the dungeons. Now it was only Eli, and it felt incredible. Sucking and licking and swallowing his distended flesh, she took him so deep that she felt the soft cushion of his pubic hair against her lips and nose, the spurting of his come into her eager throat.

Aftershocks consumed her, stealing her mind as she greedily swallowed his come. Depleted, she lay immobile, vaguely aware that he was fastening a leather belt around her waist…working something between her legs…tightening it so the plugs in her ass and cunt would stay in place. She loved the sensations.

"I love how you respond. Now, sweet slave, this is to keep you filled while we sleep." Once he had the belt secured to his satisfaction, he loosened her bonds then lay beside her, pulling her close, making her feel protected…warm…almost loved.

Satiated, she stroked Eli's head and let her emotions have free rein while he slept. A masterful Dom, a respected surgeon who shared her hoped-for specialty. A gorgeous man. Could it be possible? Could she dare hope Eli might be the answer to all her late-night fantasies?

Chapter Three

ꟹ

Early the next morning, Eli blinked at the bright sunlight that flooded the room. For a long time he lay in bed watching Maggie sleep. He could hardly believe it. She'd let go of the stress he saw in her so often when they worked together. While he'd strongly suspected she was a sub, there was nothing like a sweaty, satisfying confirmation. If she hadn't been so good at projecting that remoteness when he'd touched on her personal life, he might have done this months ago. They could have been sharing the fetishes he'd tried so hard to keep separate and distinct from his professional life.

Guess you kept your secrets hidden even better than I did, sweetheart.

Ten years ago, when he'd just finished medical school, he'd learned the hard way that the woman he'd figured would make an ideal doctor's wife hadn't been at all inclined to share his need for D/s play. The failure of the marriage that hadn't survived the first year of his residency at the Tampa veterans' hospital had sent him searching for a BDSM club. He'd found sexual satisfaction, but not a woman with whom he could form the kind of emotional and intellectual connection necessary for a successful marriage. Although he sometimes yearned for a life partner to share the ups and downs of daily living as well as his sexual preferences, Eli had pretty much resigned himself to staying single and putting up with his fellow surgeons' frequent innuendos about his sexual orientation.

Maybe he and Maggie… No, it was too soon. Still, Eli couldn't help imagining them together, not just in bed and at work, but as real, twenty-four-hour-a-day partners in life. Hell, his former wife would have had him thrown in jail if he'd ever tried to tie her down or put a plug up her ass. Maggie had begged for it.

Funny. She gave coworkers the impression of a well-bred, conservative woman. A caring woman who had the makings of a hell of a surgeon. Oh hell. He had to face it. While he was leery of the word love, he liked Maggie so much that during those brief moments of doubt about her orientation, he'd had the wild consideration of turning vanilla for her, giving up his need for sexual control. He'd envisioned taking her to meet his mother. Mom would like her, he thought as he watched her sleep, even if she wasn't one of the vapid blonde daughters of her good friends that she'd been shoving at him ever since his divorce. He smiled when he pictured his last full-time submissive, with her long, black, dyed hair, Goth makeup, and the snake she'd wanted tattooed around her neck in lieu of the traditional collar. If Mom had ever seen her, she'd have stroked out.

Eli got hard again, thinking about making Maggie his full-time sub. He'd never dared to dream he'd find a woman like her, a lady outside the bedroom, a fellow professional with whom he could share days as well as nights. She'd given him not only a hell of a fuck, but the surprise of his life. If he were to take her home, she'd make his mother happy. And she'd undoubtedly keep him on his toes while he broke down her reserve and made her respond to him, not just in bed but on every level.

Eli ran his fingers through her strawberry blonde curls. He liked her hair short like this because it made it easy to explore all the erogenous zones he'd discovered when he'd once played at a dungeon with a sub who'd been shaved bald. He'd have Maggie shave her pussy, he decided, and he'd mark her as his own not with a collar, but with a piercing only he and she would ever see.

He'd control her mind, make her trust him so completely she'd know everything he did to her would bring her pleasure. So thoroughly she'd never need to use that safe word. For the first time in his life as a Dominant, he wanted to let the world know Maggie belonged to him. He wasn't at all sure she'd go that far. Fuck, he didn't even know for sure that she shared his feelings beyond the unmistakable lust that had driven them last night.

Feelings? Eli wasn't sure how to define what he did feel for Maggie, but it was a hell of a lot more than gratitude for a mind-blowing night of sex. Damned if he'd label the emotions surging through his brain as love. Love had let him down before, made him leery of the term and all it implied. Somehow, though, the prospect seemed doable when he looked at Maggie.

He stroked her cheek, traced the delicate line of her jaw. For the first time in a long time—forever, he amended—he experienced a sense of tenderness, a need to protect this woman who'd shed her aura of emotional invincibility with her clothes last night. Imagining them together years down the road didn't send him running, as it had with other lovers.

Maybe in time they'd both tire of bondage games. Many of his acquaintances in the BDSM community had told him the ultimate pleasure happened for them when they'd given their hearts, and taken their slave's love to cherish in return.

First, though, Eli had to establish their relationship as Master and slave. Maggie obviously expected it, reveled in submitting. He opened her toy drawer and took out the nipple clamps he'd noticed last night. While she slept he stroked her breasts, pinching the nipples then clamping them when she began to whimper and pant. Bending, he bathed the distended nubs with his tongue.

"Ow! That hurts. But it feels so good, too. Use your teeth. Please, Master." Maggie's sleepy plea had his cock rising to full attention.

He drew one nipple into his mouth and sucked, then clamped down on it with his teeth until she let out a little scream. His testicles drew up, and his cock swelled and hardened further. "Want more?"

"Oh yes, please."

He bit her, harder, then reached between her legs and pulled aside the belt that held the vibrator and butt plug in place. "Good girl. You're wet for me. I like that." Her slick, swollen pussy called out to him. The smell of sex permeated the air around them. Eli's cock throbbed. But first…

He pulled away and stood up. "Take off the harness. Get up and shower. You can take the dildos out, but leave the clips alone. I want your nipples hot and red, like they are now." Bending, he took one in his mouth and sucked it, hard.

"Yes, Master." When she looked at him, he saw desire in her eyes. But also worry. Drawing her close, he kissed her long and hard and sent her to the shower with a terse command, but first he held her gaze long enough to convey that she wasn't alone in her feelings about last night. Hell, he didn't want her ever to feel alone.

If he didn't get dressed and get out of her bed, he wouldn't be able to resist fucking her again. That wouldn't do, since he had surgery scheduled in less than an hour and he knew she'd have rounds to make before taking her turn working in the free clinic. Later, he promised himself as he gathered up his scrubs and pulled them on.

How far would Maggie go toward following his orders? Eli intended to find out. Taking a pad he found by the phone on top of her bedside table, he scribbled out his orders, along with a note of apology for stranding her here alone. After laying out the clothes he wanted her to wear, he propped the pad on top of the pile and left his car keys on top. As he hurried out of Maggie's apartment to grab a taxi, he glanced at his watch.

He'd see her again in less than seven hours unless a problem with a clinic patient brought him to her office or both of them to the ER or surgery. Seven hours until he'd take her to his private place at Rio Brava and put his collar around her slender neck.

He hoped to hell he'd read her right and that she wanted him for a full-time Master, not just a quick, handy lay.

And maybe the amazing would happen and they'd decide they needed each other forever. He had a worrisome but unexpectedly pleasurable feeling that keeping her would make his own life whole in a way he'd never known.

* * * * *

"What's got you smiling, Eli?"

Mark Blackstone, the senior partner in their practice, was sprawled in an overstuffed chair when Eli came into the surgeons' lounge, stripped off his mask and gloves and tossed them in the trash. "Mooney's breastbone and rib reconstruction went a lot better than I expected. Looks like I may get to escape this afternoon, earlier than I'd thought. You done for the day?"

"No such luck. A construction worker up in Fredericksburg just cut off three of his fingers with a circular saw. I'm taking a breather while they airlift him here and get him prepped for surgery."

"Looks like you'll be here awhile." Eli often wondered how Mark managed his killer schedule with the gimpy leg that often had him limping after long hours in the OR.

"Yeah. Lynn's going to have a fit. We were supposed to take the kids over to Kurt and Shelly's for dinner."

"Maybe Kurt won't be able to make it either." Eli had seen their other partner early this morning when they shared coffee and rolls in the cafeteria. "He's got a case going on now that may take him the better part of the day, or so he said. Shattered femur, courtesy of last night's bull-riding event at the local rodeo. Guess I'll be the only one making it to the office to take appointments."

"Probably. Some days..." Mark shook his head. "If we hadn't all been suckers for punishment, we wouldn't have gone into specialties where almost every case is an emergency.

The carpal tunnel release I just finished was a rare, scheduled pleasure."

"You do know, don't you, that if you and Kurt weren't so damn good at reattaching limbs, you could get the occasional evening and weekend off?" Eli was good, too, but he wasn't the only thoracic surgeon on staff who could handle serious chest injuries. This weekend, Bill Everett had first call. "I don't have that problem, for which I'm eternally grateful, especially today."

"Lucky SOB. So that nurse who said she saw a hot-looking, third-year resident driving your SUV into the parking lot this morning wasn't mistaken after all? Could it be our last bachelor's about to bite the dust?"

Eli didn't know about that. The notion that he could persuade Maggie to go for more than kinky sex might be way off base. "You'll be the first to know if that ever happens. Margaret and I worked together last night, with Kurt and one of the ortho residents. The patient bled out. She kept saying that if I'd been there before she opened his chest, we could have saved him. I didn't think she ought to be left alone, so I took her for a drink to calm her down. She was still pretty shaky, so I drove her home and left her with my car so she could get to work today."

That was the truth, even if the timing of his departure wasn't quite true. It was bad enough that his mother stayed on his back about settling down. He didn't need himself or Maggie becoming gossip fodder for the entire damn hospital staff.

"Thought you might have had a better night than I did. Lynn and I've hit the ten-year mark, and in a good many ways our relationship's gone stale." Mark paused when the slapping sounds of helicopter blades began resounding from a pad outside the ER. "Not that I don't still love her, because I do. That's probably the unlucky construction worker now. I'd better start getting ready for a marathon—that is, if the severed fingers are in any shape to try to reattach."

"Do you ever hope they won't be?"

Mark grinned as he got up and stretched. "Nope. I love my work, even when it interferes with my love life. Have a little extra fun for me. I'd better call Lynn and give her the bad news."

"Okay. I'll be seeing everybody's post-op patients in the office until about three," Eli said, hoping to hell nothing would come up to keep him from Maggie a minute longer than necessary.

* * * * *

Margaret was glad it was Friday, a quiet day in the free clinic with no surgeries on the schedule and only a few patients scheduled for thoracic surgery consultations. She almost wished for an emergency, anything that would take her mind off Eli and the provocative message he'd left, a message now tucked neatly into the pocket of her lab coat. Sending her last scheduled patient on his way, she went into one of the small cubicles that served as offices for specialty residents when they came to the Clinic.

What was she getting herself into, tearing down boundaries she'd set, boundaries that clearly said work and play don't mix. Taking Eli as her Master could hurt her, destroy the hard-won self control that made her a good surgeon. Her old Master had fit into a small compartment of her life, a secret space she'd never let interfere with her public persona. Eli would invade her whole life…usurp the time when she could pretend she was in total control.

It was inevitable, she supposed, that the afterglow of such an amazing night couldn't hold out long against her worries. This was a whole new book she and Eli had opened up between them. Taking a Master who was a big part of her professional life was bound to result in some complications. And anxieties.

Taking his note out of the pocket of her lab coat, she reread the instructions he'd left for her. Yes. He was an overwhelmingly intuitive Dom in that he'd given her something to distract her, orders as precise as his instructions when he talked her through a new procedure. Her cunt contracted and her nipples began to tingle.

He could get her hot without even being in the same building, and she couldn't have that. Stuffing the note back into her pocket, she tried to concentrate on something—anything—but the man who'd imprinted himself indelibly on her mind.

She picked up a group photo taken of her and Dale with her parents and sister last year. Unlike Dale, a general contractor who'd been self-educated and a little rough around the edges, Eli would fit in well with her conservative, academically inclined family members. Not that they wouldn't find some fault with him. As much as she loved her mom and dad, she'd learned they couldn't be pleased. Fifteen-hundred SATs should have been perfect ones, *magna cum laudes* should have been *summas*. Her number-three ranking in med school would only have pleased them if it had been number one.

They'd fault Eli for something, she was certain. Who was she kidding? Her parents wouldn't approve of Eli a whole lot more than they'd liked Dale. She could almost hear her mother whining that Eli didn't look like a doctor, that he was too big, too muscular, too authoritatively male. No way was he at all like the quiet, scholarly neighbor boy her parents had always encouraged her to seek out as a mate. Maybe, just maybe, she'd never have to introduce them.

Wishful thinking, Margaret. No way would Eli let her shove him into the sex compartment of her life and exclude him from the rest. He'd proven this last night, in spades, that he might very well resist every attempt she might make to run things with that overwhelming, masterful hand of his. But would he keep the respect he'd always shown her as a doctor? His friendship and his mentoring of her residency meant as much as what they'd shared last night.

She didn't have to think about that now. Or about whether she'd impress Eli's mother who, if hospital gossip was accurate, was on a perpetual mission to pair her son with one of a string of her friends' daughters. Margaret pulled out Eli's note and read it again.

Sub, hell. From what he'd written, she gathered Eli intended that she be his slave. If she could have, she'd have ignored the note. But she couldn't. He'd gambled she'd go all the way to find satisfaction, and he'd been right on.

The note had caught her eye the moment she'd come out of the shower, sore but supremely satisfied. Disappointed that he'd left, even though she knew he had an early surgery call, she'd followed each scribbled order. She'd made a conscious effort to ignore the small voice in her head that kept questioning her sanity. But she couldn't help appreciating the thought he'd expressed about the underwear he'd picked for her to wear. *I'll be thinking about you wearing these things, getting hard. Counting the hours until I can take them off you. Take you completely, in every way.*

"By the way, Dr. Berman, you look sexy in that dress," the unit clerk had said when she arrived at the hospital for Friday clinics. She'd sounded surprised. So surprised it made her self-conscious until she found a lab coat. Usually she wore the sleeveless Kelly green sheath with a matching jacket, but Eli had specifically ordered her not to wear it.

She felt sexy. How could she not when she had her tall, muscular new Master set firmly in her mind?

Eli had to have known she'd feel exposed in the satin half-bra and matching garter belt he chose for her, especially since he'd strictly forbidden her to put on panties. The lace tops of sheer thigh-high stockings abraded her inner thighs when she walked on the spike-heeled black pumps he'd set on the bed. She never wore high heels to work. Well, she guessed she did now since he'd commanded it. Wiggling her toes inside the shoes, she willed her feet to stop hurting. He had to have been sending a deliberate message because he knew the heels were impractical. A message that she was to consider his will before her own, accept the pain along with the prospect of ecstasy to come.

Good thing the lab coat covered up her nipples that showed up rock hard and obvious through her lightweight bra and dress. At least Eli had been thoughtful enough to order that she take off the nipple clamps he'd put on her before her shower.

Would he come by her office early? Sometimes he did, if he had time, to check over charts of patients she'd seen. If he came today, she imagined he would want proof she'd obeyed him to the letter. Her cunt clenched when she imagined Eli slipping a hand under her skirt. If he did he'd discover she had shaved her pussy as per his order. Cool air from a floor grate slithered up her legs, reminded her how much more sensitive her private flesh was now, devoid of hair.

She smiled when she thought about it. She was soft there now, as soft as his muscular chest and abdomen. She liked that he had so little body hair, guessed he kept himself smooth because of the body-building contests she'd heard he entered on a regular basis.

Feeling her bare pussy wouldn't be enough, she thought. He'd insert two long, thick fingers in her cunt, rewarding her with a tweak of her G-spot when he discovered she'd found and inserted the diaphragm he'd suggested. He'd have her open her mouth, check out the round silver barbell she'd inserted in her tongue in place of the clear, flat disk she usually wore to keep the piercing open. She could hardly wait to take him in her mouth, rub the ball over his thick, swollen cock head.

"Wear a piece of real tongue jewelry, not that retainer, but remember not to let anyone else see it," he'd written. Clamping her mouth shut, she rubbed the ball slowly against her palate. It felt good, made her eager to run her tongue over every inch

of Eli's hard, hot body, experience the vibrations when the ball in her tongue collided with the ends of the barbell securing his Ampellang.

The mock turtleneck collar of her dress hid a love bite just below her hairline at the back of her neck. Gently she found and rubbed the swollen flesh. He must have noticed the small injury and considered it when choosing this dress, a small concession to propriety and professionalism. Just thinking of it calmed some of her other worries. The dress was evidence that he recognized their need for discretion. That he was thoughtful, considerate of her feelings and their respective positions. A quality her old Master had never demonstrated.

And then, in contrast to that, she thought of things far from the realm of respect and discretion. Like Eli taking her, making her take his hot flesh into her mouth and cunt and anus. Her juices began to flow, heating and soothing her well-used, stretched tissues.

Good thing the attendings hadn't called for Grand Rounds today. She'd have had a hell of a time reviewing a case with the tongue ring in her mouth. Tentatively, she slid her tongue across her upper lip, gauging the weight of the tongue ring. It was heavier than the one she'd worn for her old Master's pleasure, heavy enough to make her diction less distinct. And it gave her voice a seductive sounding edge. She could hardly wait until the day was done, so she could go to Eli. Serve him.

His two final orders awaited her attention. "At precisely three thirty p.m., insert this vibrator in your pretty cunt, and think about how much better it will feel when it's my cock in there instead. Don't come, though. Your orgasms all belong to me."

Margaret glanced at her watch. Three twenty. If she hurried, she could make it to the ladies' room in time. Purse in hand, she walked purposefully to the restroom and locked the door, then fished out the vibrator, an egg-shaped, purple gel device she'd bought but never used. Her earlier examination showed it was electronic, but since it had no switch, it was obvious that it was remotely controlled. Since most remote control toys required proximity, it made her shudder to think Eli might arrange to be close enough, somewhere within a few yards of that restroom door, in order to control her pleasure. Hiking up her tight skirt and spreading her legs, she inserted it, pushing it as high up in her vagina as she could manage with her fingers.

She was already wet. And hot. How could she do this and function like the calm professional she was supposed to be? Especially when Eli got around to setting the vibrator in motion?

She had no choice. Her inner muscles clenched to keep the egg securely where she'd put it, and she stepped hesitantly out of the privacy of the restroom, glancing down the hall both ways then making for her office as quickly as she could without dislodging the vibrator.

Having the thing fall out and bounce merrily down the hallway would not be funny. Well, it would be, but it would also prove highly embarrassing if her nurse or one of the first-year residents saw it happen. At some point she'd have to establish some ground rules for their relationship, but at the moment her overworked libido compelled her to follow Eli's last orders.

Just as she'd begun to believe she could control the needy sensations that snaked through her body, the vibrator began to gyrate. It wiggled back and forth, around and around, its buzz inaudible but transmitted from her cunt straight to her already overloaded brain. Even though she tried to control herself, she breathed hard as she walked carefully down the hall to her office. She found concentrating on the latest JAMA journal totally impossible, no matter how hard she tried to focus on what should have been an interesting article on a new technique for resecting diseased lungs.

As time went on, the gentle vibrations grew stronger. She squirmed in her chair, glanced at the wall clock. Damn, she still had to sit here another hour or more. Reading was really a lost cause now. She gave up, and stared at Eli's message—his last command.

Could she? Dare she declare her subservience to a colleague? Acknowledge his control over her private life? Could she be his slave in the bedroom and his equal outside it?

Would Eli want to flaunt their relationship? Margaret didn't think so, but she couldn't help remembering Dale and the gold collar he'd given her. He'd taken pleasure in attaching a black leather leash to it when he felt like leading her around the public dungeons. Once when they were on vacation where no one they knew was likely to see them, he'd even made her walk along with him on a public street, as though she'd been a pet bitch. She'd felt that horribly degrading yet strangely erotic, worse than the worst spankings he'd often administered behind closed doors until she screamed with the pleasure-pain of it.

She'd sworn when he left that she'd never enter into a D/s relationship on that level again. But here she was, jumping headlong into the fire in spite of herself. Eli had sneaked into her life as a friend and mentor. He'd switched gears quickly enough when she finally let him know she liked her sex rough and a little kinky.

His last command would change Margaret's life if she chose to obey. *I want you to wear my collar. If you agree, hold out your hand to me. I'll meet you in your office as soon as I've seen all my patients.*

He'd obviously want their relationship out in the open. It could hardly be otherwise, with them working together nearly every day. She hoped he'd feel the need as much as she to keep the true nature of that relationship strictly between them. Her old Master had needed to exert his will on her before others, and he'd satisfied that need by sharing her with fellow Doms in public dungeons, humiliating her while letting her remain masked to conceal her identity. Maybe Eli would want that, too, but she doubted it.

No, Eli wouldn't flaunt their lifestyle. He couldn't, not and protect his own career. Perhaps, she hoped, he would forgo the local sex clubs, collar her in the privacy of the dungeon he'd whispered about last night, far away from prying eyes. Not that she'd mind the occasional club scene, the feel of Eli and another lover touching her, arousing her, taking her to heights she reluctantly admitted she'd enjoyed. But she would relish the privacy to worship her Master's magnificent body, accept the pain he'd inflict in order to bring her pleasure.

When Margaret reached to answer the phone, the vibrations of the egg intensified, as though Eli had sensed she'd be doubting the wisdom of this and wanted to remind her she needed him. When he walked through her office door, a predatory grin on his face and a cell phone in his hand, she set down the receiver. The thud of the door closing behind him made her jump with anticipation.

A moment earlier she hadn't been certain she'd do it, but when he looked at her, she knew. Eli was her future. Her Master. She might as well admit to him what she'd already acknowledged to herself. She stood, head bowed, and brought his hand to her lips. He smiled, as if he'd had none of the doubts that had tormented her, turned his hand to grasp hers, and sandwiched it between his palms.

"Have you done everything I asked you to?" As if to test her further, he kicked up the speed on the vibrator to its highest level, reaching out to steady her when she swayed forward, shuddering. His arms firmly around her, he turned them toward the door. "Good thing I remembered to close it."

"Yes, Master. I followed your orders to the letter."

"I see you did."

Damn, but she was hot. Blood slammed into his cock when he smelled the musk of her arousal floating like an aura around her, blending with the light floral scent of her cologne.

His musk now. No one would have recognized it as that. He'd have noted what he thought was a musky, sexy perfume if he hadn't eaten her pussy and flailed her responsive little clit with his tongue. Her tongue darted out, wetting the lips that had felt so good on him last night.

His cock swelled painfully against the soft cotton of his boxers, and his balls tightened. God, but he wished he dared take her here, ease the ache he'd had all day. The ache that had intensified the moment he walked through her office door.

"You'd tell me if you had doubts, wouldn't you?" If she was going to back out, he wanted to know now, before they took the next step. "I want you as my submissive, as long as you want me as your Master," he said, even though, in his mind, he wondered what would happen if he decided he wanted her as his lifetime sex slave.

Whoa, slow down, Eli. Savor it. But with a collar, even though she might think it was too soon for that. He wanted to make it clear he wasn't looking for some temporary fun and games, and to give her one last chance to blow him off for another few months, the way she had after that first kiss.

She bit her lower lip but held his gaze. From the aroused state of her body, the needy look in her eyes, he guessed she wanted him, too "No doubts about us. But..."

"But what? I've known you long enough that last night just cinched it for me," he said slowly, cupping her chin. "I'm sure you want me, too. Tell me, Maggie, what's holding you back?"

"I don't want any of our colleagues to know about our lifestyle." She looked afraid, but she spoke with certainty.

Though part of him wanted to flaunt her in the dungeon at Club Rio Brava, he knew he wouldn't. At least not as long as he felt this need to protect her, to keep her for himself, not share her with some other Dom no matter how discreet he might be. But he couldn't let her believe he was giving in too easily. He already knew she was a hardcore sub, the kind who needed a firm hand and a sense that she had a true Master, in order to let go with him, give him the trust he found himself wanting from her. "What if I'm not okay with keeping it a secret?"

"You could take me to a dungeon. We could wear masks," she told him, her voice small when she spoke, smaller still when she lowered her gaze to the floor. "That's what my first Master often did."

He could tell from her tone that she hadn't liked that. Had her former Master shared her? Humiliated her before fellow Doms and Dommes? He recalled one Dom at a BDSM club near the Riverwalk, the first dungeon he'd checked out after moving to San Antonio. The guy had been a sadist if he'd ever seen one. He'd offered his pretty slave to anyone who would take her. Though she'd been masked, and her hair had been long and blonde, she'd reminded him in some ways of the prim and proper third-year resident he'd met earlier that day, so much that when the sub's Master invited him to fuck her, Eli had turned down the offer.

Now, when he saw the frightened look in Maggie's eyes, he wondered again if she'd been abused that way, and if she'd done the dungeon scenes she spoke of only to please her Master. Eli reached out and touched her, framing her face between his hands. "Unless you want to, we won't frequent the dungeons. I belong to a club you might enjoy, but that will be your choice."

At the easing of her expression, he nodded. "If we ever go, it will be because you ask for it. And it will be at my club, where all the members are sworn to secrecy as well as having careers that wouldn't survive having their sexual kinks made known. Come on. My personal dungeon awaits us."

When he noticed her hands trembling as she gathered her purse from a drawer, Eli turned down the vibrator. When he imagined her cunt slick and wet and eager for the satisfaction he'd soon provide, he could barely resist locking the door, sweeping the papers off her desk, and fucking her on the scarred surface of her desk. Instead, he drew her close, tamping down the baser instincts she had a way of igniting and resting his cheek on top of her auburn curls.

"Oh, yes. You feel so good." Her breathy hiss got him even hotter. Then she opened her legs, as though she wouldn't mind if he were to take her right here, right now.

"Stop that or I'll fuck you here and now. We wouldn't want anybody walking in on us, now would we?"

Her movement slow, reluctant, she stepped back, her eyes glazed with passion. She'd held her hand out to him. She wanted to be his. Now, not later, if he read her right. The enormity of her choice hit him, made him almost as impatient as she. He pulled her to him, hard, and slid a hand inside her lab coat. He had to touch her, fondle her prominent nipples that beckoned him even through the lab coat and that green silk dress he'd ordered her to wear. "Let's get out of here to somewhere private."

"All right, Master."

She stood on tiptoe and laid her hands on his shoulders, lifting her face for his kiss. He could hardly wait to collar her…to put the ring he'd bought where no one else would ever see it. Maybe someday, if she agreed, they'd make their bonding permanent and legal, and he'd slide a rock of a diamond onto her finger.

That unexpected thought shocked the hell out of him, coming as it had from out of nowhere. Eli couldn't help but wonder if he'd been changing for a long time now in what he wanted from a relationship, and if his night with Maggie had opened a door where those ideas could take over his imagination. As if she knew his mind was churning, she didn't say anything, just held his hand as they walked out to the parking lot.

* * * * *

A few minutes later, they were hurtling west on San Antonio's outer loop.

"Where are we going?" Maggie asked once Eli turned onto a farm road that wound around some gently rolling hills.

Eli lifted her skirt and cupped her bare, freshly denuded pussy. "My weekend place. It's out by Riomedina, along the river near Club Rio Brava. Have you ever heard any of the other doctors talk about it?" Several other doctors on staff at University belonged to the club, and Eli wondered if Maggie had ever gone there with one of them.

"I don't think so."

Good. He wanted to be the only Dom in her life. Another surprise since he'd never thought of himself as particularly possessive. "I'll take you there sometime. Meanwhile, I love feeling your pussy so soft and bare for me. Wet, too. Are you anxious for us to get there?"

"I'm burning."

Tweaking her clit as he drove along, he stoked her flames. "Did you manage to get fitted for a diaphragm?"

"No, Master. I already had one." Her legs went slack, giving him room to fondle her more thoroughly. "That feels good. So good."

"I'm glad. I don't want you on the Pill. Too many side effects."

"I haven't taken any for a while now."

"We'll take other precautions, but I want you to promise you'll let me know if careful's not good enough." Though Eli would rather she didn't get pregnant, at least not right away, the idea of having a kid or two with her wasn't as scary as it would have been with every other woman he'd fucked over the years.

"I will. Oh, yes." She arched her back, giving him even better access to her satiny flesh.

"Feel good?" With his thumb, he circled her clit. God, did he love how she responded. His cock reared up, as though reminding him it had been over eight hours since the last time they'd made love.

"You feel incredible. You make me crazy to take your big, hard cock inside my cunt. To feel all of you, stroke your incredibly smooth skin." Her soft fingers drifted over his forearm. "I like that you're not very hairy..."

He chuckled. "I keep my body hair waxed off because I like to enter bodybuilding contests. I've thought about letting it grow back between competitions, but the prospect of itching for weeks while it's growing out changes my mind every time. I could always shave all over, but it's bad enough to have to shave my face and neck every day without adding a few acres more of real estate to that ritual. Maybe someday I'll go have it removed with a laser. How about you? Don't you feel hornier now, with your cunt all smooth and silky? Don't you think you'll like it better when we fuck?" He was throbbing now. If he didn't fuck her soon he thought he'd die.

Margaret was so hot she wouldn't have cared if Eli fucked her in front of half their colleagues. All she wanted was for him to relieve the ache that had her in a frenzy of sexual frustration. Now.

As if he'd read her mind, Eli turned onto a narrow road that meandered along a river—the Medina if she wasn't mistaken. After a few minutes he turned in to a secluded scenic overlook surrounded by dense shrubs, cottonwoods and towering pine trees. The shrubs already had begun showing fall colors of red and gold, and they lent a screen that at least gave the illusion of privacy.

"Spread your legs," he ordered, his tone commanding. From the taut set of his features, she guessed he must be as eager as she. When she obeyed, he reached inside her and took the vibrator from her cunt. "God, baby, I love how you're already hot and wet for me."

He slid over to the center passenger seat, fumbling with his zipper. "Help me get out of these pants. I can't wait another minute to fuck you."

With trembling hands she unbuttoned his boxers and freed his huge, rigid cock. While she fumbled to free his testicles, he unbuttoned her dress, lifted her breasts out of the cups of her bra and tugged on her bare nipples. "Bite them, please, Master."

Lifting her as though she weighed no more than a feather, he set her down astride his thighs. His cock head brushed her clit, sent delicious sensations sizzling along her nerve endings. "Oh, please, don't make me wait." Her cunt gushed when he pulled her down, impaling her. He bent his head, took a nipple in his mouth and sucked hard.

As though he was as desperate as she for satisfaction, he fucked her hard, raising his hips and pulling her down on his cock until he was in her to his balls. Hands on her ass cheeks, he lifted her almost off him and then slammed her down, harder and deeper with every thrust.

He was breathing hard. So was she. The heady sensation of arousal spread through her body. She wanted to come. Now. Every time he found her G-spot with his monster, pierced cock and its barbell, her need grew more desperate. Her inner muscles clenched his cock, begging silently for release.

She couldn't come without permission. If she did, he'd be within his rights to punish her. "May I come, Master?"

"Am I really your Master?" His breath, moist and warm against her breast, sent waves of intense arousal straight to her cunt.

Raising her hands to cup his cheeks, she looked into his deep brown eyes. "You're really my Master." She paused, trying to hold back the flood of pleasure that threatened to explode. "Please. Fuck me hard. Make me come." With both hands she pressed his mouth against her breast, silently urging him to bite her, hurt her, make her come.

"Easy, baby. Relax. Just let me love you. Come for me now." He must have known what she needed, for he sank his teeth into that sensitive flesh. He pinched her other nipple, hard. It hurt, but it felt so good.

Oh God, she was coming, overwhelmed by the incredible feelings. Delicious pain, enormous pleasure and more. His arms tightened around her, protective and sheltering as her cunt clenched hard around his huge, fiery cock. Warmth suffused her body. That warmth had everything to do with the emotions that flowed between them, little to do with the mind-boggling physical reaction to a skilled master's touch. She hadn't come like this since…since ever.

Delicious stretching, scorching heat. Accompanied by emotions having as much to do with love as with passion, the sensations carried her over the top, not once but many times. Margaret loved it when Eli came in her, his hot semen bathing her cunt in hot, delicious bursts that intensified the waves of sexual fulfillment. When they finally stilled, she collapsed against him, breathing in the smell of the leather seats and his woodsy cologne…the arousing aroma of sex. "Thank you, Master."

"My pleasure. Thank you." He bent, took her mouth in a kiss that spoke more of devotion than desire.

Suddenly she wanted to taste him, this master she sensed would always be kind, would never subject his lover to humiliation. "May I suck your cock now?" she asked, rising as she did from his lap.

"Oh, yeah. My cock is yours. For your pleasure as well as mine."

Crouching on the plush carpeting, Margaret took him in her mouth, tasting the heady mix of his climax and hers as she licked it away. God, but he had a beautiful cock, long and thick. She licked every inch, loving it, then took the dark, plumlike crown into her mouth and tongued his slit while he burrowed his fingers into her hair, holding her captive ever so gently—lovingly, she'd almost say.

"Stop or we'll be spending the night here, and I've got other plans." Gently he raised her head and drew her back up onto the seat. "We'll have plenty of time to play once we get to my place on the river."

"Yes, Master." Her cunt still tingling from her massive climax, she snuggled next to him. The reassuring pressure of his fingers on her thigh as he resumed driving reminded her how much he pleased her. And set off a flurry of unexpected emotion she could only describe as love.

Chapter Four

ꟹ

"We're nearly there." Eli turned onto another narrow paved road, eager to have his woman share the place he'd built to escape the city, get back to nature the way it must have been before urban sprawl began to take over the old West. "Look to your right. That's the dungeon I was telling you about. Club Rio Brava." The rugged-looking building sat back from the road, almost hidden among a grove of tall pecan trees that looked eerie now that their leaves were almost gone. At the sudden tension he sensed in her, Eli again wondered what the bastard who'd had her before had done to her. Leaning over and taking her hand in a firm grip, he commanded her attention. "Hey, remember what I said. We'll do the club thing only when it's what you want. We're not going there tonight, or ever unless you want it. My weekend place is a little farther, on the bank of the river."

Darkness had fallen, cloaking trees in shadow but for the golden glow of a full harvest moon. "I'm going to hood you now," he told Maggie after pulling to a stop in front of his place.

"I hate the dark," she told him. Still, she bent her head obligingly and let him lower the lightweight hood over her face. He recalled that she kept a night light on in the bedroom at her apartment, wondered what long-ago experience had made her cringe from darkness. Something else he'd have to learn about her, he thought, a pleasurable study that might take a lifetime.

Excitement had him fumbling where his hands were usually steady, and it took extra seconds to lace the hood snugly. "There. This won't be for long. I have a colleague—you don't know him, but he's another fancier of our lifestyle—who drove out here earlier. He will place my ring, and then he'll leave. I'd do it myself, but I never want you to associate me with pain that doesn't produce pleasure."

"As you wish, Master." Her voice, always soft, was muted even more by the hood. "A ring?"

"A mark of my possession, if you will." He sensed her continuing unease, wanted to alleviate it. "One no one but you and I will ever know about, but which will enhance the pleasure for both of us. I promise."

Eli took her hand and pulled her from the car. "It's dark already, but there's a full moon hanging over the water." A breeze blew off the river, ruffled his hair. Fallen leaves crackled beneath their feet,

She trembled a little, nearly stumbled when she suddenly stopped walking. "What was that noise?"

"That's the call some woods creature is making to his mate. Nothing to be afraid of." Eli laced his fingers through hers. "You'll get used to the sounds soon enough." He hoped she would, anyhow, for retreating from the city to commune with nature was as important to his emotional wellbeing as satisfying his need for sexual dominance. He loved the sound of rushing water and the feel of a cool breeze that blew off the spring-fed river. And the distinctive sounds and smells that abounded in this country setting.

Cool, damp air hung along the path beneath tall cottonwoods and other native trees. The porch light of his cabin glowed, its yellow light beckoning him. He started walking faster when he felt Maggie shiver. Excitement coupled with a tinge of fear, he imagined, for the fall air was brisk but not unpleasantly chilly.

"Okay. We've got six steps here," he said, pulling her close and wrapping his arm around her. Boards creaked below their feet, punctuated by a bobcat's screech as they mounted the stairs.

"Oh!" Maggie stumbled, but Eli was able to grab her and steady her against his body. "What was that?"

"You caught your heel between two boards. Here, I'll carry you the rest of the way." He scooped her up, loving the way it felt when she trustingly looped her arms around his neck. "Welcome to the place I go to get away from it all. Three bedrooms, two baths, a fully equipped kitchen, a fireplace in the great room, and a very special playroom downstairs. I hope you'll approve the changes I had made to accommodate our lifestyle. Since you can't see, I'll take you downstairs to our private playground."

A dungeon that really was a dungeon, his contractor friend had commented when Eli had described what he wanted for a basement playroom a few months earlier. He'd never used it before, never wanted to bring a sub to his special place of refuge. Eli's anticipation built as he carried Maggie down the steep stairs. There it was. And there was his friend, an anesthesiologist he'd met at Club Rio Brava who was finishing a subspecialty residency in Dallas. Nodding, Eli strode to the padded table in the center of the room and laid Maggie down.

"What?" She turned her head from side to side, as though she was trying to acclimate herself to her surroundings.

"You're in our playroom. My friend is already here. Be still while I take off your clothes." As gently as he could, for she obviously was uneasy, Eli slid off her shoes. The stockings and garter belt followed. God, but she had a gorgeous pussy, all pink and satiny smooth. He couldn't help it, he had to taste her. Bending over her, he tongued her clit for a moment, enjoying the way she squirmed as the tiny bud grew hard and elongated.

Then, mindful of his friend's presence, he stood and finished undressing her. Skimming his fingers along the taut, satiny skin of her torso, he asked, "Where would you like your ring?"

A Dom who gave his sub a choice? Margaret liked that. She considered the possibilities. Nipple? Navel? Her clit throbbed just then, and she made up her mind. She reached up blindly, stroked his stubbled chin. "My clit, please, Master."

Eli caressed her still-swollen clit then stepped back. "I hoped you'd choose this hot little piece of flesh."

She'd always wanted a clit piercing but never had the nerve to get one. Now the decision was his, but he'd given her a choice. Margaret opened her legs and relaxed, closing her eyes behind the hood. She fantasized about Eli tugging at a little gold ring with his teeth, sending arousing shards of sensation to her cunt that would radiate all through her body.

What felt like a wide restraining belt tightened around her middle, before someone—not Eli, she thought, because these hands wore gloves—brought her arms in close to her body and fastened her wrists into cuffs apparently fastened to the sides of the belt. "Put her legs up in the stirrups and we'll get this done." The voice was deep, definitely masculine, but she couldn't place it. No surprise, since Eli had said she wouldn't know him. She recognized Eli's touch a moment later when he stroked her calves before settling her feet into devices that felt a lot like the stirrups on a GYN examining table.

"Take a deep breath now," the stranger told her just before the pungent odor of an icy disinfectant he swabbed along her slit began to sting her nostrils. "You're going to feel a little pinch."

Little? It was all she could do to hold back a yelp when he sank a needle through her clit. It hurt. A lot. Perversely it also sent a shock wave of sexual pleasure through her, almost climactic in its intensity.

"All done," Eli said, blowing gently on what she imagined was her new clit ring. That sent another delicious little orgasm coursing through her veins.

"Well, I imagine you can take care of your woman now." Margaret sensed the stranger had stepped back, heard his footsteps as he ascended the steps. "I expect you to return the favor to me one day. I'll be going. I have my own lady waiting for me back at Club Rio Brava."

"Anytime. Thanks." As she listened to the man leave, she realized she'd tensed, almost expecting Eli to offer her to the other Dom. But Eli wasn't her old Master. She needed to relax, enjoy him. Enjoy this. Margaret wanted to trust him. Needed to trust him. She needed to sweep away old memories, make room for new ones they'd make together.

When Tom had left, Eli removed her hood then stroked her belly, her breasts. "You're so fucking sexy. I'm hard as stone, just looking at my ring on your pretty clit." Very gently he touched it, setting off another pang of arousal. "I love looking at it, wish I dared play with it now, wiggle it around with my tongue. Guess I'll have to be satisfied playing with these beauties until you heal." He pinched her nipples lightly then cupped her breasts.

"Now I'm your sex slave. I belong to you, for as long as you want me."

"I'll always want you, Maggie. I'm not an animal, though. I want more from you than just sexual submission."

His look was so intense it frightened her, though his hands were gentle. Soothing as well as highly arousing. "I know. I'm just not comfortable with the "more" part. It's so new..."

"For me, too, sweetheart." He bent, brushed his lips over hers, the stiff hairs of his mustache tickling the sensitive skin of her upper lip. "Know this. I'll never hurt you. You can let go with me emotionally as well as physically, the way you can't with another human being."

Eli's gaze locked on her clit ring, gold and delicate, a sparkling ruby winking at him from the small captive bead. Looking would be all he dared do until she healed. "Hate to do this, baby, but we don't want you getting an infection." He positioned a sterile vinyl shield and smoothed its adhesive edges down to protect her new piercing from bacteria that might be lurking in the air, or on his hands and mouth. "Your cunt's off limits for the next few days… I almost wish you'd wanted something else pierced."

"I'm sorry, Master."

He realized it had startled her that he'd wanted her to make her choice of where her piercing should be, even if it impacted their intimacy for a short time. That her desire mattered to him. "Don't be sorry. Anticipation will make it so much sweeter once you're healed." That wasn't exactly true, because it would be pure hell for him to deny himself the pleasure of burying his cock in her sweet cunt, of taking her impudent bud between his teeth and making her squirm with desire.

Suddenly it hit him. He hadn't even considered inviting Tom to join in their sexual games. During the years he'd lived the BDSM lifestyle, Eli had taken part in countless ménages, even a few orgies, and he'd never before failed to make the courteous offer to share his sub. Sharing was practically expected at the club up the road, as well as every other dungeon where he'd ever played.

He'd do something else for Tom, maybe another piercing for the other man's favorite sub, Loretta—that is if Tom could find another spot on her body to be pierced. Damn it, Eli wanted Maggie all to himself. Was he in love? That was a distinct possibility. He was definitely obsessed. He knew he'd have to fight this unfamiliar possessive streak before he'd share her with another Dom, even for her own pleasure.

Maggie smiled, her tongue darting between her lips as though she wanted to taste him even while she lay passive on the table, her legs in stirrups, baring her freshly shaved pussy to his hungry gaze. Her plump labia glistened, beckoned him. "Let me please you, Master."

Her eagerness touched him, aroused him. She seemed to love everything he'd done so far to her incredibly responsive body. His slave. No, a partner he wanted to bring to ecstasy every way he could, whom he'd protect with his life and never allow to be hurt.

Eli glanced along the dungeon walls, letting his gaze linger on the bondage swing along one of the mirrored walls. His cock turned hard as rock when he pictured Maggie there, her anus beckoning him as she lay at the proper angle and height for him to penetrate her there. He'd fondle her round, responsive breasts, place love bites on the back of her neck, in the sensitive spot he'd discovered last night, just below her hairline.

Yeah. He had to claim her there, fill her tight rear passage with his cock, make her whimper, moan and shout her satisfaction again while he took in every expression in her eyes, each curve of her body, reflected in the mirrors and imprinting themselves in his memory. Working quickly, he loosened her bonds before rubbing his fingers through her soft auburn curls. She looked wanton, no longer the staid, conservative colleague but a temptress, eager for him to take her.

He had to taste her now. Covering her mouth, coaxing her to open to him, he tongue-fucked her there, slow and easy, as gently as he intended to fuck her ass with his cock. He lifted her off the table and carried her to the swing, never breaking the kiss until he laid her there, face down, and positioned her hips and thighs in the slings on either side of the center swing. "Give me your hands, baby."

"Anything you say, Master." Her trust humbled him. Very gently, he fastened one hand at a time into Velcro cuffs attached to the thigh slings.

Then he reached for her collar to fasten it to the farthest strap on the swing. Damn. He'd forgotten to collar her. Reaching in his pocket, he took out a soft leather collar and crouched down in front of her. "That gold ring in your clit's the sign that you're mine. But I want you to wear this while we're all alone out here," he said, showing her the wide black leather collar with gold clasp and d-rings where he imagined he might sometimes want to attach a leash. "I'll never ask you to wear it where others can see."

"Thank you." Lifting her head, baring her throat, she looked at him while he fastened it and affixed the tiny gold padlock for which he'd keep the key. "I trust you to care for me, Master."

"I will. I promise to bring you pleasure, fulfill all the fantasies you've ever had. And, Maggie, trust that I'll never hurt you."

"I want to trust you completely."

"Then, as your Master, I'll make sure you can. You're mine now." Completing her bondage, Eli looped Velcro ties through the collar's d-ring and secured them to the swing.

Looking at herself in the mirror, Margaret realized how helpless she was. No matter which of the images she looked at in the four mirrored walls, she saw herself, totally submissive to her new Master. She loved it. Loved being totally possessed by Eli, loved anticipating what he'd do next to make her come. Suspended in the swing, her breasts hanging free, her cunt and anus lay open, inviting her Master to stand behind her, take her in any way he chose. She envisioned him naked, stepping up to her, his cock resting against her buttocks, the large barbell that pierced it providing a cool contrast to the heat of his aroused flesh. He'd stand there, teasing her, his balls bouncing against her swollen slit until she begged him to fuck her, let her come.

She felt terribly, deliciously exposed. Erotically helpless. No need to make decisions now. Eli would make them for her. Her clit throbbed. Yes, the piercing hurt some, but there was no doubt about her arousal. Anticipation built as she imagined him touching her, suckling her, reddening her flesh with all the accouterments of the Dom he was, tools she was certain he had somewhere in this posh, secluded dungeon. The swing hung at just the right level so his cock would line up perfectly with her wet, needy pussy if he stood between her legs.

He smiled down at her, his eyes glittering with lust, though he made no move to return from the other side of the room. From the intent look on his handsome face, she guessed he must have been contemplating what delicious tortures he'd use to heighten her pleasure and his own.

She'd always loved how Eli looked, massive and powerful, as though he could take everyone's problems on his broad shoulders and solve them. She saw those shoulders now as he stripped off a pale blue polo shirt. Thick biceps tensed, and when he reached for his belt, his abdominal muscles rippled.

He curled his belt up in one large hand, as though he knew she was imagining him using it to warm her ass. Shooting her an intent look, he tossed the belt away and shoved his pants down, stepping out of them as soon as he took off his shoes.

Somehow he looked as sexy in boxers as he would have stark naked. The cotton fabric bulged, barely able to restrain his erection. When would he take it off, come and administer whatever discipline he felt his new slave needed?

Eli stepped closer, laid a hand on his cock. Slowly, he slid his hands under the waistband of his shorts and shoved them down, freeing his massive erection. "I'm going to fuck your ass, baby, but not just yet." Gathering some things from a drawer, he brought them along as he approached her. "Easy, now, I'm about to clamp your nipples.

"Yes, Master." She wanted to scream with the initial pain. Then, when he tightened the clamps on both nipples, she could barely keep from shouting out with the ecstasy that radiated all through her body. The pressure built, grew so intense she closed her eyes and moaned.

"Look." She couldn't ignore his hoarsely growled order.

Glancing at the closest mirror, she saw it, a thick gold chain with a weight dangling from it, attached to the nipple clamps, pulling rhythmically against her tightly clamped nipples. "Oh, yesss, Master. Fuck me, please."

"I will." Bending, he took her lips and plunged his tongue deep down her throat. Too soon he broke the kiss, sucked her lower lip between his teeth for just a moment before letting go. "I'm not going anywhere, my precious slave. Not until I have you screaming with pleasure.

Moving behind her, Eli adjusted the height of the swing. Then he bent over her, and nipped that sensitive spot on the back of her neck, just below her hairline—the one he'd bruised last night. With every touch of his hands, each moist breath he took, her arousal grew. Slowly, without the urgency that drove her, he traced along the curve of her spine. "You're one gorgeous woman, and you're all mine," he murmured, tracing around her asshole with one finger.

Margaret soaked in each touch, every breath. The touch of his tongue as he licked his way down her spine was as erotic a sensation as she recalled ever having experienced. The reflection aroused her, a picture of her helplessness, his mastery. He'd leashed his strength, restrained bulging muscles that quivered as he held back. His concern for her welfare was evident every time he touched her. She should have expected it, for he treated his patients with a similar concern.

When he stroked her legs, he sighed. "You don't know how many times I've looked at you, imagined your long, beautiful legs wrapped around my waist. My neck."

"Unfasten me and I'll make that fantasy come true." Truth was, she didn't want him to release her yet. She loved the feeling of helplessness, trusted he'd deliver even greater pleasure than he had last night...or along the side of a deserted road an hour earlier.

"Not yet." As though wanting to distract her, he slid his hands up her inner thighs and up her torso until he found her tightly clamped breasts. He pinched the tips of her nipples sharply then soothed them by rubbing gently over them with his thumbs. She wasn't expecting the sudden pain when he sank his teeth into her buttock.

"Mmm. You taste good." He soothed the bite with long, slow laps of his tongue. When he bent his head down further and used his tongue to lick the sensitive skin around her anus, her cunt contracted, anticipating…

Then he stopped, and she thought she'd die of unsatisfied lust.

Eli stood there, looking down at his slave. His Maggie.

His collar marked her as his property, from the top of her head to her small, shapely feet. God, but he loved the way her breasts swayed like peaches ripe for picking, the nipples darkened and puckered within the clamps. A sheer layer of sweat on her brow and the dark, needy look in her eyes gave silent proof of her arousal. Between her pale, slick labia the tiny stone in her clit ring caught his eye when he straightened and feasted his gaze on her plump, pink pussy.

When the piercing healed, he'd suck and lick her clit every night until she begged for mercy. Nothing turned him on more than the idea of feasting on his woman's smooth-shaved sex. Now just looking at the ring, his permanent mark of ownership, had him so ready that his cock stood straight up, curled against his belly. His mouth watered to lap up the glistening honey that dribbled invitingly from her cunt. Soon he'd be able to toy with the ring in her sensitive little bud, hear her squeal with delight. Temporary restraint would be hard, but the future pleasure would be worth it. Not only because he'd wanted to stake his claim either. Maggie's clit was so responsive, so sensitive, it was made to be adorned.

He had to take her. Fumbling with the wrapper, he pulled out a heavily lubricated condom and rolled it on. His cock throbbed, demanding that he fuck her now, mark her his in the most basic of ways.

Her flushed cheeks and swollen lips marked her desperation as she stared at him in the mirror. "Please, Master, I need your cock inside me," she begged, squirming as much as her bonds allowed when she looked at his sheathed erection in the mirrors that surrounded them.

"My cock needs to be inside you, too." Eli took some water-soluble lubricant and smeared it over the condom, then stepped behind her and tugged at the chain attached to her nipple clamps. "I love playing with your breasts, too."

"Oh yes, Master, that feels…incredible." She sounded breathy, and her nipples were swollen and rigid. Her reaction stoked Eli's own arousal, made him urgent to take her now.

"It's about to feel a lot better. I'm going to fuck your plump, pretty ass, but first I want you to come. Come for your Master."

She whimpered.

"Don't worry, all I want is your pleasure. A good master would never damage his most prized possession." He knelt behind her and dipped his head to her glistening slit. Then he reached and cupped the round globes of her breasts in both hands. God, how he loved to play with them, to squeeze and knead them while she moaned with pleasure. Her honey flowed, and when he lapped it from her slit, he felt her clit swell and harden beneath the protective dressing. She tried to shift, as though she wanted him to suck her there, but he didn't dare oblige her. "Soon, baby. Soon."

"God, yes," she said when he offered his fingers. She caught two of them in her mouth, licking and sucking them as though they were his cock while she rubbed her sopping pussy against his mouth, seemingly desperate for him to give her a climax. He was getting desperate, too. If he didn't fuck her soon and release his pent-up semen, he'd explode.

He tongue-fucked her cunt, as deep and fast as he could, drawing soft whimpers. When he stopped, he licked backward along her slit and ringed her puckered asshole, teasing the tight opening with short stabs of his tongue.

"I need your big, hard cock inside me. Please, Master." She whimpered when he withdrew his fingers.

"Relax, Maggie. You know your cunt's off limits for a few days. But don't worry. I'm going to make you come. I'm going to fuck your ass. You'll love it." Then he ringed her ass again, stiffening his tongue and plunging the tip of it inside the small, puckered opening. Rising, he retrieved the tube of lubricant and worked a generous glob of it around and in her anus. She felt tight, almost as though she'd never been ass-fucked before, so he squirted out more and applied it to the condom he had on.

His eyes were glowing with hot lust when Maggie gazed at his reflection. The way he deliberately readied his sheathed cock with more glistening lubricant made her shiver more with anticipation than from any fear that Eli might hurt her. Her anus twitched, the lubricant he'd applied cooling tissue swollen from their play the night before. She could hardly wait to feel him stretching her, reaming her with his massive, pierced tool.

Her pussy contracted when he ringed her once more with the head of his cock. She tensed, expecting him to claim her ass as forcefully as he'd taken her pussy the night before. Instead, he worked one finger past her tight anal sphincter, then a second. "Breathe deep, baby. Relax. This is going to feel good. Real good." He withdrew his fingers and moved into her slowly, carefully. She took another deep breath, panted and restrained a cry when her flesh protested his invasion. Their reflection showed his huge cock poised, buried only to its pierced head in her rear passage, the other end of its long, thick shaft separating their bodies.

"Open up for me, Maggie. You can take it all. Easy now. Keep breathing easy. Relax and let me fuck your tight, sweet ass."

The idea of him taking her this way with his huge, pierced cock frightened her. But it aroused her more. She couldn't tear her gaze away as he sank into her, inch by inch, until she thought she'd split apart. The touch of his hands on her buttocks soothed her. His quiet words of pleasure, encouragement, helped the pain of his penetration give way to a feeling of fullness that promised pleasure.

She looked once more in the mirror. Her Master, breathing hard, his hands grasping her naked buttocks. Herself, his slave, helplessly bound by his will. By her own volition. When he slid his hands along her body, found her breasts and cupped them in his hands, they looked as one. Incredibly erotic as he buried his cock to the balls and stilled his movement. She wanted more.

"That hurts so good. Your cock's so big. So hot."

"Your ass is tight, baby. I'm not moving. Breathe deep. Relax."

She tried. "I feel...full. So, so full. Please, fuck me. Fuck me hard."

When he all but withdrew and then sank back into her, she gasped. Pain gave way to intense pressure. Heat rushed through her body, and when he reached beneath her and tugged at the chain that hung between the nipple clamps, she went on sensual overload. Her cunt constricted, demanding to be filled, and her clit swelled more against her master's very private sign of possession.

With each slow, rhythmic stroke of his cock into her anus, the last of the discomfort faded, replaced by a delicious sense of fullness...of anticipation. Her climax began and spread quickly through her body, shattering into thousands of tiny needles of ecstasy when Eli let go with a shout. The jerking spasms of his cock set off a series of small aftershocks that left her drained.

So drained that she barely registered it when he loosened her bonds, lifted her from the swing and carried her upstairs. Much later as they lay in a rough-hewn pine bed beneath a large skylight, Maggie looked up at the starry sky. Eli Calhoun obviously deserved the title of Master. He'd certainly mastered her.

Chapter Five

ᘓ

The sun sparkled through brilliant autumn foliage when Eli looked through the skylight the following morning, his hard-on prodding Maggie's flat, taut belly. She was a sleepyhead, all warm and cuddly and relaxed the way he wanted her always to be with him.

They'd get up and go outside, walk along the banks of the lake, hear the leaves crackling beneath their feet while a brisk breeze tousled her hair. Here, they had no patients, no obligations other than to each other. He intended to make the best of this solitary time with his lover—his love.

Yes, she was his love. No doubt about it. He'd let her rest a little longer while he made breakfast. Bending, he dropped a soft kiss on her slack lips before quietly dressing and heading downstairs.

Together. Since the end of his brief marriage, Eli had used that word only in terms of the portion of his life he spent with a sub in bed, the hours shared with his residents in the OR or on rounds, the stolen moments of friendship snatched between cases or after hours. He'd kept his feelings in neat compartments—sex, work, recreational activities with his friends and colleagues.

Maggie had pried open the doors to all of him. He should be running for cover, but all he wanted to do was stay, build toward the sort of relationship he'd promised himself he'd never risk again.

While birds chirped in the cottonwood outside the kitchen door, Eli brewed coffee, set out glasses of juice and scrounged through the cupboard to find the makings for some breakfast fajitas. They were going to relax…and do some serious talking about their future. Sometime between yesterday and now, he'd realized Maggie was his perfect mate. He wasn't about to let her go or let their work interfere unnecessarily with their life together.

A worrisome thought crossed his mind. What if Maggie only wanted sex? Stolen hours away from the mainstream of their personal and professional lives? The idyllic feeling of the past few moments disappeared, replaced with doubts. If she did…hell, it had been ten years, and still he remembered the disappointment of his failed marriage, the feeling of lost love, betrayal. He was moving too fast, wasn't he, caught up like some kid in a rush of feelings? Eli gripped the handle of the skillet, his other hand clenching into a tight fist.

Fuck, he should hope that's what she wanted. After all, it was what he wanted too. Or did he? His emotions warred—desire, respect, friendship…possessiveness. He'd tear apart that junior resident who was always drooling over Maggie when they went on rounds.

Eli had to get a grip. *Think…think of the sub, not the woman. Concentrate on sensation. Plenty of time later to sort out logistics.*

When he climbed the stairs to the loft and went back into the bedroom, Maggie was still asleep. Eli visually traced the gentle curve of her spine, then bent and placed a wet kiss on the intriguing dimples on her rounded buttocks. He loved seeing her wearing his collar, its dark expanse a stark contrast with her ivory skin. Damn it, a week ago he hadn't imagined her even letting him into her life, much less that she'd prove herself to be the submissive of his dreams.

"Wake up, sleepyhead. I've fixed us some fajitas." When she smiled at him, he couldn't resist taking her mouth, tangling her tongue with his. "I want to take you for a walk, show you where I go to get away from it all."

"That sounds like fun, Master." Her husky, sleepy voice made him reconsider going out, contemplate crawling back in bed instead and easing the ache in his balls. Damn, but she'd keep him in a constant state of arousal.

He rose and dragged out some faded sweats from a drawer. "Put these on. They'll be way too big on you, but I like the idea of you wearing my clothes. Besides, all you have with you is hardly appropriate to traipse around in the woods." If he didn't get her covered up fast, he'd be joining her again in bed. And he had thinking to do, thinking best done with his brain and not his cock.

* * * * *

Outside with sun dappling the grounds through a stand of sturdy trees, Eli's cabin looked much like other weekend hideaways Margaret had seen. When she looked down a footpath strewn with fallen leaves, she saw blue, briskly running water. The river, she guessed.

Only a few other cabins dotted the view, but she imagined they weren't as isolated as it seemed. Eli's collar warmed her throat, reminded her she'd given herself into his keeping the night before. Her clit tingled when she walked, his ring a constant reminder as well. The loose sweats smelled woodsy, like the aftershave Eli sometimes wore. When they reached the small dock, Margaret tilted her head. "Yours?" she asked, gesturing toward the small, sleek fishing boat that rocked gently in its boathouse alongside the dock.

"Yes. Do you like to fish?"

"I don't know. I've never done it." Not much of an outdoorswoman herself, she was a bit surprised to learn Eli spent much of his free time communing with nature. She wondered how he found time for fishing and other outdoor pursuits as well as what must be a rigorous schedule at the gym and, of course, his busy career.

"Some weekend when we have more time, we'll pack a picnic and spend a day out on the water. You'll like it." His gaze hot, as if he wanted the pleasure of experiencing the physical along with the mental simulation of her company, he pulled her to him, so close the beat of his heart resounded in her breasts. Her cunt throbbed, its slick juices sliding down her thighs when he cupped her buttocks and ground his erection hard into her belly.

A small motorboat roared past the dock, sending its wake churning up the dark green water into a froth of gray-white bubbles. They weren't alone. Instinctively she started to pull away. "What if somebody recognizes us?" *Oh no, he'll be angry with me now, punish me.*

But he surprised her, resting his hands at her waist and smiling down at her. "They won't. Don't worry. No one's close enough to see us. Kneel here," he said, indicating a spot on the dock next to a roughly hewn wooden bench where he'd sat down.

No one would mistake the intent look in his dark eyes for anything but the lust of a Master—a man who knew what he wanted and expected it to be provided without question. Margaret had seen that look before, acceded to a Master's control. With Eli, though, she sensed he wanted not just satisfaction of his sexual desires and control over hers. He was looking for more than sex.

And just like that, instead of Eli, she was thinking of another Master, the one who'd wanted to rob her of the self-determination she'd worked so hard to attain. Not that he'd been cruel, because he wasn't. But like many Doms, he'd driven home his power by imposing his will without any consideration for her feelings, her concerns.

If she'd read Eli right, he was a man who'd want to own her body and soul, to command every aspect of her life. He'd fully engage her emotions in every way. If she gave in, would Margaret Berman the woman disappear, leaving only Maggie, Eli's submissive? The prospect terrified her.

But God, she wanted to give in to him fully. It would be so easy to give in and peel away the protective reserve that had saved her from emotional pain before, when relationships had sputtered and died like embers in a fireplace on a winter night.

"Maggie, look at me." He tipped up her face so she met his gaze, his grip gentle, contrasting with the stern tone of his voice. "I'm going to talk. While you listen, you can put this in your tongue and tickle my cock with it."

Maybe the serious look on his face had signaled only eagerness to explore more sexual pathways, nothing more. Perhaps he had no more than hours of pleasure on his mind. Margaret hoped so. Attempting a smile, she took the tongue ring with its tiny vibrator and replaced the plain gold one she'd put on yesterday morning. "How do I turn it on?"

"I do." He held up a small remote control, rotating its control with his forefinger and making the barbell vibrate against her tongue. His heated gaze held desire, of course, but she thought she sensed something more. Something that touched her heart as well as her libido.

The vibrations felt weird. Arousing, especially when she thought about the thrumming sensations she could create in his cock by tangling the tongue ring with the barbell in his Ampellang. She felt herself grow wetter. "Would you like for me to suck your cock, Master?"

"Yes, please do."

Already engorged, his cock twitched when she drew her face close and blew on it. First, though, she'd sample the taste and texture of the smooth, dark rose surface of his scrotum. He tasted clean yet musky, and while she tongued him there, she paused frequently to suck first one testicle then the other into her mouth. From his rapid breathing, she guessed he found that highly arousing. The vibrations spread the delicious sensations slowly through her body.

Soon he was hard as rock, and she longed to cup his sex, but no good sub moved her hands without her master's permission. When she almost toppled over, he steadied her. "I have as much a duty to you as my lover as you have to me. You don't have to get permission to move or to hold a posture like this if it's not comfortable."

Eli sounded sincere, but still Margaret hesitated before dropping her pose and resting her hands on his muscular thighs. Not wanting to displease him, she kept her head still and continued licking his balls until she elicited a moan. Then she ran her tongue over his long, rigid shaft. The feeling of him ruffling her hair, digging his fingers in and finding the erogenous zone at the crown of her head, stimulated her even more than the vibrations or the clean, male taste of him. Just when she thought she'd driven him past his desire to talk, as he'd said he would, he spoke, though his voice was hoarse, ragged in its desire.

"I've known I was a Dom for about fifteen years, since I was nothing but a green kid exploring his sexuality. I get off being in control sexually." He paused, his words hanging between them as though he expected a response. "I was married briefly when I first started my residency, to a woman who wanted nothing but plain vanilla sex, and since then I've had subs who've provided everything but plain vanilla. Until now, I've never found a sub with whom I could imagine sharing a life. Maggie, I'll never interfere with your career or humiliate you the way I'm guessing your last Master may have done. But I want more than a fuck buddy on weekends. I'm hoping you do, too."

She did, even more than she needed the control he offered. Somehow he'd known intuitively her misgivings, her fears. He was wrong about her old Master being cruel but right that she'd dreamed of a Master with whom she could share everything—not just sexual kinks.

"I'm thirty-seven years old, and part of me apparently is ready to settle down. I've learned that just any sub won't satisfy me any longer. I want a woman to love. To share more with than just *this*." He lifted her face, made her stop sucking him now to meet his gaze. "I want you. Even before I guessed you hid a submissive nature behind the armor of reserve you wear, I ached to have you. You gave me wet dreams, made me want you so much that I was even willing to restrain the dominant side of me. I'd planned to do that the other night. I want you 24/7. I want to walk into your office and kiss you any time I feel like it, in front of anybody who cares to look. Maggie, tell me you'll let our relationship come out into the open."

When she looked into his eyes, she saw desire. More important, she sensed he was sincere. She loved the idea of a partner, almost as much as she yearned to have her Master. But that longing terrified her as much as it aroused her. One part of her wanted to run as fast as she could, escape the trap of commitment. Another larger part of her brain admonished her to stay and hope Eli would never want to let her go.

"Well, will you? Don't keep me guessing. I don't give a damn whether you wear my collar when we're not alone, but I expect you to wear my ring."

"I'm wearing that already." It tickled and tingled, reminding her it was beneath the dressing over her clit. Reminding her she belonged to him.

He lifted her left hand to his lips and sucked the third finger into his mouth. "This is the kind of ring I'm talking about. The kind that goes here, where everybody can see."

What? She hadn't dreamed, hadn't dared to even consider Eli might want that kind of commitment. Not now, probably not ever. Maggie wanted to say yes. Instead, she took advantage of the fact he'd let her go when he picked up her hand to duck her head and close her mouth over his thick cock head. Using her tongue, she rotated the barbell in his piercing. He let her do it, though from his stillness, she wasn't going to get away with it without a response. But she had to be careful, consider all the changes being his full-time slave would entail. Visualizing a life with her Master being a big part of her professional life—an omnipresent reminder of her subservience—troubled her even as the prospect intrigued her.

"Well?"

From Eli's husky growl, Margaret surmised that she'd managed to get him even hornier. But he still expected an answer to his proposal—a verbal one. That became obvious when he laid his hands on her shoulders and said, "Stop that for now, baby."

"You want us to live together?" She couldn't even consider marriage at the moment, even though the mention of a ring implied that.

"I want you to marry me. Eventually. We can just live together for a while if that's what you want." He slipped his arms around her, drew her up onto his lap. "We've been friends for ages. We're professional colleagues." His gaze softened. "And you can't deny we're damn good together in bed. What more could you ask for?"

She didn't know. "I'm Jewish," she blurted out, grasping for any reason to say no.

"So what?"

"Our parents—they may not approve."

"Maggie Berman, quit making excuses. I'm not going to interfere with your religion, and I doubt you're going to mess around with my beliefs. Don't worry. My mom will love you. She's been angling for me to find a good woman and settle down ever since I finished my residency and moved back to Texas." Eli paused, and his expression turned serious. "Don't tell me your parents would object to you marrying someone who doesn't share their faith."

They would, but then Margaret hadn't spent a lot of time during recent years trying to please her sober, academic-minded and very demanding parents. Long ago she'd found that making the effort was futile. "Yes, but I've spent most of my life disappointing them, even when I tried not to. It's…it's just… Oh, I don't know."

"Baby, I can't imagine you ever disappointing anybody. Particularly your folks. Damn it, parents are supposed to love kids as they are, and not very many could ask for more than you've already given them. College. Med school. You're doing great in a specialty residency program that's rough for anybody to get into." Eli's expression was fierce, as though he truly couldn't fathom her parents feeling anything other than pride in her accomplishments.

Come on, Eli. Take away my choice. Order me to marry you. He had no problems ordering her to service him in any and every manner imaginable. No difficulties making her come at his command, bombarding her with more erotic sensations than she'd ever felt before. Truth be known, he had no problem making her heart go mushy with emotions having nothing to do with his mastery of her in bed.

"Can't make up your mind, Maggie girl?"

"I…I—no. No, Master." She couldn't control the tremor that went through her body when she realized she'd displeased him.

"Baby, I won't hurt you. Ever. The only way I'll punish you is by denying you this." He lifted and turned her to straddle him, then rubbed his cock against her through her sweats. "And that would be awfully hard to do." With a gentle hand, he cupped her breast, then lifted her chin and looked into her eyes. "I never want to make you cry."

"So, it's either marry you or lose you as a master?"

"I wouldn't say that. But I want us to be together, as friends and lovers to our colleagues and friends, and as my much-loved sex slave when we're alone. Be honest. You want that, too." He slid a hand inside her sweats, stroked her wet, hot slit. "Your cunt's telling me yes, but I want to hear it from your pretty lips, too."

She wanted him. It wasn't just her weeping pussy. With every bit of her being she screamed for Eli to take her now. He'd said he wanted a woman to love, but did he love her? How could she ask for that declaration this soon? But it wasn't too soon. It felt as though they'd known each other forever, and truth was, she loved him. But… *Say you love me. Me. Not your resident. Not your friend. And not your sex slave, either.* "I can't. Not yet."

"I want you too much to let you seal me off into one corner of your life. I want it all." He stroked her hand, his touch incredibly gentle, incredibly arousing. "Think about what we've got together. Do you really want to lose it by saying no?"

What is love if not desire...and respect? Margaret didn't think she'd be able to argue with her body or her heart. She couldn't see him every day at the hospital and not want to throw herself into his arms. He'd said he would give her time, but she had a feeling seven years wouldn't be long enough to alleviate her worries.

Damn it, she was a surgeon. She made split-second decisions in the OR, usually with decent results. Why not make one now, reach out and take what she wanted more than anything? She took a deep breath, drew on the courage that had let her step up and try to snatch a patient from the jaws of death. "I don't need any time to decide. Not if you love me." Then she fixed her gaze on their joined hands. Waited. Seconds ticked away, along with her ability to breathe, to hope...

Then he spoke, his voice quiet, confident, compelling. "Baby, I love you. Never thought I'd feel this way again, but I do." Eli's smile turned as warm as a summer day, though the breeze had picked up and she'd just been shivering despite having on his warm sweats. "I do. Now, let's enjoy our weekend. We're going to have a busy time making wedding plans."

She couldn't help laughing. Her Master didn't waste time here, any more than he did in surgery. "I just said I'd marry you, and you won't give me a little time to get accustomed to the idea?"

"Nope," he said, grinning back at her. "I'm not giving you time to change your mind."

Damn, but she liked having a Master who knew what he wanted and wasn't shy about going after it. "All right. Now may I finish sucking you off, please?"

"Feel free, baby. I'm not about to tell you no. But first, let's go back in the house. I want to taste every inch of your luscious body and make you come. You're mine now. All mine."

* * * * *

Inside, seductive music caressed her ears. Music Margaret hadn't noticed was playing when they'd gone outside an hour earlier. When Eli lifted her in his arms and carried her not to the dungeon but upstairs to the loft where they'd slept, she felt…loved.

Not merely wanted.

The sweet scent of vanilla rose in the air when he tossed bath oil crystals into the Jacuzzi tub. Fat candles flickered in the windowsill, their reflections bouncing off the angled window and skylights.

"You have beautiful breasts," Eli murmured when he'd lifted his sweatshirt over her head. "Tempting." He bent, kissed each aching nipple, then straightened and caressed her cheek. "I do love you, you know."

She sensed something different in his touch, a promise of devotion she'd never recognized in his deep voice before. It was almost as though he were seducing a beloved innocent, not mastering his slave. "Please, Master. Make me…"

"You don't need bonds. Not now. Trust that I'll take good care of you. That I'll make you come for me." He slid the sweatpants down her legs, his large hands caressing her, massaging her calves and thighs. Kneeling, he examined the dressing on her pierced clit, his touch gentle. Arousing. "The dressing's waterproof. Come on, join me in the tub," he said when he stood and stripped off his own clothes.

The tub was deeper than it looked, Margaret realized as soon as she stepped in. Warm bubbles tickled her breasts as they burst against her body. Eli settled behind her, his erection a fiery probe nudging the crack of her ass. Would he…

She spread her legs, inviting him in, eager for the stretching feeling of pleasure-pain when he'd penetrate her anus with his huge, hot cock. No. Not her body but his, to do with as he would.

"No hurry, now. Come, sit on my lap."

Her cunt clenched with anticipation as she settled on his hard thighs. His erection nestled inside her labia, hot and throbbing. His hands cupped her breasts, squeezing and tugging at them until the nipples tightened and poked insistently at his palms. "Oh, yes, Master. Please."

"Like that, don't you?" Shifting, he took each nipple between his thumbs and index fingers and rolled them, pulling them to where they barely broke the fragrant froth on the surface of the water.

Her cunt clenched, and a sense of urgency began to grow in the pit of her stomach. The pressure and the tiny kisses of breaking bubbles of oil on the tips of her nipples helped her arousal build to a fever pitch. She wriggled, as if she could take his cock inside her on her own, soothe the urgent need to be filled. Taken.

"Please. You won't hurt me. I need you inside me. Don't make me wait any longer. Fuck me now." She didn't care that he might punish her. She had to have him inside her, filling the throbbing emptiness…giving her his hot semen…triggering her own climax.

"Relax, sweetheart. You know I don't dare fuck you now, or play with my clit ring the way I want to."

"You won't hurt me. Not as much as it will hurt if you refuse." She clamped down on her lips, waited for her punishment. "I'm sorry, Master. Do with me as you will."

Eli felt her body tense, as though she expected a rebuke. She'd agreed to marry him, but he knew it would take more than a ring on her finger to allay doubts born of previous relationships and maybe even of the family she thought she could never please. He looked forward to being the doctor who'd heal those wounds, teach her to trust and love. Accept him as her Master again. And he'd start proving it now. He chafed her nipples once more, then set her off him. "Sit right here. And tell me if I hurt you. If you don't, I'll redden your pretty ass." Stretching out so he could brace his feet against the other side of the tub, he lifted her until her hot, wet pussy cradled his cock.

"Lean back," he said, guiding her down then lifting her enough so he could take her from the rear. Reminding himself to go easy, he grasped her hips, lifted her and positioned his cock at the welcome entrance to her vagina. "Like that? I thought you would." He helped her slide down on him, take him in. "That's it, baby. Take me slow and easy. Feel yourself stretching, accepting me, taking my cock and making it your own."

"Oh yes, Master."

She was hot and wet. And so tight he was almost afraid to move for fear of hurting her, but she gave him no choice. Once she'd taken him in, she began to move up and down, setting the water in motion. Its gentle waves caressed his arms, his chest, his back. When she spread her legs further, he reached between them and stroked her incredibly smooth pussy lips, mindful not to brush against her clit.

Her delighted moan told him she was close. So was he. Pressure built in his balls. He fucked her carefully as she fucked herself on his cock. With his free hand, he reached up and fed a finger to her mouth just as she screamed out with ecstasy. He couldn't hold out longer. As her cunt clenched around his cock, he came—hot, fast spurts of semen that seemed to fuel her own climax.

"I never came before when I wasn't confined." Hours later Maggie smiled over at Eli as they lay in bed, an amazed look in her beautiful eyes.

He smiled. "You're confined. With or without the ropes and cuffs and toys, and your mind knows it. It knows I'm your Master." He rolled over, cupped her face between his hands as he leaned over her. "But I'm as bound to you as you are to me. For the first time in my life, I've been mastered by love."

Epilogue

ꝸ

Once Maggie had agreed to a lifetime commitment with Eli, things started moving like a tumbleweed across a barren field. Nothing would do Eli but to spread the word—now, not later—to everybody they ran into once they got back to San Antonio. Within a day, they'd moved her few possessions to his spacious new condo unit not far from the Riverwalk.

No one, not even the hospital administrator who could have pointed out that attendings weren't allowed to fraternize with residents, seemed to mind that she and Eli had gotten together so suddenly. His partners welcomed her to their group, and their wives embraced her as one of them, without the slightest hesitation. Lynn Blackstone and Shelly Silverman even managed to squeeze a surprise engagement party into everybody's busy schedule in a matter of three days.

Maggie was happy but exhausted from the flurry of activity. She'd smiled until her face felt frozen, accepting congratulations from everyone at the hospital, from senior attendings to the pretty Mexican woman whose job was to tidy the surgery lounge.

Now all they had left to do was inform their parents. Maggie was sure Eli had saved that for last because she was so certain her parents would raise objections.

"I'll go first," he told her, sitting in front of the phone on a glass-topped cocktail table.

"Thank you, Master." She sat, snuggled against his powerful body, on the large brown leather sectional that took up most of the living room in his condo—now her home as well. Trying to calm her nerves, she looked at framed photos of Eli's weekend cottage and one of the Medina River that she thought must have been taken at sunrise. The photos brought memories of the dungeon where they played, the peaceful sound of forest animals outside the cabin, the gently running water tumbling over limestone and some fallen tree limbs only a few hundred feet from the front door. One visit there, and she loved the place because it told her good things about who Eli was, setting aside the obvious facts that he was a gorgeous specimen of a man, a loving master and a surgeon with compassion as well as skill.

It didn't work, trying to take her mind off facing her parents. Although she tried hard to squelch the fear that was building in her gut, she was pretty sure that Eli sensed her discomfort.

"It's all right, sweetheart. Mom will love you just like she loves me." He put the phone on speaker and brought her left hand to his lips. One at the time, he kissed each finger, finishing up with the one where he'd put a perfect diamond solitaire last night, to the delight of the other guests at their engagement party.

"Hello, Eli. It's good to hear from you." Eli's mother sounded the way Maggie had imagined she would after looking at her photo on Eli's bureau—sweet, with just a hint of a Texas country twang in her voice. A welcoming sound. A sound that chased away some of her trepidation.

"Hi, Mom. I've got a surprise for you. Maggie Berman's here beside me, and she's foolish enough to have agreed to be my wife. Say 'Hi,' sweetheart."

Maggie shot Eli a surprised look. "How are you, Mrs. Calhoun?"

"Oh, my God, my boy's certain to give me a heart attack yet if he doesn't quit springing surprises on me! Tell me all about yourself. How you and Eli met, where and when you're gonna tie the knot. How long has my naughty son been keeping you all to himself?"

Maggie squeezed Eli's hand for courage, but still her voice came out squeaky, not at all like the self-confident surgeon she knew she should project. "We work together, ma'am. I'm one of the surgical residents Eli supervises. We've known each other about six months, since he came to San Antonio and started working at the hospital, but..."

Eli broke in. "She's too embarrassed to tell you I swept her off her feet less than a week ago, Mom. I'm past the age of dawdling now that I've found the woman I want to live with for the rest of our lives. The wedding will be as soon as you can get yourself off the ranch and down here to see us tie the knot."

"Wait a minute, Eli. Have you thought that Maggie might like a bit more of a ceremony than it sounds like you're planning?"

His mother obviously didn't realize Eli was a Dom, but Maggie appreciated her concern. "It's all right, ma'am. We both want a small wedding, just our friends here—and families who want to come."

"That's good then. My son never did want to wait once he made up his mind what it was he wanted." She paused, as if she was thinking of Eli as a child...a teenager...a young man graduating from medical school. Maggie could hear the love and pride in her voice and knew Eli had never known anything but his mom's love and pride. "You'll have your job, making my big lug of a son toe the line. I'll see how soon I can get somebody to cover for me at the Founder's Day celebration and let you know how soon I can get away."

"Thank you." She smiled at Eli. *I like your mom.*

He grinned back at her then spoke. "Do it quickly, Mom. I want to lasso this filly before she gets away."

"Now, son. Be patient. How far away do Maggie's parents live?" She paused then spoke to Maggie. "Will it take more than a day or two to get your folks down to San Antonio? You don't want to rush them."

"They live in Chicago." Maggie doubted her mom and dad would make the trip. After all, the last event in her life that they'd shared with her was...hell, she didn't remember. Was it her high school graduation, when she'd been valedictorian? Of course. They only attended events where she was being honored as number one. "If they want to come, they can get here in a matter of hours."

"If they want to come? You mean they might not?" Eli's mom sounded scandalized, but no less enthusiastic than she'd been before Maggie's revelation.

Eli spoke, his tone sympathetic. "We haven't told Mr. and Mrs. Berman yet. I wanted to let you know first."

"Of course. Welcome to the family, Maggie. We're all gonna love you, just like Eli does."

After exchanging goodbyes, she hung up. "Dial your folks' number now, sweetheart."

"They're not likely to welcome you with open arms the way your mom did me." Oh, yes. They'd be civil. Never let it be said that David and Miriam Berman ever behaved in a less than socially correct manner. But she didn't want Eli to expect the sort of spontaneous joy she'd heard from his mom. Reluctantly, she dialed the number that hadn't changed for as long as she could remember.

Then she took several shallow breaths as the phone rang once, twice, three times. Maybe they'd be out. She hoped so.

No such luck. Maggie heard the click of the receiver, the stern sound of her father's voice. "Berman residence."

Not "hello." He couldn't even give in that little bit to popular culture. It was if he and her mother were caught in a time warp and had never been able to break free. "It's me, Margaret," she said, trying to keep her voice steady even though her body was trembling uncontrollably. "I'm engaged."

A sharp intake of breath came through the speakers, loud and clear. "Engaged?"

She was about to speak when Eli clamped a hand over her mouth. "Yes. I'm Elijah Calhoun, and Maggie and I plan to get married as soon as it can be arranged. We want you to come share our big day."

Her father sputtered. "This is a shock. Mother and I have never met you, Mr. Calhoun."

"Doctor Calhoun," Maggie said, slipping out from under Eli's hand over her mouth. "I'm one of Eli's residents in thoracic surgery—chest traumas are his specialty, and I've been taking a rotation with him." *Please, God, let my father not subject Eli to the third degree. For once, make him happy for us.*

"Mother! Margaret has some disturbing news," her father called out.

That made her furious as well as hurt. "I didn't mean to disturb you, only to tell you I'm in love and thrilled that Eli has asked me to marry him. We're going to do it in the next week or two, as soon as his mom can get here. Nothing big, just a few good friends and hopefully our respective parents."

Eli took over, thankfully, though Maggie would have spared him. While she'd expected him to exert the sort of control he demonstrated when dealing with difficult OR staff, he stayed amazingly low key, answering her cold, formal parents' pointed questions even though they were asked in a disapproving tone, barely within the definition of civility. "Yes. I have no intention of holding your daughter back professionally," he responded to the question of whether he intended to allow her to pursue her career. He answered questions as to his ability to support her, his background…even his ethnic background, a whole lot more cheerfully than she'd imagined he would.

"What day can you get here to witness your daughter's wedding?" Eli asked, neatly cutting off the inquisition before the anger apparent in his expression and in his tightly clenched fists spilled over into his voice.

"I don't know," Maggie's mother said, her tone hesitant. "David?"

Maggie heard the familiar sound of her father clearing his throat, letting out a loud sigh. They weren't going to come. Just as she thought. But Eli kept on the pressure. "Well, Mr. Berman. Do we wait for you to get here, or does your silence mean you're not coming?"

"We will let you know," her father finally said. "Mother and I need to talk."

Hugging Maggie, Eli brushed gentle kisses over her face, licking away the tears she hadn't been able to hold back. "Don't know if they'll come see us get married or not, but I hope they do, for your sake."

"Thank you. As long as your mom comes, I'll be content." And that was the truth. Maggie might never have parents who loved her for herself, but she had Eli, her Master and her love. "You really love me, don't you?"

"I do. Gotta practice for saying that on our big day." With that, he swept her into his arms and carried her to their bedroom as though she weighed no more than a baby. "And in the meantime, while I practice, you could help my concentration by…" He murmured a suggestion to her that she was sure could not only wreck his concentration, but shatter her as well. A suggestion she recognized, with a tilt of her heart, was his way of taking her mind off the pain of the last few moments. Her Master, who always looked after her heart as well as her body. "And," he continued with a glint in his eyes, "if you're good, I'll tie you up and eat your pussy until you scream."

And she was good. Very, very good.

The End

SWITCHING CONTROL

Trademarks Acknowledgement

ꙮ

The author acknowledges the trademarked status and trademark owners of the following wordmarks mentioned in this work of fiction:

Barbie: Mattel, Inc.

BMW: Bayerische Motoren Werke Aktiengesellschaft

Dolce & Gabbana: Gabbana, Stefano & Dolce, Domenico

Ferrari: Ferrari S.p.A.

Jacuzzi: Jacuzzi, Inc.

Lexus: Toyota Jidosha Kabushiki Kaisha TA Toyota Motor Corporation

Rolex: Rolex Watch USA

Chapter One

ꟃ

"Lookin' good, Tom."

Tom could say the same for his pal Eli Calhoun. The burly surgeon looked as comfortable in a tux as he did in the more familiar surgical scrubs. Eli's wife Maggie fit right in, too, wearing a shiny black dress that hugged her curves. Lucky bastard! Eli had hit the jackpot when he found her, a gorgeous woman no one would ever guess was his sex slave as well as his colleague and wife. From Eli's grin and relaxed stance, Tom surmised that he was having a good time at the ball despite his preference for more high-energy pursuits like cracking chests, bodybuilding and acting out BDSM scenes. "Thanks. Every now and then we have to keep up the pretense of being civilized. You two having fun?"

"It's not too bad." Eli smiled down at Maggie. "I'm still not big on these dress-up shows, but enduring them's a lot easier since I know I'll be taking Maggie home. How about you?"

"I'm okay. Doing the command performance tonight with my mom and my date." Speaking of Jo, she'd broken away from a group of San Antonio businesswomen and was headed their way, her blonde hair gleaming around her shoulders and her hot body encased in something light blue and shiny and slit to show off one perfect leg. Killer heels had her hips swaying when she walked, in a way Tom imagined had every man in the room imagining those legs wrapped around his waist.

He'd had those fantasies, too, until they'd tried having sex a while back. But he'd learned quickly that she was all promise and no delivery. "Have you two met Johanna

Carlisle? Jo, these are my colleagues, Eli and Maggie Calhoun."

Jo was arm candy, no doubt about it. Tom had no doubt that the picture they made together worked in this crowd. Jo in her finery, diamonds glittering around her neck and in her earlobes, her perfectly manicured hand resting in his as she greeted his friends. His mom liked seeing him with Jo at affairs like these, told him regularly that she wished he'd finally settle down and put a ring on her finger.

But he and Jo had been down that road, and both of them soon realized they were not sexually compatible. Jo was vanilla all the way. She considered oral sex kink, and after that one very awkward evening he realized, despite her diplomatic withdrawal from bed, that she considered his interests just short of perversion. At the very least she'd realized he wasn't the gentle lover of her Regency fantasies. However, by some miracle, they'd somehow managed to stay friends, such that it was mutually beneficial to them to attend galas like this together.

He certainly couldn't bring one of the subs he played with at the Club, like Snake Woman. Tom stared into his drink and sighed, wishing he didn't envy Eli so much. Seemed right now he had to be platonic friends with women in his social life and only a sexual complement to the subs inside the club. Would he ever find someone like Maggie, who could straddle both worlds? Someone he could love as well as desire?

It wasn't that he hadn't begun to give a lot of thought to settling down with Jo. She was witty, gorgeous, well-educated, and successful as a family practice associate in one of the biggest law firms in San Antonio. She had all the qualities he should have been looking for in a mate—except for one. Tom had learned young that vanilla wasn't his flavor when it came to sex. And Jo was as vanilla as a woman could be, from the gleaming blonde hair she usually kept fashionably confined in some sort of twist to the pink, pedicured toes that peeked out of spike-heeled sandals. In between she had a body made to showcase the tasteful designer gown his mother had gushed over.

I want to fuck her. My way, though. Maybe she's not all that plain vanilla after all. Right, Latimore. The minute you dragged out a flogger, she'd have the cops slapping you in cuffs and escorting you off to jail.

Still, she's got all the other qualities you want in a wife. Otherwise you wouldn't be thinking of proposing.

Jo's hand felt warm through the fabric of his coat, and the subtle scent of her cologne had him halfway hard. Every sign she gave told him that if he took her home tonight, she'd let him fuck her. Testing the waters, he slipped an arm around her waist, laying his hand ever so carefully above her hipbone. "I don't think I mentioned it before, but you look mighty pretty tonight."

"Thank you. You're not too bad yourself." Her tone was soft, almost submissive.

She was no submissive. But she was good company, and she fit in with society's idea of what a doctor-socialite's mate should be. Hell, he didn't know. Something was holding him back yet pushing him toward her. As inhibited as Jo was in bed, she wasn't as bad a lover as the subs he'd taken at Club Rio Brava would be as life partners. The idea of bringing Snake Woman, his most frequent partner in club scenes, to a function like this was so ridiculous as to make him shake his head.

Professor Higgins had transformed Eliza Doolittle into a lady in *Pygmalion*. But Tom figured that not even Higgins could transform Snake Woman. Of course, what did it say about him that he chose her most often when he went to the Club? If he was going to be honest with himself, he'd admit he chose the sub most likely to satisfy him sexually but least likely to meet his emotional needs because he'd just about given up finding one who could do both. With Snake Woman, he wouldn't fool himself with any illusions, as he had with Jo.

Snake Woman—he didn't even know her real name—was too far gone to give a damn about how she appeared in the real world, interested only—as far as Tom could discern—in satisfying her sexual compulsion to be totally controlled. "Want to stop by the buffet?" he asked, hoping no one had noticed his moment of introspection.

"Yes, for a few minutes. The spread looks pretty good. Maggie?" Eli looked down at his wife and smiled.

"I'll take some of the veggies and dip, love." Maggie turned to Jo. "All right. This is my first year in San Antonio, and I can't get Eli to tell me much about Fiesta except that he's going to take me to the opening event at the Alamo. Maybe you can fill me in while the men get us some *hors d'oeuvres*."

"Tom could tell you more about the history. His great-great grandfather was one of the founders, and he's on the committee for the River Parade. Basically, Fiesta's ten days of eating, partying and celebrating the heroes of the Alamo. It's been happening in springtime now for nearly a hundred years. I think there were only a few years it was canceled because of war or maybe during the Great Depression. You won't want to miss the parade, or the Oyster Bake over on St. Mary's campus. Tom?" Jo shot him a smile before he could head to the buffet table.

She was obviously in her element, a born-and-bred local firmly entrenched in the traditional spring festivities and obviously impressed by his pedigree. "Jo's exaggerating. It was my great grandfather who helped get the whole thing started. The men in my family all started reproducing late. Anyhow, you two won't want to miss the River Parade. It's unique, plus you can watch it from one of the restaurants along the Riverwalk. If you two ladies will excuse me, I'm going to join Eli and get us some snacks."

For a few minutes they sat, sipping champagne and munching delicious but not very filling appetizers. Tom could tell Eli was getting tired of the small talk. So was he.

Eli took his and Maggie's plates and handed them to a roving waiter. "I think we'll take off and get to bed early," Eli said, his muscular arms reaching around his wife's slender waist and cupping her belly protectively. "It was nice to meet you, Jo." With that, Eli and Maggie disappeared into the crowd.

"They're sweet, obviously newlyweds," Jo said, her voice and smile sincere as she laid a hand over Tom's and gave it a squeeze. "I'll bet you'd like to make your escape, too, wouldn't you?"

He would. Maybe he could develop a taste for vanilla if he tried hard enough. It wasn't as if Jo would accept sharing him with the subs at Club Rio Brava the way his mother had turned a blind eye to his dad's frequent overnight absences. And he respected her too much to marry her and cheat behind her back. "We'd better go tell Mom goodnight."

"All right."

* * * * *

Several months later

"I'm relieved we pulled this case off." Eli Calhoun wadded up his mask and gown and tossed them into the bin after they'd both walked into the surgeons' lounge following a particularly grueling Thursday afternoon case. "So what's happening with you, Tom?"

"Not much. Work and more work, and an occasional night out at the club."

Eli grinned. "What about that gorgeous blonde you've been showing off at all the hospital functions? Anything going on there?"

"Nope." There never had been, beyond the friendship Tom and Jo enjoyed. "We go out once in a while, but I doubt that will happen often, now that she's found the guy I imagine she'll eventually marry. I could love her, except..."

"Except you're into domination and she's not the type to submit? I sensed that when you introduced her to Maggie and me." Eli opened his locker and started changing into street clothes. "Speaking of Maggie, I'd better hurry. We're going out for dinner since she's off call now."

Tom tried to tamp down the envy he couldn't help feeling. "Morning sickness getting to her, huh?" he asked in a teasing tone.

"A little." Eli's grin conveyed a lot of pride, as if he were the only man on earth to make his woman pregnant. "We're taking it easy now, nesting. I don't want her to overdo it, which is why I convinced her to go out on leave."

"You're one lucky SOB, you know." Not too many Doms could find a sex slave who shared not only their professions but also their places in local society. Tom certainly had never run across such an ideal woman.

"Yeah, I know. I'm hoping you find someone like her, my friend." Eli paused then laughed. "Not that someone as ugly as you deserves a woman as great as Maggie, of course. If you find her, you'll probably have to hide your Dom hat and beg her to give you the time of day."

"You're nuts. If you can latch on to a woman like Maggie then I should be able to do it, too. After all, you may have muscles on your muscles, but your social graces leave a lot to be desired."

"What can I say? I'm just a ranch boy, deep inside. I've got other qualities, though. Ones Maggie thinks more about than whether or not I pick up the right fork or remember to open the car door for her."

Despite the touch of understanding underlying the humor in Eli's voice, it did give Tom food for thought. The last couple of times he'd been to the Club, he'd been leaving as he noticed a Domme on the floor. She hadn't seen him, but something about her had tugged at him. Although she'd been wielding a flogger on the wimpy ass of a groveling male sub, he'd sensed something vulnerable about her. Maybe it was that slightly wounded look in her eyes, or the fact she didn't seem to be enjoying what she was doing the way he always did when he was with a sub. Or maybe it was her lush, rounded curves that attracted him. Or the heavy nipple rings he had trouble imagining a Domme choosing for herself.

He'd disregarded the instant attraction because of course he didn't lean that way. But maybe he should take a closer look. If she was there tonight and unoccupied, perhaps he'd invite her to play with him and Snake Woman and see what happened. If nothing else, he could resolve this niggling feeling about her.

"How're you liking marriage?" Tom asked.

"To Maggie? I love it. Love her."

"You don't miss the BDSM scene?" He and Eli had finished medical school the same year and discovered early on that they shared a need to dominate their sex partners. Tom had invited Eli to join Club Rio Brava when he came to San Antonio last year to join Mark Blackstone and Kurt Silverman's trauma surgery team.

Eli shook his head. "We make our own scenes. Not as much now as before we found out about the baby. Once in a while we drop in at the club, but I don't need it the way I used to, and I'm certain Maggie doesn't, either." Approaching forty as Tom was now, Eli had settled down with a woman who shared his lifestyle but who outwardly seemed as conventional and socially savvy as Jo.

"Enjoy your night off. Tell Maggie I offered congratulations to you both." Tom put on a clean set of scrubs and grabbed his pants and shirt out of the locker. He was off to Club Rio Brava, but the prospect of slaking his lust had dulled by comparison to the life his friend had lucked into.

* * * * *

What the hell was the matter with him? Tom kept stopping, almost turning back toward San Antonio every few miles. For a long time he sat in his car at a shady spot on the winding road along the river, thinking. Trying to weigh his conflicting needs for kinky sex against an equally strong desire for a lifetime relationship with a woman who fulfilled all his nonsexual requirements for a partner.

A soft breeze set in motion the new, bright green leaves that were beginning to sprout. Pussy willows swayed down at the river's edge where water lapped against them, higher than usual following last week's rains.

Nature was starting anew. As he'd tried to do.

Tom understood now why his dad had lived two lives, one with him and his soft-spoken, beautiful mother and the other with a string of subs at the club a little farther down the road. Too bad Tom wasn't cut out to follow his father's example, at least as far as his sex life went. He wasn't into subterfuge, and he wasn't into women who wouldn't demand fidelity.

Fuck it. He might have had Jo in mind when he'd bought a three-carat diamond at that estate auction three months ago and stashed it away in the wall safe in his bedroom. But he hadn't given it to her. Now he never would. She'd cut him loose, which didn't bother him nearly as much as it should have if what he felt for her was love.

His mom had been disappointed when she'd learned Jo was getting serious about one of the partners at her office. Johanna suited her just fine as a potential daughter-in-law. *Too bad.* It was he, not his mom, who'd have to live with the woman. And he wanted a woman who loved playing kinky games.

Tom's recent effort at making a fresh start with his personal life was over. Turning the key in the ignition, he listened to the engine purr for a minute then headed out for the last half-mile of his journey back to hedonistic pleasure. No strings, no pretense.

When he got to the rustic clubhouse, Tom slid out of his car and went inside. His cock was hard as stone, and he needed to ease his lust and his frustration with a real, live woman—not with the animated Barbie doll he'd tried for the last three months to tell himself he loved. He tried not to care that his partner for the evening would have to be one of the club subs. Yeah, he'd have loved having a partner to share every facet of his life, but he wasn't seeing that happening, and he didn't mind all that much. He was here for sex, the kinkier, the better. Besides, he thought the red vintage BMW at the end of the parking lot might have been Snake Woman's, and he lengthened his stride, anxious to see the sub with the serpent once more.

* * * * *

The hot Dom who'd just walked in took her breath away. Selina Harrison paused mid-stroke in flogging the air. It was a slow night at the club, and not a single promising male had crawled into the playroom looking for a Domme to take him in hand. Too bad Selina had cut off her most recent needy sub months ago. Now she feasted her eyes on the tall, lanky guy with a dimple in his chin and a twinkle in his eye. She wondered at the surgical scrubs he had on. Leather was the usual club attire for most of the male Doms. Still, those blue scrubs draped nicely over his broad shoulders...and hinted at an impressive sex beneath the string that kept the pants from slipping down and giving her a clear, unimpeded view.

For him she'd almost get on her knees and take his orders. Hell, forget the almost. She'd do it in a New York minute if he ever gave her the time of day. Which was highly unlikely.

He made her want to submit, something she hadn't thought about for five long years since she'd vowed never again to set herself up for mistreatment by a cruel Dom. Maybe it was the scrubs, or the kind look on his handsome face that wasn't quite overshadowed by his obvious lust.

Quit with the fantasies. This is the kind of guy who comes here for his jollies and then goes home and crawls into bed with a size-four society princess. Just like most of the members of this club.

Her mouth watered when she watched him claim Snake Woman, the only club submissive who hadn't been taken when he came in. With an arousing economy of motion, he secured her to a St. Andrew's Cross not three feet from where Selina stood. God, but the guy moved as gracefully as a mountain lion.

He obviously wasn't turned off by major kink, because Snake Woman certainly qualified as kinky—in spades. She probably was a size four, that is if she ever put on clothes—but nothing else about her would remind her Dom of the moment of his gorgeous vanilla wife or girlfriend.

Not many women had the balls to shave their heads. Snake Woman had gone that one step further, and had a wicked-looking reticulated python tattooed, its head staring down at her face, its body coiling around and around her neck, breasts and belly, over her pussy and down her left thigh to her ankle. From what she'd heard in the dressing room, Snake Woman had maintained the look long after the Master who'd commanded it had become ancient history. Just looking at the creature's broad head staring down at Snake Woman's face gave Selina the creeps.

The Dom started out by stroking the head of the serpent, his touch gentle, sensuous, as if his purpose was to give pleasure, not take it. From the ecstatic sounds the serpent made, Selina guessed his touch to her tattooed scalp must have been a real turn-on. Now he was tracing the snake's body that slithered around the woman's small breasts on its way down her torso, moving slowly, his fingers teasing by sliding off the tattooed flesh to stroke pale, human skin. With one finger, he caught and tugged at the silver chain that joined dainty rings dangling from her distended nipples, and when she moaned he clamped first one nipple then the other as she wriggled in apparent ecstasy.

Selina's own pierced nipples tingled, the weight of the large rings she wore in them a constant turn-on when, like tonight, she was without a partner, amusing herself by limbering up her whipping arm. When he ran the tip of his tongue over the tips of the sub's nipples until she writhed orgasmically on the cross, Selina imagined him licking her that way, biting her own needy flesh as her pussy clenched and sent hot fluid dribbling along her slit and down her thigh.

Omigod. She had to bite her own tongue to keep from yelling, begging him to leave Snake Woman and sample her honey. The musky smell of sex that swirled all around them had Selina caught up in the scene, savoring the role of voyeur. She couldn't help reaching down and playing with her own ringed clit when he started to lick his partner's hairless, tattooed mound. He caught her clit ring and held it between his gleaming white teeth. Snake Woman moaned then, and when he caught the chain between her breasts and pulled it taut she writhed with pleasure and let out an orgasmic howl.

Selina was so hot, she couldn't suppress a deep moan, and that apparently drew the Dom's attention. "Come join us," he said, his voice a deep, irresistibly sexy rumble. "And give me that flogger."

When she met his gaze, she sensed he was testing her, gently demanding her to do something submissive. In that moment Snake Woman faded into the background of Selina's mind. There was only the Dom...and her, being drawn back into her long-ago dream that she'd find a man who could compel her submission. It wasn't just the physical pleasure she craved, but the emotional surrender she wanted to give him. A gift, not his due. Unfortunately her childish dream had blazed very briefly before it had become a nightmare.

This is not a good idea, Selina. The voice in her head spoke in a whisper, as if it had to warn her but didn't expect her to heed its advice. As if it didn't want her to say no, but to embrace her deepest feelings, dispel the fear. The Dom must have read her mind because the look in his eyes darkened, commanded her to step toward him, offering her flogger—and herself.

"Good girl," he murmured, feathering a knuckle across her cheek before taking the metal-tipped leather she held out to him, a hesitant offer of surrender.

When he took the flogger, she steeled herself to feel its sting on her breasts or cunt, since the rest of her was mostly encased inside a leather cat suit. But the touch of the leather on her ringed nipples was more of a caress, as soft yet confident on her body as the Dom's voice sounded to her ears. "On your knees and suck my cock. Use your tongue." He adjusted the cross, bringing the sub's cunt level with his mouth while Selina went to her knees.

It was probably her imagination—her fantasy—but it seemed when he turned his attention back to the woman on the cross that he wished it were just the two of them. To keep her fantasy alive, she told herself he was a gentleman who knew it wasn't right to tie up a girl and leave her unfulfilled.

His long fingers nimble, he untied the waistband of his scrubs and slid them and his underwear down and off with one efficient motion. Selina gasped. He was awesome. Hard-muscled thighs, taut belly, evidence that he was no couch potato. For a moment she did nothing but look, savor his well-conditioned lower body.

Then she focused on his big, gently curving cock. The silver Prince Albert ring was thick and heavy—titanium if she didn't miss her guess. When she looked closer and cupped his heavy testicles in both hands she realized he also had a guiche piercing adorned with a small, thick ring. "Oh."

"Like it?" His words were muffled against the lucky sub's pussy, but Selina could tell he liked having the hardware played with. Catching the guiche ring on her little finger, she took his cock in her mouth and swirled her tongue around the plum-shaped head. The ring in his PA tickled her throat. Could she take it? God but she wanted to consume him, make him writhe and moan the way he was torturing Snake Woman. Making herself relax, she tilted her head back.

It wasn't easy, but she managed to control her gag reflex while she swallowed against his satiny shaft. She squeezed his balls firmly in both hands as she deep-throated him. Her pussy creamed, clenched. Her asshole twitched. She wanted to submit to him, have him claim all her needy holes.

She had to be crazy, getting off on being on her knees, sucking off a Dom she didn't know from Adam. Worse, she was imagining how it would feel if she were the one secured to that cross, writhing with climax after climax, totally under the control of a Dominant lover whose goal was apparently to give as well as receive pleasure.

His hips thrust in and out, and when she sucked hard, he moaned against Snake Woman's pussy. She felt his cock swell further against her throat, gently demanding more. The salty taste of him, the sheen of sweat on his taut belly, made her want to draw out his climax. Take it for herself rather than let him save it for someone else. She started to swallow convulsively, move her lips harder against the base of his cock. As he started coming, feeding her spurt after spurt of steamy ejaculate, she gently squeezed his sac, wanting all he had to give.

He must have read her mind because he stopped licking Snake Woman's cunt, released her from the cross, and drew Selina to her feet. This was a big man all over, with more of a swimmer's body than a weightlifter's or football player's. She liked that he was strong enough to heft her substantial weight without any obvious effort—and nice enough not to comment that inside the cat suit was a "cat" her last sub had described as fat while they'd been breaking up.

That was okay. The worm, as she'd called him, had been a hundred-fifty-pound weakling in addition to being a sniveling, groveling sub who couldn't get it up without being flogged until his ass cheeks bled and having his balls stretched until they nearly fell off. Selina figured she was a lot better off without him.

Right now the Dom's eyes bored into her. Lifting his hands from her waist, he cupped her breasts then hooked his forefingers through the rings in her nipples and drew her to him until his strong heartbeat pounded against her flesh and his still-hard cock prodded her leather-covered belly. "I'd like to get to know you, Mistress. Somewhere away from here."

Mistress? Selina had almost forgotten she was here at Club Rio Brava, dressed and acting the part of a Domme. But he remembered and apparently chose to make use of the club rule that allowed two Dominants to reveal their identities to each other and interact outside the dungeon. "I'd like that, too, Master. My name is Selina Harrison."

"I'm Tom Latimore. Meet you outside. My car's the black Lexus parked right by the door."

Tom Latimore. The name rang bells somewhere deep in her head. Of course! He'd been the hot guy she and all of her girlfriends had drooled over when he'd come to his cousin's sweet-sixteen party. He'd been a college man, home for a visit from some Ivy League school out East. She wouldn't expect that he'd remember her. After all, she'd been a shy, overweight fifteen-year-old who'd spent most of that party hiding behind a potted palm, sharing her loneliness with a plate of rich snacks.

But she had no trouble remembering how he'd stopped to talk with her as if he'd been interested in what a gawky wallflower had to say. Or the warmth of his hand when he held it out and asked her to dance. For years she'd held on to the memory of her first dance, of the prince singling her out of a crowd full of older, prettier, skinnier girls. Girls with self-confidence to spare. After that party, her favorite fantasy had been that he'd come home again once she grew up and ask her for a date.

She should have recognized him right away, she supposed, since he hadn't been masked. After all, other than picking up a few character lines on his handsome face, he hadn't changed all that much.

Her heart beat faster, and her pulse raced as she hurried to shower and change, thinking all the time that when she went outside to meet him, she'd see a pumpkin instead of that Lexus he'd mentioned.

Chapter Two

ஐ

Tom leaned back against the supple leather seat, amazed at how eager he was to spend time with Selina outside the club. His cock hardened, as though remembering the delicious feel of her full lips, her soft fingers. The memories were indelibly etched in his mind, along with those of her dominating subs yet not seeming quite comfortable about doing it.

What would she be like outside the club? And what would she be wearing in place of the black leather? He had a sneaking suspicion she might not be a Domme by nature, found himself hoping she was up for making a switch.

When he'd asked her to join him and Snake Woman she'd hesitated, almost as if she wanted to but was afraid. Of what? It was damn unusual for a Domme to switch, in his considerable experience. Most seemed not to have much interest in a man who didn't crawl on his knees before them. But Selina? He couldn't quite figure what it was about her, but he'd almost have sworn she was only pretending…or possibly escaping from a submissive role that had once caused her pain.

He liked her roundish face, full lips and even features, what he could see of them in the cutout face section of her leather mask. No sane man could have failed to notice her generous breasts, creamy skin peeking from the holes in the cat suit, rouged nipples sporting thick silver rings big enough for him to hook two fingers through. The rest of her—well, other than most of her face, her nipples and her inviting, cleanly shaved cunt—had been encased head to toe in the form-fitting black leather costume for her play at the club. From the unnaturally firm way her waist had felt when he brought her to her feet, he guessed she had on a corset underneath. She was no reed-thin lightweight. As a matter of fact he was certain his fashion-conscious mother would call her hefty.

That is if the two should ever meet, which he doubted. But then Selina wasn't Snake Woman. Tom cringed when he considered how often he'd played sex scenes with the submissive serpent, but then, he had no reason to believe Selina would fit in a whole lot better with his social and professional acquaintances than the bald, tattooed woman who got off on significant pain.

Hefty didn't bother him. But he preferred to think of Selina being generously curved, could hardly wait to sample the naked woman beneath all that leather. Too many women these days killed off all their natural curves with crazy diets and liposuction, leaving nothing but bones for a man to hold on to. Given the choice, Tom liked a happy medium.

Then he saw her coming through the door, standing on the porch. Backlit by Club Rio Brava's soft incandescent porch lights, she looked more like a suburban matron than the hard-core Domme she portrayed in the club. In tailored black slacks and a loose-fitting soft gray sweater, her face framed with short, wavy sable hair, Selina had a look about her that even his mother could appreciate. Tom managed to untangle his legs and get out of the car, succeeding in reaching her in time to open the passenger door and seat her inside.

* * * * *

Tom obviously belonged to the upper class San Antonio society Selina had deserted some ten years earlier. Of course almost every member of Club Rio Brava did, except for a few newcomers who'd been recommended for membership, and a few favored subs like Snake Woman whose memberships had been sponsored by their former Masters. Still, Selina didn't realize just how upper class Tom was until she saw the discreet sticker on his window that identified him as a member of the oldest and most prestigious of the clubs that sponsored Fiesta.

Not that a socialite couldn't be a pervert, of course. Her ex had been a poster boy for Perverts-with-a-Pedigree, if indeed such an organization existed. But instinct told her Tom Latimore was no pervert, just a hot Dom she could hardly wait to serve. She wanted to be confident he'd never harm her. Trying to think of him as that nice college boy who'd made it a point to dance with her, she pushed aside the hurtful memories that had made her decide once her marriage was over that she'd never submit to any man again. "What?" she asked, belatedly realizing Tom had asked her a question.

"I asked if you'd like to go to your place or mine. Or someplace neutral like an all-night restaurant." He sounded amused at having caught her napping, so to speak.

Well, she wanted him to fuck her, and she didn't think a restaurant was the ideal place for that. Besides, the last thing she needed was to feed her face at this time of night if she wanted the latest diet she'd started to work. "Yours."

She'd have invited him to the condo she'd bought after her divorce, but she wanted to see where he lived, find out how far he went toward bowing to convention beyond the conservative khaki slacks and subtly hidden western boots he'd switched into from those blue scrubs he'd worn for the club scene. Besides, her bed was mussed, and she had things strewn all over the place. It wasn't as though she'd expected to bring a lover home.

He drove expertly, no extra motion expended until after he turned off the outer loop and stopped at a stoplight. As if he sensed her nervousness he reached over and brushed her cheek then pulled her to him for a kiss. No more than a brushing of lips to lips, it pleased her more than the strictly carnal touches she'd experienced from a string of faceless subs.

"You know, Selina, I want you in my bed, but that's not all. I have this feeling...the feeling I want to get to know not just your body but *you*."

Men liked to fuck her, but they'd never wooed her. Until now. She resisted the urge to pinch herself, see if he was real or only a dream that would end as soon as they'd slaked their mutual lust.

"We're here," he told her, shutting off the engine when he'd pulled into a reserved parking space on the first story of the parking garage. She was about to let herself out when he opened the passenger door and helped her out.

As they walked around to his building, she imagined she was glowing, basking in his consideration, the manners she'd never before experienced from a sexual Dominant.

* * * * *

"Be it ever so humble…and all that." Tom led her off the elevator and fit a key card into the door of one of the penthouse condos a few blocks from University Hospital, where he'd mentioned he worked. "Come on in and make yourself at home."

"Home" was a jumble of Southwest and contemporary, a sort of eclectic cross between ranch house and city showplace. Selina kicked off her shoes, crossed to the window and looked out at the distant lights from the Riverwalk and those of University Hospital less than a block away. "Not very humble, by my way of thinking. Seriously, it's gorgeous." She especially liked the lived-in look, open journals and a single used coffee mug marring an otherwise pristine setting.

"Want to see my etchings?" She liked the way his eyes twinkled when he gestured toward the hallway and issued the clichéd invitation.

"Why not?" A long time ago Selina had decided to ditch feminine subterfuge and go after what she wanted. Now, though, she wanted Tom to take her, steal away her choices and fucking make her come. Putting on her best Domme façade, she started down the hallway. "What are you waiting for, an engraved invitation?"

"No, honey, I already issued one. One that will give you pleasure like you've never known, playing with cringing little slave boys." He came up behind her, his body radiating heat. Before she could take a breath, he had his hands under her sweater and was cupping her breasts, tugging at the rings behind the sturdy fabric of her bra. He was taking over and she liked it, the certainty of his mastery without the slightest overtone of brutality. She couldn't have refused him no matter how hard she might try. "Understand this. I'm the one in charge here. And you're going to come like you've never come before. I ought to run a chain through these and tie you to a wall. Make you play with them while I use a flogger to strike your impudent butt. Would you like it if I use dildos to warm your ass and cunt before I fuck you?"

She shuddered at the thought of him making her helpless the way her ex had often done. Hurting her more each time than he had the last. "No restraints. Please." Everything else he suggested had her heart beating faster, every cell in her body anticipating what she hadn't had for years. Mastery. A strong man asserting his will on her body and heart. Compelling her acceptance and pleasure without commanding her submission, which she'd give him willingly.

A look of concern creased his brow, as though her fear of being restrained confused him. Then he reached out, brushed her cheek again the way he'd done in the car, a reassurance amid the sexual heat and pressure that surrounded them. "No restraints then. I promise." That touch, those few words, helped her relax, let her arousal build.

He stilled his hand, steering her to a doorway on the left, into a large room dominated by a king-size, four-poster bed draped with a Lone Star patterned quilt. A sheepskin lay folded at the foot of the bed, its texture soft and inviting. As inviting as a leather flogger he'd just set on the night stand, only it added to her arousal, and the excitement she always experienced at the promise of sensual pain. When she glanced the other way, a reflection greeted her from the mirrored wall.

His hands firmly on her waist, he stood behind her. Every throbbing prod of his cock against her ass cheeks made her want him more. A shudder made its way through her body, reminding her she was afraid. But not of him. Not now, not after that soft reassurance amid the sensual command of a Master. It made her believe he wouldn't hurt her…at least not physically. What had her wanting to bolt was the disgusted look she imagined crossing his handsome face when he saw her in the bright light of the room. He'd be seeing, not the in-control Domme he'd met at the club but instead a scared, overweight woman. A woman with more insecurities than she wanted anyone to see.

As if he read her fear, he drew her closer. "All I want tonight is to make you feel good. Give you pleasure. Make you let go and share all the sensations that go with great sex. I want you to come until you can't come any more. Then I want to sleep with you, feel your heart beating next to mine."

"I want that, too." Not that Selina thought she would ever get it. Might as well let her fears loose, voice them before he could do it. "But I'm afraid when you see me you're not going to want that anymore."

"I see you, baby. I see a woman who makes my cock rise with anticipation. With clothes or without, you're going to turn me on." He squeezed her corseted waist. "Come on, let's get these things off you. I can tell you all night long that I like my women with a little meat on their bones, but you're not going to believe me until I show you."

How did he know? Was she that obvious? Steeling herself for the disappointment she was certain she'd see in his eyes, she peeled off her sweater and looped her thumbs into the elastic waistband of her slacks before he did it for her. For a long time she stood there, feeling his gaze on her, wishing to God she'd stuck with that diet the last time and cursing the lingerie manufacturers who pretty much limited the kind of support she needed to ugly black or white garments without the least bit of potential for sexual titillation.

Tom cleared his throat. "Come on, don't make me wait. Want some help with the corset?"

"No." All she needed was for him to unlace the thing and watch her waistline inflate like a balloon on steroids. "I'd like to leave it on if that's okay with you." At that moment Selina realized one of the benefits of masquerading as a Domme. No sub would dare insist she disrobe any more than she wanted to. And if he intended to pursue a relationship, he'd keep his mouth shut about her excess flab.

No such luck with a Master, and Tom definitely was that. When she made no move to finish disrobing, he shed his own clothes and took her in his arms. His touch was strong yet gentle when he unhooked her bra and bared her breasts. "Beautiful," he murmured, cupping them, raising them so he could unfasten the bow that held her corset lacing tight.

She held her breath, as if that might lessen the shock of his seeing her waist expand by a full four inches when the corset came off. "How do you stand wearing this thing?" he asked, rubbing his fingers over the reddened flesh he was uncovering. "It can't be good for you."

Oh, yeah, she'd almost forgotten this gorgeous man had mentioned he was a doctor as well as a Dom. "Go ahead, tell me I need to lose about sixty or seventy pounds before I end up with heart trouble and high blood pressure. Everybody else does."

"Right now I want to touch and squeeze and love all however many pounds of you there are. I'll leave the weight management lectures to whichever of my lucky colleagues may be taking care of you for that." As if punctuating his statement, he slid her panties down and bent to kiss the rose tattoo on the inside of one quivering thigh. "I like this."

She was naked. Completely naked. The light was incredibly bright, casting its evil illumination on every flabby inch of her as well as on every lean, perfectly sculpted muscle on Tom's magnificent body. When he stood, she saw his cock, hard as stone and rising up against his flat belly. His PA ring brushed his navel. "Told you I'd like it. I like you, honey, a lot. So does my cock. Now lie down on that sheepskin and let me show you I can give pleasure as well as take it."

His words were reassuring, but they couldn't drown out the damning litany in her own head. When she turned back the quilt, spread the sheepskin in the center of the big bed, and lay down, she felt like a specimen pinned down for examination under a high-powered microscope. Even the soft fuzz of the sheepskin caressing her backside didn't distract her from that glaring illumination. The recessed overhead lights seemed as though they all were focused on nothing but her much-less-than-perfect body. "The lights. Turn them off. Please."

"No, baby. It turns me on to look at you. Close your eyes if you don't want to see me, too." He turned away for a minute, as if giving her time to become accustomed to the light and the fact he wasn't going to turn it off.

She did want to look at him. Who wouldn't? The guy was sex personified, obviously in charge all the way, yet he didn't show any signs of being a domineering bastard with a mean streak, like her ex-husband and a few of the Doms she'd encountered in the BDSM community. Of course, she remembered that abusers never start out as abusers, as well as the fact that she carried the lasting legacy of her abusive ex-husband. The lack of confidence and feeling of self-loathing had practically ruined her for a good relationship even if one fell into her lap. Lying back against the cushion of the sheepskin, watching him choose toys from the nightstand drawer, Selina tried not to think about how she must look compared with the slender Snake Woman and every other partner that Tom had ever played sex games with.

Who'd have ever imagined the toughest Domme at Club Rio Brava was a fraud? Out of the corner of his eye Tom watched Selina. What the hell had happened in her past to steal her self-confidence? Sure, she was too heavy. The physician in him couldn't help acknowledging that. But she was fucking beautiful, with skin soft as a baby's and the most beautiful violet-colored eyes he'd ever seen. Lush lips made for sucking cock…bountiful tits tipped with large rosy nipples. He liked the way her clit peeked impudently out from pouting pink cunt lips he was fairly sure had been rid permanently of pubic hair.

And he loved the sweet, submissive voice that gave her away every time she tried to play the Domme. He knew that voice from somewhere, liked the warm recollection that wouldn't quite come clear. It was as if he'd known her at some point in the distant past, not as a sex object but as a young, naïve girl. Not quite a child yet not fully mature, either. He'd remember eventually. Now all that mattered was to give her pleasure, and take it for himself as well.

His gaze settled on the marks left by that goddamn corset. If Selina were to become his slave, he'd forbid her to wear the torture device unless she seriously needed punishment, because it hurt him to see the cruel ridges it made on her soft, tender flesh. He'd also talk her into growing out that short matronly bob that did nothing for her pretty face but emphasize her lack of confidence in her appearance. He imagined her hair long, a dark silken mass he could sink his fingers into, command her attention to him.

Rifling through the nightstand drawer, he finally found what he'd been looking for. The large, vibrating butt plug and matching dildo he'd bought and stored away but never used had made their way back to the left rear corner of the drawer, past the wrapped condoms and a tube of lubricant that had gotten occasional use. He started to take out the handcuffs, too, but changed his mind. Something in Selina's past had apparently frightened her about being restrained, and he didn't want to spook her.

At the moment his only goal was to hold her, touch her, wipe away the doubts that showed in her eyes and make her come. Setting down the toys, he picked up the flogger from the nightstand and let the silken strands slide idly over Selina's soft, pale skin. The small tremors of her flesh didn't escape his attention. "Relax, honey. Don't think, just feel." He bent, sucking one prominent ringed nipple between his teeth and flailing it with his tongue. The metals collided, his tongue ring reverberating with the impact and sending waves of sexual pleasure through him. When he heard her moan, he knew she liked it, too. "You know, I've never seen such beautiful breasts." He turned his head and gave the same attention to her other distended nipple.

"Oh, yes. Bite me. Harder. Please," she added as if only now remembering she was not the one in charge.

Giving her nipple one last swipe with his tongue, Tom raised his head and trailed the flogger down her body, along the reddened flesh bitten into by those corset stays. Seeing those marks infuriated him, made him want to lash out and hurt whoever had made her feel she needed to injure her beautiful skin. "I should punish you for hurting yourself this way. But I find all I want to do is bring you pleasure." She spread her legs as he moved the flogger lower, obviously eager for him to push her quickly to climax. "We have all night, honey. No need to rush." He hoped that was so, and that no case would come along tonight that couldn't wait a few hours until daylight. Fortunately he was number three on the call list so it wasn't likely he'd draw an emergency case this late in the evening.

Her baby-soft cunt drew his attention, and he couldn't resist bending and drawing her hard little clit into his mouth, using his tongue to rotate the tiny gold barbell that adorned it. He had the feeling she could come quickly that way, but he wanted to give her more. Taking one last nip at the hard little nub, he picked up the dildo and rubbed it along her sopping slit. "I love how you're wet for me."

She moaned, her hips tilting upward in blatant invitation. Tom slid the dildo home then bent again and lapped at her clit with his tongue as he spread her legs wider, bending them slightly at the knees. "I'm going to take your ass, too. Does that excite you?" He ringed her anus with a finger then slipped it just beyond her anal sphincter.

"God, yes." Her enthusiastic words trailed off as though she weren't any too sure about what she wanted. "I want you that way. But you're too big."

"Trust me. I won't hurt you. You're going to want it so bad, that when I fuck your ass, all you'll feel is incredible pleasure." Withdrawing his finger, he reached for the lubricant he'd laid out and coated the butt plug before inserting it carefully up her ass. "Feel good?"

She shuddered, but she writhed with arousal at the double stimulation. Tom stroked her thighs, tracing the faded rose tattoo just below her left cunt lip, increasing the pressure with his fingers as he felt the tension building inside her. His cock was hot as fire, his balls about to burst. He thought about her lips, about the warm wetness of her mouth, how it had felt when she'd swallowed his flesh, consumed his climax. At the club, he'd barely thought of Snake Woman while Selina had given him head, even though his own face had been buried between the other woman's legs while he brought her to climax with his tongue. All he wanted then and now was to give Selina the best orgasms of her life.

Despite his earlier thoughts, Tom couldn't help but return to his wishful fantasy of a woman who could share his life as well as a club membership. Selina made it impossible for him not to think about it. He'd been a fool to give up so soon, immersing himself with subs like Snake Woman while Selina had been just a few feet away, giving him a chance to entertain the idea again…

Not as a master, but as a lover. Just as he would be her lover but never her slave. He had to have all of her, bury his cock to the balls in the wet heat of her cunt…fuck the deep, soft cleavage between her generous breasts. His fingers itched to tunnel in her hair, hold her mouth steady to take his deep thrusts. He'd calm her fears and claim the dark, tight cavern of her rear…

Don't restrain me. Please. Her words stopped him from mounting her, pinning her to the bed with his own body. They didn't deter him from leaning over her, bringing her massive breasts together with both hands so he could suck both ringed nipples while she came to the edge, pushed on by the toys vibrating in her cunt and ass. His tongue flailing tissue already distended from the weight of the nipple rings.

"God, yes." She came hard. Fast. Her body shook with the intensity of her climax. Tom couldn't wait. He changed positions, snatched the dildo from her sopping cunt, and sank his aching cock deep in her willing body. Her nipples pierced his chest when he claimed her mouth and tongue-fucked her there.

But it was her cunt that gripped him. Wet velvet, so hot, incredibly pleasurable. As though she wanted never to let him go, she squeezed his cock with muscles as tight as a clenched fist while the vibrations of the butt plug, separated from his cock only by the thin membrane dividing the two passages, thrummed through their genitals, increasing the delicious sensation. Only when he he'd brought her to climax twice more did he relinquish control and come inside her.

Chapter Three

ഇ

And only when he came back to his senses several minutes later did Tom realize he'd forgotten to put on a condom.

He never forgot. "Uh, Selina?" he said, drawing her attention to his naked, wrung-out cock.

"It's all right. I'm on the Pill. I'm clean and I'm sure you are, too."

Relief poured over him. But not nearly as much of a reprieve as he'd have felt if it had been Snake Woman or Johanna reassuring him that he hadn't taken an unacceptable risk.

Maybe the risk with Selina wouldn't be all that unacceptable.

He wasn't finished, and he got the idea from her eager look when he withdrew the butt plug that she wasn't, either. "Come on, let's play in the water," he said, taking her hand and tugging her with him. The trip took longer than usual as he sampled the salty taste of her perfect skin and she shyly explored his body, seemingly overwhelmed at the fact that he couldn't keep his hands off her.

Like most of the women who'd seen the sunken Jacuzzi his decorator had made to look as if it were outdoors, Selina's eyes widened with delight. That bunch of tropical greenery he had to remember to water every week did add the illusion of being out in nature, which was why he liked it so. Without the slightest hesitation she followed him into the water. "This is beautiful. Reminds me of a tropical rainforest," she told him as she settled beside him and lay back against the jets.

Her breasts seemed to float, partially hidden by the swirling water yet allowing him to look his fill, to take them in his hands and lift them so he could lick droplets of water from her large, rosy nipples. "Like what you see?" he asked when she shifted her gaze to take in the dark blue tile walls and stark white fixtures set on a blue-veined marble floor.

"Oh yes." Her gaze settled on the bidet, and for a moment his muscles tensed. Jo had thrown a fit when she first noticed it, accusing him of all sorts of perversions, some of which Tom had never before considered in connection with the high-end device common in Europe but not often found in American homes.

"You like the bidet?" he asked.

Selina's whole face lit up when she smiled. "I love it. Had one installed last year at my house. How about you?"

"It comes in handy sometimes." Reaching under the foam from the jets, Tom found and cupped Selina's ass cheek. "For cleaning places that are hard to get to." Like assholes, he thought, wondering if Selina might be into enemas as well as douches.

"Mmmm. You're right about that. Do you use it yourself or just save it for your guests?" When she began to slide her hand beneath his hip, he caught her wrist, laid her hand on his thigh.

The idea of her playing with him that way made him a little nervous. "You don't need to do that, Selina."

"But what if I want to? What if I know it will bring you pleasure?"

Tom studied her, and for some reason Eli's words came back to him. *"You might have to get down on your knees and beg."* Maybe a key to gaining Selina's full confidence was to let her exercise her familiar Domme routine in a controlled way. Besides, from his experience in a few ménage scenes, he knew as well as Selina that anal play could bring him pleasure, too, along with the uncomfortable, out-of-control feeling he had never been able to overcome completely.

"Then please me," he said, letting her wrist go but moving his own fingers more deeply, eliciting a moan from her as he demonstrated that he still held the reins. Following his lead, she found his anus and ringed it, applying enough pressure to start him on the way to another hard-on. "Did you ever take a plug…or another man's cock here?"

Tom had, in ménage scenes, but he hadn't been able to relax and get into the scenes, and wasn't too fond of where this conversation seemed to be leading. Still, he couldn't deny she knew how to stimulate him and how to position her finger once she worked it up his ass to massage his prostate. "Maybe. Stop it, honey, or you're going to make me come again. And I'm saving that for you." Shifting his hand, he worked first one finger then two up her ass and began to stretch the tight hole by splaying then closing his fingers. "Here."

"Two can do that," she said, her breathing shallow and fast. When she slid in a second finger and began to pump them, his cock came to full attention. "I think I want that vibrating plug up your ass while you fuck mine."

"If you ask me nicely, I just might allow that." He could tell the constant subtle reminders were having an effect on her. That hesitation, as if she'd expected more censure, was followed by a pleasing flush as she reacted positively to his firm reminder that he was in the one in control. She wanted a Dom—he was sure of it. Some bastard had apparently taught her not to trust. He'd have to work on that. Tom wasn't intimidated by a high-maintenance woman—at least not one who engaged his mind and body like this one. "Want to do it in here? Now?"

"Oh, yes. You do know how to get a woman hot. Stand up." When he did, she removed her fingers from his ass and grabbed the butt plug. "Where are the condoms?"

He stepped out of the tub, reached between two plants and opened a drawer. "Here. One for the plug and one for me," he said, handing her one of the two foil packets he'd fished out. "Go ahead, honey, get your jollies. Unless you want to…" Gesturing toward the bidet, he held his breath until she took his hand and stepped out of the tub.

"I'd love to. You first, though. That is, if you don't mind."

"Can't say I mind at all. Do your worst." The feeling of the warm spray tickling his ass was surprisingly sensual, yet not as much so as when he changed places with her and watched her struggle to maintain self-control while she cleansed herself the way he'd just done. If he hadn't felt his cock throbbing, he wouldn't have believed it could have gotten so hard so soon, considering he'd come twice in the past two hours or so. But it was, and his balls felt hot and tight. The head of his cock swelled around the PA ring, so much so he dreaded removing it, but maybe… He stuck his finger through the ring, wiggled it at her. "Want me to take this out?"

Her agile tongue went out as if to lick off the pearl of lubrication that glistened around the ring. "Leave it in. I've never taken a cock with a ring that thick—not up the ass, anyway. Bend over while I'm cleaning up, and I'll give you this." The butt plug already wore a lubricated condom, Tom noticed as he spread his ass cheeks for Selina's pleasure. It wasn't just any woman he'd let put something up his ass, but somehow he liked the thought of Selina claiming him as he intended to claim her. "Eager, are you?" she asked, her tone teasing.

He didn't know about eager, at least as it applied to having his ass fucked by his own butt plug, but his cock apparently could hardly wait to ream Selina's tight, dark hole. It would already be as warm as his own from the same sort of internal cleansing. When she pressed the tip of the plug against his anal sphincter, he made a conscious effort to relax and enjoy the unfamiliar invasion.

"Take it easy, lover. For a big guy you're awfully tight here, but I'm going slow." She went down on her knees behind him, pushed the first narrow bump of the graduated bead plug inside then paused. Tom inhaled deeply when the next one popped inside. "Can you take it all?"

"Yeah. I can take it." The stretching feeling as she inserted the plug actually wasn't that unpleasant, probably because it was her wielding the toy. He'd had his doubts, but this wasn't at all like what he remembered from infrequent ménage scenes where he'd had to struggle to accept another man's cock when that was called for in the script. "The warm water relaxed me." Actually it was Selina who'd relaxed him, made him feel as if her main purpose was to please him as much as he wanted to please her. Sexually, for sure. But he was certain that feeling spread outside the natural need for orgasm, to something much, much more.

He hoped Selina felt that way, too.

"Oh yes." She rotated the plug, setting the vibrator in motion at the same time she pushed the rest of the plug into his rectum. Its broad base buzzed against his hole. His balls ached, drawing up tight against the base of his cock when he stood. Eyes closed against the stimulus that threatened to have him shooting his load before the party even began, he felt her soft, warm breath, the wet motion of her tongue as she licked around his PA, the softness of her hands when she ran them down the length of his shaft and sac. "I'm putting a condom on you now."

Slick with lubrication, warm from Selina's hands, the condom went on easily as though she'd done this more than once. Good. While some men wanted to break in virgins, Tom had always appreciated a woman who knew what she was doing about sex. When she rose, her big breasts swayed sassily, tempting him to take them, taste them, tug at the rings that seemed so incongruous compared with the dainty barbell in her clit. A welcoming smile on her face, she moved to the vanity, bent over it, and presented him with her plump, inviting ass.

Her buttocks felt like warm silk when he grabbed the soft flesh, parted it, found her warm, damp asshole and massaged it. "You ready, love?" he asked, concerned like he'd never been before that taking him anally might cause her more pain than pleasure.

"Oh, yes. Please."

No protests. No doubt in her voice. No hesitation. Any doubt that she was his dream lover dissolved when she whined and wiggled her butt. "You've got a beautiful ass. I can't wait to sink into you here." Still he was cautious, sliding first one then two fingers inside while rubbing her clit with his thumb.

"Please, don't wait. Take me now." He heard desperation in her tone that matched his own.

"Hold on, oh eager one. I can't wait much longer, either."

Positioning his cock, he pressed forward into her warm, tight hole. One inch, then two, little by little he filled her, her moans and whimpers egging him on until he'd given her his full eight inches and his balls nestled against her labia. Reaching around her, he kneaded her breasts, tugging at her nipple rings. "I'm going to fuck you now," he told her before beginning to withdraw slowly then fill her again, over and over, trying all the time to ignore the vibrations in his own ass that kept threatening to shove him over the edge.

"Yes. Oh, yes, Master, fuck me hard."

Spreadeagled, laid out over the marble vanity in all her glory for her Master's pleasure, her cunt dripping as he reamed her ass and played with her nipples, Selina tried to concentrate on the vibrations coursing through them both from the vibrator inserted in his ass. But she couldn't. His warm, dry skin brushed hers as he bent over her to steady her for his thrusts. His well-lubricated cock slid in and out of her rear, not the punishment she'd expected thanks to memories of her ex's brutal poundings, but rather a sensuous, sexual claiming that had begun when Tom had allowed them both to prepare for the mutual invasion.

She felt her lips go slack, ready to take him there, too. Wanting him to take all of her, make her his own. Wanting him, for this, but so much more. Her cunt clenched, and she concentrated on the friction of his cock going in and out behind it. "God, yes, don't stop!" she screamed as waves of pleasure began, overwhelming in their intensity. He didn't stop but fucked her harder, digging his long fingers into the sensitive flesh of her breasts while he tugged hard on her tingling nipples. "Don't...omigod, don't stop."

It went on forever, the charged sensations that raced through her body and his. She'd never... "Please fuck my cunt, Master. Oh, God, I've never come like this before."

He paused, pulled out and tossed away the condom. Then he spread her legs wide and slid his hot cock into her cunt. "Hold on, honey, it just gets better. Play with your nipples for me so I can watch you. I'm about to give you the ride of your life."

His fingers dug into the flesh at her waist, holding her steady as he pounded into her like a jackhammer. She raised her upper body, grabbed the rings in her nipples, rotated and tugged at them until she started to come again.

"Look at yourself." That wasn't a request but an order. A Master's order.

Though she'd sworn she'd never submit again, he'd been disabusing her of that notion from that first encounter at the club. Selina couldn't imagine herself doing anything but following his every order. She gasped at the sight of him, eyes wide open, his fingers buried in the flesh at her waist, slamming into her from behind while he watched her playing with her breasts at his command. Her mouth opened as she gasped for breath, desperate for him to claim her there, too.

"I can tell you want to suck me off. We'll do that, too. But later. I want you to squeeze me now. Milk my cock. Do it until I come inside your hot, wet cunt." He fucked her harder...slower...deeper as she tightened her muscles around his massive cock. "Oh, yeah, like that." His cock jerked, and the spurts of hot semen triggered an orgasm she didn't think she could manage. When he slumped over her back and wrapped his arms around her, she wished, impossibly, that this might be more than a night of pleasure…more than the temporary answer to all her sexual fantasies.

There was something about him. About them, together, bringing those fantasies to life, making them seem more real than imaginary, more permanent than just a one-night stand between two sexually needy people whose paths had crossed due to a quirk of fate.

"Honey, I think I love you. I know damn well you're the best lover I've ever had. Let's go to bed and get some sleep. Mornings come damn early around here." His deep voice poured over her like velvet, made her take a deep breath and enjoy the way his breath tickled her neck, the gentle stroking of one hand on her belly while he cupped her mound with the other. While what had come before felt like her wildest fantasies come to life, this felt…comfortable. Right.

When she crawled in bed, he lay on his side behind her, his body heat warming her, lulling her still-pounding heart to slow down. His even breathing against her neck tickled—but in a nice way, she thought as she drifted off to sleep, his words still resonating in her heart. *"I think I love you…"*

Chapter Four

ꟸ

Selina's warm, soft butt pillowed Tom's half-hard cock when the alarm clock woke him from a sound, peaceful sleep. God but she'd wrung him out last night. Rolling away reluctantly and silencing the damn clock, he got up and took one last look at her, curled on her side in the middle of his bed.

Fuck if she didn't look as though this was where she belonged. True, she was no sleek blonde trophy like Jo. But no woman had gotten him so hard, so fast, for so long. Not since he'd been a horny teenager with a hard-on for anything female that moved and a penchant for controlling his girlfriends.

For the first time in years, Tom called in sick. A resident could do the pre-op evaluations he had scheduled for this morning, and if he was lucky the OR supervisor would be able to coerce another of the anesthesiologists to fill in for him in OR Three this afternoon. If she could, his weekend could start right now. A full three days when he could get to know Selina, not just in bed but out. Meanwhile he'd shower, dress, make breakfast—and then wake her up.

I know her from somewhere. Selina Harrison. The name sounded vaguely familiar. To have become a member at the club she had to have had connections that caused their paths to cross sometime. Her ex? An old lover? Even her father might have sponsored her membership at Club Rio Brava. Searching his memory, Tom drew a blank, that is until a vague picture began to form. Of course! He'd met Selina at a sweet-sixteen party he'd attended for Cousin Tracy, teased her about hiding out among the potted greenery instead of coming out to dance. That was why she looked vaguely familiar, even after more than fifteen years. He recalled Tracy having mentioned something about Selina a few years ago—something about her having just ended a disastrous marriage and moving back to San Antonio.

It came back to him, that night when he'd gone up to a shy, plump girl with long black hair and a hesitant smile. She'd intrigued him, so he'd sat and chatted with her, and when she glanced wistfully toward the dance floor he'd taken her hand and led her out on the floor. He'd liked her softness, the budding curves that had felt so much better in his arms than the skeletal bodies of some of his recent dates. But he'd been a college man, twenty years old, and she'd been jailbait.

Crazy. He'd thought about her a long time after that night, considered looking her up once he came back home to stay. But time and distance had intervened, and by the time he finished medical school and a residency in Houston, she'd moved on with her own life, too.

He damn well should have tried harder. If he had… Fuck it, he had her now and this was no time for regrets. It was time to look toward the future. A future he envisioned with Selina.

As Tom chopped vegetables for an omelet, his one culinary masterpiece, he recalled last night, pondered details that at the time had gotten lost in a fever of lust. The rose tattoo high on the inside of her thigh, faded with age, intrigued him, as did those unusually heavy rings that had been fed through Selina's large nipples and welded shut. They had to have hurt her for a long time, he imagined, recalling his latest experience of stretching his PA by hanging too heavy a stainless steel weight from the ring. The nipple rings seemed incongruous, particularly when he contrasted them with the dainty gold barbell that adorned her clit.

He didn't mind the body jewelry. Since he had piercings, too, it would have been damn hypocritical for him to complain. The tattoo didn't bother him, either, since it wasn't located where everybody who saw her would notice, like the cobra head emblazoned on Snake Woman's cleanly shaved skull. He just wondered. Selina's markings seemed to represent other times in her life—experiences that had combined to make her the sometimes Dominant, often submissive lover who'd captured his imagination as well as his cock.

He pictured her decked out in black leather as she'd been at the club, every inch the Domme, covered head to toe but for her facial features, magnificent breasts and slick pink cunt. He wondered, too, about the mask. Though club members typically didn't cover their faces, Selina had chosen to frame her face with a continuation of the black leather cat suit. Less concealing than the mask he owned that hid all his features, providing slits for his eyes and nose and a larger, circular opening through which he could thrust his tongue, it told him she wasn't all that anxious to advertise her identity, even at Club Rio Brava. While he never wore his mask there except to participate in certain group scenes, he had to admit hers added to the mystique that surrounded Selina.

Without the trappings, though, Selina proved even more a mystery…a woman who obviously wanted to submit to a dominant lover yet seemed terrified at the thought of being restrained. A woman who was so afraid of falling under the wrong sort of master's control that she masqueraded as a Domme. Or was she a switch?

That wouldn't bother Tom much if she were. His cock hardened when he thought about her using a flogger on his bare ass, handcuffing him and having her way with his compliant body. She certainly didn't shy away from adventurous sexual games, no matter who was in charge. He liked that.

And he had a feeling he'd like Selina in a nonsexual way, too. He intended to find out.

"Good morning. Whatever you're cooking smells awfully good." Selina came up behind him, smelling of his shampoo and soap. When he turned to kiss her, he noticed she had on one of his dress shirts, unbuttoned to display her impressive cleavage. "Sorry. I couldn't find one I could button," she said, raising her gaze to meet his.

"The better for me to see these." Smiling, he brushed back the shirt to expose both her breasts, caught his index fingers through the rings and pulled her to him for a long, deep kiss. "I hope you like eggs."

"I do. I can only eat a little, though. And coffee. Lots of coffee." She looked him over, heat in those deep purple eyes as she looked pointedly at the boxer shorts that did little to hide his growing erection. "Aren't you going to work?"

"No. We're going to play, that is unless you have something pressing to do." He hoped she didn't, that they could extend this fantasy encounter over the next few days…maybe longer. "Sit down and let's get some nourishment."

Once the omelet was gone, Tom reached across the table and took Selina's hand. "I think it's time we shared a little more about ourselves than sex, don't you?"

She bit her lower lip then laced her fingers through his. "What do you want to know?"

"Everything." He read her hesitation, smiled to put her at ease. "If you want, I'll start out. I'm Tom Latimore, born and raised on a ranch northwest of town. Went to Yale for undergrad, University of Texas for my MD. I'm thirty-nine years old, an anesthesiologist at University Hospital. Never married, but I'd been thinking about proposing to the wrong woman. Until I met you." Pausing, he ran his thumb over the back of her hand. "Your turn."

She settled her gaze on her empty plate. "Selina Harrison. I'm thirty-five, divorced, living on a trust fund from Grandpa and the alimony from my not-so-darling ex. I dropped out of SMU my sophomore year with dreams of white satin gowns and happily ever after. Love, honor and obey, with emphasis on the *obey*."

Tom untangled their fingers and lifted her chin. "He controlled you and you liked it, didn't you?" From her tone and the unshed tears that glistened in her eyes, he guessed he'd hit the nail on the head. "He had your nipples pierced." It wasn't a question. He knew without her saying that she'd never have chosen the heavy, ugly rings for herself. Dainty, slender barbells would have been her own choice, jewels not unlike the one in her clit. The thought of her being pierced with a large-bore needle, of thick, heavy rings being forced through brand-new holes and welded shut made him see red.

She cupped one breast in her hands, and tears flowed down her cheeks. "It hurt so much…for so long. He'd thread a chain through the rings and use it to secure me to the wall of our room."

Tom imagined her chained up, helpless. He wished the bastard were within reach because he'd like to pierce him in some very tender spot—like his balls—and use the ring to chain him in a firepit. "I'm sorry, honey. You chose your genital piercing yourself, right?"

"Yes. After the divorce. My pussy looked so plain after I had the hair removed…"

"No need to explain. I like it. Like playing with it, feeling your little clit get hard for me." He went to his knees beside her, brushed his shirt out of the way. "Spread your legs. Keep talking while I finish my breakfast. Tell me about this," he said, tracing the tattoo with his tongue and rolling the stainless steel ball suggestively over the petals just below her outer labia.

She whimpered then cupped his head in her hands and pressed him closer. "He wanted me to get it before our wedding, so he could show it off to his friends when he took off my garter. But he didn't get to do it. Mother insisted the garter should go around my calf, not my thigh." She gasped when he started to tongue her clit, then cupped his head in her hands and pressed him closer. "That feels so, so good," she said, sliding forward and giving him full access to her sweet, wet slit.

"What happened?" Tom's deep voice resonated against Selina's swollen flesh, making the little barbell vibrate and arousing her even more.

"I didn't obey him the way he wanted. No matter how I tried to please him, it wasn't enough. I was too fat, too disgusting. At the divorce hearing he sneered at me and said he didn't know how he put up with me for nearly ten years. Don't I disgust you?"

He raised his head, his expression fierce. "Damn it, I don't lick the pussies of women who disgust me." Then, when he saw her tears, he smiled, took her hands and drew them to his lips. "You don't disgust me at all. You turn me on more than any woman I've ever taken. Honey, the bastard you married had no right to hurt you."

She might as well tell him everything. Why she'd turned Domme. Why she doubted she'd ever trust another man, even Tom, enough to let him make her completely helpless. "Hurt me? He did everything he could think of to cause me pain. I got off on the physical part of it but not the humiliation he started dishing out near the end of our relationship."

"Sounds like he was a real loser." Though Tom's oath floated on the air, hardly more than a whisper, his revulsion was evident.

Selina hesitated. But there was no getting around it. If she was to have any hope at all of having a relationship with Tom, she needed for him to understand the life she'd lived—a life she never intended to return to, no matter what. "Once he stripped me naked and put me in a wooden yoke—you know, the kind oxen wear when they're pulling wagons. He fastened it to a fence post so I had to stay bent over and steady myself with my hands, and then he hooked my breasts to a milking machine, the kind they use to milk dairy cows." The pain came back, made her shudder, almost as much as the next memory. It helped that Tom was holding both her hands, rubbing his thumbs in circular motions over her palms. "Part of me wanted to scream, run as fast as I could, as far as I could. But

I'd gone so deep into submission to his every whim, I kept quiet. I hoped that by submitting like that I was making him happy, and I tried to ignore the shame of having some of the ranch hands see me that way, but…"

She had to tell him, say it out loud and purge the hurt and shame from her mind. But remembering brought back the pain, the feelings of inadequacy she doubted would ever go completely away. Tears ran down her cheeks like a raging river as she tried to stop herself from trembling, gather the words that might send Tom running for cover. She bit her lower lip, welcomed the pain as she steeled herself to relive that last, awful day before…

"The last straw was when he stripped me naked and tied me to the paddock fence by running a chain through my nipple rings. He invited all the ranch hands to come fuck my ass and pussy while he chopped off my hair and shaved my head."

Tom's grip on her hands became painful. "Damn him. I don't blame you for leaving."

"Bad thing was, I didn't. I must have come a dozen times. I'd have stayed if he'd let me, but when it was over he jerked off all over my scalp, unlocked the chain and dumped me into the Ferrari he'd bought me for my birthday. He told me to get lost, that he had no more use for a fat, ugly whore." She couldn't believe she was saying this to him, but then again, looking back, she couldn't believe she'd allowed Les to do that to her. As his demands had become more and more extreme, the fact her whole world had become him—no job, no friends, living isolated on his ranch, nothing but waiting for him to come home at night—she kept submitting, hoping to hold on to a love she'd never had to begin with. She'd talked to the therapists and understood the whole phenomenon, but she wasn't sure if it would make her appear any less pathetic to Tom—or to herself. Tom was going to hate her now. She just knew it.

But it didn't seem as though he hated her. His touch gentle, he stroked her pussy, and when he lifted his head and met her gaze, she saw fire in his eyes. Fire and tears, as though he hurt for her, hated only what Les had put her through.

"You're not ugly. You're beautiful. Don't believe anything less. I love looking at you, touching you, fucking you." His words sounded so sincere she almost believed him, and when he lowered his head again and licked her slit with incredible tenderness, she wanted nothing more than to give back to him, take him into her and provide him all the pleasure she'd once offered her ex. But Tom was apparently determined to push her over the edge, as if doing that would wash away the hurt that had driven her now for four long years.

Longer, if she were honest with herself because Les had turned mean almost before the honeymoon had ended.

Omigod. Tom had his tongue in her cunt, licking and teasing and going for her G-spot with that arousing metal ball. "Oh, yes, like that!" she screamed as the first waves of her climax rushed over her.

It wasn't over yet, this fantasy come to life. When Tom told her to go to his bedroom and wait for him in bed, Selina was quick to obey. Every cell in her body longed for the rush that came every time Tom touched her. But maybe because she was still raw from what she'd just told him, as she drew off his shirt and saw herself in the hated mirror, her doubts returned. The sunshine caught and accentuated every roll, each imperfection no one could fail to notice—and disparage.

Lying on the bed, she curled into herself. Try as she might, she couldn't hide her self-disgust. Or the snide voice inside her that said this was nothing more than a fanciful interlude…and that Tom would soon come to his senses and throw her out, the way Les had done so long ago.

Chapter Five

ജ

It was almost as though fate had brought Selina at a time when he'd finally figured out he needed more than just a D/s relationship at the club and a friendship that provided him an escort to take out in public. He'd never expected to find it in just one female body, although he'd hoped.

It was too early to be sure, yet Tom was. Selina would be his perfect mate. A sexual submissive who'd fit in with his friends and colleagues. One his mother would welcome into the family. More important, he'd discovered that she needed sexual domination as much as he needed to provide it. Tom sat staring out his kitchen window, mentally enumerating what he had to do before demanding that Selina become his slave.

But this was going too fast. They'd just met last night, after all, unless he was going to count that chance encounter years ago. So maybe he'd slow himself down, take some time with her. That meant extricating himself from the OR rotation for long enough that he and Selina could properly explore their new relationship. Not at all sure this was going to be possible, Tom dialed the surgery scheduling desk and prepared to grovel.

God, but he hated having to beg. At least the conversation with the OR supervisor wasn't as bad as he'd imagined it might be, probably because it was the slow season for elective cases, a time of year many of the surgeons scheduled their own vacations. He managed to get the next two weeks off, and all it cost him was a promise to take first call for emergencies on the next three major holidays.

Oh no. What was Selina going to think about that? He hoped to hell she wasn't big on taking part in family gatherings or watching fireworks displays. Oh well, she'd have to get used to the fact that she'd have to share him with his job. Memorial Day was coming up in less than sixty days, so he still had a little time to drop the news on her at the right moment.

Now his only obstacle was Selina herself. And how to make her believe he'd never hurt her the way her sonofabitch ex-husband had. He had an idea just how to do it. It involved a very public announcement of their relationship, and a new piercing, one no one except him would ever see. No, not a new one, but the removal of the rings he imagined had to remind her of ol' Les every time she looked at them. He'd borrow a colleague's office and a surgical saw to get rid of them, and replace them with ones that held special meaning to him—to them.

But first he had to take her again. Push her—and himself—over the edge. He was like a teenager with his first lover, fully charged and insatiable. There was a difference, though. A big difference. With Selina it wasn't just lust, as it had been with the string of casual subs he'd played with at BDSM clubs. He wanted not only to dominate her sexually, but also to earn a spot in her battered heart. If he dared, he'd hunt down Selina's ex-husband and punish him for hurting her so much she was afraid to let go and fully accept his own domination. What he could and would do was try to wash away her deep-set doubts she had about her own worth, her own attractiveness.

That last, he definitely had a handle on. Rising, Tom strode to the bedroom, hoped she'd be waiting as he'd ordered. He'd bring her around, and if in doing so he had to accept a temporary switch of power now and then, that was okay, too.

* * * * *

When he went upstairs, he found Selina on his bed, her body bathed in sunlight from the bank of windows. Knees raised to her belly, arms obscuring his view of her magnificent breasts, she lay still, her eyes closed although he could tell by her shallow breathing that she was awake. Hiding herself in a way, yet open to be taken. A picture of submission, yet more. One of a sort of hopelessness he didn't like seeing from his lover.

He was going to have to do something to bolster her self-confidence. Show her he found her desirable. Shedding his clothes, Tom stretched out behind Selina and stroked the reddened indentations the corset stays had made on her back. "Your skin's so soft. So pretty. Too pretty for you to hurt yourself like this." He followed his hand with his tongue, sliding it along the ugly grooves as he massaged her rounded buttocks.

"I'm not pretty. There's no need for you to lie." Her voice was small, muffled by the pillow. She sounded resigned, and that set his temper off until he reminded himself what she'd been through.

Tom rolled away then came back, this time sitting on his haunches next to her. Staying close yet not close enough to intimidate. "I'm not lying, Selina. I'm telling it as I see it. There's no way you can fail to know you turn me on. You've got to believe me when I say the chemistry between us is worth exploring further. Turn over. Show me you're not afraid I won't like what I see." When she obeyed, he saw her eyes, wide open, scared, their expression a lot like that of a deer he'd once observed closely through the telescopic sight on his rifle. "Come on, baby, where's the hot Domme who captivated me out at the club, looking on and cracking her whip into the air? She wasn't afraid of showing off her stuff."

Tears spilled over and wet her face when she looked up at him. They tore at him. God, the last thing he wanted was for her to cry again. "Let me see you smile."

Her lips turned up slightly. But she still had that haunted look in her eyes. He cursed himself silently for having insisted she share the highlights of her life with him, when what had gone on before had little or no significance compared with the emotions and passion running hot between them now. Smiling down at her, he stroked her cheeks, brushed the tears away. "That's more like it. Now come up here and give me a kiss."

The salt from her tears stained her lips, emphasized her vulnerability. The hard grip of her hands on his shoulders told him she was trying ever so hard to be strong, maintain control. The tremor in her fingers confirmed her doubts. He had to get through to her, make her believe he wanted her with all her hangups, not just any woman who happened to be available to satisfy his lust.

He cradled her face between his hands, concentrated on the feel of their lips locked together, their bodies growing more aroused by the moment. Heat radiated from them, a cocoon of warmth surrounding them. Silent testimony to the connection between him and her, testimony he refused to let her deny or compare with old relationships, old hurts.

"This time's for us," he said, his lips still close to hers. "I'm going to make love to you, no props and no power switches, just me getting to know the real Selina Harrison and you starting to trust that I want you not just to fuck—but to learn every inch of you, inside as well as out. Okay?"

She nodded, the gesture hesitant yet encouraging, and when she did he nibbled a path from her jaw to the hollow between her breasts. Her heart beat strongly against his cheek as he stroked her throat, her chest, ignoring the heavy nipple rings and concentrating on fondling the tips of her nipples, tracing around them. "So pretty. So *mine*." Gently he cupped her breasts and kneaded them with his fingertips.

As if the marks from her corset fascinated Tom, he traced them first with his fingers and then with his tongue. Selina moaned with the pure pleasure of being seduced, not mastered, with feeling his hot, damp breath on her flesh, the sensations of heat and moisture and of being possessed. Could her fantasy man be real? Could Tom truly want more than just a convenient vessel for his desire?

She wanted so much to believe. To take that leap of faith that once had propelled her into the arms of a monster. But she was afraid the loving domination would morph into uncaring meanness once she dropped the façade of control and…

Oh God. His morning stubble slid along her belly, the abrasion incredibly arousing. Without her consciously directing them, her legs opened, giving him access to her wet, swollen pussy. His tongue, minus the tongue ring he'd been wearing last night, felt like warm velvet as he lapped up her cream. His hot breath stoked her fires, made her desperate to have him take her. Any way he wanted. She raised her arms, wrapped her fingers around the headboard as she lifted her knees and opened herself fully for his pleasure and her own.

He left no doubt that he was in control when he stretched out over her, on his knees between her legs, one hand steadying himself above her by grasping her entwined wrists as he claimed her lips once more. An alarm went through her head at the feeling of helplessness, of him pinning her beneath him with nothing more than his substantial body weight and the loose grip of his hand on wrists she herself had positioned to be restrained. He calmed her quickly, though, with the gentle suction of his mouth on hers, the sensual feeling of his warm skin against hers. "Fuck me, please," she said when he raised up and shifted to where his rigid cock lay poised to enter her needy pussy.

"My pleasure." Slowly, carefully, he slid into her swollen body. She loved his heat, his hardness, the incredible feeling of fullness and the arousing friction from the jewelry in his cock. Most of all she appreciated the care he took to deliver those delicious sensations that radiated through her, enhancing the arousal that had been building since he'd joined her on the bed and brushed away her tears.

It wasn't quite orgasm—she'd found that to experience that she needed a certain amount of pain and fear. But what she was feeling came close enough that she wanted him to keep it up, make her feel cherished. As beautiful as he'd said he found her, despite her own doubt that a man like Tom could actually see beauty where most men saw only her excess weight. "Oh, yes. Don't stop. Fuck me harder, faster."

He bent and nipped her neck. "Patience, now. I want you to experience sex with me, without the trappings we both seem to need. For the first time in years, I'm loving vanilla sex, and I think you're liking it, too, from the hot, wet feeling of you surrounding me."

She was. But she wanted to come. His slow, deep penetration increased her arousal. More than that it fed the hope that he was feeling something more than lust, some emotional connection she wished she dared to reciprocate.

Heat built up inside her. As though Tom knew she needed more, he fucked her harder, faster, gathering her close to his body and whispering words of affection, of sex, as her climax built. "Come for me now," he ground out through clenched teeth. That was enough, that Master's order and one last hard thrust. For the first time in her life she exploded, without physical domination, with only the knowledge that for the moment he controlled her. Without force. Without restraints. Without kink or toys or the accouterments of the lifestyle that had brought them together. His triumphant shout and the sensation of his climax spurting inside her womb set off another wave of ecstasy before he gathered her in his arms and cuddled her as though she were precious… desirable… beloved.

* * * * *

"Are you going to take me back to the club to pick up my car?" she asked when they left his condo a few hours later.

He grinned. "Not yet. I like having you under my control. Besides, I don't think I want you driving that Ferrari. Maybe I'll borrow it and push it off a hillside."

The look she shot his way was one of mild horror, as though he'd just reminded her she'd told him about the part that car had played in the final humiliation of her marriage. "No you don't! I'm not about to be chained up to be your sex slave whenever you take a notion you want to fuck." She stopped dead still. "I'm sorry, I shouldn't have reacted like that, but..."

"Honey, it's okay. I'm glad you value yourself enough to make sure you're treated right. You deserve that. Every woman ought to demand that, sub or not." Despite the facts that it was broad daylight and they were out on a busy street, he bent his head and kissed her. Damn it, he'd get her to trust him, but he allowed it might take time considering all her ex had put her through. "If I really did something that possessive, I'd buy you something new. Not a Ferrari, though. I'm afraid I'm not that rich."

She reached over and squeezed his hand. "I wouldn't care if it was a compact sedan—I just don't want ever again to have to depend on a man for my wheels."

Or anything else, for that matter. She didn't say it, but her determination to hold on to her independence came through loud and clear.

Tom figured he was in for a lot of persuading if he was to bring her around. It came to him as he walked around to the driver's side that she'd probably never gotten to pick out any car for herself. Not before her escape, and not since then, either, because she most likely felt she'd be foolish to get rid of that six-figure sports car that had likely been part of her divorce settlement. "How about me letting you pick out your next car for yourself?" Tom found himself wanting to coax smiles from Selina, to drive all the hurt and sadness out of her memories. He wanted to protect her and see not only to her pleasure but her happiness.

For the first time in his life he was beginning to understand why the knights of legend lived and sometimes laid down their lives to win the love of their ladies.

"I'd like that—if you're really determined to lure me to become your new sex slave." Her comment came out like a joke, but he heard the doubt and worry in her voice. Taking her hand, he brought it to his lips then held on to it.

He wasn't about to spook her. Especially now, when he was pretty sure she was the woman he wanted to spend the rest of his life with. "Not just a slave, honey. A lover...and a friend. Tonight we're going out to celebrate the first night of Fiesta." He'd originally planned to skip the opening night of the Oyster Bake at St. Mary's, but since his mother was one of the alumnae who would be overseeing the event, it would be a great way to introduce her and Selina in a more or less neutral environment.

"I don't know." He could almost hear her mind at work, mulling the pros and cons of joining him where many of her old friends might see them. "Once I got married, I quit getting involved with Fiesta. Afterward, I never bothered with it."

He understood that. Selina had probably been too bruised and battered to want to socialize. Abused women often withdrew into a cocoon that included only themselves and their abusers. "Don't you think it's time to come out of your shell?" he asked as he settled her on the passenger seat and closed the door.

"I'll go with you," she said. Tom didn't delude himself into thinking she was pleased about it. To be honest, he didn't blame her for wanting to avoid reminders of the ancient past. He couldn't help being proud of her for trying to set aside her recriminations and join him for a social outing. "You'll need to take me home first, though, so I can change clothes."

Chapter Six

ꟾ

What on earth was she going to wear? It had been a lot of years since she'd gone to an Oyster Bake, but she vaguely remembered a scene full of San Antonio society women wearing pale, floaty dresses and lightweight sweaters to ward off the early spring breeze. Well, she hoped styles had changed since then because she'd given up floaty, frilly dresses about the time she said good-bye to size fourteen. Wishing she dared venture out in jeans and a top like a lot of the tourists wore, Selina rifled through her closet, singling out three outfits and tossing them on her bed.

She gave her selections a critical once-over. The black linen dress, one of her favorites, wouldn't do because the only way she could zip it was if she put on her corset, and Tom had forbidden her to wear it again. "Well, Selina, you can either show off your fat in the other dress or try to hide it under the slacks and tunic," she mumbled. Neither choice appealed.

"Tom?" Hopefully he was still in the living room where he could hear her.

"Need a hand?" He poked his head through the door, making her unpleasantly conscious that all she had on were a bra and panties.

"Which one of these do you like?" Selina tensed as he gave the once-over to both possibilities she'd found. Probably his true answer would be "neither". She didn't like them that much either, but there was a limit as to what garments did a decent job camouflaging a few of her excess pounds and were made in size eighteen.

"The purple one. It goes with your eyes."

That was why she'd bought the amethyst jersey dress, even though it clung to her fat more than she'd like it to and drew attention she'd just as soon not encourage. "All right. Give me a few minutes, and I'll be ready. You know, I'm nervous about this. Really nervous."

"Don't be. Getting back into the swing of Fiesta is sort of like riding a bike after a long time. You don't forget how to do it."

He was right. She shouldn't be afraid. At least she shouldn't let him know if she was. But he had a way of drawing out all the things she'd kept hidden underneath that leather cat suit for so long, and she couldn't deny she liked having him as a confidante as well as a Master. "I know. Go on out and I'll get ready. It won't take long."

"Okay. I'm going. But don't you dare come out wearing one of those torture devices, or I'll have to spank you. I'd stay and watch, but I might decide what I really want to do is toss you on that bed and make love until we both pass out from hunger and exhaustion." Dropping a casual kiss on her cheek, he made his way out of the bedroom, leaving her with the impossible task of making herself presentable.

When she walked out to meet him a few minutes later, an overnight bag in her hand, he stood and relieved her of the bag. Selina tried hard to concentrate on him, forget they were going somewhere they'd likely see old friends. Mutual friends. God forbid, they might even run into his mother and hers. Make that probably. She'd almost forgotten, but now here she was, her flesh clammy, her fat cells quaking so much she was certain that Tom couldn't help noticing.

Tom was a hunk, a prize any woman would be proud to claim. And she was the ugly duckling, no longer protected from stares by her leather cat suit and mask. No longer safe behind the persona of a make-believe Domme where she was sure not to be hurt, able to command others instead of being commanded. What she really wanted to do was run and hide, protect herself from hurt she felt was inevitable. But she couldn't do that. Not as long as there was a chance in a million that Tom could care for her enough to want to be her Master, not just for a short interlude. He'd told her this afternoon that they'd be spending the next two weeks together. Time enough to fall in love, she mused, not too happily because she didn't dare reach out and grab the possibility he might even want to make their affair a permanent thing.

Feeling more naked than if she actually had been wearing her birthday suit, Selina settled herself on the leather passenger seat of Tom's car and willed herself to be invisible.

* * * * *

How in hell could she think she was anything but beautiful? Eager to show her off, Tom lengthened his stride then slowed down when he realized Selina was having a hard time keeping up in those high heeled sandals she had on. No wonder. He couldn't imagine trying to walk on what might as well be stilts. Still, they did great things for her shapely legs so he wasn't about to suggest she wear flats next time. "Come on, slowpoke, I've got a taste for some roasted oysters."

Her smile seemed tentative, but she managed to hold his gaze. "All right. You'll have to forgive me if I don't move quite as fast as you."

"You're forgiven. I can wait a few minutes for my oysters so long as I can look at your gorgeous legs. I like the way those shoes draw attention to them." He lowered his voice and whispered in her ear. "Almost as much as I like feeling them wrapped around my hips when we're making love." The way the sun filtered through new, bright green leaves on massive red oak trees that lined the pathway to the St. Mary's campus, it cast her in patterns of light and dark, accentuated her hair and the silky smoothness of her skin. "Come on, I'm ready to show you off. Don't be nervous." He wasn't. He couldn't wait to introduce Selina to his vanilla friends.

"Hey, Tom!"

Tom turned and shot a glance backward. It was Mark and Lynn Blackstone with their three kids in tow. Oh God, he'd been scheduled in to do the anesthesia on two of Mark's cases this morning. He was in for a hard time, he was sure, about taking his impromptu vacation. "Don't say a word, my friend. How'd your cases go this morning?" he asked when the other couple caught up to him and Selina.

"Well, no thanks to you." Mark's acid words contrasted with his grin. "I take it this lovely lady's the reason for you taking off."

"Yeah. Selina, this is Mark and Lynn Blackstone. He's out of sorts because I took myself off his cases today. Mark, you'll have to introduce the kids. I've heard a lot about them, but this is the first time I've ever seen them. Guys, meet Selina Harrison. My girlfriend." He took her hand and rubbed his thumb over her palm when he realized she was trembling. He wished he could wrap his arms around her, show his friends how proud he was that she was with him. Instead he put an arm around her, a more civilized gesture of affection that seemed to put her more at ease.

"Hi, Selina." Lynn had a definite twinkle in her eyes that reminded Tom she was known around the hospital as an inveterate matchmaker. "Meet Beth and Brandy. They're twelve, and Skipper's almost four. Tom, you've been hiding Selina from us," she added, her tone chiding.

"Not hiding, nosy one. Selina and I have just discovered each other. Come on, I'm sure your kids are anxious to try out the scary rides and eat all sorts of junk food at the concessions. And I'm ready to try some of those oysters. Never eat them except here." It never ceased to amaze him, how Lynn and Mark couldn't seem to keep their hands off each other, after all the years they'd been married.

As they walked along together, Tom realized Selina hadn't uttered a word. She apparently was finding this social outing more intimidating by the minute. "Chin up, sweetheart," he whispered as he bent his head and dropped a kiss on her cheek. He thanked his lucky stars that easygoing Mark and Lynn were the first friends they'd come across.

Crowds of noisy teenagers and parents trying to keep up with excited kids converged onto the already crowded Oyster Bake scene. A plaintive country singer competed with sounds of Spanish guitars and castanets that were coming from another bandstand across the way. Tom loved all the Fiesta events, and he needed for Selina to enjoy them, too. "How about we go find my mother and get the introduction over with? Then we can melt into the crowd and have some fun."

"What if she doesn't like me?" Coming to a complete halt on the narrow sidewalk, Selina looked up at Tom, seemingly not noticing the hordes of people detouring around them and spilling off the pavement onto the neatly manicured grass.

"Why wouldn't she?" He knew the retort wasn't likely to bolster her confidence, but he couldn't manage to hide his irritation. "You're just the kind of woman Mother expects me to marry. Good background, San Antonio roots, all that goes with it. That said, I've been a grown man for a lot of years, and I don't have to ask her if she likes the women I choose."

"I imagine your mom will think a lot like mine, and mine hasn't had a pleasant word for me since I divorced Les and came back here. She's almost sixty years old and still wears a size six. I sort of imagine your mother's pretty much the same, right down to thinking I'm an embarrassment because I'm fat, not to mention the fact I couldn't manage to hold on to a husband most of her friends considered a great catch. Or that the only job I can get is as a volunteer since I didn't finish college or learn a trade." Selina looked as though she were about to cry, so Tom grabbed her hand and led her off the sidewalk to a concrete bench between a pair of Texas redbud trees.

He sat and pulled her down beside him. For God's sake, he'd never seen a woman so afraid of criticism. But then, he hadn't had to live his life subjected to a beast of a mate and a hypercritical parent. "Stop agonizing, sweetheart. As far as I'm concerned, you're the woman I want to sleep with, live with. To me you're just what the doctor ordered. Beautiful, sexy as hell, the perfect woman, the perfect sexual submissive who can hold her own in my real life as well as my fantasies. Fuck it, the only person you need to please is me. I couldn't care less that you're overweight, and I'm proud of you for managing to escape the monster you married. As far as working, your only job will be to take care of me and reach out and realize your own potential."

"At one time I wanted to teach elementary school," she offered in a tiny voice.

"You could still do that if you really want to, but wouldn't you rather have your own house full of kids?" He hoped he wasn't going too fast, but he was determined to quash her insecurity, whatever it took.

Choking back a sob, she nodded her head.

"Then smile for me. Show me you can be just as confident as you seemed, wielding that flogger at the club like a pro. Dry those tears and act like you love me." He laid his hand on her knee, stroked it in a circular pattern until her trembling stopped. Then he lifted her chin, forced her to look at him. "Am I your Master or not?"

"You are. And I do love you. But it's too soon…"

"No buts about it. I love you, too, and I say we're going to enjoy Fiesta together. We're going to say hello to family and old friends, eat some oysters and have a beer or two. Afterward I'm going to take you back to my place and fuck you until we're both too tired to move. I've got some other plans for us tomorrow. Come on now, let's have some fun." With that Tom stood and held out his hand.

* * * * *

She had to admit it felt good to be part of the enthusiastic crowd, savoring the filtered sunlight that offset the coolness of a sharp afternoon breeze. Tom's constant attentiveness helped her fight her inclination to find a shady spot and hide rather than mingle with the crowd, almost as much as his offhand declaration of love boosted her self image. As they approached the raised platform where Tom had said his mother would be, Selina tried hard to absorb some of his optimism, to tamp down the sense of impending disaster that had her fighting a strong urge to run for cover.

"There she is," Tom said, winding his way through the sea of bodies toward the platform. "I'm going to tell her you're my future wife."

Oh, no! "For heaven's sake, Tom, why?"

He grinned. "Because it's true. We love each other. We're dynamite in bed. And it's not as if we just met yesterday. We've known each other for twenty years."

"Omigod, I didn't think you'd remember that dance." She'd never forget it, but when she tried to remember whether she'd been pimply that night instead of just fat and painfully shy, she drew a blank. "I did. For a long time you were the Prince Charming of all my teenage fantasies."

Taking her hand and bringing it to his lips, he laughed. "I had a hard time persuading myself you were jailbait. Thank God you're all grown up and even hotter now than you were back then."

"But isn't it a little quick to start thinking about something as permanent as marriage?" Selina could only imagine the shock such an announcement would cause his mother. Hers, too.

"Not at all. I've got two weeks' vacation, and I intend to spend every minute of it with you. I couldn't ask for a better match than you, even if I tried."

More than a little bit overwhelmed, Selina looked up at him. "Shouldn't we wait, test our feelings?"

"I've been waiting twenty years for you, even if I was too stupid to know it until now. And you say you love me. So consider us engaged, and get used to the idea of marrying me very soon. Put on a happy face, sweetheart. Mom has noticed us coming her way."

Selina was able to pick Tom's mother out from three women conversing at the edge of the platform. She looked a lot like Tom—same twinkling eyes, lips that curved up in a welcoming smile. Not quite as determinedly youthful as her own mom, Tom's was well-preserved, with glowing skin and a nice figure, although she'd let her hair go natural, a salt and pepper shade that seemed to fit her style. She wore sensible gray heels with a pale gray dress. It was conservative yet festive because of the silk designer scarf and a huge Dolce & Gabbana handbag in colors that picked up the bright tones of the scarf.

The woman was well put together. Calm, collected, full of self-confidence—everything Selina wasn't. Before Tom and Selina reached her, she'd broken away from her friends. "Tom! What a lovely surprise," she said, her arms outstretched for a hug when they finally found their way to her side. "And dear, you must introduce me to your friend."

"Mother, this is Selina Harrison. Selina, my mother, Helen Latimore. And Selina's not just my friend—she's my fiancée."

Mrs. Latimore hesitated just a moment, but Selina sensed her horror before her lips tightened and she spoke in a low, controlled tone to her son. Why on earth couldn't Tom have waited? "I'm sure I must know Selina's family, dear. Still, your announcement comes as a surprise." An understatement if Selina had ever heard one.

"A surprise to us, too." Tom grinned, louse that he was, as he snaked out his arms and drew Selina close. "I took one look at her and lost my heart."

Selina felt every movement of her eyes as Mrs. Latimore gave her the once-over, imagined the horror that must have been going through the older woman's head. Her obviously precious only child—Tom had mentioned he had no siblings—getting himself caught up by a dumpy, gauche woman who was so damn scared she could barely manage to put together two coherent words.

When Tom's mother held out her hand, Selina managed to take it. She hoped she achieved a smile, but she wasn't at all sure. "It's good to meet you, Selina. Forgive my temporary shock at Tom's announcement. I'm glad he's finally decided to settle down. I've despaired of having grandchildren to spoil before I'm too old to enjoy them. Hmm. Harrison. I believe I know your mother, dear."

"I'm happy to meet you, too." Selina didn't dare say anything else. Not now. Not when it appeared that Tom's mother was actually taking his announcement fairly well.

Tom squeezed Selina's hand. "Let's go somewhere a little more private and chat a little while. Mother?"

"There's hardly anyone in the little Mexican restaurant next door. I imagine we can find a quiet table."

Selina was all for hiding. Especially now that she'd seemed to pass muster with Tom's mother. She didn't want the glow to go, which she was sure it would if she had to confront her own mother. Just after dark, she and Tom said their goodbyes, bought some oysters to take home and headed back to his condo. By the time they got there, he had her in a sexual frenzy, driving along the back streets with one hand on the wheel, the other doing exquisite things to her pussy.

"I'm hungry to try some of these oysters, see if they really get us horny," he said as he got out of the car and retrieved a large bag the vendor had packed in ice. "Don't know if it's possible to get any hotter than you've already made me."

* * * * *

"Take off your clothes and sit up here," Tom said, patting the kitchen counter as he shucked the oysters and set them on a bed of crushed ice he'd dumped into a jelly roll pan. "Want cocktail sauce?"

"Yes, please." Selina did as he asked while he opened the refrigerator and came out with a bottle of the red, horseradish-laden condiment. "Where are the crackers?"

"Here." He grabbed a box out of the cabinet and came to her, his erection obvious through the lightweight khaki pants. "Anybody ever eat oysters out of your hot little cunt?"

"N-no." Surely he wouldn't. Or would he? She slid out to the edge of the countertop at his urging, let him put her legs over his shoulders and bury his face in her pussy. His tongue snaked out, filled her, sent waves of excitement racing through her body.

By the time Tom stopped and reached onto the tray for an icy oyster that chilled her flesh as he worked it up her cunt, she was too hot to think about protesting. After all, she'd had stranger things than that shoved up her vagina. Besides, every cell in her body was singing, anticipating the delightful heat of his pierced tongue when he fished it out.

"Mmm. Good. Almost as tasty as your juices by themselves." His hot breath tickled her labia. "Give me another one."

"Want cocktail sauce?" She wondered if the stuff would burn her insides but wasn't about to say so, not when her pussy creamed at the thought of his tongue snaking inside, retrieving it, pushing her toward the edge in a way she'd never experienced before.

"Just your pussy juice, sweetheart. Be a good girl and eat your share because I'm not fucking you until all the oysters are gone."

"Okay." After handing him another of them, she leaned back, let her own oyster slide down her throat, the sharp taste of the sauce tickling her taste buds while his talented tongue brought her to the edge of orgasm. One at the time, he inserted the oysters and sucked them out until there was nothing but empty shells left on the tray.

She had to have him, feel his huge cock invade her body, force her climax. Ready to beg, she slid her legs off his shoulders, spread them wider and let out a moan.

"Ready for this, sweetheart?" He stood back a little, his eyes on her sex as he unzipped his pants and slid them and his underwear off to reveal his pulsating cock and testicles tight with desire.

"Please, yes." She was more than ready. "Take me, please."

The change in his pocket jingled when his pants hit the tile floor. His hands tightened on her splayed knees as he stepped between her legs and impaled her on his cock. Her pussy sucked him in, squeezed him on each inward thrust as shards of ecstasy spread through her like a wildfire.

"Play with your nipples for me," he ordered, and when she loosened her top and obeyed him she hardly thought about the heavy rings, only about the delicious feeling of touching them, making them swell for her lover to tight, puckered points.

He lifted her legs over his shoulders again, changing the angle of penetration. Stuffing her fuller than she'd ever been, never missing a beat as he fucked her faster, deeper, harder. He glistened with sweat. She could see the pulsing of a vein in his neck, the tightening of his expression as he held back, wanting…

"Yes, sweetheart, I want to come. With you. Not alone." He slowed his thrusts, moved in a circular motion, seeking and finding the G-spot that set her off, made her scream with the pleasure-pain of it. "That's it. Oh, yeah, squeeze me now." When he let out a bellow of triumph, she felt him come inside her, spurt after spurt of hot ejaculate that set her to coming again.

"I love you," he whispered in her ear once his breathing had eased.

And she loved him. But she wasn't ready yet to believe this was real, wasn't completely convinced she was more to him than a sexual toy to be discarded once the newness wore off.

What she was ready for was to enjoy it while it lasted. Later, after they'd showered and toweled each other dry, she lay in the dark, listening to him breathe and wondering what he had in store for her tomorrow.

* * * * *

"Wake up, sleepyhead." Tom noticed how soundly Selina slept, which was a good thing since his workday started early. He'd hate to have to tiptoe around to keep from waking her once his vacation was over.

Rolling over and opening her eyes, she looked up at him and greeted him with a sleepy smile. He couldn't resist bending and kissing her. "What?" she asked, a surprised look on her face.

Obviously she wasn't used to getting up early, but then she didn't have to, now or ever. He kind of liked the idea of her being home when he left, and there when he came back from the hospital, as old-fashioned as that might be. "Time to get up, sweetheart, we've got a busy day ahead of us."

"Okay. Give me a little while to get ready."

"Sure." He was glad he'd taken the loose diamond he'd bought out of the safe behind an abstract painting on the wall before she woke up. While waiting for her to change, he called a jeweler across the street from the hospital and made an appointment, letting him know he already had the center stone but wanted Selina to pick the setting. Good thing he'd had the sixth sense that had kept him from proposing to Jo. She wouldn't have liked the old-fashioned rose-cut stone, but he had a feeling Selina would.

About fifteen minutes later Selina came out, looking good enough to eat in the pants outfit he hadn't picked for her last night. "I'm ready, I think."

"Okay. We'll have breakfast after our first stop." Getting up and checking his pocket for the box that held the diamond, he followed her out the door. "We'll come back and get the car. Our first stop is less than two blocks down the street."

When they turned in between two glass windows filled with sparkly stones and Rolex watches, Selina looked confused. "Why are we stopping here?"

"For your ring. I'm a guy who likes to stake his claim." His hand at her back, they stepped inside. "Hey, Sol, I'd like for you to meet Selina, my fiancée."

The elderly jeweler beamed as he showed them to a back room where he'd laid out a large selection of platinum and gold settings. "You have the stone you mentioned?" When Tom handed it over, the jeweler picked up his loupe and studied it. "Beautiful. A family piece?" he asked.

"I bought it at auction a while ago. Didn't know until yesterday I'd find a use for it so soon." He turned to Selina. "If you'd prefer another stone, we can trade this one in."

"Omigod, don't do that. It's gorgeous. I love it. But it's so big, I'd like a simple setting." She looked over the tray Sol pushed her way then turned to Tom. "Please. You pick it out."

He'd noticed she seemed to prefer silver jewelry, so he picked a plain platinum setting and band. "How about these, and a matching plain band for me?"

She smiled and nodded. Sol smiled. Tom asked how long it would take to set the stone and arranged to come back for the rings later in the day. "Thanks, Sol."

* * * * *

Selina was thrilled yet none too sure about the wisdom of Tom's insistence that they marry right away. Marriage had done her wrong before, in spades, but she knew for certain she wanted Tom, and she understood he came with his own set of rules.

"Where are we going now?" she asked when he pulled up in front of a medical building not far from the hospital where he worked, helped her out of the car and herded her into a third-floor office. Her hackles went up. As far as she knew, anesthesiologists didn't usually practice out of an office, and Tom had mentioned he did his work at the hospital. The last time a man had taken her to a doctor's office it had been her ex, and he'd been furious when the bariatric surgeon had refused to staple her stomach to force her to lose weight. "I don't meet the criteria for weight-loss surgery," she said before she could hold back the words.

He smiled. "I know. Remember, I'm a doctor. We're not here for a surgical consult or to look into liposuction or anything else. Remember, I like you just the way you are, but if you want to slim down, I'll hold your hand and help any nonmedical way I can."

"I'm sorry..." She cursed silently because she'd jumped to conclusions—again. It wasn't right, wasn't fair to Tom that she carried all this hurtful old baggage.

"Don't be. I'm not. We're here because those rings in your nipples offend me. I'm going to get rid of them."

Oh, no. She'd thought of that, but decided against having them sawed off when she realized she'd be left with huge, ugly holes. "I'm afraid the holes won't close," she said as he led her into an exam room where a wicked-looking saw had been laid out on a small table beside the chair where he told her to sit.

"How'd you like to have these instead?" Reaching in his pocket, he fished out a small box. Inside, when he snapped open the lid, she saw a pair of delicate platinum barbells with diamond-studded captive beads. "They come off. If you like, I'll buy you a pair for every day of the week."

What a Master! Interested not only in her physical pleasure but also in soothing her emotional hangups, Tom brought her practically to tears. She'd chosen badly before—but now she believed he'd finally bring her the ultimate pleasure she'd sought. Loving control, dished up with the hottest sex she'd ever imagined.

She pulled off her sweater and bra and sat very still while Tom cut off the hated rings. Surprisingly her flesh contracted, not a lot but enough that the beautiful new jewelry filled the space. "You do it, sweetheart," he urged, apparently aware that if she tightened the captive beads herself, she'd know he was allowing her the measure of control she needed to feel safe.

"You know, Doc, I think I love you," she said, blinking back tears when he bent and tenderly drew first one nipple and then the other into his mouth.

Looking into her eyes, he murmured, "I know I love you. Now let's go grab the rings before we brave the storm and go spring the news on your mother. It's already spitting drops of rain outside."

"My mother?" Rain was the least of Selina's worries. She could just imagine the scene, the hurtful barbs that at least she could count on being blunted because of Tom's presence. Oh no. She wasn't up for this.

"I called her, said we'd arrive at her house in time for lunch. She didn't seem particularly surprised, so I don't doubt that my mother clued her in."

"All right." As long as Tom was by her side, she could live through the inevitable inquisition.

And he was right. Her mother seemed almost content, smiled and made nice over the asparagus salad and cheese biscuits. She even brushed a kiss on Tom's cheek and welcomed him to the family as they were leaving.

* * * * *

"Well, the worst is over. We've got smooth sailing now," Tom told Selina later after arranging for Maggie and Eli to bring her car back from Club Rio Brava on Monday. He made a mental note to check out a lot that was for sale out there, near the riverfront lot where his two friends had their private dungeon. He liked his condo, didn't too much mind hers for that matter. But Tom envisioned building a place out there that would accommodate their kinks and also provide room for a couple of kids. Come to think of it, they probably should seek out a house closer to the hospital, too, because they'd probably outgrow either of their places pretty quickly.

"Want to go play at the club tonight? I'll even arrange a ménage if that would turn you on."

When she reached over and stroked his cock through his dark slacks, her new ring glittered in the dim light. A scented candle flickered on the end table next to the leather sectional couch where they sat together until Selina slid off and knelt at his feet. "You turn me on, Master. If it pleases you, though, share me with your friend." From the look in her eyes, he guessed she was saying so just to please him, not because she was anxious to have two Doms at the same time.

Surprisingly, Tom found he wasn't interested in taking part with Selina in a ménage. He wanted her to himself, and he wasn't particularly interested in switching partners even if Eli might want to at some point—which he seriously doubted. Tilting her head so she had to look at his face, he said, "I think I'll keep you to myself for a while. We can go play at the club, but you'll only be playing with me. And me with you," he added when he saw her unsure expression. "You know, we're going to have to work on this insecurity of yours. But meanwhile if you want an extra cock or two, you'll have to be satisfied with me and a couple of dildos."

That coaxed a laugh out of her. "You're more than enough for me. Believe me on that."

"Then believe I'll always tell you the truth. You're beautiful to me, sexy as hell. You get me hard just looking at me with those gorgeous eyes, and when you touch me, it sets off an explosion in my gut that's hotter than an oil-well fire. I want you in my bed and my life, for the rest of our lives. If we play games, it will be you I'll want to come home with. Not Elle or Snake Woman or any of the other subs who hang out at Club Rio Brava." Tom took Selina's hand. "And I hope you'll always want to go home with me."

"Elle?" Selina shot him a confused look.

"I'm sure you've seen her at the club. She's an unattached sub, like Snake Woman. Just not as flamboyant, and I doubt she'd consider getting shaved or tattooed. Petite. Jet black hair. She's a resident at the hospital. I ran into her at the club, recognized her. No, sweetheart, we've never played. It would have been embarrassing to have to see each other every day at work and realize we'd had kinky sex together. Particularly since she's got a vanilla boyfriend. Lynn's brother Trace. I understand they're pretty serious. You'll most likely meet him before too long. Of all the attendings, Mark, Kurt and Eli are the ones I generally socialize with."

"Are they…"

"Are they into BDSM play? Just Eli and Maggie, as far as I know. Kurt and his wife are still acting like newlyweds after ten years and three kids plus one from Kurt's first marriage."

"I haven't met them, have I?"

"I doubt it. This week they're in Atlanta for his oldest son's graduation from college. You'll meet them before the end of Fiesta because they'll be back in time to attend our wedding reception."

"Mark and Lynn seem as though they're down-to-earth folks." Selina reached for Tom's belt and loosened it, rubbing her fingers along the bare skin she'd uncovered, delving her finger into his belly button. Tom laughed. "I've always suspected they're pretty hot for each other, but as far as I know they're not into our lifestyle. In any case the four of us sort of gravitated toward each other. Eli and I shared an apartment during med school, and neither of us managed to keep our sexual proclivities secret."

"Oh."

"Yeah. You know, sweetheart, I like seeing you on your knees. Makes me want to stuff my cock into your pretty mouth and have you suck me off while I give you another token of my love."

She squeezed his obvious erection, smiled up at him. "Don't you think we have on too many clothes?"

"We do, at that. First one naked gets to suck cock or pussy." He watched her practically tear off the neat black suit and go back on her knees. Her eagerness got him hotter than he'd ever been, so he stopped teasing her and ripped off his shirt and slacks. "I think you won," he told her as he laid the jeans beside him on the couch and sat on the edge of the leather seat, his hard-on jutting out, ready for her to take it between her lips.

"I did, didn't I? You know, you've got a beautiful penis." With that she licked a drop of moisture off the head before opening her mouth and taking him inside. Her tongue felt like moist velvet caressing his flesh.

Her breath tickled him, and the slurping sound of her suckling him practically had him coming before she'd even warmed up. Reaching in his shirt pocket he found the heavy platinum chain with its barbell closure. When she went down on him completely, swallowing him, using her hands to fondle his balls, he fit the collar around her neck and twisted the barbells until they locked with a metallic clink.

She raised her head, smiled as she slid her fingers along her collar. A smile that conveyed pleasure, certainty…no fear or anxiety at all. "Thank you, Master," she said, and she lowered her head again, took his straining cock once more.

Knowing she was his had as strong an effect as any aphrodisiac. He felt himself swell as she swallowed against him, felt her soft hands exploring his belly, his thighs. Pressure built quickly. He wasn't lasting long this time. Grasping her head in both his hands, he made her take him deeper, and when she did he exploded, filling her with his hot, wet seed.

He'd never felt so powerful yet so humble when he lifted her face to his and tasted his own climax on her glistening lips, or when he admired the satin patina of his collar against her soft, silky skin. A gentle symbol of ownership, but whether it symbolized his possession or hers he wasn't certain.

Epilogue

A year later…

ꟹ

"I'm going to miss this place." Selina had argued against leaving the condo, but she knew Tom was right. They needed more bedrooms and space to entertain. But it was the specially equipped dungeon in the house they'd built that had finally persuaded her they needed to move.

"Me, too." Tom came up behind her and splayed his fingers over her significantly smaller belly. She'd managed to come within five pounds of her weight-loss goal since they'd married the last night of Fiesta, although if she wasn't dead wrong, that wouldn't last long. "Still hanging in there, honey?"

"Uh-huh." Five days now since her period hadn't come. Three since an EPT showed up positive. They'd spent yesterday with Eli and Maggie, and for the first time Selina had realized how much she wanted a similarly conventional home life and the kids their friends all seemed to enjoy so much. "I hope this isn't a false alarm," she said, leaning her head back and listening to Tom's steady heartbeat.

"Me, too. But I'm glad we put in that room so we can indulge our kinky tastes away from the kiddies' curious little eyes and ears. Come on, let's fuck in the hot tub one last time before the movers come. I want to watch your face in the mirror when you come."

Oh, yeah. Selina's hot master still had it all…the perfect prescription for her submission. "Your wish is my command," she said, turning into his arms and raising her lips for his kiss.

UNEXPECTED CONTROL

Trademarks Acknowledgement

The author acknowledges the trademarked status and trademark owners of the following wordmarks mentioned in this work of fiction:

Dallas Cowboys: Dallas Cowboys Football Club, Ltd.

Demerol: Alba Pharmaceutical Company/Sanofi-Aventis U.S.

Google: Google, Inc.

Harvard: President and Fellows of Harvard College

Jaguar: Jaguar Cars Limited

Johnnie Walker Red: John Walker & Sons Ltd./Diageo plc

MySpace: News Corporation

Shiner Bock: Gambrinus Importing Company, Inc.

Prologue

ꝏ

All this lovey-dovey togetherness was enough to make pediatric surgeon Elle Drake want to scream. She'd never imagined she might see the intense, serious neurosurgeon, Mark Blackstone, catching his wife under the mistletoe and fondling her breast while giving her a quick, hard kiss. Or that Mark's partner, Kurt Silverman, could actually relax. Drink in hand, he was laughing with the OR supervisor he swore kept a voodoo doll of him to jab with pins every time he had to have her call in extra staff for the emergency cases that often presented themselves on nights and weekends.

Elle had been at the party less than fifteen minutes and already she'd run into three fellow staff members she'd also seen at Club Rio Brava. Unfortunately, any of the usual thoughts she might have had about sharing a Dom with another woman to deal with her sexual frustration were pointless. Maggie and Eli Calhoun were joined at the hip—and hot anesthesiologist and Dominant Tom Latimore had recently found his life partner in former club Domme Selina Harrison. Elle didn't imagine either of the women would be amenable to sharing. Come to think of it, she wouldn't be, either. Following her thirty-second birthday last month, Elle had started to wonder if she should walk away from the club scene and find a good man to settle down with, even if he was vanilla.

So here she was, all dolled up at University Trauma Group's annual holiday party, waiting to meet her dinner partner, the nearest thing she'd had to a blind date since her freshman year in college. What would Lynn's younger brother be like? Not for the first time since agreeing to be a party date for Mark's brother-in-law, she wondered what she'd said yes to.

Idiot, you know why. Recently she'd come to the conclusion that her trips to Club Rio Brava, the exclusive BDSM club, were leaving her emotionally unsatisfied, no matter how many times the faceless Doms forced her to shed her inhibitions and come. She'd even thought about walking away from the club, but she didn't have much hope that a vanilla guy could satisfy her. After all, she'd tried several before, and they'd left her as physically wanting as…

Damn her sexual quirks, she was a wreck when it came to relationships. She just couldn't seem to mesh her emotional need for a happily-ever-after with a decent man with her physical need to be dominated sexually.

But Eli had found his partner outside the club. Why couldn't she do it, too? Smoothing the iridescent blue taffeta of the long skirt she'd paired with a black silk-knit top, Elle let herself feel a sense of anticipation. Maybe this time she'd luck into her ideal man—a guy like Eli, who'd played Dom to her sub a few times before finding Maggie.

Trace Williams might be drop-dead gorgeous. He probably was, considering that Mark's wife still looked like a beauty queen after however many years of marriage and four kids. But Elle didn't even want to calculate the odds that Trace would be into BDSM games. No. She'd enjoy a pleasant evening of conversation, mingle with the cream of University Hospital's medical staff, and continue with her own split life—respectable surgeon by day, secret submissive once the lights went down.

"Selina, you're looking great," Elle said to the former Domme who'd apparently made a switch when she hooked Tom. She'd also lost thirty or forty pounds since Tom had swept her off for a quickie Vegas wedding last spring. "Marriage must agree with you."

"Yes." Selina's smile said more than that simple word. "Shelly, Lynn and Maggie have gone all out for this party." She gestured toward the heavily laden buffet centered with a large menorah nestled on a bed of glossy evergreen leaves and delphinium blossoms. A fragrant blue-spruce Christmas tree with sparkling lights and balls cast shadows on Elle and Selina from its place in the center of a huge living room, and sprays of mistletoe with blue and silver ribbon decorated every doorway. "There must be millions of calories in all that food."

"Probably. It all looks delicious, though." Elle eyed a plate of small round cookies with chocolate centers. Hard to resist, even though she wouldn't dare swipe one and see if they were as good as they looked—not until somebody else started decimating the spread.

"Oh, there you are." Elle turned at the sound of Lynn's voice, but it was the man she was with who took her breath away. "This is Trace. Trace, Elle."

Omigod. The guy *was* killer good-looking, with a twenty-four karat smile and dark-brown hair that looked as if it could use a trim. But it was the deep brown eyes raking her from head to toe that had her speechless—as tongue-tied as if he were stripping her naked in front of the entire, mostly vanilla crowd. "Hi, Trace," she managed.

He took a step toward her, took her hand in a confident grip. Working hands, she thought as she experienced the not-unpleasant sensation of calluses abrading her palm. "Hello, beautiful. Come on, let's let my sister and Selina visit while we grab a drink and get to know each other. I keep telling Lynn every year that they should just hire a caterer for this bash or hold it at the country club, but she and Shelly are determined to do it on their own."

He might be vanilla, but it was obvious from the way he jumped right in as if they'd known each other for years that Trace Williams didn't lack self-confidence. Elle tilted her head and smiled up at him. "Really? I thought I saw some people in caterer's uniforms, coming in and out of the kitchen."

"They're here to serve. Lynn and Shelly did all the cooking. And they spend days every year, decorating the house where the party's held."

"Oh." Elle couldn't imagine herself spending days creating anything like this politically correct wonderland. "The only signs of holidays in my apartment are some candles in a window and a wreath I picked up at the grocery store." What on earth was she babbling about? Damn it, Elle hadn't let a man fluster her this way for years, if ever. The idea of going on her knees to Trace, having him take her over, had her body heating with inexplicable anticipation.

Come on, Elle, you're weaving Dom fantasies about a guy you just met. A guy you know isn't a Dom. Or is he? She wondered if she was picking up on familiar vibes from him, but no! It had to be false hope. She knew he wasn't into BDSM. If he were, she undoubtedly would have run across him at Club Rio Brava, because he was part of the San Antonio elite even though he wasn't a doctor, and the club directors would have welcomed him.

Still, he seemed almost dominant when he maneuvered her toward the patio and caught her in the doorway underneath a beribboned leaf of mistletoe, bent his head and drew her much closer than was seemly in front of all these people. The kiss he claimed went on long enough to ignite a fire inside her. Him, too, if the sudden hardness against her belly was a fair indicator.

Maybe... No. Trace was as hot a man as she'd run across in years, but he was no Dom. She'd enjoy the evening with him and walk away.

Sure she would. As he walked her to her car when the party was over, she found herself saying yes to dinner at the Riverwalk on her next day off, and a country club's annual holiday dance the following weekend. And to God only knew what else. She'd risk the hurt when she tried to come for him and couldn't, hold on to the miniscule chance he'd be the one man to ring her bells without providing her that element of mastery she needed to let go her inhibitions.

Chapter One

Almost a year later…

ꟷ

God, but he loved her. Trace watched Elle, a city girl who seemed to take to ranch life as if she'd been born to it. The cold wind whipped her sable hair as they rounded the corner of the paddock fence on horseback and headed for the barn.

"My ears are freezing."

"So are mine, sweetheart. I'm sorry. The weatherman predicted a day a lot warmer than I'm feeling." He shouldn't have been so eager, should have waited for Saturday night and taken her to some romantic restaurant. "Come on, let's get inside."

"Great idea." Elle shivered as she dismounted and paused to stroke the nose of the glossy blood-bay mare before handing the reins to a stable hand. "I enjoyed the ride, Trace, and I'm sure Beauty here will get you a nice colt from Diego, but it's damn cold outside."

"May I blame it on the weatherman? I wouldn't have planned a long ride for us if I had any idea the temperature would drop like the stock market did in the crash of 1929." He didn't blame Elle if she was pissed. After all, he'd made her believe coming out here this afternoon was a matter of life and death—figuratively speaking.

Her smile took the bite off her words. "I thought you must have had some more compelling reason than wanting me to exercise your new mare when you insisted that I come out today. I'll forgive you, and the weatherman, though. It's been good to relax after a nerve-racking morning in surgery. Come on. I want my surprise. Don't keep me in suspense any longer." She pulled up the collar of her jacket, shivering in the crisp bite of mid-November air.

"Your wish is my command." Trace wanted to wrap her in a cocoon that would shield her gentle soul from the inevitable stresses of her profession. But first he wanted to thaw her out. "Let's get you inside and warmed up first." He was used to being out in the elements, but she wasn't. That's why he hadn't stopped and proposed at one of her favorite places by the ice-glazed stream. "Lynn and Mark wouldn't be happy if I let you freeze out here. Neither would your little patients."

She took his gloved hand and brought it to her lips. "No, they wouldn't. First one inside gets to make a pot of hot cocoa." She took off then paused until he caught up with her on the pool deck. "Look. It's really getting cold. Steam's rising off the water."

"I'm too busy looking at you, sweetheart." Opening the kitchen door first, he scooped her up in his arms, the way he anticipated doing again on their wedding night. He kicked open the door and strode across the deck to the kitchen door. "Close the door for me. I don't want to put you down just yet."

"All right. How do you stay so warm?" She snuggled up against him, nibbled at his ear. "How about that cocoa you promised?"

"It's coming. Water's already hot and ready." He captured her lips, found them willing but still cold. She'd been reluctant to drive out here, and he chalked up her dragging her feet to the fact that she was worried about one of her patients, a three-year-old she'd told him had practically died after running his tricycle out in the street. But he sensed something more. Something that scared him, made him reluctant to open his mouth and risk rejection.

Trace had wanted to propose here on the ranch, in a romantic setting, one they'd revisit thirty years from now when they recalled this day. But the weather hadn't cooperated, the temperature dropping fifteen degrees in the last two hours. The usually calm wind was whipping trees around, chilling every living thing down to the bone. When he noticed Elle had on only a lightweight sweater under the suede jacket she'd just taken off, he knew she must have been miserable outside.

"More cocoa?" He really wanted them to adjourn to his bedroom, where he'd done a quick tidying up and set out candles and a bunch of long-stemmed roses on the table beside the bed. He'd started a small fire in the fireplace, too. The diamond ring he'd bought yesterday sat on the table in the jeweler's distinctive box, just waiting, and the covers on the bed were folded back.

When she shook her head and smiled, he took that as a hint that she was as anxious to make love as he was. "Then let's go upstairs."

She was tiny, light as a feather in his arms as he took the stairs two at the time. Yeah, she was strong in many ways. Had to be, to fight death in kids the way she did. But when she was with him, he wanted to take care of her, shield her from harm, emotional as well as physical. Once in the room, he set her on the edge of the bed and came down beside her.

"I love you, you know." He took her hand, traced a circle on her palm.

"What's the occasion for the flowers and candles?" Elle gestured toward the table.

He started to tell her but changed his mind. "You'll see. First, I want to make love to you. Warm you up after that chilly ride. Unless you're not in the mood."

"How could I not be when you've gone to all this trouble?" She inclined her head toward the fireplace, sighed. "I've always loved watching a fire in the bedroom. Mom and Dad had one in their bedroom when I was a little girl." Trace detected a hint of a tremor in her voice, wondered what kind of memories that fire might be dredging up in her mind.

He knew Elle and her mother weren't close. That was evident when they ran into her last spring at one of the Fiesta events. Elle never talked much about her childhood other than mentioning she was an only child, and that her mom and dad hadn't gotten along. The only time he'd noticed much emotion on the rare occasions she talked about her family was when she told him her dad had died when she was barely in her teens. Trace sensed she'd buried some baggage pretty deeply, and though he didn't know exactly what that baggage entailed, he figured it had something to do with growing up in a house full of discord. He was determined not to cause her any distress if he could help it. Maybe that was why he felt overprotective of Elle now.

The best way to distract her from whatever memories that fire had kindled would be to get her into bed, do everything he knew how to make her come. Very calmly, even though he wanted to rip off her clothes and claim her hard and fast, he undressed her and then himself. Elle was too precious, too delicate. She deserved the slow, sweet foreplay, the respect he owed the woman he wanted for the rest of his life.

"Lie down, sweetheart." She was fucking beautiful, and not just on the outside—although that didn't hurt. When he looked at her firm, round breasts he imagined nourishing their baby someday, blood went rushing to his cock, but he just kept looking at her, stroking the pulse point at her throat, running his hands lightly over her breasts, her ribcage. He loved the softness of her, the waist he could span with his hands, her flat belly and the hairless pussy that beckoned his hands and mouth. He couldn't resist laying his hand on her plump mound, feeling the satin smoothness. "How do you keep the hair from growing back?"

"I had it permanently removed. With laser treatments. Just like I had all the hair taken off my arms and legs. Black hair shows when it's growing out, almost as much as your five o'clock shadow." She laid her hand over his. "This shocked you the first time you saw it, didn't it?"

"A little. I like it, though. And I've been wondering how you managed to keep this so soft and smooth."

She laughed. "So why did you wait so long to ask?"

"I didn't want to embarrass you. But I've been thinking I might like to try getting rid of some excess hair, myself." He'd often wondered if he irritated her skin down there with his tangle of pubic hair.

"You don't have to. If you want, though, I'll shave you. Give you an idea of how it would feel to be totally naked before making it permanent."

When she tangled her fingers in his pubic hair and played with his balls, he felt as though his cock would explode. "Anytime, love. If you weren't a surgeon, though, I might feel a little threatened if you approached the family jewels with a razor."

"I'll be very, very careful."

"Just like I intend to be with you." The feel of her satiny skin beneath his fingers when he found her clit and stroked it made him want to forget about the foreplay, mount her and fuck her hard, but he clamped down on those barbaric thoughts and lowered his head. Light nips to her thighs had her squirming quickly enough, so he took her clit between his teeth and flailed it with his tongue.

"Oooh."

"Like this, do you?"

"Feels good. Don't stop."

Trace returned to his task, gratified but wanting, needing more of a response from her. A scream of pleasure, maybe, or even a whispered *omigod*. But Elle was always a lady. Quiet, dignified. Screams apparently weren't her thing. It didn't matter. He loved being with her, adored everything about her. He wanted her to be his wife, for always. For all those things, he could do without the loud, frantic sexual responses he'd been used to getting from other lovers over the years.

Her hands felt good in his hair, stroking his scalp while he tongue-fucked her. She seemed to like it from the way her juices were flowing now, slick and salty. The earthy smell of sex had his heart racing.

Why wouldn't he get on with it, take control and push her over the edge? Elle pulled his face away from her pussy, tugged him up her body. "Trace," she whispered before he took her mouth. He smelled of sex—hers as well as the unmistakable scent of aroused male. His muscular chest had her pinned to the bed, and his cock throbbed against her cunt. The way he touched her, so gently, made her feel loved. It also frustrated her so much she wanted to scream. He was hot. Obviously ready, at least physically.

Why wouldn't he stuff that monster cock down her throat, make her go down on him the way he'd just done on her? So many times she'd wanted to go on her knees, take him in her mouth and feel him come deep in her throat, but he'd never asked. Never shown her he might want oral sex from her.

Of course she could have opened up her mouth and asked, or just gone to her knees and done it on her own. But every time she started to do it, Elle heard her mother's voice in her head, as if she were there and looking in. *"A good girl would never force the issue, reveal those unnatural urges."*

So she could turn into a complete wanton under the hands of a strange Dom at the club, but she wouldn't dare ask the man she loved if she could. God, was she fucked up in the head!

She locked her arms around Trace's narrow waist, urged him closer. She was no weak kitten who needed kid-gloves treatment. She didn't need for him to treat her like a terrified virgin, as if he thought she'd bolt at the first sign he intended to take her—by force if necessary. "Make love to me now," she whispered, when what she really meant was *"Please, Master, fuck me hard. Tie me up. You can't hurt me, not enough that it's going to interfere with the pleasure."* Not for the first time, she felt the grip of despair that told her she should end this relationship before they both ended up getting hurt.

But she had a feeling that breaking up with Trace even now would break her heart.

He felt so good, all hard muscle built by hard work, not hours in a gym. And he made her happy in so many ways. Damn it, she'd gone and fallen in love with a vanilla man, but she so badly wanted him to be a Dom. This was never going to work.

His cock felt velvety soft when he sank slowly and gently into her sopping cunt. The stretching sensation, the heat and throbbing of him as he moved in her. She tried to concentrate on the delicious friction and heat, banish the need for him to rob her of her choices and push her over the edge. It worked, but only to the point that when he finally dropped his head to her shoulder and shuddered with the force of his climax, she felt a tiny twinge, enough that she tightened her legs around his waist, tried to maintain the little kernel of hope that this time he'd make her come. Really come. She turned her head, found his mouth, claimed his ragged breath as her own.

Fool. She should have known she couldn't come without kink. No matter how much she loved Trace—and she did, too much to let him think he wasn't satisfying her. It was her problem, her lack. Not his. When he stopped shuddering and gathered her in his arms, she pretended. But she suspected that if he didn't know now, he'd soon realize her coming was only an act.

Can you stay the night?" As he often did after they made love, he wondered if her climax had been faked. But he was certain her affection wasn't. She cuddled up to him like a friendly pup, her cheek on his chest, her arm draped over his back, fingers lightly kneading his butt.

She lifted her head, met his gaze. "I'm afraid not. I've got an early case in the morning."

Trace tried to hide his disappointment, but he wasn't sure...hell, he wasn't sure of anything with Elle, except that he'd fallen in love for the first time in his thirty-five years of living and that he wanted to stake his claim. "We'll skip the champagne until next time, then. Stay here for a little while. I have something for you."

"A present? I love presents."

"Good, sweetheart." Getting up, he didn't bother with clothes but strode to the table by the fireplace and took the ring box. When he came back to the bed he went to his knees. "Marry me. Be my love and my partner. I don't mind sharing you with your patients—not much at least—but I want you to belong to me not just now but for the rest of our lives."

He opened the box, hoping she'd be pleased with the good-size diamond solitaire on a slender, etched, platinum band. When she didn't move to take it right away, his confidence took a hard swat. "Don't you like it?" Damn it, he should have dragged Lynn along to pick out the ring.

Elle reached over and caressed his cheek. "It's beautiful. There's nothing I'd love more than being your wife..."

He heard the *but* in her voice, saw it in the confused expression on her face. "Need some time to think about it? If you do, that's okay." It wasn't, but Trace could practically feel her slipping away emotionally. Maybe he'd gone too fast, assumed too much. "Just so long as you keep on thinking positive."

"I will. Can I let you know in a week or so, after I've had time to think it over? It's not that I don't love you, because I do, more than I've ever loved a man."

Trace wondered if she was thinking about Lynn and Mark, Shelly and Kurt Silverman, their new partner Eli Calhoun and his bride. He hoped so. If any couples could encourage her to take the plunge, they could. Even after years of marriage and a handful of kids, the older couples acted like newlyweds, and Maggie seemed over the moon with Eli and their baby boy.

"Take all the time you want, love. It's a pretty big decision, turning your back on being single. But we can make it together, I'm sure." He wasn't at all certain despite his brave words, but he'd give Elle the gift of space she seemed to need so badly. "Just remember I love you, too. There's nothing on Earth I wouldn't do for you…or with you."

Chapter Two

ꙮ

Damn it, Elle. What the hell is wrong with you? Any other woman would kill to have Trace propose to her.

A big part of her longed to say yes. Trace Williams was everything a woman could ask for in a man. Intelligent, fun to be with and drop-dead gorgeous. They both loved funny movies and taking long rides along the creek at his ranch. He even shared her love for line dancing and a few icy Shiner Bock drafts. And it wasn't as if the guy were an itinerant cowboy. He had an MBA from Harvard and was as rich as Croesus. Elle loved being around him, appreciated the way he fit in with her coworkers at the hospital, dreamed about having a little boy with his mischievous smile. So why was it she'd just balked at accepting his ring?

Idiot. It's because what you want is a collar.

Elle stood outside the door at Club Rio Brava, drawn by the promise of a hot encounter with one or more of the nameless, masked club Doms charged with satisfying the needs of closet subs like her. But she hesitated. There was something sleazy about satisfying her sexual needs here at the club when she'd just told Trace she'd give some serious thought to his proposal.

It wasn't that she worried he'd get wind of her visiting the BDSM club where she'd been a member for several years. The club's motto rang in her ears. *What goes on here stays here.* She had no doubt this was true, because the affluent club members took that vow very seriously indeed. Still…

Along with drilling the idea that sex was bad and no decent woman enjoyed it, Mom had always taught her that her word was sacred, that going back on it was one of the worst sins she could commit.

Elle pondered the question of whether getting off with a stranger would constitute a breach of that semi-promise she'd made Trace before getting up out of his bed and coming here.

Her conscience hissed out "yes" so loudly the word rang in her ears. It wasn't Trace's fault he didn't satisfy her in bed. She hadn't ever let him know she was a sexual submissive, able to come only if her partner or partners applied a certain amount of force and kink.

But her body yelled "no". Her pussy ached for the sort of satisfaction she hadn't gotten tonight. She ached for the hot, wild release she knew would await her if she stepped into the inner chambers of Club Rio Brava. She wanted a Dom to force away her inhibitions, take away her choices so she wouldn't need to feel guilty for all her wicked needs.

But she wouldn't indulge herself. Not tonight, when the memory of Trace's sweet lovemaking was fresh on her mind. Not when she was supposed to be considering his proposal.

Somehow Elle dredged up the strength to take her hand off the highly polished brass doorknob and walk back to her car. Her heart longed for a friend and lover, a partner to share life's joys and sorrows. Trace fit the bill in almost every way. She couldn't picture any of the masked Doms inside the club being able to satisfy any need except her obsession with being dominated during sex, even if he were willing to try.

Elle wanted a Dom, but not for the impersonal BDSM play participated in at the club by everybody except members in full-time relationships, like Eli and Maggie. Like Tom Latimore and his Selina. How the hell could she tell Trace that if he wanted to satisfy her sexually, he'd have to dominate her, push her past the inhibitions built up since she'd been a little girl at her prissy mother's knee.

She'd never forgotten the arguments, her precious daddy bellowing at Mom, saying awful things to her about wanting good sex, and blaming his failures with investments and his love for single malt Scotch whisky on Mom not giving him any loving at home. Sometimes at night when Elle slept, her mom's usual reply, *"Get it from your sluts. Only they could enjoy your pawing"* rang out in her ears as clearly as it had when she'd been six years old, trembling on the stairway and witnessing the hate that frequently erupted between the two most important people in her life.

Daddy had been the most important man on Earth. Her hero. Elle's fantasy as she was growing into a woman had her seeing him kissing away Mom's anger and making her submit to his wishes. If he'd done that, maybe he'd still be alive and all their lives would have turned out differently. Maybe that was what drove her to want a dominant man in her own life.

* * * * *

Trace was reasonably sure Elle loved him. It seemed she just didn't much like making love with him, though, and that stung. He searched his memory, analyzing his technique for any flaws that might have turned Elle off. Too much love talk? Not enough? Maybe he hadn't discovered the types of foreplay that turned her every way but loose. Or…no, he wasn't too rough. He'd taken pains to be gentle, to take sex slow and treat her like the precious lover she was.

He'd known from the first that she'd grown up without a father. She'd mentioned a couple of times when they first started dating that before he'd died he and her mother had argued all the time and occasionally come to blows. Whether she'd meant to or not, Elle had given him the impression that the thought of having a sexual relationship made her uneasy because of those childhood memories. But she'd never shown any fear when they made love. And her skill in bed made him believe she'd enjoyed some decent sexual experiences in the past.

Not that her experience bothered him. On the contrary, he liked the way she didn't flinch when he ate her pussy. And the ease with which she explored his body, although that could have come from her being a doctor. He hadn't expected that at thirty-two, she'd be a simpering virgin. Not with her dynamite looks and…

Well, she was highly intelligent, well-spoken and just plain fun to be with, but it was her looks that must have attracted males like flies from the minute she hit puberty.

Perplexed, Trace lay in bed, staring up at the stars through the skylight that gave the room a feel of wide-open spaces. The lingering scent of Elle's female musk and her sexy-as-hell French perfume swirled around him. If he had a grain of sense he'd dump her and find a woman who welcomed his cock as much as his company.

But the pretty lady doctor had burrowed under his skin, ruined him for other women. Imagining how much better life would be if Elle were with him, he got up, padded to the window and stared out toward the horse barns. He could practically feel the heat of her curvaceous little body flush against him, her hand on his hip. They'd have watched the silvery moon glowing through the skylight above his bed, and he'd have enjoyed watching her soft sable curls shine in the reflected light. He'd been looking forward to enjoying the afterglow of their lovemaking, that special closeness lovers often share.

But Elle obviously hadn't had snuggling on her mind. "I've got to get on home," she'd told him practically the minute he'd proposed. She'd even rolled onto her back, resisting his effort to keep her close. Then she'd put on her clothes, dropped a casual kiss on his lips, and told him once more that she'd think over his proposal. The way she had practically run out as if the hounds of hell were chasing her would have been funny if it hadn't been so embarrassing.

Could it have been that Elle just plain didn't have much of a sex drive? That didn't seem likely since she'd never refused him when he initiated lovemaking, even out at their favorite spot along the stream or in the barn. He just plain didn't understand.

Where the fuck had he gone wrong? Trace stood there staring out the window, thinking back on the times he and Elle had made love over the past nine or ten months, trying to remember if he knew for sure she'd ever come. Yes. That one time in the barn when he'd gone at her like a bull on a cow in heat. He'd felt terrible afterward for having let go his control, but he was pretty sure she'd come.

As bad as he hated to, he was going to ask Lynn and Mark for some advice.

* * * * *

"You want to marry a woman who doesn't like having sex with you?" Mark shot him a look that said *"What kind of fucking moron are you, anyhow?"* as if he'd said the words out loud.

"Now, Mark, there's this thing called love." Lynn had always been a sucker for the happily-ever-after full of hearts and flowers, like most women Trace knew. She also was the one who'd prodded Mark to set up that first blind date where Trace met Elle. She'd sung Elle's praises, telling him about the beautiful pediatric surgeon who often referred bone trauma patients to Mark or Kurt. At the time his sister had made no bones about the fact she thought he and Elle would make a perfect match. Lynn's expression morphed from teasing to serious when she turned back to Trace. "What makes you think Elle doesn't like sex? Do you think she's frigid?"

Trace didn't, but the question made him want to squirm. He hated dissecting his sex life with his sister—even more, he felt uncomfortable spouting off his concerns in front of Mark. Lynn and Mark had always struck him as being ideal for each other, even more so in the last couple of years since their youngest was born. Since then it seemed they must have done something that had put a newlywed sort of excitement back into their fifteen-year-old marriage.

Still, Trace adored Elle. If only he could get into her pretty, steel-trap mind and find out what it was he needed to do to set off fireworks in their bed. "She doesn't...well, put it this way. Last night I thought the lovemaking was damn good. Hell, I've never gotten any complaints on my technique. Not even from Elle. But she jumped out of bed as if she'd been bee-stung and took off. I can't imagine it was because she had an early day in surgery."

Mark laughed. "You're right on that. Elle didn't have surgery today, early or otherwise. She does her cases on Thursday, other than the occasional emergency like the one yesterday morning. And she has afternoon office hours if I'm not mistaken."

"Oh." So it was just as Trace had suspected. Elle hadn't wanted to stay. But her last words had been that she'd think over his proposal. That gave him a smidgeon of hope. "What the hell?"

Lynn laid a hand on his forearm, her touch much like the ones he'd seen her bestow on her kids when they skinned their knees or had a bad day at school. "Maybe you're just too nice. Some women like..."

"...a lover who pushes the envelope. Right, honey?" The look Mark shot at Lynn made her squirm so obviously not even a brother could fail to notice.

"Maybe. You know, Maggie mentioned that she thought she recognized Elle in the dressing room one time at...at a club she and Eli belong to." Lynn looked at Mark, her expression hesitant.

Mark grinned. "I bet you're right. Trace, has it ever occurred to you that Elle...that she might need a little push?"

"What?"

"It might take some role-playing to get her hot. Some imaginative foreplay." He hesitated, as if he wasn't sure Trace understood what he meant. "You know, handcuffs. Blindfolds.

Maybe even a spanking or the bite of one of your riding crops." Mark shot Lynn a look that clearly was asking for help.

"For instance, tie her down and tease her until she's so hot she begs you to make love to her," Lynn suggested with a cheeky grin.

Trace's cock twitched when he imagined dominating Elle that way, but he cringed at the thought of what she'd do to him when he let her loose. "You want me to die young, sis?"

"I want you to live happy." When Lynn paused, Trace wondered if this conversation was embarrassing her half as much as it was humiliating him. "You're a sweetie, maybe too much so. A lot of women like a man who's forceful in bed. Trust me." She winked at Mark, who pretended not to notice.

Later, when Trace got up to leave, Mark followed him to his car. But he didn't leave. Instead he leaned against the car, his coffee mug in hand. "Are you using your tickets for the Cowboys' game on Sunday?"

"I don't know yet. If you and Lynn want to leave the kids home, you can have two, though. I know I won't be taking any guests other than Elle." She liked football, but a game wasn't exactly the place he had in mind to test out Mark and Lynn's suggestions. "On second thought, you can have all four tickets if you want them. My two nieces might like to go, too."

"Thanks, pal. I'll send somebody over to the ranch to get them."

"No problem." Except that Trace wanted his weekend with Elle to himself. "I'll be coming in to town Friday night to pick up Elle. I'll stop by here and leave them for you."

Mark's expression turned serious. "Okay, Trace, I'm going to put it to you straight. Lynn was trying to beat around the bush. I don't know why. Maybe because she's your sister, or because she was respecting Elle's privacy, but I can tell this is the real deal for you and she's breaking your heart. And I happen to think—well, we both do—that you're good for Elle.

"So here's the deal. What Lynn was trying to tell you is that we think Elle may be a sexual submissive. Like Eli and Maggie, she's into hard-core bondage and discipline, the kind that apparently goes on in BDSM clubs. Not that I'd suggest that you ask Eli for a recommendation to his club right away, but making a trip to the local triple-X toy store might do a world of good. It has for us."

Trace hoped to hell he didn't look as shocked as he felt. "Okay. I'm game to try almost anything," Trace said as he slid behind the wheel.

"By the way, Elle's not on call this coming weekend. Just in case you might want to spirit her away."

* * * * *

On the way home from Lynn and Mark's place, Trace mulled over what they'd said. Elle, a sexual submissive? Right. If he tried dominating her, she'd most likely chop off his balls. Well, maybe not, he thought when he remembered the one time they'd come in from a ride around the ranch and he'd fucked her in an empty stall, with her hanging onto the rough wood wall, her legs trapped in the tight jeans he'd slid down below her knees. Her tight cunt had been wet and swollen, and she'd moaned with pleasure the harder and faster he'd pounded into her.

As a matter of fact, when he looked back he realized that was the only time he could remember when he was positive Elle's orgasm had been real. And he'd felt like apologizing to her afterward once he regained his voice. Maybe his mom had taught him a little too well that he needed to treat women with tenderness, respect.

So maybe he'd give Mark's suggestion a try. He opened the door and stepped inside his empty house, imagining her there, greeting him with a submissive smile. All he had to lose was Elle, and it seemed he'd been doing a decent job of that by playing Mr. Nice Guy. He headed for his office and turned on the computer.

Dominance and submission. Trace hesitated for a minute before hitting "Enter" and waiting for Google to come up with some possible sites. The first one he clicked on featured an interesting array of what looked like medieval instruments of torture, and some damn arousing shots of chicks in various stages of undress who were bound and seemed to be enjoying what Trace would say amounted to some serious abuse.

Obviously that wasn't something he wanted to pursue with anybody, much less the woman he loved. He shook his head and tried another site. And another. What the hell? He had trouble believing anybody sane would enjoy inflicting serious pain on his partner, or that any woman could get off on being hurt. Then he hit on a website where some Dom went into the psychology of why some people were Dominants, others submissive. It pointed him to a MySpace page where an anonymous woman had talked about what she needed in her lover.

Trace clicked on the link.

This was more what he was looking for. Against a typically feminine-looking background that featured white roses on a pink screen was a message. It made sense to Trace, where the hardcore BDSM sites hadn't. He could deal with this, he thought, re-reading what the woman had written, about the responsibilities she faced, how she needed to escape them, hand over control to a dominant lover.

"All my life I've had to lead others, but in sex I have to have a leader. I need a man to take control of my body and my senses to overcome my inhibitions, and make me find pleasure in the acts my mother taught me were horribly wrong.

I want a Dom who understands what I need and knows what it takes to bring me along, a Dom who loves me and who wants to give me pleasure.

"A gentle Dom who'll kiss away the bruises from his lash, who'll support me in daylight as well as during the long nights in his bed. I want a man who loves me and fulfills my every fantasy.

"A strong man. A leader. A lover I can lean on, count on, not just for tonight but for all time."

The woman had issued quite an order. As he re-read the passage, Trace wondered if he could ever be all those things to Elle. He'd never thought she might have deeply ingrained inhibitions that gentle loving by an equal couldn't sweep away. But she'd mentioned her dysfunctional family, the prudish mother and the philandering, hard-drinking dad.

Trace hoped Elle would find gentle domination enough to bring her along because he'd hate having to resort to the damn pillories and adjustable crosses, and the many physical torture devices he'd seen demonstrated during his brief research. He'd do it, though, if he had to.

He loved Elle, and if he had to act the Dom to have her, he'd gladly play the role. In fact, as he thought back to that day in the stable, and the times he'd wanted to play a little rougher with her, he decided it might not be a chore at all. Thinking about ordering her to his bed, restraining her there while he indulged every carnal thought he'd ever had, sent blood south so fast he was feeling lightheaded and his cock was straining to get free of his jeans and play. Maybe Elle wasn't the only one who'd lose some inhibitions if he took the reins.

Chapter Three

ℌ

Alone in her apartment, Elle almost wished for an emergency to call her back to the hospital. Even if this *was* beginning her weekend off call. She had too damn much time to think about Trace and the proposal she knew she had to turn down.

It wasn't as if Elle didn't love him, because she did, with every beat of her heart. It certainly wasn't as though he weren't one hot dude, because the rugged rancher was every bit the dark-haired, brown-eyed lover she'd conjured up in the best of her late-night fantasies. If only he didn't save the well-worn, oiled, leather whip he kept coiled neatly on his saddle horn for easing along recalcitrant heifers. She'd rather he used it to remind her he was her boss.

Except for that one time…

Not that he'd actually used that whip on her. Or even alluded to it. He hadn't needed to. They'd come in from a ride along the creek that ran through one wooded section of his property. All it had taken was his suggestion, made with the slightest hint of demand, and a pointed look at the rough wood wall of the empty stall where he'd led her, his hot gaze boring into her body as she slid her jeans down to her knees and stood there gripping the wall, waiting…

She hadn't had to wait long. His breath had been hot, his work-roughened hands intent as he positioned her, his voice deliciously raspy as he told her exactly what he intended to do.

I'm gonna fuck you 'til you scream like a mare when she's taking it from Diego. And he had. For the first time outside Club Rio Brava, Elle had come. Without toys. Without a kinky scene or a pair of hot Doms. Without anything except her and Trace and his favorite mount, a big black stallion who'd watched with his ears perked toward her as she reached for and found her peak. She guessed that in itself was some sort of kink, voyeurism as real as if the voyeur had been human, taking in every thrust, every parry, ogling their glistening bodies straining as they raced to pleasure.

She still didn't know what had come over him that day. Maybe just being outdoors and unable to have their hands on each other for a long day of riding horses out to check a spot on the ranch boundary where the fence had been torn down had fed his lust…and hers. Whatever it was, he hadn't repeated it, and she hadn't been brave enough to let him know how much she loved it. And sadly, maybe that was why he hadn't repeated it. Damn!

Her pussy throbbed with the memory of it. Restless, she went into her bedroom, stripped and lay across the bed, desperate for release. Picking up a thick, purple, silicone dildo—a damn poor substitute for a lover's eager cock—she rubbed it along her swollen slit. Trying to concentrate on sensation and set aside her jumbled feelings, she pretended she was in Club Rio Brava getting it on with one of the masked Dominants who'd singled her out for a night of fun and games. That didn't work. Trace was on her mind. It was his long, thick cock she imagined taking her, forcing her to reach out and grab those hot sensations her body wasn't willing to let loose on its own. Fuck it, why did she have to go and fall in love? And if she had, why couldn't she have fallen for a Dom who'd make her shed all her sexual hang-ups?

Elle had the feeling she knew that answer. The masked Doms who made her come six ways from Sunday forced her to fulfill her secret fantasies. Fantasies so dark, so outside the realm of her reality that she dared not whisper them in the light of day, not even to the man she loved and was considering marrying.

Trace was real, not some faceless partner. A man from her real world that she could love in the light of day, without shame or need for secrecy. Rubbing the dildo slowly over her clit, she imagined it was his callused fingers, his touch as delicate and reverent as the Doms' were often harsh and demanding. Slick, scalding tears slid down her cheeks because a huge part of her wanted everything Trace was offering.

It wouldn't be fair, lying in his arms at night pretending to be satisfied when her pussy kept on throbbing for more than his sweet vanilla loving. And Elle couldn't imagine herself yelling out, demanding that he get down and dirty and fucking make her come. If there was anything her mom had taught her, it was that ladies didn't push. Of course, Mom would have a hemorrhage if she ever figured out that Elle had learned her lessons about what good girls do a bit too well, and that she'd had to resort to taking temporary partners at Club Rio Brava. It wouldn't matter that Elle had to search out men who were willing and able to push her past that ladylike reserve, over the top to sensations of ecstasy she'd only imagined. Sensations she'd never experience again if she gave in to her own deepest desires and agreed to become Trace's wife.

Unless…

Unless she told him. Elle might lose him if she did, but if she didn't, they'd be in for some hard times if they actually made it to the altar. Better miserable without him than miserable trying to be the vanilla lover she wasn't.

Now all she had to do was figure out how to impart her secret she'd kept very well up until now.

* * * * *

Trace had never before given up on anything he really wanted, and he wasn't about to do it now. Early on Friday evening, he started to dial Elle then decided to wait until he was almost there. Surprise her, he thought, shrugging into a shearling-lined leather jacket over a flannel work shirt and his usual jeans. Good, he thought, noting the temperature on the way to his car. It had warmed up some this afternoon. As he pulled out of the ranch driveway onto the highway, he picked up his cell phone and speed-dialed Elle's number. This time he wasn't taking no for an answer. Just hearing her soft "hello" after the second ring got him hard.

He tried to keep his voice stern, confident. "I'm coming into town and dropping off tickets for the Cowboys' game to Mark and Lynn. I'll pick you up in about forty-five minutes. You're spending the weekend with me at the ranch, and there won't be any sneaking away from me this time."

He heard her indrawn breath, felt a long pause before she said, "Okay." That she didn't argue shocked him, but he wasn't about to complain.

Neither was he going to indulge in the flowers-and-candy banter he doubted would solidify his characterization of a sexual dominant. "Wear something sexy," he said in his best imitation of a drill sergeant barking orders, before hanging up and maneuvering onto the San Antonio beltway.

* * * * *

Three-quarters of an hour? Staying the weekend? What had come over Trace? Elle had hardly recognized his commanding voice, the air of command she'd never experienced with him. All the thoughts that had been tumbling in her head since his proposal seemed to come to a screeching halt when he'd practically ordered her to be ready. A fantasy in her head, or a tentative dream coming true? She didn't know. It seemed to be a sign that it was time for her to be brave, risk it all.

Sexy? Elle would show him sexy, and in doing so she'd reveal what it took to satisfy her sexually. Rifling through the bag she took to the club, Elle grabbed a black lace thong and lace-up leather bustier. Damn. Getting the laces tightened up the back without any help was quite a task, but she managed. Taking a good look in the full-length mirror, she fluffed her hair and frowned. She had no idea what had come over Trace, but she'd chalk his sudden demands up to a benevolent fate.

Makeup. She needed makeup, a lot more than the ladylike application she wore for work and on their frequent dates. She stepped into the bathroom and took out the war paint—dark eye liner, mascara, sparkly eye shadow, rose-colored lipstick and pale pink blush. No time for fresh foundation or concealer. Despite her initial surge of confidence, Elle noticed her hands shaking as she recreated the look she'd adopted for her visits to the club.

A coil of anticipation swirled in her vitals, the way she sometimes felt at Rio Brava. Exhilaration and nervousness competed in her head. While one part of her loved that this was happening with Trace, another part of her worried about what was going to happen. Maybe she'd misread his air of command and he'd just been cranky when he called. She slipped her feet into black stiletto heels, grabbed a sheepskin-lined khaki trench coat, and she was ready.

Ready to gamble that Trace would accept her kink and want her anyhow...maybe even want to join her in the sexual games she needed to make her come. Her pussy twitched with anticipation and more than a little fear.

Whatever she did, she didn't want to lose him.

By the time he knocked and she went to the door to let him in, Elle was shivering, partly with sexual excitement but also with the trepidation she couldn't shake. What if Trace's idea of dressing sexy was a little black sheath dress and killer heels? "Come in," she said, smiling up at him as she held the front of her coat closed to hide what she had on underneath it.

Before she could reach up on tiptoe to give him a kiss, he took her mouth. Unlike his usual casual pecks, this kiss demanded the speeding pulse and jackhammer heartbeat that had her breathless as he forced his tongue between her lips and dragged her against his hard, fit body. He used his hands to knead her butt and moved his hips against hers as if he intended to fuck her then and there. When he finally let her go, she stepped back and looked him in the eye.

He didn't flinch. "Come on. Did you pack a suitcase?"

"No." Where was he going with this unfamiliar macho posturing?

He caught her elbow and practically dragged her to her bedroom. Damn, he'd never done that before. "Grab a bag and toss in some jeans and a shirt, and whatever you want to wear to your office on Monday. Hurry." He gave her a sharp slap on the ass that made her juices start to flow and her nipples tingle.

This wasn't the Trace she knew and loved, but she wasn't about to question the change. The air in her bedroom felt charged, and her skin tingled at the prospect that something had happened. It seemed that something had swept away her old vanilla Trace and replaced him with somebody who showed every symptom of being a Dom.

Hurrying, she opened up a small piece of luggage and tossed in the items he mentioned—plus some extra underwear and a couple of pairs of shoes. "Okay, I'm ready," she said, her voice not quite steady as she dropped the lid of the weekender with a loud thud.

"Not quite so fast, sweetheart. I saw something in that drawer that I want to see on you." Opening the underwear drawer she'd just closed, he selected a purple lace thong and a matching shelf bra that left her nipples bare. "Dare I imagine you wear things like this to work?"

"You may imagine me wearing them anywhere you want to." She didn't think he'd appreciate her telling him that she'd bought them for the club but never yet worn them.

"You won't be wearing them anywhere except in my bedroom," he rasped, grasping her shoulders. His kiss was hard, demanding, his tongue forcing her lips to open and let him in. Was it her imagination, or did he press her tighter than he'd ever done before against his pulsating erection? Was he insistent on making her submit to his newly raging lust? Her pussy twitched with anticipation. Her heart beat faster, and if he hadn't been so obviously intent on controlling this scene, she'd have suggested they stay there. All she could do was gasp for breath when he let her go.

"Hold that thought, sweetheart. We're off now for the ranch." His voice sounded deeper, huskier than usual, his breath coming hard when he broke their embrace. "Come on." He picked up her suitcase, took her hand, and practically dragged her out the door of her apartment and onto the brightly lit street.

* * * * *

A gentle night breeze caressed her bare thighs beneath her trench coat. The sounds of castanets and guitars drifted over them as Trace led her by a Tex-Mex restaurant across the street from her place. The heat of his hand at her waist excited her as she glanced down at the erection pressing insistently at the snug jeans he wore. God but he was gorgeous, and tonight he projected a raw sexuality she'd never noticed before. Everywhere their bodies touched, she tingled with anticipation.

"Get in," he said as he opened the passenger door of his Jaguar and guided her down onto the soft leather seat. He circled the car with a confident, predatory stride and a long, heated glance through the front windshield then slid behind the wheel. When he turned the key, the powerful engine purred to life, its sound almost as arousing as the closeness they shared, sitting hip to hip, his hand on the gear shift just inches from her thigh.

Trace exuded confidence, competence, everything she'd always looked for in a lifetime partner. His striking good looks reminded her of her dad. Thankfully, though, he was everything her father hadn't been before he drowned life's disappointments in Johnnie Walker Red, leaving her and her mom in genteel poverty. Tonight Trace projected dominance, too, in the possessive way he laid his hand on her bare thigh once he'd gotten onto the Outer Loop and settled down at highway speed. Elle laid her hand over his, traced around his long, callused fingers with her fingertip.

"If you don't stop that, I'm going to pull over at the next exit with a decent motel and teach you what teasing will get you," he growled, catching her hand and laying it over his jeans-clad erection. "See what you do to me?"

"I see." Elle stroked the hot, rigid flesh, felt it strain harder against her hand. "Do you know what I've got on under this trench coat?"

"I got a look while you were packing. Never realized until then that you were into leather. I've dreamed about you wearing chaps and cowboy boots and nothing else--well, maybe a straw cowboy hat to protect your soft cheeks from the noonday sun." He laughed and squeezed none too gently on her thigh. "We'd take a ride, stop at the creek and make love in the shade of those mesquite trees while the cattle watch us. Maybe one of the ranch hands might ride by."

The idea had Elle practically panting, hoping Trace would stop the car and take her right now. But two could play his game. "You like having sex while others watch?"

"There's something that turns me on about the risk of others seeing us. That excites you, too, doesn't it?"

She recalled Trace's big black stallion watching them that day in the barn, his round, expressive eyes seeming to take in every thrust, his snorts and whinnies plaintive, as though he wanted his own mare to cover. It was all she could do to keep from moaning at the intense arousal that coursed through her body "Yes. How about you?"

Trace chuckled. "The idea of taking you, anywhere, anytime, keeps me rock hard and ready. But you know that, don't you, my kinky little darling?" He paused, giving all his attention to the road as they merged onto northbound Highway 281 from the Outer Loop. "It won't be long now. Are you ready for what's coming?"

"I can hardly wait." And that was the truth. The mellow sound of Trace's voice, the low growl of the car's powerful engine as it ate up miles, the smells of leather and sex and a faint woodsy whiff of his aftershave hit her senses hard. Her pussy felt swollen and damp against the lace of her thong, and her whole body ached for him to take her. To force down her inhibitions and bring her wildest fantasies into real life. Real time. "I'm so wet for you," she said, hardly believing she'd uttered the words, not to a masked Dom at Club Rio Brava, but to the man she loved and wanted to marry. Her best friend in the real world where they both lived.

A fat, golden moon lit their way as they drove along. Elle looked at his face, smiled when she saw the tight set of his jaw and realized he was as aroused as she. The excitement built around them, and by the time he turned into the long, tree-shaded drive that meandered through his ranch land toward his house on top of a rocky plateau, her pussy was wet and swollen, ready for submission.

Chapter Four

ꟾ

Trace stopped the car on the private ranch road, near their favorite tree beside the stream. "Time to take care of this," Trace said, deliberately sliding his hand between Elle's legs. "You meant it when you said you were already wet." Her female musk filled the air, intensifying his own arousal.

After grabbing a blanket off the backseat and walking around the car to let Elle out, he said, "Take off the coat. Don't worry, I'm gonna keep you warm." He felt weird, giving orders instead of making requests, but that was what he gathered sexual submissives expected. When she dropped the garment onto the ground he practically swallowed his tongue. The brief glimpse of black leather and lace back at her apartment had been a mere prelude to the sight of her standing in the moonlight, all pale skin except for the stiletto heels that emphasized the luscious shape of her legs, a lace G-string and a skin-tight leather thing that pushed her breasts up and cinched her waist so tight it was small enough for him to interlock his thumbs while encircling it with his hands. He could hardly wait to warm her nipples that already were puckering from the cold air. When she inclined her head, her sable hair framed her face, made him want to bury his hands in the soft curls.

"You'd better run for the shelter of our favorite tree or I'll take you right here," he growled, punctuating his words with a hard kiss and a sweep of his hands down her back until he reached her nearly naked ass and pulled her tight against his hungry cock. Despite the fact it was only forty-five or fifty degrees, he wanted to take her out here, under their favorite tree, give her a taste of what he'd teased her with in the car, the idea of somebody watching. "When I said wear something sexy, I never imagined you'd show up in something like this." He broke the kiss and nuzzled one earlobe then bent and picked up her coat.

"If I'm not mistaken, you like it," she said, her voice husky as she ground her hips against his straining cock. "A lot."

"You'd better bet I like it. Now move." He punctuated his order with a another light slap on her bare ass before watching her sway on those stiletto heels—but not for long because his heart was beating double-time and his cock was throbbing with carnal anticipation. Damn, he was starting to see the appeal of dominating a lover. Especially when Elle stepped out from under the canopy of the huge cottonwood tree they'd claimed as their special place and struck a pose that practically shouted *Come and fuck me now*.

Nothing on Earth could have kept Trace away. He strode to her and inhaled her intoxicating female scent for a split second before laying down her coat, spreading the blanket, lying on it and dragging her down on top of him. Her breasts spilled out of the black leather, rose-tipped and creamy. He sampled first one, then the other, gently at first then harder when she began to moan and writhe on top of him.

"Like that?"

Her nails dug hard into his back. "Oh, yes. Please bite me. God but that feels good."

He nipped her once more then raised his head. "You should have told me you like it rough. You know all I want to do is make you happy."

"You do…Master." The "Master" part shook him a little, but in a good way. All he wanted to do was take care of her, and if it only took a little macho action, it suited him just fine.

A golden moon shone down on them through the branches of the tree, highlighting the hard, intent look on Trace's face as he sat up, shed his jacket and used it to wrap around her shivering shoulders. He had the in-control look of a Master, yet different from the ones she'd played with at the club. Hot lust and a sense of possession, entitlement mingled in his expression, but those emotions were tempered by an emotional commitment he couldn't hide. The sound of water rushing over the small boulders in the creek and the touch of his hands on her body that matched the rhythm of nature had Elle on the verge of coming as she never had before with so little foreplay.

She wanted to tear off her clothes and his, feel the heat of their bodies mingling, joining, heedless of the cold air, the lowing of cattle in the field across the creek. In the distance, she heard the familiar yodel of a wrangler singing, as they often did to soothe the cows and keep themselves company. "Please," she said, her senses bombarded with the sights and smells and sounds of nature…and of Trace.

"Please what?" His voice was breathless, his touch certain, masterful.

"Please fuck me now. I need you so much." And not just for sex, even though her body screamed for satisfaction.

He rolled her over on her back and came down on top of her. "I don't think you're ready yet, love. You're going to have to scream for it first. Come on. Tell me what you want, what you really want."

Damn it, he knew what she wanted. Why was he torturing her like this? His mind games had her hotter than a lash had ever done. When he pinched her nipples with his callused fingers, his touch excited her more than a cruel Dom's stinging nipple clamps. His hot tongue invading her mouth was better than any ball gag, and his substantial weight pinning her to the blanket held her as securely as any restraints could. She writhed beneath him, needing more.

"Hold that thought. And tell me how the hell I get you out of this outfit." Trace moved away but not for long, ripping off his clothes. "You want me to tear it off you?"

Elle couldn't care less. She just wanted to be naked for him, to feel the heat and weight of him pressing her so hard against the blanket that she could feel each blade of grass marking her flesh. "Yes. Please. Don't make me wait any longer."

His hands trembled as he searched for and found the fastenings of her bustier. Each brush of his knuckles when he loosened the strings aroused her as much as if he'd cut the strings and ripped the garment from her body. He wasn't so careful with the G- string. One hard yank and it was off. He crushed it in his hand, brought it to his lips briefly before tossing it aside. Then he peeled off his jeans, spread her legs and buried his face between them.

His hot breath scorched her clit, and his fingers dug into the sensitive flesh of her inner thighs. The sensations were painful, as much so as if he had her on the rack. She couldn't help writhing when he caught her clit between his teeth and flailed it with his tongue. God, she was going to come and there was nothing she could do to stop it.

"Not yet, love. I haven't given you permission." His words reverberated in her pussy, her breasts. She nearly screamed with the effort of holding back the orgasm that was just beyond her reach. "I see eyes out there watching us. I bet they smelled sex and it's driving them crazy. As crazy as it's driving me."

She saw eyes, three pairs of them glowing in the night, their gazes seemingly fixated on Trace's dark head and her wide-open pussy. When he shifted his hands and cupped her breasts, the eyes moved. Were there humans out there? Or did the eyes belong to cows or some wild creatures intent on devouring them? It didn't matter. All Elle wanted to do was come, and then to torture Trace the way he was torturing her.

As if he read her mind, he shifted, obscuring her view of their silent voyeurs by straddling her face and feeding her his swollen cock. "Suck me," he ordered, his voice pained enough that she knew his restraint was costing him. Somehow that made her feel better as she dug her nails into her palms to take her mind off the acute pleasure-pain he was inflicting on her.

It didn't help. Her entire being focused on the feel of his cock stuffing her mouth. His tongue worked its magic on her clit then plunged deeply into her pussy. She nearly came when he slid his fingers along her slick wet slit and rimmed her puckered rear hole. Those eerie observing eyes enhanced her arousal. She fantasized that it was human voyeurs watching them, imagined them beating their cocks, spewing their seed along the expanse of grassy pasture.

But it didn't really matter. Human or animal, their visitors enhanced the sexual tension. She had to fight like hell not to come right now, to wait for her Master to give her permission. She tried to concentrate on the sound of the rushing water, the occasional chirp of some native bird from the tangle of blackberry canes across the creek. It wasn't working. She sucked harder on his cock, running her tongue along the prominent vein on its backside. Maybe if she could drive him crazy…

Chapter Five

ꟸ

His kinky darling was driving him to distraction. He wasn't going to last much longer, the way she was sucking him like a pro. Trace pulled away and spun, dragging Elle's thighs over his shoulders, hardly noticing the digging of her stiletto heels into the flesh of his back. If she wanted it rough, that's how she'd get it. Just once he dragged the tip of his cock along her slit before plunging inside her sopping cunt.

"Oh, please. Don't stop. My God, I love your cock. Fuck me hard and fast and please, please let me come."

Was this his woman he'd thought preferred her sex quiet and proper? God, had he been clueless. He'd never been so hard in his life. "Not now, but soon. What if I told you those were some of my wranglers watching us? Would that get you hotter?"

"No."

"Liar," he rasped against her ear. "You can't honestly tell me the idea of people looking while we fuck doesn't turn you on."

She didn't answer right away because she was breathing too hard to talk. He knew damn well the idea excited her. It aroused the hell out of him, too, and that surprised him because he'd always been a pretty damn private person. Of course, he was fairly sure their voyeurs were curious cows, not cowboys. But right now he didn't care if half the world was watching, because he was hotter than hell even though it was barely forty degrees and the breeze was starting to kick up. "Well, are you going to tell me you don't like having people watch us having sex?"

"Maybe I like it just a little bit." She turned her head and bit his earlobe. "May I please come? I can't wait much longer."

Trace had never been so aroused. His cock felt like it was going to burst. His balls ached. His heart was beating so fast he should have been worried about a heart attack, but he wasn't. The only thing on his mind right now was exploding inside his woman, feeling her tight, juicy cunt spasm around his cock as he poured out his seed. "Neither can I," he muttered, spreading her legs wider and driving into her hard and fast. His balls tightened. He couldn't hold back any longer.

"Now! Come for me. Don't hold back. God, yes. Squeeze my cock like you're never going to let it go." He came, his hot sperm spurting, mingling with her slick fluids. Fuck but it felt incredible! When she obeyed, she clutched his cock so hard it was as if they were one body. One soul.

Her heels dug into his back but he didn't care. He plunged in one last time, felt the last of his release spurt against the soft tissue of her cervix. He caught her scream of pleasure in his mouth, grasped the sides of her head with both hands, digging his fingers into the soft mass of her hair. He tried to say something, to tell her how much this meant to him, but he was spent. So spent, it was all he could do to lift himself off her body and gather her in his arms.

Elle lifted her head from his shoulder, studying this whole new Trace, a compilation of all the wonderful things she knew about him—and now the intriguing field of things she didn't. "Why did you wait so long?" Then before he could answer, she bit her lip, realizing… "I don't know how you guessed, and maybe I don't want to know, but…did you do this just for me? Did it turn you on, too?"

It occurred to her then that, as terrible as it would have been for her to pretend to be vanilla for Trace, she loved him too much to put him in the same situation, where he was having to be something he was not. But his quick grin melted away her worries and his eyes flashed with renewed lust when he laid her hand on his cock, which was already stirring again. "Oh, yeah, it turns me on."

"Then why didn't you do it sooner?"

Drawing his mouth close to her ear, he whispered, "I didn't try it sooner because I'm a damn fool. A fool who loves you."

"I love you, too, and I want you to be my Master." She lifted her head from his shoulder and looked at him, saw the love shining in his beautiful brown eyes. While he wasn't sure, he thought that might have been an answer to his proposal, but he wasn't going to risk asking for confirmation yet. For one thing, the love shining in her eyes and the commitment in her voice had rendered him speechless. He rubbed his fingers along her spine, his touch gentle now as she snuggled as close as she could get, intertwining her legs with his, reminding him she must be freezing now that the heat of the moment had passed.

"We'd better get out of here and into the house before we turn into ice statues," he said, disentangling their legs and helping her to her feet. "Here, put on your coat." When she did, he rearranged his own clothes and folded the blanket.

When she bent and retrieved those super-sexy scraps of clothes she'd worn, his heart started pounding fast again. "I ought to punish you for not telling me."

"Not telling you what?" she asked, her tone all innocence as she settled onto the car seat and put her hands against a heater vent.

Trace shot her a grin as he put the car in motion. "You know what. We could have saved a lot of time and worry if you'd just told me up front that you're into kinky sex games."

"I wanted to be everything you wanted me to be. I thought you were looking for pure vanilla."

"Vanilla? That sounds boring. Is that really what you thought of me?"

"As much as you thought I was as staid and conventional in bed as I have to be on the job."

Trace laughed. "I imagine most men, not just the ones who like the whips and chains and dominating their partners in front of others, like to feel in charge with their women. I admit, when I first started looking into Dominance and submission, I wasn't sure since I'm not into torture, either giving or receiving it. But then I looked in the right places and started imagining you that way, me in control of you.

"Based on that, honey, it seems to me that if you'd told me you wanted a sexual dominant in bed, I'd have been happy to oblige." He gave her a serious look. "It was driving me crazy, suspecting I wasn't getting you off. I love you."

"And I love you, too, my reluctant Master."

Trace cleared his throat. "So now that we've revealed our kinky tastes, can we move ahead? If you want to be tied up and gagged, I'll do it. I'll even punish you when you're naughty if you'll be satisfied with a few swats on your luscious ass. I love dominating you, sweetheart, but I can't hurt you, and I don't think I'll ever be able to share you with another Dom, which I've heard some subs like." He swallowed, his hand tightening on hers. "Is that something you want?"

"I told you I want you for my Master." She brought his hand to her lips after he stopped the car in front of his house. "I've never been as satisfied as I was just now, and that includes all the club scenes I've been in. But then I've never been in love with any of the club Doms I've—"

"No. I don't need to hear about your other lovers." Trace didn't want to hear about the club and the Doms. Not now, when his heart was practically bursting with happiness at what she'd said first. Maybe later he'd want to know more about those scenes, and what she'd liked. He knew he'd do almost anything to make her scream the way she had earlier tonight. But now was just for them. Not for revelations about past lovers, hers or his.

With that he slid out from under the steering wheel and strode around the car to let her out. "Come on, let's continue this conversation in my bed. As I recall, we've got some unfinished business to take care of there."

Elle looked up at him. Tears glistened in her eyes when she met his gaze. "I was afraid. Afraid you'd be scandalized if you found out it takes more than gentle loving to turn me on."

"You're a genius, but in some ways you're an idiot. Damn it, I guess I've been one, too, thinking all along you were a hard-nosed professional woman who'd sue me or worse if I treated you with anything but the utmost respect. I just hope you're not expecting us to add on a personal dungeon filled with things like restraints on the walls and other scary devices meant to hurt you, because that's not in me to do."

"All that isn't necessary. What I need is for you to tell me, not ask me, what you want, let me know how I can please you. You know, until tonight I never knew you wanted me to suck your cock." She reached down, cupped his balls.

Damn, he couldn't believe that with a simple touch she had his cock stirring again already. "Keep it up and you'll turn me into a satyr," he said, keeping his tone light. "How about letting me open the door so we can go inside the house and start all over again?"

"You're not supposed to ask—you're supposed to give orders, my gentle Master." Her teasing look took the sting out of the reminder.

He supposed this "Master" business would take a little time to get used to, but he was game. "Okay. How's this? Get your luscious little butt upstairs. I want to get you in my bed and fuck you until you can't see straight."

She laughed, the sweet sound warming Trace's heart. More relaxed than he'd ever seen her, she reached up and cupped his face between her hands. "That's fine, but you don't have to act as fierce as all that. I've grown used to you pretty much wrapping me up in love and devotion."

Her smile made him feel damn good. For the first time since he'd decided to take Mark's advice and encourage her to submit sexually, Trace had the feeling this was going to work. "Then, my kinky love, let's get to bed so I can practice being forceful."

* * * * *

Elle could hardly believe it. Her sweet, loving Trace scooped her up, carried her upstairs and tossed her unceremoniously on his bed. From a bag on his dresser, he fished out a very real-looking pair of handcuffs and showed her he knew how to use them. He also knew how to use his hands and mouth to drive her up, up, up. It seemed like hours that he inflicted his sensual torture while she lay helpless, her cuffed wrists secured to the headboard and her ankles tied with mismatched silk ties to the broad, sturdy footboard. Deep kisses drugged her as effectively as a shot of Demerol. When he drew a nipple into his mouth and suckled her, using his tongue to make the flesh tighten and elongate, it sent tremors of arousal through her.

"Want my cock?" She hardly had time to answer before he moved and straddled her face.

Yes, she wanted it. Wanted to please him. If he hadn't had her mouth occupied sucking his cock, she'd have begged him to let her arms loose so she could pay proper homage to her Master the way a good slave should. Her fingers itched to explore his groin, fondle his balls, play with the sensitive flesh around his anal opening. When she thought about him claiming her rear hole, her sex tightened with anticipation.

He tasted good, so good. Clean and strong, the least bit salty yet smooth as fresh cream on her tongue. With callused hands he traced the length of her body, skimming all her erogenous places but never quite giving them all the attention they craved.

His gentle torture went on forever, until the rising sun peeked through the skylight as he rose and knelt between her legs. Although she wanted him to fuck her hard and fast, it seemed he was determined to take her his way. Slow, loving, each motion deliberate, he played her helpless body like a fine instrument, dragging out not only her sexual responses but her emotions.

There was nothing tentative about the way he claimed her cunt, but as if he knew she wanted him hard and fast and hurting, he fucked her slow and deep, grinding his balls against her opening as the tip of his big cock nudged her cervix then retreated.

"Come now," he ordered, his voice rough, tortured. To her surprise, she did, stimulated by the staccato bursts of his semen as he tightened his grip on her hips and shouted out his pleasure. Her own rolling orgasm moved her as much as—no, more than the mind-blowing, violent climax he'd brought her to by the creek.

Trace had obviously done some research into Domination and submission. It showed in the way he'd bound her, however loosely, taking away her freedom to protest. As fully as if he'd chained her to a St. Andrew's cross, he'd confined her, made her helpless to resist his domination. "Thank you," she whispered when he loosened her bonds then rolled onto his side and drew her in his arms.

"My pleasure." His rumbly purr reminded her of a satisfied cat. "You don't need to thank me, though."

"Oh, yes I do. You understood I needed for you to take control, take away my compulsion to feel guilty for liking everything you were doing to me. You let me enjoy the sensual ride, and you made me come on your command without having to hurt me at all."

No doubt about it now. Elle adored Trace. She loved him for sensing there had been something wrong about their lovemaking, and for setting out to fix it without her having to make humiliating explanations she'd once thought would send him running away.

"What's on your mind, sweetheart?"

Elle found her Master's lips, traced them with her tongue. "Just thinking about how lucky I am. How somehow I found you, and how much I love you for figuring me out, for letting me know you can satisfy my sexual kinks as well as any club Dom. Not to mention that I love you for being the rock I can lean on when I'm down, and the lover who makes me happy out of bed as well as in it."

"I want to make you even happier. Tell me all about the things you've learned from other Doms that make your hot little cunt go crazy."

"Well..."

He lifted her chin, made her look into his eyes. "Consider that a command, my darling slave."

"I'd like for you to feel free to take any part of me you want. Any time. Anywhere. With any part of you. With toys. And I wouldn't mind having you take me in front of people." *God, don't let him make me come out and tell him I like anal sex, or that I enjoy double penetration and having people watch while I'm writhing with pleasure.*

He slid a hand down her back, into the crack of her ass. "You want me to fuck you here?" When he slipped one finger beyond her anal sphincter she trembled just a little. "You're awfully tight here. Having my cock inside this hole would have to feel like heaven."

"To me, too." With Trace, Elle found no need to be shy, the way she would have with most vanilla people. After all, Trace was her lover. Her Master, a sexual Dominant in disguise. "You know, Master, you're a wolf in sheep's clothing."

"Actually I'm naked. And, amazingly, I'm getting hard again. Are you going to need tying up again, or can I just order you onto your belly, hands over your head and ass in the air?"

Her pussy clenched with anticipation. "I'll follow your orders...but you're so big, you're going to need some lube."

"I know. Believe it or not, I've done this before, just not as often as I've fucked pussies. Be right back." When he got up and padded across the bedroom, Elle hurried to position herself the way her Master wanted her.

Yeah, Trace had ass-fucked a woman, but never before had he been so eager to claim one this way. As he grabbed a large vibrating dildo, a condom and a tube of lubricant from his toy store bag, it came to him that what he was about to do was going to be a promise. A total claiming of the woman he loved. Before, having anal sex had been to satisfy his or someone's curiosity, to see what it felt like to ram his cock up his partner of the moment's tight rear passage. Armed with his tools, he turned back to the bed, happy to see that Elle had followed his orders.

"That's a good little slave." He bent and lightly bit her right buttock. "I'm gonna fill up both your holes and you're gonna like it." Lubricating the purple gel dildo, he inserted it in her dripping cunt, making sure the flared end was positioned correctly to stimulate her rigid, swollen clit. His balls tightened and his cock swelled to full erection even though he'd come less than an hour ago.

"Oooh. That feels good."

Trace laughed. "Not as good as it will feel when I fill up your other hole with this." Nudging the base of the dildo with his cock, he donned a condom and slathered lubricant over it. Then he packed more of the slippery, water-based stuff into her asshole and positioned himself at her anal opening. "Tell me if I'm hurting you. I mean it." He didn't trust her not to grin and bear it, to suffer serious pain in the pursuit of pleasure.

"You won't. I promise." She sounded eager. Her ass twitched against the head of his sheathed cock. "Fuck me, Master. Please."

Slowly, carefully, he pushed past her anal sphincter then stilled until her muscles began to relax, accept his cock. "Good slave. I'm going to fuck you now." This was no time for force, just a slow, delicious thrust until she had all of him. "Okay?" he asked.

"Oh, yes." The motion of the vibrator reverberated through her flesh, stimulating him as well as her. He held on to her firm, round butt cheeks, loving the feeling of tightness, the excitement of trying something forbidden with his woman. Pressure built in him. She moaned with every thrust he made, each touch of his fingers as he slid them under her to squeeze her breasts. "Come for me now, sweetheart," he said, and when she began to shake and whimper he couldn't help it. For the third time since early evening, he was coming.

Damn it, she was going to kill him if they kept it up like this. But what a way to die.

* * * * *

When Elle woke up she was alone, wrapped up in the soft bed linens on Trace's bed. The clock on his bedside table said ten o'clock. She never slept this late, usually was at the hospital making rounds by seven. But she felt refreshed. Satisfied. Stretching, she got up and peered out a semi-frosted window. There was Trace, swimming laps in the crystal blue water of his heated pool. Steam rose off the water, but she had no trouble watching his well-developed muscles ripple with each strong stroke. God but she loved him, wanted him here and now. She craved more of his sweet loving, more heated sex, more...well, just more of everything. More of Trace.

She was going to take the plunge, marry him. Maybe even have a couple of dark-haired, brown-eyed babies who looked like their daddy, before she was too old and set in her ways for motherhood. Not that she planned to give up her career. She'd worked too long and hard to get where she was, and it made her feel good to help her patients get well and live productive lives.

If she married Trace, her mother would be happy. After all, he had every quality that Mom held as sacred. Money her dad had squandered, social standing that would give Mom something to brag about to her friends. Trace had all that in spades. Her mother would also appreciate his good looks and the casual but impeccable manners no one could fault. Not that pleasing Mom was a reason she would say yes.

She'd marry him because she knew Trace would make her happy. And because she believed she could make him happy, too.

After last night, Elle had no doubts. Every muscle in her body ached deliciously. Every cell practically sang with the memory of how he'd played her, first hard and then ever so gently but leaving her with no doubt whatsoever that he was her Master.

He dived deep then surfaced and levered himself out of the pool. Water glistened over his nude, tanned body, its motion calling attention to his rapidly rising cock. He dried off and shrugged into a wool robe before coming up to the room and sitting beside her on the chaise lounge, a huge grin on his face.

"Well, will you?" he asked.

She couldn't resist toying with him, just a little. "Will I what?"

"You know damn well what I'm talking about. Will—you—marry—me? Be my permanent sex slave when we're alone together, my beloved companion all the time?"

"You're my Master. If you tell me to marry you, I won't have any choice." Not that she had a choice anyway, loving him the way she did.

"Damn it, just say yes."

God but she loved him, even the part that didn't seem to realize she'd given him her body and her heart, something she'd never done before. "I just did, in every possible way, these past few hours, but *yes*. A thousand times yes, Trace."

Dripping water over her naked body, Trace took her hand and slid on the beautiful diamond solitaire he'd offered for the first time a few days ago. It was hard now to imagine that she'd had her doubts, that she'd been so wrong to think they'd always be incompatible sexually. "Marry me, Elle. Marry me as soon as you can put together whatever kind of shindig suits your fancy. I can hardly wait to have you at my beck and call in bed, in life, for always."

Tears welled in Elle's eyes when she met his gaze and saw the raw emotion there. "Yes, I'll marry you. Soon. Masters like you are hard to come by. I don't dare let you out of my wicked clutches."

"Not a chance, my darling. I need a lot of practice at this Dom stuff, and I can't wait to begin. Slip on some jeans and a coat, and come with me. You liked it that time we fucked in the barn while Diego watched us. Now you're going to get a chance to watch him do his thing."

* * * * *

Just in time, Trace thought, noting with satisfaction as they approached the paddock beside the barn, that the blood-bay mare he'd selected for breeding was already restrained. "Watch how Beauty trembles. Do you think she's waiting eagerly for a stud to cover her? I bet she is. See how she tosses her head. Listen to her whinny. It's not too much different from how you moaned before I finally put my cock inside you last night."

She looked around, as if someone were there to overhear. Yeah, Elle did get hot at the idea of strangers watching, imagining what they'd spent last night and this morning doing. So did he, now that he thought about it. Voyeurs, that's what they both were, but he liked it. Loved her. Would do damn near anything it took to keep her happy.

Even before he saw his ranch manager leading Diego from the barn, Trace felt the ground shake when the big stud bellowed a mating call. "Sounds like Diego's eager today," he said as he lifted Elle onto the top fence rail and climbed up beside her.

"Oh, yes." Then she gasped. "He's…omigod, he's huge. Trace, won't he hurt her?"

"No, love. Beauty's going to enjoy getting fucked as much as you do, and if we're lucky she'll produce us a fine colt or filly right around our first anniversary. Look, she's twitching her tail and rolling her eyes. Did you know that's the way mares flirt?"

She leaned hard against his chest, and he drew his arms around her waist. "They're not so much different from humans then, are they? Oh, no. Watch Diego. He's biting her neck. Why doesn't his handler stop him?"

Trace stifled a grin. He knew he'd gone and gotten himself a city girl, so he was just going to have to teach her some lessons. Although they'd been together almost a year, she hadn't spent a lot of time around the ranch, and he'd managed to keep the breeding part of the business out of her sight. He leaned over and nipped her neck. "Now tell me, how did that feel to you?"

"Mmmm. Felt good. You think Beauty likes it when Diego bites her? I bet she does." Elle glanced at the horses and let out a little scream when the big black stallion reared up and thrust wildly until he managed to seat the tip of his huge phallus inside Beauty.

The crisp air, sounds of hooves pounding and horses whinnying in the pasture, the satisfied feel of Elle's arm around his waist combined to make Trace feel damn lucky he'd chosen to take over his grandmother's ranch instead of becoming a doctor like his dad. This was where he belonged. Where he and Elle would raise their children in the open space of the country.

"How long do they stay coupled?" Elle asked.

"Not long at all. For them it's pretty much downhill now. I'm half tempted to take you back down to the creek again and fuck you against our special tree. From the back this time, so I can play with your pretty breasts and nip at your neck."

Elle turned in his arms. Her pulse was fast, her voice breathless when she spoke. "You're tempting me, my darling Master. But I know you wouldn't, not in broad daylight with all your wranglers chasing cows out by that creek. I get off on having voyeurs join club scenes, but for now, I'm just fine with the illusion of being looked at rather than the reality. Besides, it's damn cold to be making love outside when we've got a perfectly good bed in the house."

Trace gave her a quick kiss. "You're right. It is a little chilly, and I don't have the balls to turn exhibitionist right now, but hold the thought. We'll have plenty of warm, moonlit nights to make memories underneath that tree. We'd better get back to the house now. We've got family to call and a wedding to plan."

* * * * *

Funny. Now that she'd accepted Trace as her Master, his slightest touch had her tingling with anticipation. Elle closed her eyes as they snuggled on the couch in the den and mentally visualized the three possibilities he'd suggested as places on his ranch he'd like for them to make their marriage vows.

She loved them all. The pasture beside the creek was her sentimental favorite. She couldn't help feeling, though, that it was their own private spot, too sacred to open to all their friends and family. Besides, even though Trace assured her it could be done, she didn't think a lot of their guests would appreciate a reception served from a chuck wagon. She ran her nails along his forearm, enjoying the tactile sensations as she considered the other options.

Although the lawn in front of his sprawling ranch house was flat and perfectly manicured, ideal for setting up chairs and a massive white tent, there was something cliché about getting married in a setting much like they'd seen at estate-like, suburban San Antonio homes like Kurt and Shelly's—or Lynn and Mark's. No, Elle wanted something different, something she and Trace could remember for a lifetime as having been uniquely theirs.

"The garden behind the pool." Trace had laughed when he showed it to her, and at first Elle laughed, too. Fenced with delicate wrought iron topping a six-foot brick wall, it was behind the house, out of sight of the pool area. Trace told her it had once been a formal-style garden that had been allowed to go back to nature sometime before he and Lynn were born. Old-fashioned roses clung to the wall, a riot of waxy green leaves and delicate pink flowers whose tendrils curled around and tumbled over carcasses of what used to be boxwood hedges. Elle imagined them as they used to be before years of neglect had taken their toll.

"You've got to be kidding." The warmth of Trace's hand as he grasped hers and brought it to his lips did a lot toward taking the edge off his reaction.

"Not at all." Elle shuddered a little when he nipped at her knuckles. "Just imagine us getting married underneath that huge wisteria vine in the corner, with the guests sitting on benches in the center of the garden."

"You want our guests to watch us get married while they sit in the middle of that bramble of weeds and runaway rosebushes?"

Elle couldn't help laughing. "Of course not. I was sort of imagining we'd have the place cleaned up. Can't you imagine it, minus all the dead stuff and weeds, with the climbing roses trimmed into submission? We could always plant some colorful flowers to give the garden a festive look."

When she opened her eyes and looked up at him he didn't look entirely convinced, despite the wry grin on his handsome face. "If you say so, sweetheart. I'm not entirely sure I want to wait to marry you until we can turn that eyesore into a showplace."

"Four months? Is that too long?" She imagined getting married in April, when nature would be transitioning from winter to spring.

Trace lowered his head and nibbled the sensitive flesh along her shoulder while he loosened her shirt and freed one breast. "I guess not. But I don't see how that garden is going to suddenly look great after forty or more years of neglect." He drew one of her nipples between his lips and flailed it with his tongue.

Then he pulled back and looked her in the eye. "Sorry, sweetheart. If you want that eyesore turned into a fit scene for our wedding four months from now, I'll make it happen. As long as I don't have to wait all that time to have you in my bed every night. It's not that long a drive to the hospital from here, and I'll let you use the Jaguar. I can take one of the ranch trucks if I need to go somewhere while you're at work."

"All right." She wanted his mouth on her, his cock invading her. What was it that suddenly had her reacting to every subtle bit of his gentle foreplay now? She hadn't earlier, before he'd shown her he had another side, a dominant one that allowed her no choice but to follow a Master's command. Elle didn't know, but her body apparently did, because she felt herself getting wet and swollen between her legs, ready for whatever Trace might have in mind. With every wet, hot stroke of his tongue on her nipple, each glide of his hands along her aroused body, she wanted him more. "Master, may I touch you, too?"

He bit her, not hard enough to hurt but more than enough to rouse her senses to a fever pitch. "Oh yeah, you can touch me anytime." Then he pulled away long enough to shed his boots and jeans and undress her without his usual finesse.

"Do you like taking it here?" He rimmed her asshole with a finger then worked it slowly inside. "You seemed to, last night."

"I..." Just like last night, answering the question directly embarrassed her. For just a moment, she almost slipped back into what she'd done before, denying what she wanted so that he wouldn't think she was *that* kind of girl. Trace might not know a lot directly about what went on in BDSM dungeons, but he'd shown a keen interest in learning what pleasures she'd discovered there, and he had a natural skill at being a Dominant. She'd be a fool to deny herself. She was going to have all the pleasures of a BDSM dungeon with her future husband, even if they never set foot in one.

She'd been right to tell him. There was no place for lies or evasions between them. "Yes, Master, I like it if it gives you pleasure. Do you want to put your huge, hard cock up my ass again?"

"God, yes, but I don't want to hurt you." Tentatively, he delved a little deeper with his finger and made her let out a little moan. How could she ever have thought he was anything but a wonderful lover? "We'll take it slow and easy then. Kneel on the floor and rest your gorgeous body on the couch."

Nothing could have stopped her from obeying. Her heart pounded in her chest when he reached in his desk drawer and pulled out some lube, a wrapped condom and a large, thick dildo. After donning the condom, he strapped on the dildo behind his own throbbing tool and lubricated both with slick, transparent gel. "This is supposed to make you hot," he told her as he knelt behind her and packed more of the stuff in her swollen pussy—and her tight, yearning ass.

Hot? Elle was burning from the inside out. Trace couldn't have known she'd been aroused the entire time they'd been searching for wedding sites and talking about guest lists and receptions. Or had he known? Had he read her arousal at his slightest touch?

Apparently, because he was wasting no time now. Holding her hips steady, he seated the dildo in her pussy slowly, as he entered her ass. She felt full. So full. So completely taken, mastered. "I love you so much," she told him between moans of pleasure-pain. Ecstasy.

"I love you, too." Trace moved slowly, determined to show her just how much by holding back his own racing need. "Your ass is so tight and hot, it's all I can do to hold back."

"Don't, then." When he'd have slowed the pace even more, Elle pushed back into him, taking all his length, clasping him with her inner muscles, enslaving him as much as he'd mastered her.

"Come, now," he gasped. "Can't hold back. Sorry."

"Oh, God yes."

He felt the tremors through the dildo, the tension that flowed through her flesh to his. As he felt the spasms, the spurts of his hot seed, he collapsed over her back. His last conscious thought was that she had the softest skin he'd ever felt.

Epilogue

The following April, at the ranch

&

Four months later, as Elle walked down the aisle, she was acutely conscious of Trace's gaze scorching her skin. He wanted her now—she could tell from the tight set of his lips, the bald yearning in his deep brown eyes. God but she wanted him, too, as if they hadn't made love just this morning. She couldn't understand what it was about him that kept her hot all the time. Hotter than any club Dom had ever made her...even though he'd never chained her to a cross or made her cringe in pain before giving her release. Maybe because her heart and soul were as tied to him as her body.

That made her recall the mantra he'd found at MySpace.com, the one he'd told her about that had inspired his journey into the world of Dominance and submission.

"All my life I've had to lead others, but in sex I have to have a leader. I need a man to take control of my body and my senses to overcome my inhibitions, and make me find pleasure in the acts my mother taught me were horribly wrong.

I want a Dom who understands what I need and knows what it takes to bring me along, a Dom who loves me and who wants to give me pleasure.

"A gentle Dom who'll kiss away the bruises from his lash, who'll support me in daylight as well as during the long nights in his bed. I want a man who loves me and fulfills my every fantasy.

"A strong man. A leader. A lover I can lean on, count on, not just for tonight but for all time."

Elle had thought at first that Trace had made up the words, until one night when he showed her the website. The words weren't what she'd ever have said. She prided herself too much on being pragmatic, never fantasizing. But Trace had taught her different. He'd shown her the truth of that stranger's words. Today she had no doubts. No misgivings. She knew Trace was everything she needed in a lover…a lifetime companion, a man who'd meet her every need.

As Trace watched Elle greet old friends and new acquaintances at their reception, the look on her face made him feel like a million dollars. Strong, powerful and invincible. Though the spoken vows they'd made at twilight were to love, honor and cherish each other, she'd whispered in his ear that she was taking him as her Master. Her only Master. For as long as they both lived.

Surrounded by friends and family on the land he loved, Trace said a silent prayer of thanks for Elle, who outshone the garden that she'd restored into a showplace. She'd bowed to convention, chosen a long, white gown embroidered with purple wisterias and pale green leaves. God but she was beautiful. And she was his.

Lynn had hardly recognized the restored garden, and Mark had asked why Lynn had held their wedding on the front lawn instead of this magical place. "It wasn't so magical fifteen years ago," she said with a smile. "Elle resurrected it from an eyesore full of weeds, just like she turned my little brother from a tomcatting womanizer into a one-woman man."

Trace smiled. He had been a skirt-chaser until he found Elle. Now he was perfectly content to stay home, be her husband…and her Master when the lights were dimmed. "You get the credit for finding me the woman of my dreams," he told Mark. "Much as I'd like to spirit her away right now, I suppose I should go visit some with our guests."

He needed his Elle fix, badly, so he joined her on her way to speak to her mother. He brought her fingers to his lips, delaying her steps. "Let's leave our guests to celebrate and go inside before we have to hurry off to our honeymoon. I've got some things I'm longing to do with my kinky, darling bride."

Elle gazed up at him adoringly. She needed to get away with him as well, be alone with her new husband, show him in every way she could that he was the most important thing in her world. Tormenting them both, she leaned in next to him and whispered so softly she hoped no one else could hear. "I'm with you, Master. I don't know where you found it, but you came up with the perfect combination of Dom and protector. I love you more than I can say."

Trace suppressed the urge to whisk her away, and faced his new mother-in-law. The woman, who had always impressed Trace as a cold fish more interested in her daughter's security than in her pleasure, seemed to have softened in the romantic atmosphere of the garden setting, though. "How are you, Ms. Drake?"

"Well, thank you. The wedding was beautiful. I had my doubts about that garden, but it turned out just fine. You know I expect you to take care of my daughter. It seems you're making her quite happy so far."

Trace smiled at his mother-in-law. "You don't need to worry, ma'am, I'll take good care of Elle as long as I live, and I'll do my best to never hurt her."

"Thank you, son. I can't ask for more than that." Tears welled up in the older woman's eyes, and Trace wondered if she was thinking of a time, years ago, when she'd gone into marriage with stars in her eyes—stars that Elle had told him went out, long before her father died.

He and Elle made the rounds, chatting with friends between trips to a catered buffet for sliced prime rib and savory side dishes. Just as they were about to cut the giant wedding cake and make their escape, Eli and Maggie came up to wish them well. "If you ever miss the club scene, Maggie and I are always available to join you," Eli told Elle before giving her and Trace a huge bear hug. "For something more private than a full-fledged scene at Club Rio Brava."

"Thanks. I'll keep that in mind." Trace could hardly be jealous of the burly surgeon, not when Eli he was obviously so obsessed with his own wife. "Later, though."

Now he wanted Elle to himself on the sunny Bahamas beach where he'd booked the honeymoon suite at a luxury hotel on a cliff over the Atlantic. He had several ideas of how he'd keep her so happily exhausted that she'd never regret having given up her club full of Doms for just one. Him.

The End

LEARNING CONTROL

ཡ

Trademarks Acknowledgement

ꟸ

The author acknowledges the trademarked status and trademark owners of the following wordmarks mentioned in this work of fiction:

FedEx: Federal Express Corporation

Ford: Ford Motor Company

Jaws of Life: Hurst Performance, Inc.

Mercedes: Daimler Chrysler AG Corporation

Velcro: Velcro Industries B.V. Limited Liability Company

Prologue

ജ

Putting the kids to bed, slipping into a sexy nightgown and waiting…

For the past few months this had been a pattern and Lynn Blackstone didn't much like it. She'd almost think her husband of nearly fifteen years was cheating if she didn't know that if he was, she'd have heard about it from his partners, or rather from their wives.

She stared into the full-length mirror on one wall of the master bedroom. There'd been some changes since she and Mark had first met, even though she'd always taken care of herself. She supposed she shouldn't have been surprised to see wear and tear. After all, all that time had to have exacted a toll somewhere. Still…

She wore the same size she'd worn ever since she and Mark got married, in spite of having had four kids. Other than a few laugh lines around her eyes and mouth, she'd so far beaten off most outward signs of aging. But she felt old. Unwanted. In some ways, she'd become like the comfortable slippers her husband put on after a day of exhausting surgery. Except Mark had been slipping into those slippers a lot more often than he'd been slipping into her lately.

It wasn't as if he had said anything. But he'd been putting in even longer hours than usual, accepting emergency room calls when he could have signed off to other surgeons qualified to repair trauma injuries to peripheral nerves and the musculo-skeletal system, even if they weren't as good as he was. Tonight, though, she had no reason to be angry, because Mark was working with both of his partners, trying to piece together what was left of a sixteen-year-old kid who'd tangled with a semi on the inner loop at rush hour.

Opening her dresser drawer, she got the dildo that stood in for her husband most nights—but not very well. Lying back on the bed, she inserted it and let its vibrations trick her body if not her mind into believing it was Mark fucking her, bringing her to a much-needed release.

Pressure built in her pussy, but the vibrator didn't do it to push her over the edge. "Damn it all." No toy could make up for the hot loving she wasn't getting from her husband. Unable to control her frustration and fury, she grabbed the dildo and tossed it across the room. It gyrated obscenely, its motor whirring noisily now that her body wasn't absorbing the vibrations. Something had to give, and she was pretty sure she'd given enough.

What she wanted was her husband back in place of the constantly absent moneymaking machine he'd become. What if just once he'd walk in the room, look at her with lust in his gorgeous dark-brown eyes and make love with her the way they used to…

She smiled. "We Got Married in a Fever" fit them to a "T" back then, except they were in San Antonio, not Jackson. The fire kept on burning for a lot of years, until recently when Mark had started working harder, growing more distant every day.

In fact, at one time, they were very adventurous. Mark had gotten into tying her up and playing kink games, mastering her for their mutual pleasure. They'd toyed with getting more involved in the BDSM scene, joining a club he'd learned about from another doctor on staff at the hospital. He'd even visited the club, talked to her about what he'd seen. If she hadn't gotten pregnant with their oldest about then, they'd have joined and taken their BDSM play to the next step. For a long time their vanilla sex life had been plentiful and good, even with the kink restricted as it was because there were always kids who might overhear them.

Whether it was Mark's absence or her own maturation in the last year or so, Lynn had been hungering lately for that overwhelming, all-encompassing feeling that came with being taken over by Mark's Dominant side, surrendering to him completely.

What had made the fire go out? They were the same people, just a few years older. They both loved their kids. Mark still treated her like a princess in lots of ways. She glanced down at the gorgeous sapphire-and-diamond tennis bracelet on her wrist. He'd brought it home from a medical conference he'd attended in New York a few weeks ago and put it on her before going straight to sleep.

Lynn felt like screaming. She didn't want to be the cut-out trophy wife on whom he hung jewels. She'd rather have him than the costly presents he'd been showering on her, and she was ready to tell him so. The frequency of the gifts had grown in direct opposition with the way his interest in her as a woman had seemed to fizzle out.

After she got up and washed the vibrator, she put the bracelet away and straightened the blown-up photo of them that he'd chosen to cover the wall safe. It broke her heart to look at it, remember how they'd been when it was taken a few months after they married, carefree and so in love they could barely keep their hands off each other.

When she heard the distinctive crunch of car tires on the crushed limestone driveway, Lynn lit a fragrant candle on the night stand, crawled back in bed and arranged her silk nightgown.

A perfect site for a seduction. Maybe tonight…

* * * * *

It was all Mark could do to crawl out of his car. Nine hours on his feet in surgery at the end of a full day's work had just about done him in. He glanced at the upstairs window at a soft glow that came from the master bedroom. Knowing Lynn was up there waiting sent blood rushing to his groin, made him walk a little faster despite the shooting pain in his thigh and a pounding headache he attributed to the harsh, bright lights in the operating room.

The trek to the house and up the long, curved staircase pretty much cooled the lust that always overcame him whenever he thought about his wife. By the time he reached the room and saw her there, relaxing on their king-size bed, he knew sex was a no-go. Not only because he could barely stand up, although that was part of it. He had just six hours before he had to be back in surgery, doing a dicey secondary ulnar nerve repair He owed the patient the best job he could do, and that meant he needed all the sleep he could get.

Slowly, every muscle in his shoulders burning from exhaustion, he stripped down. Before he looked at Lynn, he felt her gaze on him, so hot it practically burned his naked skin. When he sat on the bed and took her hand, he saw the saddest look he'd ever seen on her beautiful face. "Sorry I woke you, babe," he murmured, climbing into bed and reaching over to give her a quick kiss. "Long night again, but with a little luck, the patient ought to make it."

She hesitated then spoke. "Good. Mark, don't you think you should lighten up your caseload? You look so tired…"

She didn't have to spell it out. Mark knew she was tired, too. Tired of spending lonely nights after the kids were bedded down. Tired of more things than he could bring to mind at one in the morning.

Not that she ever complained. Hers had always been a true submissive personality. His mind drifted back to those years when they'd gotten pretty deep into BDSM games. "Yeah. I should."

"But you know you won't." Resignation hung from every word. "Go on, sleep now. I know you've got an early case tomorrow."

"I love you. Someday I'll make up to you for all these nights you've been spending alone lately." And he would. Somehow. If only the stock market hadn't crashed around his shoulders, leaving not a whole lot of cushion to fall back on if he decided to slow down or brought in a new associate the way Kurt had done earlier in the year.

But it had. And he couldn't stay awake all night and do justice to that case in the morning. Sighing, Mark rolled onto his side and counted sheep until he dropped off to sleep.

Chapter One

Three months later

ꟸ

This was the part about practicing medicine that Mark could easily have done without. He glanced across the conference table at his partners before returning his attention to all the predictions of doom and gloom being spouted by Doris Cabell, their practice manager he liked a whole lot better when she wasn't telling them they couldn't afford to bring in another associate, or anything else for that matter.

"You may actually have to scale down the staff you have. Not you doctors, of course, but some employees in the physical therapy, radiology and clerical departments."

"Why?" Orthopedic surgeon Kurt Silverman never minced words, just cut to the chase. Mark wanted to know, too. At least he thought he did.

Cabell looked at Kurt with expressionless, slate-gray eyes that reminded Mark of a great white shark he'd seen on a TV news show between cases yesterday. "Two big auto insurance companies filed for bankruptcy last month. Unfortunately, one of them is your largest debtor. Your attorneys say we'll be lucky to get ten cents on the dollar, and even then it may take years."

So their receivables were up, but there wasn't much chance they'd ever see a significant chunk of that money. Doris didn't have to point out that much of their group's revenue came from patients injured in some kind of insured accident, and that many of those patients wouldn't likely have the money or the will to pay out of pocket if their insurers failed.

Great. Just great. Mark halfway listened while Doris pointed out other depressing facts they already knew, such as that the practice had to cover fixed costs for this new building and equipment, and that variable expenses were rising as well. He looked across the table at Eli Calhoun, the thoracic surgeon who'd bought in less than a year ago as a junior partner. Eli looked positively green. Mark would, too, if he'd just found out his year-end bonus from the practice was likely to be a big, fat zero. Eli hadn't been out of the Air Force long enough to have amassed a big nest egg from his surgery fees.

Kurt looked none too happy, either, but he was in the best financial position of them all. Sure, his portfolio had shrunk like everybody else's, but he'd been smart enough to stick with more or less recession-proof investments.

"We can't skip doing the holiday party next month," Kurt said. "Everybody expects us to have it every year. We'll save some bucks by doing it at my place instead of a hotel or club, and I'll tell Shelly to take it easy on the refreshments. I don't want to skip bonuses for the employees, although we can pare them down if we have to."

Maybe things would get better by this time next year, but Mark wasn't holding his breath. "Good idea, Kurt. I'm sure Lynn will help out with the party." Kurt already had an assistant just out of his orthopedics residency, but he paid the man's salary from his own fees. Mark couldn't afford to do that, so he'd have to keep on taking every case he could get and praying the patients' insurance companies wouldn't keep going out of business.

* * * * *

Speaking of cases, he had one booked for an hour from now. No point in going home for dinner once the meeting had ended. Instead Mark joined Eli at the hospital cafeteria across the street, envying Kurt for getting to go home early for once.

"We'll be okay," Eli said. Then he looked over at Mark. "Won't we?"

Mark must have been wearing his worries on his face. Although he didn't want to alarm Eli, he needed to talk with someone. Six months ago, everything had been going great. He'd interviewed some surgeons fresh from residency, would have hired one if the salary he'd offered had attracted somebody trained as he was, with residencies in orthopedics as well as neurosurgery. Now he couldn't have hired one even if he'd managed to find a good one who'd work mostly for experience. Not and keep Lynn and the kids in the way he'd promised himself he would, back when they were living in a studio apartment at a rundown apartment complex near the hospital.

Of course they hadn't actually had to live so frugally, if he'd have set aside his pride and accepted help from her wealthy family. But he'd been determined they'd do it on their own and promised himself he'd give Lynn everything she'd had as a child, and more. In fifteen years, he'd achieved all he'd dreamed of. They had the big two-story house, two new foreign cars every few years. In the past few years he'd even been able to shower her with jewelry worth more than the hefty stash of family heirlooms she'd inherited when her mother died. And he'd paid off his medical school loans and started salting away that money for his kids' higher education.

"Mark?" Eli repeated. "We will be all right, won't we?"

"Yeah. We'll be okay. I'm just thinking that the belt-tightening's going to be hard on Lynn. I was just wondering whether she'll miss me while I work nearly all my waking hours, as much as she'll miss me adding to her jewelry collection."

Eli laughed. "Maggie's okay with us having to make a few sacrifices. Guess we're both used to living from paycheck to paycheck. At least, with the market down the way it is, we were able to find a house in town that we can afford. It'll be a whole lot more comfortable than my apartment, particularly after the baby arrives. Maggie will go back to the hospital and finish her residency, and then come join me while she studies for her specialty boards." Eli dug into his lasagna. Mystery meat, they called the cheesy casserole that might include beef, chicken or pork on any given night. Sometimes even leftover shrimp or crabmeat. "I don't envy you and Kurt with your big houses and families to take care of. Guess I should be happy I'm the poor doc in the group."

Mark stuck with his usual tuna salad and pie—blueberry today, his favorite. "You know, I was as poor as any medical student, with no family to fall back on and school loans mounting. I used to wonder how long it would take me to pay them back. When I first saw Lynn, I was sitting right in this cafeteria making a meal of soup and crackers."

"Fell hard, did you? I know I did with Maggie, even though I figured I'd get thrown off staff for lusting after one of the residents on my service. Lynn's hot as hell now. She had to have been a perfect ten back then."

"She was. Still is, at least to me." Not only had Lynn set off Mark's libido and been just as hot for him as he'd been for her, she hadn't cared that he had no money, or that the only place they had to fuck had been an empty resident's sleeping room where a resident might barge in any minute. "I think we must have broken in every on-call room in this hospital that summer."

"So how long did it take you to rope and tie her?"

Eli apparently was into ropes and ties, because he often mentioned how much Maggie enjoyed it when they spiced up sex with toys and light bondage. "Not long, once we realized we meshed not only in our interests but in the variety of kinks we liked in bed. We got married as soon as I finished med school the following spring." Those had been fun times. Times when Mark had lived to get back to his wife and their enthusiastic sex play.

"I didn't know you and Lynn were ever into BDSM games."

"We were, before the kids started coming along." Mark recalled how they'd started off with toy blindfolds and handcuffs and a purple silicone gel dildo he used to accuse Lynn of liking more than she liked his cock. She'd come back with a smart remark about the dildo being more readily accessible than he was, most of the time. He'd even bought a flogger and practiced using it to tan her gorgeous ass without inflicting any real damage. "After that," he said, amending his denial, "we pretty much turned vanilla. Sometimes I miss it, but lately I've been working such miserable long hours I don't often have the energy for sex at all."

"Ever hear of Club Rio Brava?" Eli's voice dropped to a whisper.

"Yeah. I even went there once, not long after I finished my residency and joined the medical staff here. One of the radiologists—he's no longer in town—asked me if I'd like to join. Lynn and I almost did, but then we found out she was pregnant. Just as well, I guess, because back then I wasn't especially anxious to display my scars to a bunch of strangers. You know, she's gotten me over that, for the most part. In the years we've been together, she's never once flinched when she's seen or touched my gimpy leg. I damn near lost my leg, and what's left is not pretty."

Eli grinned. "You can always cover up that leg. It's your cock that draws the subs' attention. I can understand, though, why the pregnancy made you decide to pass. Maggie and I hardly ever go out there now that we're expecting."

Mark nodded. "So you understand why we decided not to."

"Yes, I do. But now your girls must be old enough that they'd figure out what was going on if Mom and Dad did anything but the mildest BDSM play at home, unless Lynn's a whole lot quieter than Maggie."

"She isn't." At least she wasn't, if Mark's time-dulled memory was spot-on. "Maybe you're right, and the Club would be a nice place to get away where we can check the inhibitions caused by family life at the door."

Lynn had always insisted that Mark be the boss when it came to all things outside the bedroom. Come to think of it, she didn't assert herself much when it came to sex—she wanted him to initiate the action, show her what he wanted her to do. Was it possible she might want not only more sex but Dominant sex?

Mark suspected Lynn had been stressed and unhappy off and on for some time now. She hadn't said much about it though. After all, to be fair, he was leaving her in a no-win situation, wasn't he? He'd worked his ass off to get this practice off the ground, and Lynn loved him too much to beat him up about being a great bread winner simply because she was lonely. But truth was, he was lonely, too. He missed her and the kids. He didn't want to wake up one day with everything money could buy and find she'd left him because the one thing he couldn't buy, time for her and the kids, was the one thing she'd needed most of all.

Strange as it sounded, maybe Eli's whispered invitation, the titillating possibility, was a way to get them launched back in the right direction, turn his focus to the one thing that should be able to tear him away from his love for his career—love of his wife and her beautiful body.

He looked Eli straight in the eye. "Are you inviting me to this not-so-secret club?"

"Yeah. I am. Interested?"

"I'm not sure." Mark couldn't bring Lynn, not right away, not until he saw the club again and refreshed his mind as to what went on there. Still, in spite of being tired while another case awaited him, his cock stirred at the thought. "Even though she thought she'd like club play back then, we've gotten older. The idea of joining a BDSM club might turn Lynn off."

"But then it might turn her on. How about it if I get Maggie to sound her out about it?" Eli paused for a minute, shot Mark an amused look. "Well?"

"That would be better than if I brought up the subject. I teased Lynn a month or so ago when I found a brand-new clit-stimulating dildo in her dresser drawer. She'd tossed out her old one when Lissa found it in the night stand by our bed. She was about five years old when she asked Lynn what it was for."

"Guess Maggie and I will be having problems like that when our kids start getting nosy." Eli put his napkin on top of his plate and slid back his chair. "We'd better get upstairs. Time flies when you're having fun."

"Uh, Eli, is there any possibility I could make a solo trip out there? Decide if I think we'd both enjoy some kinky sex play away from home?"

"Sure. When would you like to go?"

Mark shrugged. "Maybe a night next week, if there ends up being one when both of us are off the call list."

"You got it." Setting his tray beside Mark's on the conveyor belt, Eli headed for the elevators at a pace Mark couldn't match. When Mark joined him in the line for the next elevator, he couldn't resist teasing Eli a little. "Didn't you ever hear the story about the hare and the tortoise?" When Eli looked puzzled, Mark went on. "Welcome to the practice, my friend. It's taken you all this time to learn I'll catch up eventually and to quit deliberately slowing down so I can keep pace. About the practice and the economy, it will work itself out. And we won't starve. Medicine's virtually recession-proof, unless you're a cosmetic surgeon."

* * * * *

Mark was working again tonight. No big surprise. At least he had called ahead to let her know. Lynn set down the phone and went to her closet, looking for something different to wear to the girls' school play tomorrow night.

She really ought to reorganize things. Where on earth was that royal blue silk slip dress she'd bought last year when she and Mark went to Dallas for a medical conference? Oh no. She spied it on the closet floor where it had slid off its hanger at some point. "Damn it, I guess I'll have to think of something else to wear." When she bent to grab the dress, she felt something else underneath it. A small object wrapped in cloth almost as soft as the garment that was going to have to go straight to the dry cleaner.

The flogger Mark had brought her on their third anniversary. She hadn't been able to toss it out with the dildo after Lissa had found her stash of toys. Kneeling on the carpeted floor, she unwrapped it, rubbed her palm lightly over its braided handle then grasped it. Recalling how the leather tails had tickled her buttocks when Mark wielded it, the bite that got her wet and ready for whatever her Master had in mind, she sat and held it for a long time.

Tears ran down her cheeks. Memories flooded her brain.

Her thoughts drifted back to those carefree times when she was a sophomore physical therapy student and Mark an extern doing a summer rotation in orthopedics at University Hospital. She'd fallen in instant lust when she first saw the dark-haired, buff medical student whose shy manner didn't quite fit with his obviously healthy ego. Not even his limp or the awful scars on his right leg from a teenage car accident made her think twice. Mark Blackstone was who Lynn had wanted, and who she ultimately got.

Despite dire warnings from her mom, she hadn't cared that she was a down-home ranch girl from the hill country northwest of San Antonio, and he was a Jewish boy from southern California, going to med school at UT up in Austin. They had a whirlwind affair that summer, and the following year they married as soon as he graduated.

She'd give anything to go back to those carefree days when Mark saved time for her even though he was just starting a grueling dual residency program. The nights, the sex that pushed all the limits she'd been taught, where Mark always alleviated her guilty conscience for liking everything he did to her, by exerting total command over her body, her reactions.

This flogger, wrapped and put away so carefully, symbolized something they had lost. Lynn wouldn't have wanted to go back, exactly. But she knew this was part of what was missing in her relationship with her husband now.

She wanted it back. Not the youth and not the financial struggles that went with loving her stubborn Master who wouldn't touch her inherited wealth. She wanted once again to be the center of his world. The Master around whom her life revolved.

Setting the blue dress in the dry-cleaning hamper, Lynn rewrapped the flogger in the same silk scarf, now faded with time, that she'd used so long ago. And she placed it on the night stand next to the bed before going back to the closet and selecting the first appropriate dress she found for the coming event. After all, whether or not the girls' moms had seen her wear the outfit before meant nothing.

When the phone rang again, she hurried to answer it. "Hi, Maggie," she said when she recognized the soft voice as belonging to Eli Calhoun's wife.

It seemed she was alone tonight, too. Lynn was glad to invite Maggie over for hot cocoa, biscotti and girl-talk. She liked the young, pretty resident Eli had married last year, envied her the carefree way she was handling her first pregnancy. In less than half an hour, Maggie was knocking at her door.

* * * * *

"Did you find Mark getting less interested in sex while you were pregnant?" Maggie laid a hand on her burgeoning belly. "Maybe it's just me, but..."

"I doubt it. Any loss of interest in bedroom play right now is more likely to be because everyone in the practice, even Kurt, seems to be working nonstop. It's been weeks since Mark and I had sex, and I'm not pregnant." Sometimes Lynn wished she were, but four kids were enough to handle when Mark wasn't often in the mix. The nanny helped, but nothing could make up for a father's loving discipline. "Are you having complications with the baby?"

"No. But—I'm not sure whether you know this, but we're into playing BDSM games. Eli's afraid to get really physical for fear of hurting me or Junior—and I miss it. Eli mentioned something that made me think you might like BDSM, too."

At first Lynn didn't know how to respond. It had been so long ago. Mark must have mentioned their games to Eli. "I—uh...Mark and I experimented with the lifestyle before the girls got old enough to find some of our toys and ask questions." Lynn couldn't help smiling when she recalled that day when Mark had brought home the flogger she'd just found, other days when he'd found a new toy to stimulate her. She'd loved it when he restrained her, binding her to the bed and ordering her to suck his cock. *Face it, Lynn, you liked it all, the loss of control, acceptance of his Dominance.* "But that was years ago. We used to enjoy a very active though vanilla sex life until recently, when Mark started coming home late every night with nothing on his mind but sleep."

"Eli said Mark's interested in visiting the BDSM club we belong to. He apparently wants to check it out and see if he thinks we'd scandalize you."

"Scandalize me?" Lynn looked at Maggie, astonished. "Mark's the one who'd more likely be scandalized. I think I've thought about it far more than he has, at least recently. Of course..." She felt a wistful pang, remembering. "He used to be the one who always took the lead. Tell me, what goes on in this club?"

Maggie did, her cheeks getting rosy as she described the private rooms, the devices designed to titillate and arouse the subs and give the Doms the kind of power trips they seemed to get off on. "You know, a real Dom does everything in his power to bring his lover pleasure, even to the point of sharing her with another Dom sometimes, or hurting her if that's the only way he can make her come."

"The only thing I don't much like is pain." That part of BDSM wasn't something Mark had ever been interested in, either, Lynn recalled. He'd never even put welts on her behind when he used the flogger, just aroused her intensely with the light stings, the idea that if he wanted to, he could inflict some serious damage with those leather tails.

"Some women can't come without pain. They've grown up being taught sex is dirty or wrong and can't get past the taboos they've built up in their minds, unless there's pain involved in sex."

"Do you?" Maggie didn't strike Lynn as a woman who'd put up with any real pain, but then you never knew.

"I used to. Since we fell in love and married, I find I don't need real pain to come, just the feeling that Eli's controlling me. And he's gotten gentler, too, as if he's come to trust that I love him so much I'll do anything to please him, without him applying any force at all. Sex has become more of a mutual thing, but we still enjoy BDSM play, and the senses of voyeurism and exhibitionism we can indulge at the club."

The idea of being restrained, asked to give over complete control of her body and will to Mark, appealed to Lynn so much that she asked more questions. With each answer, she became more certain she wanted to try this—anything to revive Mark's libido, make sex more important to him than the wealth he kept working so hard to amass.

The fact that Mark was looking into this club for the two of them gave Lynn hope that he still cared. That he still desired her. This was proof he realized something was missing in their relationship and that he wanted to fix it, share pleasure with her again. For the first time in months, she anticipated more than a kiss and a pat on the ass when Mark got home late at night.

"Want to go toy shopping?" she asked, eager to experiment as she figured out how to make Mark realize that while he might be nudging past forty-five, he still had a lot of testosterone that needed regular nourishing.

"Sure." Maggie grinned as Lynn brought a laptop to the kitchen table and turned it on. When Maggie selected a set of vibrating nipple rings, she licked her lips with anticipation, and Lynn noticed her silver tongue ring. "Eli got me a pair of those. They're not much use now, because my nipples are so sensitive I practically jump out of my skin when he sucks them, however gently. The trials of pregnancy," she said with an exaggerated sigh.

"Mine were sensitive then, too. Even afterward, as long as I was nursing the boys. I've thought about having them pierced, but I don't know if Mark would like that."

"Can't tell you whether or not Eli likes them, because I don't have nipple piercings. They're too hard to hide under scrubs and too much trouble to take out and reinsert. My clit's pierced though, and I love the feel of that. And my tongue ring, although I have to wear a clear acrylic retainer in both piercings when I'm working in the OR."

Lynn's cheeks grew hot when she imagined getting a tongue piercing and giving Mark head—something she hadn't done for a long time. She'd rub her tongue over his cock and balls, use the ring to add to his pleasure, and hers. How would it feel if he got one of the intriguing little spheres and used it on her clit? "Does it hurt?" she asked.

Maggie set down her half-eaten biscotti and looked at Lynn. "What?"

"Getting pierced."

"Oh. It depends on where you're getting a piercing. Since he's a surgeon who does a lot of peripheral nerve repair, I'm sure Mark could make most piercings relatively painless. If he'd do it, that is. Eli had a fellow Dom do my clit. A doctor, but I don't know who he is or what his specialty might be. It stung down there for a week or so, but what was worse was that Eli wouldn't fuck me until it healed, except for my mouth and ass."

Her ass? Lynn hoped she didn't look as shocked as she felt. The mouth part was okay. She'd gone down on Mark and liked it, and she loved the way he made her feel when he used his mouth on her pussy. But anal? There was something forbidden yet strangely erotic about the idea of being penetrated there. "What about the tongue piercing?" she finally managed to say.

"I've had this since I was in college. I got it done at a piercing parlor close to my dorm, and I don't recall it hurting all that much. You just have to be careful to keep the hole clean—food and such. I think you'd like it, but you'd probably have to switch off from the ball to a clear retainer whenever you're around your kids. Otherwise, Lacey and Lissa would have pretty good arguments to use if they get a notion to pierce a nose or eyebrow, or something else that would set them apart from the other girls at their preppy school."

Yes, they would, so they'd better never know. Was Lynn insane to even be considering it? It seemed extreme, to be considering a tongue piercing after just hungering for more frequent sex, but somehow this conversation, finding out what Mark was looking into, renewed in her mind the need to throw caution to the winds that had once been a vital catalyst in their marriage. She was tired of playing it safe and cautious. She'd done that for too long. Now she was going to throw herself into it and see what happened.

Lynn clicked on a good-size titanium ball and a package of discreet clear plastic discs. They joined the other toys she'd already put in her shopping cart. This should be enough for now, she thought, giving the list one last check before keying in her credit card number. "I'm going to do it." At Maggie's questioning look, she added, "Ask Mark to pierce me." Already she was getting aroused, and more determined by the minute to lure her husband away from his patients—at least some of the time.

"I think you'll enjoy it. And other piercings, too, but you should let Mark pick them out. After all, different men like different sexual stimuli." Maggie dug her beeping cell phone from her purse. "Excuse me."

When she hung up, she gathered up her things then turned to Lynn. "That was Eli. He and Mark are both out of surgery and on their way to their respective homes. I'd better go. He expects to find me in bed, waiting..."

Maggie was obviously eager. And she obviously got more than a kiss and a grunted "good night" when her gorgeous husband got home, long day or not. As she walked her friend to her car, Lynn vowed that tonight she was going to seduce Mark. He might be bone-tired, but he wasn't dead and neither was she.

It was only nine o'clock. Plenty of time to play with her husband tonight. In a few days, she'd have the toys she'd just ordered, ones she hoped would coax him into further entertaining evenings. On her way to the bedroom, Lynn checked the kids, asked Maria, the nanny, to listen for the boys, and went upstairs. Anticipating, needing, wanting to be more to Mark than a habit even now.

Looking longingly at the long-forgotten flogger, she put it and the scarf in a drawer of the night stand on Mark's side of the bed.

* * * * *

The talk he'd had with Eli stuck in Mark's head through the pretty much routine nerve transposition he'd just finished.

Surprising the OR staff, he turned down a case that had arrived in the ER while he'd been finishing up his scheduled case, and headed home. Let the guy on call for hand surgery drag himself in to try to reattach that severed finger. Eli wanted a shower and bed, and he wanted—no, needed—to fuck his beautiful wife.

For the first time in weeks if not months, Mark was raring to go, not so bone tired all he could think about was sleep. Tonight he felt a spring in his step, and even though running was a bit more than he could handle, he hurried into the house and upstairs. Something smelled sweet, aromatic, seductive when he opened the bedroom door.

His heart nearly stopped when he saw Lynn. No sexy nightgown to cloak her, just Lynn standing naked by the window, her golden skin glowing in the light from a flickering candle. His wife. Mother of their children. But tonight he saw her as a sex goddess awaiting his pleasure.

"Come here." His mouth felt dry, and his breathing turned ragged. When she sauntered across the room and went down on her knees in front of him, his cock turned rock-hard behind the scrub pants he hadn't bothered to change out of. "What do you have in mind, down there like that?" The thought of her taking him in her mouth the way she used to do made him want to make this last, almost as much as he wanted to satisfy the formerly dormant libido.

She untied his scrub pants, blew playfully on the skin she uncovered. "I want to taste you, refresh my memory. My love, I've missed you so much. Missed *this*." With her tongue she stroked his cock head while she cradled his scrotum in both hands.

"Oh yeah. I've missed it, too. That's it, baby, feels so damn good." When she took him completely in her mouth and sucked his cock, he almost lost control. "Don't stop."

"Mmmm." She stroked the insides of his thighs as she took him deeper, swallowed convulsively.

He couldn't remember her ever being so needy, so ravenous, but it felt incredible. He barely noticed his tired muscles, the exhaustion that had overcome him for so long.

For a while he'd wondered if his sex drive was heading south. It obviously wasn't. Blood slammed into his sex, made him lightheaded. He had to get control of himself or he was going to come before he'd done half the things he wanted to do to Lynn's sleek, fit body. "Stop, now. If you don't, this will be over before I've gotten to fuck you." He lifted her face, met her sparkling gaze. "And I've been thinking about your hot, sweet cunt for hours. Go lay your gorgeous little self across the bed."

She did, while he stripped off his clothes before going to his dresser and grabbing two of the ties he seldom wore. Her gaze settled on the ties, and she licked her lips. "Want me to tie you up, the way I used to?" It had been years, since before they'd left their tiny apartment, but he could see excitement in her expression.

"What made you think about this?" she asked as he tied a tie onto each wrist then secured them to the bed. There was a coy note to her voice, a sexy smile playing on her lips.

God, seeing her like this made him grab hold of the part he used to play so naturally that he wondered if he was going to fit at this club better than he'd expected. "You've been talking to Maggie. You know why. I think I need to get your mind on something other than playing mind games with your Master."

She trembled, but her whisper set his blood to raging. "I always liked it when you made me feel helpless."

"Lie back, relax and enjoy it. I'm going to fuck you until you scream for mercy, but first..." He got between her legs, raised them over his shoulders and caught her clit between his teeth. When she squirmed beneath him, he gave her a smart slap on the butt. Her honey was sweet, sweeter than he remembered, so sweet he was going to lose it. Trying to hold on, give her all the pleasure she hadn't had for so long, he made a concerted effort to silently recite all the nerve endings in an arm and hand.

It wasn't going to work. He couldn't name body parts he worked with nearly every day with total confidence and precision. Not while he was drowning himself in her sweet musk, stroking her silky skin, drinking the fluids that gushed from her hot, wet cunt. Mark slid up her body, a journey of reacquaintance, of erotic sensation…of love that had never gone away even after all the years they'd shared. "I've got to have you now," he whispered against her slack lips, smelled his own musk as her heart pounded against his chest. "We'll continue playing after…"

"Fuck me, Mark. Please fuck me now. I want to feel your big, hot cock inside me again."

She sounded desperate, almost as anxious as he was. "Not as much as I want to slide into your slippery, wet cunt and fuck you until you scream with pleasure and we both collapse in a sweaty heap." With that he shifted and drove into her, reveled in the way she welcomed him with rippling vaginal muscles, a rise of her hips to meet his desperate thrusts.

Oh yes. This was the Mark she loved, devouring her as if he'd been starving. His teeth grazed her throat, he tasted her skin with a tongue as slick and smooth as his five o'clock shadow was delightfully scratchy. She loved the way his soft chest hair tickled her breasts, teased her nipples into hard pebbles aching for his hands, his mouth. He thrust into her deeper, faster, claiming what had always been his, claiming and controlling her with each sure, fierce penetration.

"God how I love you. Love this." She wanted him to kiss her, would have framed his face in both hands and drawn his mouth to hers if she could have used her hands. He must have read her mind because he took her lips instead. Another claiming, this one as sweet as his fucking was fierce. "Open for me," he ground out, and when she did he claimed her mouth, plundered it with his tongue. His teeth grazed her lower lip, softly biting her tender flesh.

"Oh yesss," she moaned when he moved down, captured one breast, suckled her ever so gently. "Why did you wait so long?"

His only reply was a rumbly groan as he clasped both breasts, brought them together so he could lick both nipples. "I like having you under me, helpless."

She wasn't really helpless, not with her legs free, wrapped around his narrow waist, coaxing him to take her harder, make the bubble of sensation low in her belly burst in a kaleidoscope of sensations. Lust that hadn't died after all. A feeling of being mastered by her lover…her only love.

She tightened her vaginal muscles around his cock, felt the tension building inside her, sensed from the way his breathing grew ragged that he was on the edge. So was she. "Come in me, love. Come now."

He laughed, a strained sound from deep in his throat as he thrust deeper then stilled inside her. "I'm the one giving orders here, am I not?"

"You are, Master. Just as you've always been." Lynn tightened her legs around his ass, held him, squeezed on him with her inner muscles. "May I come now, please?" She couldn't wait much longer, not with waves of long-denied sensation starting to flow through her, growing stronger every second as he seemed to grow even harder inside her. God help her, she was coming and no command was going to stop her.

"You may." He held her tighter than the ties on her wrists, withdrew then slammed back into her one last time. "God yes, baby. I'm coming too." He came in hard, staccato bursts that bathed her womb, threw her over the edge in a maelstrom of sensation so strong she shook in his arms. It seemed to go on forever, the sensations pouring over her, melting her heart as well as her body to the only man she'd ever loved.

For a long time they lay there, sweat slickening their naked bodies, whispers of sex and love and commitment mingling with the heady aroma of man and woman and coming together. A harvest moon shone through the full-length French doors, and a light breeze made the candle on her night stand flicker.

Whatever happened, Lynn would never again wonder if she and Mark had been destined to get together. Were still bound not by a house, children and the material things they had, but by an abiding love—and lust that was as strong as ever. "I want us always to be this way," she told Mark. "Would you let me loose now so I can touch you, too?"

"My pleasure, sweetheart." Stretching over her, he freed her wrists then brought her hands to his lips and kissed first one and then the other palm. "I'm sorry about the past few months. Will you forgive me for getting so bogged down in work that I forgot the important things in life?"

She smiled up at him, capturing his dark, smoldering gaze and holding it. "I found our flogger earlier today and put it in your night stand drawer for you. Master."

"I can hardly wait to try it out again," he told her, his lips curling upward in a beautiful smile. "Tomorrow?"

"I'll be thinking about it all day." And Lynn would.

This wasn't the Mark she'd gotten used to lately, but it wasn't the twenty-seven-year-old resident he'd once been, either. Of course she wasn't twenty-two, either, and a lot of living had gone on in fifteen years. Still, Lynn loved it all, the throaty commands, the gentle domination…the way he mixed up his deep, abiding emotions for her with the erotic high of giving commands, controlling her body. This one night had restored the emotional closeness she felt with him, her hope for their marriage that had been flagging.

Chapter Two

ꟗ

She felt downright young the next morning when she kissed him goodbye and sent him off to work. It seemed from his hard kiss, the tongue action he almost never went for outside their bedroom, that he was rejuvenated, too. Her lips tingled and her heart did flip-flops, so much so that she wanted time alone to savor the memories.

Most of the time Lynn drove the girls to school herself, but today she turned to the nanny. "Maria, would you take Lacey and Lissa this morning?"

"Si, senora." She looked expectantly at Lynn.

"You can use my car." She didn't want the girls riding in Maria's elderly wreck of a station wagon, so she handed over the keys to her Mercedes. "Be careful."

Maria beamed. The twenty-five-year-old woman had been itching to drive the car ever since Mark had it and his own new sports car delivered a month or so ago. "I will take care. You want me to take Mikey and Jake?"

"No thanks." The twins were still sound asleep, and Lynn hoped they'd stay that way for an hour or so, so she could mull over what had caused Mark's sudden ardor. "Girls, make sure to get your book bags."

"Okay, Mom. See you at the program after school." Backpacks in hand, both girls bolted for the car, anticipating a fun ride with their young nanny.

As soon as she was alone, Lynn called Maggie and asked for the invitation she'd said Eli was going to give to Mark. Tonight…

Tonight she'd let him know too plainly for him to doubt that she wanted him to dominate her, wanted him to fulfill all the fantasies she'd been too shy to admit to. Meanwhile, she'd work up the nerve to ask him if he'd pierce her tongue.

The tone of their sexual play last night had been a little less kinky than when they were younger. She expected that to change now, because they knew each other better, trusted one another more. It made the possibilities endless. Lynn shivered, considering her earlier decision to embrace the BDSM lifestyle fully. Tonight she'd let him know.

After Maria had returned and FedEx had delivered her overnight package from the sex toy store, she arranged most of the toys in the drawer of her night stand, but kept the tongue ring and retainers by the phone. Mark would need something—she had no idea what—to pierce her tongue, and something else to thread through the hole before inserting the ring. With only a little hesitation, she put the phone on speaker and dialed Mark's cell phone.

"Hello there. I thought you'd be sleeping," he told her when he took the call. "I love hearing your voice, though."

"I'm glad. Very glad. What are you doing tonight?" Lynn crossed her fingers, hoping he'd be off call tonight.

He lowered his voice. "With any kind of luck I'll be home, getting some more kinky loving. Why?"

"I want you to pierce my tongue. Maggie said the sensations were incredible for her as well as Eli. She said that if you did it, it probably wouldn't hurt much since you're familiar with all the peripheral nerves." She reached under her robe, fingered her pussy that was already wet from thinking about submitting to her husband…completely. "Will you?"

"You're playing with yourself, you naughty slave. Don't you think you ought to ask your Master's permission before playing with his pussy?"

His teasing tone, the fact he knew her so well he'd been able to guess what she was doing from the tone of her voice, got her even hotter. This was something he hadn't done in quite a while, indulging in flirty phone sex with her.

He cleared his throat. "About your tongue, I'm not sure about the procedure being painless. Tongues aren't exactly my specialty, but I suppose I can do it and avoid hitting many if not all the major nerves. Do you have a ring or retainer to put in the hole? Tongues heal faster than almost any other part of the body, which I imagine means that the piercings close up easily when they're left without something to keep them open. Want any more body jewelry?" he asked in a teasing tone. "Some places are trickier than others to pierce."

Good. The idea of putting his mark on her, literally, seemed to intrigue him. "Not yet. I'll let you decide what other parts of me you'd like to decorate. Meanwhile I'm going to spend the time until you get home reading all about Master and slave relationships on the Internet."

She thought she heard him let out his breath hard and wondered if the idea of controlling her got him excited. She hoped she wasn't taking this further than he wanted to go. "I'm anxious to learn about them, too, but I still have patients I have to see before I come home."

Good, he didn't seem scandalized at all. She thought he even sounded intrigued about exploring the world of BDSM. "Go see your patients. They need you, but remember, my darling, I need you, too."

"Okay. I'll get together what I'll need for this little project and bring it home. God, baby, you've got me hard as rock. Love you, but I have to go for now."

* * * * *

The last thing Mark wanted was to cause Lynn unnecessary pain, so he stole some time between office patients and ate his lunch—a beef and veggie wrap from the deli down the street—in the practice's medical library.

When Eli came in, he glanced at the *Gray's Anatomy* text that Mark had laid out on the table in front of him. "What the hell are you doing, boning up on first-year med school anatomy? After fifteen years, I'd think you should know everything." He saw the pages Mark was looking at and laughed. "Don't tell me, you've got some patient who practically bit off his tongue."

"Fuck off." From the smirk on his face, Mark surmised that Eli had guessed why he was boning up on the physiology of a human tongue. "Unless you want to tell me how you pierced Maggie's tongue."

"I didn't do it. She told me she went to one of those piercing and tattoo parlors near the college where she did undergraduate studies, which should indicate it's not that big a deal to do. I've pierced some nipples and clits in my time, though, in case you need some pointers."

"Nope. At least not now. Lynn wants her tongue pierced because your wife told her what a turn-on it can be. I don't want to send her jumping off the chair when I clamp it, so I'm trying to figure out which nerves to numb first." He didn't relish having Eli know he was taking up body-piercing, but what the hell? Eli hadn't had any problem showing him and Kurt the thick jewelry he wore in his cock when they were showering after collaborating on a long surgery, just in case it would cause them any embarrassment to have a partner with such an obvious sign he was into BDSM.

Though his cock twitched at the prospect of being decorated with a sign of the lifestyle, Mark was going to pass on that. Imagining letting someone pass a needle through the sensitive flesh of his cock took care of the erection that was starting up again. But maybe, he thought, Lynn would like getting fucked by a pierced cock, and if so, it damn sure wasn't going to be anybody's but his.

He'd consider that later—much later, if for no other reason than that he was confident getting his cock pierced would put it out of the fucking business for quite a while. "Got that invitation for me?" he asked, anxious to see what kinky delights awaited him and Lynn at Club Rio Brava.

"Sent it over to Lynn. Seems she asked Maggie for one last night, too. You know, you look better than I've seen you for months. Apparently a dose of hot sex is the perfect cure for exhaustion and worries about the economy."

Mark nodded. Eli had it right. This morning, he'd made a decision to quit shortchanging himself and his family, even if it meant they might have to hold onto their cars for more than a year or two and put off resurfacing the driveway. He wouldn't need to start liquidating investments for the kids' education for another five years or more, and from the way Lynn practically devoured him last night he guessed she might rather have him regularly than a new bauble for every landmark occasion.

He got up and took the diagram he'd sketched on a legal pad. Then he went into the minor surgery supply room and collected vials of local anesthetic, needles, some suture packs and a sterile facial surgery pack that contained a drape, gloves, scrub brush and disinfectant soap. As soon as he finished with his last post-op patient a little after three, he tried to get out of the office without Doris seeing him.

It didn't work. "I've got two nonemergency secondary repairs for you. Patients are already in the hospital. I thought I'd work them in after you finished with your office patients." She looked at the bag in his hand and scowled.

"Not tonight, Doris. Reschedule them for tomorrow or the next day in my regular surgery block. I'm no longer taking routine cases outside normal hours. As a matter of fact, I'm going to be off every evening except for bona fide emergencies. My hours are going to be between seven a.m. and five p.m. except for primary trauma emergencies when I'm on call. Do you realize I've been putting in twelve hours or more every day for the past few months as well as working every weekend?"

She shrugged. "It's your practice. I thought you wanted to see that cash flow doesn't slack off."

"Money's not everything." It took all Mark could do not to fire the practice manager, but she'd been with him and Kurt since the beginning, and she'd managed well. He was snapping at her now for carrying out his and his partners' instructions, which was patently unfair. "I think we need to meet and talk tomorrow with the other partners," he told her, being careful to moderate his tone. "None of us can keep working the kind of hours we've been having you schedule us for. If we do, somebody's going to make a tragic mistake. I know times are tight, but we've got to keep things in perspective. All right?"

When she nodded, obviously surprised, he gave her a smile, feeling another weight easing, suggesting he'd taken another right step. "Now if you'll excuse me, Lynn and the kids haven't seen much of me lately. That's about to change. If my cell phone rings, it had better be a matter of somebody's life or death."

* * * * *

Mark made a production about taking one of the practice's take-home supply totes to their bedroom before coming back down to toss a softball with the girls out by the pool, and wrestle on the floor before dinner with the identical toddlers who were beside themselves to get to play with Daddy. Lynn had to pinch herself to be sure this wasn't a mirage—that Mark had left work before four p.m., not a.m. His sexy grin as he sat across the dinner table sent shivers of anticipation down her spine. Not hungry for food, she pushed around her broiled chicken breast, rice and steamed broccoli, wondering if the simple meal was enough to fuel her husband's appetite.

She could hardly wait until she had him to herself. If she wasn't wrong, she'd have a pierced tongue before tomorrow morning—and a sore but very satisfied pussy. Maybe other orifices as well, she amended, anxious to service Mark orally again, this time with the tongue ring there to enhance his pleasure. And to try out the butt plug that had arrived this morning with her other toys. Funny, she'd been having sex since she was seventeen, but she'd never experienced having any object up her butt. Of course she might enjoy it. After all, she'd thought about it, teased her own rim from time to time…

"Okay, girls. Time for you to get ready for bed and do your homework," Mark said when dinner was over. They didn't argue the way they argued with her, but did as they were told. He stood then reached over and squeezed Lynn's hand. "I think it's time for all of us to get some rest. Maria, would you settle these two rascals down?" His eyes shining with love for the little guys in their matching high chairs, he ruffled their dark hair and bent to give them each a kiss.

"We'll be upstairs if you need us. Please make sure the girls go to bed at a reasonable hour," Lynn said, hoping as she said it that there would be no interruptions, and that the thick walls would muffle any sounds that she and Mark might make.

* * * * *

Mark wasted no time stripping down and maneuvering Lynn into the shower. "If I'm going to perform surgery on you, we both need to be squeaky-clean," he told her while soaping them both down head to toe with pungent-smelling surgical soap. Bending, he kissed her hard then met her gaze. "What did my naughty wife spend today doing?"

"Well…I got some toys." She shot him a hot look.

A grin crossed his handsome face, and he squeezed one of her nipples while scrubbing her chest. "For the kids?"

"No, silly. For us. And don't forget, you've got that flogger." It had been so long, Lynn had almost forgotten how he loved to flirt with her. Part of their foreplay, he used to say. With a soapy hand he traced a path down her belly, found her clit and tweaked it. "Want to tell me about them?" He slid two fingers up her pussy and scissored them. "God, you're already wet. Don't know if I can wait to play with any toys tonight."

"Then don't. Tie me up again and take me. Make me yours. Please. Make me helpless to resist you." Out of the shower, she wrapped herself in a bath sheet and gestured toward the Velcro-fastening restraints she'd already secured to the four corners of the antique brass bed frame.

He laughed. "You mean you're not already?" His cock practically burst when he imagined claiming her, placing her under his command. "Hold on, at least let me dry off so I won't soak the bed."

What the hell had come over Lynn? What had come over him? Had they both been sublimating a mutual need for kink? He'd practically forgotten the adventurous nature of their sex life earlier in their marriage. In the more recent past, when he wasn't up to his elbows in patients, he'd actually had passing thoughts of reviving some kink in their bed. But each time, he'd convinced himself she'd likely buried her submissive nature after they started having babies, and that she'd chop his cock off for even suggesting they go back to the games they'd both loved before kids and life got in the way. Boy, had he been wrong.

It didn't matter. If she wanted to play bondage games, it was fine with him. More than fine. He straddled her shoulders as he secured those Velcro cuffs she'd bought around her slender wrists. "That's it. Taste your Master," he growled when she took the tip of his cock between her lips. "Now for your legs, because I'm going to devour my own personal cunt." In a hurry now, he bound her ankles, leaving her delightfully open for whatever he might want to do.

She wiggled her legs. "Ooh. Tie them tighter. Yes, that's it."

"What if I tortured you by refusing to play your games?" He knelt between her bound legs and slid his cock into her creamy cunt. "Later, though. Right now I'm going to fuck you. Don't say a word or I'll have to put a gag in your mouth, and I bet you forgot to buy one, didn't you?"

"Yes, I did."

He clamped a hand over her mouth then pulled it back and kissed her deeply instead. "Keep this pretty mouth shut on your own then. We wouldn't want to have Maria or the kids hear you moaning."

He fucked her slow and deep, missionary-style, but it was good. Not even the off chance that somebody might have heard them took away from the pleasure. His, that is. He had the feeling when it was over that Lynn still hadn't quite gotten what she was looking for, but then the night was still young.

After he'd unfastened her bonds, she handed him an envelope. He tore it open and read aloud. "*You are cordially invited to Club Rio Brava, where your privacy will be assured*." The ivory vellum card, as thick as a wedding invitation, bore a discreetly small address and phone number, and an engraved logo that featured a tiny pair of handcuffs. At the bottom of the message was the boldly scrawled signature of his partner, Eli.

"So, we both had the same idea, I guess. I take it you want to go and play some of these games?"

"Oh yes. And I want you around often enough that I don't start substituting my new dildo…or the butt plug I want you to use on me. I'm dying to see you in black leather with a flogger in your hand, but that's for the club." She lay back down and shot him an incredibly sexy smile. "The plug and a dildo are in the drawer."

His cock swelled once more when she made it obvious that she wanted him to stuff all her orifices. Reaching inside, he drew out a plug, still in its box, and the vibrating dildo he'd seen before and imagined her using it on herself on nights when he had to work. "You sure you want this monster rammed up your butt?" he asked when he pulled the anal plug from its box and started to smear it with lubricant.

"I bought it to stretch myself so your beautiful cock will fit." Her mouth went slack, as if she was already anticipating giving him head while the toys stimulated her other openings.

Mark had always been hesitant about trying anal sex, afraid he'd hurt her. When he'd been a resident, he saw too many women—men too—come into the emergency room with anal tears. But if she wanted it, he'd try it, very carefully. "Relax then. Imagine it's me filling your tight rear end." The thought of how it would feel to bury his cock, like the plug, into a hole so tight he'd have trouble getting in, had him fully aroused again. After inserting both toys and setting the dildo to vibrating against her hard little clit, he bent and claimed her mouth. "Open up for me now. I want to taste you like this, because after I pierce you, your mouth will be off limits for a week or so, maybe longer."

He was going to miss tangling their tongues, having her go down on him as if his semen was her greatest prize. Ending the kiss and turning his body, he straddled her face, giving her access to suck his cock while he stroked her satiny skin, teased her breasts until the nipples tightened and grew hard. "Oh yeah, how did I ever manage to persuade myself I didn't need my nightly playtime with you?" Moving lower, Mark found her clit, felt her heat and warmth as she sucked him harder, took him deeper, swallowing against him. God, it felt like heaven and hell. Heaven because she was dragging him to the edge, hell because he wanted this to last until she lost control and came for him. Her Master.

He smelled like sex, the mingled musk of him and her. Loving the sensations the smell evoked, Lynn inhaled it, sucked his cock head and stabbed the slick slit at the end with the tip of her tongue. She cupped his testicles, was surprised to learn they drew up when she exhaled on them. His pubic hair tickled her nose. She loved it, this feeling of being so full, so *taken*. The vibrations of the dildo, the stretching sensation of the anal plug, Mark's seeking hands on her outer labia and upper thighs had her on sensual overload. She wanted to swallow him, use the muscles in her throat to suck out his essence.

He felt so good on her, holding her down with a body as fit and firm now as he'd been when they were kids. Only now he was so much more skilled a lover. And she was uninhibited enough to appreciate those skills. Her cheeks brushed his lightly furred thighs, felt the scars that had never bothered her as much as they used to bother him. She maneuvered her head enough that she could stroke the scarred flesh with her cheek. With love. So much love, so much passion, so much hope that this could go on until they were old and gray.

His longish hair tickled her. She felt his hot breath on her mound, wished he'd be not so gentle, that he'd command her body and soul with barely controlled violence. She shuddered with the force of an orgasm that moved through every inch of her. Her nipples burned, her ass contracted. She swallowed him deeper, felt his testicles press against her mouth and nose as she sucked his musky organ.

"God, don't stop." A huge tremor went through his body and he came, salty and rich and a little bit bitter on her tongue. She swallowed all she could. When the spurts slowed down, he withdrew, letting her lick the pearly fluid off his magnificent cock that was still jerking a little when he turned and lapped his juices and hers off her mouth, her face. "I love you, baby. More than you'll ever know."

She met his gaze, unable to stop the tears that trickled down her cheeks. "I love you, too, so much I want to be your sex slave, see to all your needs."

He took her mouth, ravaged it, hard and fast as if he couldn't get enough, couldn't help exerting his control over her, commanding her submission.

The word rolled around in Lynn's sated brain. It meant acceding to a lover's slightest wish. Letting go. Savoring her

Master, pleasing him as he strived to please her. "My darling Master," she murmured, using her mouth to sample the five o'clock shadow on his chin and upper lip, the sensitive hollow at his throat. She wanted to be his everything, just as he was hers. Had been since that first summer when they were two kids so much in love they'd thought nothing would ever change.

It had changed, although she'd never doubted their love. The romantic love, still there somewhere, had become tarnished with the pressures of living, working and raising their kids. The girls were old enough now that she and Mark had to be careful not to be too demonstrative anywhere they might be spied upon. And their twins were into everything—whoever coined the phrase "terrible twos" knew what she'd been talking about.

Now she'd grabbed at the chance to renew the fires, and God willing, it would work. No more routine fourteen-plus-hour days for Mark, or lonely nights for her with nothing but a vibrator for company. Whatever it took, they were going to stoke the fever that had brought them together in the first place.

Mark responded to patients' needs, to their kids' pleas. So many things in his life were a struggle, or out of his control. By making him her Master, Lynn wanted to give him control over her pleasure, the way Maggie had said Eli felt for her. Maggie's words rang in her ears.

"You've got to let go of the control. You have to have some with the kids, but when you two are alone, let Mark take over."

That made sense, so much so that Lynn had taken the conversation further, learned Maggie and Eli lived in a slave/Master relationship that apparently kept both of them supremely satisfied.

As Lynn had done the Internet research she'd teased Mark about on the phone, she'd wondered if she wanted that kind of relationship for her and Mark. She knew she wanted to submit...and she wanted him to exert the sort of sexual, sensual control that made her hot and wet just thinking about it. So just maybe…they'd take it one step at a time, savor that journey.

The first step was coming now. Leaving the toys in, Mark got up and came back, some surgical instruments and a bowl of water foaming with the same kind of soap they'd showered with. "Are you sure you want this?" he asked, glancing down to the table at the sterile wrapper that held a gleaming titanium ring with its slightly curved stem.

"I'm sure."

He smiled and nodded then positioned her head on a stack of pillows at the edge of the bed. "I'm going to tie you down again to remind you not to move around, but we're going to need to do it so I can get to your mouth without straddling you. If I did that, I'd end up inside you again, and I don't believe I could perform this little procedure with that delightful distraction." He moved two of the restraints to the bed rail next to her and fastened the other ends on her arms.

His cheeky grin warmed her heart as she watched him scrub his hands and snap on some sterile gloves. When one of them slipped out of his hand, he cursed, but not too virulently. "I'm used to having a circulating nurse, but somehow this was too personal a procedure to bring one along."

"I'm glad, Master." She judged from his full cooperation at providing the tools that he wanted it, too—and that was her main concern. "If you want, you can put your marks on other parts of me, too. I'm your willing slave."

He laid a gloved hand on her right breast, grinned. "Well, maybe I'd like to see some hoops swinging from these, as well. Not right now, though. I only had time to study the anatomy of a tongue this afternoon. It's not every day I'm called upon to patch one back together." Getting serious, he picked up the scrub brush again and did a thorough cleansing of her face and lips. "Stick out your tongue, please."

He might have been talking to a stranger in his office if it weren't for the lusty twinkle in his deep brown eyes. "This won't hurt, other than a couple of little pricks where I put in the lidocaine. There you go, one's done."

It hurt like hell, but strangely the pain aroused Lynn even more. When the second injection went in, she managed not to flinch, and her vaginal walls clenched more tightly around the dildo.

"You okay?"

"Oh yes. Mark, did you know those little pricks in my tongue almost made me come?"

He lifted the first of two clamps and showed it to her. "If those almost made you come, love, these may finish doing the job if I don't wait for the anesthetic to take effect. What I'm going to do is place two clamps to decrease the blood supply before piercing you right here." He used some sort of surgical ink to mark a spot near the middle of her tongue. "Not too far back, where it might nick the root. And not so close to the end that people can't help seeing it when you talk."

He poked her with a clamp. "Feel that?"

"No, I can't feel anything." Her voice sounded fuzzy to her ears, she supposed because Mark had completely numbed her tongue. "Want it done, so I can lick my Master's cock, make him feel good."

"Quiet. I've got the clamps placed now. Be very still. You're going to feel a little pressure. No pain. I'm pushing a large gauge suture holder through, and when I'm done you may feel the suture hanging out from the top and bottom of the hole. Now I'll insert your jewelry and release the clamps. Voila, we're finished."

She tasted blood, but not as much as she'd expected. Although her tongue was numb, the roof of her mouth wasn't, so she gingerly rolled her new tongue ring against it, and her lips. "I like it, Master. Thank you."

Peeling off the gloves, Mark tossed them on the portable table and rolled it back into the bathroom. Then he came back and smiled down on her. "I'll go see this club of Eli's sometime this week. If you're very good, I may join it and take you there. When your piercing heals." He took both breasts in his hands and rolled the nipples between his fingers.

"I'll be very good, Master."

He sat on the bed and held her hand. "If you don't want me to, I'll pass on any actual participation when I go there. After all, I may like to play, but you're my only playmate."

Lynn loved him for saying that, but she'd read about what went on in BDSM clubs and was prepared to enjoy it all—after all, she trusted Mark completely, knew their marriage was solid and that experiencing the BDSM lifestyle would only enhance it. "I know we're a team, lover. I also know I want you to experience the whole club scene when you go there, so you'll know what to do with me later. No, don't look at me like that," she said when he looked at her as if she'd suddenly gone crazy. "I know you love me and I love you. But that shouldn't keep you from taking pleasure with another sub. After all, those club scenes are only make-believe."

Mark cleared his throat. "I'll give that some thought since you've clearly given me permission to play. Meanwhile, I'm going to take out that dildo and fuck you again until you beg for mercy."

"Will you untie me? Please, Master, I want to make you feel good, too."

Kissing each finger on each hand, as if she were a precious possession, he freed them. While she reached out to hold him, he turned and released her ankles, taking the time to massage the welts she'd caused by pulling at her bonds. "Turn over on your stomach."

His tone left no doubt he'd issued a command, not a request. Lynn loved it, basked in knowing she was the center of his world, just as he was the focus of all her lust, her best friend and the Master she'd only now discovered after all the years of living a conventional life. A lie they didn't know was one, a huge lie they finally were washing away by baring their souls and letting their real needs free. The light bite of the flogger on her bare butt and thighs didn't hurt her, it just made her want him more. "Oh Master, that feels so good," she whispered when he set the toy aside, savoring the feel of him slowly removing the dildo, spreading her, pressing the slick head of his cock between her pussy lips and sliding inside until she felt his flesh pressing against her cervix.

"Squeeze me, baby. Oh God, you're so hot. And so fucking beautiful I want to crawl inside you." Mark moaned then reached under her to knead her breasts, every once in a while tugging the nipples and rolling them between his fingers until they felt like icy-hot, tingling extensions of her spasming cunt.

Her ass felt full, too, reminding her the plug was still seated inside her body. Wanting to feel every sensation, Lynn slid her new tongue ring along her upper lip, imagined she was licking Mark instead of her own flesh. Pressure built inside her, everywhere he touched her, so strong she almost cried out. Then it burst, a shimmering ball of ecstasy that enfolded her, and him, in an almost unbearable excess of sensation, an orgasm like none she'd experienced before.

Chapter Three

ꝏ

A few days later Mark made his way to Club Rio Brava, eager to learn everything he could about the BDSM lifestyle. It amazed him how Lynn, after years of vanilla loving, had decided she wanted to be his sex slave again. When he pulled off the outer loop west of San Antonio, he stopped to get his bearings. Unfamiliar with the area around Riomedina, he stopped and gave his GPS system the address Eli had thoughtfully provided.

Dense shrubs and red-and-gold leaves falling from towering trees reminded him of the ranch where Lynn had grown up, specifically that spot down by the creek where they'd often picnicked under the shade of a huge old cottonwood while their horses drank their fill from fast-flowing water. Here, though, there were more houses, small ranchettes someone had carved out of a larger holding. It was peaceful out here, quiet but for the muted sound of a lazy river in the distance.

"Turn right into the next driveway," said the mechanical, pseudo-sexy voice inside the GPS. When Mark did, he saw it. A large, rustic-looking building that made him think about barbecue and Texas hoedowns sat at the end of a well-kept blacktop road, behind a parking lot that was closer to empty than full. Good. The fewer curious eyes who witnessed his visit to Club Rio Brava, the better. Sliding into a parking spot up front between a full-size SUV and a monster pickup, he checked to make sure he had his invitation and headed for the front porch.

He took a deep breath and rang the doorbell.

"May I have your invitation, sir?"

Mark handed it over, feeling foolish to be stared down by a dark-haired woman dressed in something black and clinging. In those stripper heels, she towered over him. Damn intimidating, he thought, not used to seeing many women who towered over his six-two frame, no matter what kind of shoes they had on. He shot a smile her way. No need to broadcast his case of nerves.

His hostess didn't look like anybody who'd submit to a man. Ever. Mark couldn't help noticing the silver-handled whip tucked into the snug belt around her waist, or the blood-red polish on her talon-like nails. "Is it in order?" he asked when she scrutinized what he couldn't help thinking of as his ticket to debauchery.

"Of course. Come on in. Any friend of Eli's is a friend of ours."

Mark stepped inside the dungeon. Damn, it would probably cost him at least two big surgery fees to join, from the polished look of mostly new equipment in here. Not to mention opulent wall hangings and what looked like genuine Turkish rugs. Smells of woodsy incense mingled with that of sex and candle wax. Amazed, he looked around, trying to school his expression to one of bored acceptance until his hostess ushered him to a mirror of one-way glass from which he had an excellent view of the large, well-appointed torture chamber they'd just walked through. "Sorry there are so few members using the club right now. Business picks up nights and weekends."

Omigod, some members apparently had sex in here, right in front of God and everybody. That shocked hell out of him, yet he found the idea strangely arousing. Still, with Lynn… "You do have private rooms, don't you?" Damn if he could imagine himself performing for an audience, baring his imperfect body to a bunch of strangers or letting his wife be ogled while they played.

"Yes, we do. But your identity will remain secure wherever you go in this house. Once you leave the dressing rooms you will be masked," his hostess commented. "It's a condition of entrance to the common halls and public torture chambers." She must have noticed him staring at a masked Dom fucking the ass of a trussed-up but very orgasmic-sounding sub whose face was also obscured. Her hood, in fact, covered her entire face except the tip of her nose and her scarlet-tinted lips. Yeah, Mark thought, a mask in this place would definitely be a must.

After all, it would do no good for the reputation he'd worked so hard to earn, being caught in here, where he'd managed to identify at least half-a-dozen laws being violated. He had no doubt a cop or a lawyer would have been able to spot more.

What the fuck had Lynn gotten them into? Yeah, the idea of making her come six ways from Sunday turned him hard as stone. What red-blooded guy wouldn't like to have his woman become a total slave to his desires? Although he hadn't expected his own reactions, he'd soon realized he liked those games. Tying her up, refusing to let her go until they were both worn out from all the sex, kept Mark's mind on sex more than it had been in…fuck, forever.

"Here's the toy store," his hostess said. "Would you like some time to yourself, to shop for your slave?"

It bothered him when the woman referred to Lynn as a slave. Though she wanted to become one, at least in a sexual sense, Mark couldn't help considering them equals. He loathed men who used their greater strength to force their wills on women—unless, as he'd learned when he brought home that flogger, a little pain could give the woman pleasure. "No, thank you." Then they caught his eye. A pair of handcuffs, metal and very real looking but for the fact they were shiny scarlet-colored instead of chrome. "I'll take those," he amended. "She'll like them."

"Surely. You know, you seem reluctant. May I guess it's your partner who wants to get involved in the BDSM scene?"

"Not entirely." Was he so obviously ill at ease? "A couple of our friends put the idea into our heads that we both needed breaks, her from making decisions—she has to do it all the time at home because my work schedule's a real bitch—and me from continuing being a workaholic until I fell over dead. So now I'm supposed to turn myself into a full-fledged Dom and make my wife my bedroom slave."

Mark didn't know why the words were just spilling out of his mouth. But then again, patients opened up to him because he was a doctor, supposedly knowledgeable about their needs. It seemed logical in a way that he'd talk with this staff member like patients did with him, seeking guidance and reassurance.

Seeing people fucking and sucking right in front of everyone in the torture chamber as well as whoever might be watching from behind the one-way windows reluctantly fascinated him. He and Lynn hadn't played publicly in those early years, but they'd certainly fantasized enough about it before she got unexpectedly pregnant with their older daughter. Here was the reality facing him, and he wasn't sure if that made him eager or anxious.

A bald sub with a snake tattooed literally from head to foot was displayed on a St. Andrew's Cross while three Doms took turns fucking all her orifices. Another Dom across the room was busy dripping melted wax over a male submissive's exposed penis. Those sights alone almost sent Mark running for the door. "What the hell?"

"That's Snake Woman. She's a bit over the top," said his guide. "As for the two guys, the Dom there is into wax torture. Look, he's molding the stuff onto the sub's cock like it's a condom. Different strokes…"

Watching Snake Woman and her Doms was getting Mark hot, making him want to join in the purely carnal acts, to command the actions of a masked sub, mete out whatever pleasure-pain it took for her to come. He felt guilty as hell when his arousal grew obvious, but he'd learned some time ago that his cock had a mind of its own. This place turned him on. Blood flowed to his cock when he glanced through the one-way glass again and saw a sub giving head to one Dom while another one fucked her. "I don't want to share my wife like that," he said, protesting his own arousal more than the unspoken suggestion of a ménage.

"That's strictly up to you as her Master. Some of our members are into that scene. Some aren't. The member who recommended you used to thrive on threesomes. Not lately, though, since he fell in love and married his sub. Commitment tends to lead to monogamous relationships between Masters and slaves, just as it does in vanilla relationships."

That made sense. "You're certain members' anonymity is assured?" The hospital administrators wouldn't like hearing that he was playing in the BDSM club, any more than Lynn's brother would enjoy finding out that his proper older sister was getting her jollies as a closet sub.

"The club is very private. You pick your name, and once you walk through that door into the dungeon in your mask, that's your only identity. It's the same for your slave. She is your wife, isn't she?"

"Yes." Moments later, having signed up and chosen Master M as his club name, Mark put on a lace-on leather half-mask that he hoped would protect his identity. Gathering his courage, he donned it and ventured for the first time into the world of hardcore BDSM.

For the first few minutes he felt ill at ease in the chamber, fully dressed while most of the participants were naked or decked out in various provocative pieces of leather. Arousal soon wiped out his discomfort, though, when a gruff-voiced Master handed his hooded slave a new dildo still in its packaging and ordered her to see to the pleasure of Master M.

It embarrassed the hell out of him, and he felt guilty as hell even though Lynn had encouraged him to play, but there was something about standing there in the corner of the dungeon with his pants bunched around his ankles, a cool breeze playing on the lower part of his face and his naked ass.

Something erotic about watching a strange woman's black-shrouded head bobbing up and down on his exposed cock, feeling her fingers brush his sac while she worked the dildo up his ass. It bothered him that, after the initial pain subsided, he actually liked the stretching sensation as the plug stretched his anal passage.

Oh God. She was sucking the come out of him, swallowing his cock while she ass-fucked him with the dildo and lightly squeezed his balls. His qualms forgotten, he clasped her head in his hands, forced her to deep-throat him when he shot his load.

"Thank you, Master M, and welcome to Club Rio Brava," she murmured after licking the last of his come off his cock. Then she turned back to her Master, her head bowed. "Would you like for me to service you now?"

Her Master shrugged, apparently unconcerned that his slave had just gotten a stranger off. "Go over and position yourself on that fucking swing. Master M, I echo my slave's welcome. Come anytime," he said, chuckling as he donned a condom and rammed his impressive, pierced cock up his slave's puckered asshole. His cleanly shaved ball sac bounced against her plump pink labia with every stroke. Being hairless, the way Mark had noticed both of them were, had to enhance the sensations of sex.

Before he left, Mark spent another hour watching, and another wad of money, buying trappings of the lifestyle he was pretty sure now he and Lynn were going to enjoy. He could hardly wait to see her in the stretchy black cat suit with cutouts for her nipples and pussy, swaying on the six-inch heels he'd bought. Or the red corset and black thigh-high stockings that would leave her breasts and cunt completely bare.

When he started looking at club attire for himself, he wondered what she'd like best. Something simple, like this pair of skintight black leather pants. They'd keep his bad leg out of sight while exposing his crotch. Yeah, Lynn would like them, a lot. It didn't matter, because she could always pick him out something else, so long as it covered up a fair amount of him below the waist. Thinking she'd get a kick out of seeing him in a cock harness like the one he'd noticed one of the Doms wearing earlier, he tossed one in his cart. Like a jock strap except that it had a round hole for a cock and balls to be squeezed through, one just like it had seemed to draw subs' attention to the buff Dom who'd had one on.

Maybe he'd wear it with the pants, which let everything hang out, or at home where only Lynn could see…

A collar. He needed to buy her a collar. In a glass case he found a large selection, from ten-dollar choker chains to one thick gold collar with its own gold-linked leash that sold for several thousand dollars. After perusing them a long time, he picked out a black leather choker about an inch wide that had a matching leash attached to a brass hasp at the front.

When he checked out, the might-as-well-be-naked sub at the counter showed him how to work the lock on the clasp. "That way you can decide if she can take it off, because you keep the key," she said with a conspiratorial wink. "It's actually metal, covered with the leather. That way, it's always around your slave's neck unless you take it off. Snake Woman's new Master makes her wear hers all the time."

Mark figured Lynn wouldn't want to wear it except here at the club or in their bedroom, but he had no doubt the member called Snake Woman didn't mind being marked 24/7 as a sex slave. After all, her bald head and the snake tattoo that began on her forehead and coiled around her body pretty much gave anybody who looked the idea that she liked kink and belonged to somebody who liked it even more. "Thanks. I imagine I'll see you around."

On the way out, Mark made appointments for himself and Lynn at the club's spa. He needed a haircut, and he wanted to get them both shaved down from neck to foot. That thought, of both of them totally smooth, skin to skin with no hair in the way, was getting him rock-hard again as he packed most of his new toys in his new locker at the club. Kids or no kids, though, he had to take the scarlet handcuffs home. A present for Lynn, a hell of a lot cheaper than diamonds and gold but a lot more potentially pleasurable.

* * * * *

"Turn the door lock and give me your hands," Mark said that night after they'd tucked the kids in bed and retired to their bedroom.

Lynn stared down at the cold metal in her cupped hands. A pair of scarlet handcuffs and an elaborate-looking key. "Why?"

"The key's your Club Rio Brava present, a day early. The cuffs are your signal that I'm ready to become your Master. Tomorrow I want you to get Maria to stay the night. We're going out to play—as Master and slave."

He'd done it. He'd really gone and joined the dungeon Maggie had told her was such a sexual turn-on. Her pussy already wet at the prospect, Lynn set the key on the bedside table and handed him back the handcuffs. "Want to use them now?"

"Oh yeah." With one deft motion, Mark cuffed her hands behind her back then dropped to his knees. "Now I'm about to make you feel good. Really good."

"Oooh, that feels so delicious. Don't stop." His tongue felt like hot wet velvet on her clit, lapping and drawing the sensitive little bud between his teeth. She strained at her bonds, wanting to bury her fingers in his dark, soft hair and hold him there, coax him to tongue-fuck her until she came. But she couldn't. She was helpless to his sexual onslaught. "I love it," she gasped as the first waves of a long-awaited climax rippled through her body. "Love you."

When he got up, pulled her onto the bed and positioned her on her knees at its center, she knew it wasn't over. His big, beautiful cock was rigid, his sac drawn tight against his body.

A creamy drop of lubrication glistened at its tip. "I love your cock, you know," she murmured when he turned her and unfastened the cuffs, only to restrain her hands again after having her lie face down on the bed, ass in the air. If only he'd pronounce her own tongue healed so she could use the tongue ring to drive him wild…

"And I love your pussy." He slapped her smartly on the ass. "I'm thinking we'll celebrate your tongue being healed up tomorrow if you're a good slave. Now I'm about to show you how much that hairy little muff means to me, before it's gone."

His whispered order started another twinge of excitement in her belly. Obviously he was going to have her shaved. She imagined him doing it himself while others watched, the way she'd seen in a short video on the Internet. But that wouldn't be Mark's style. "I can't wait." Spreading her legs farther apart, she wiggled her ass in invitation. The feel of him rubbing his cock along her slit, the heady smell of sex that filled the air, the knowledge that he had taken her and marked her his, heightened her anticipation. When he plunged into her cunt from the unfamiliar angle, she yelped at the pressure of his thick cock pressing on her G-spot. Not that it hurt. The sudden claiming sent sensation bursting through her, not just there but all over.

"Quiet or you'll wake the kids. Tomorrow you can yell all you want," he cautioned, grasping her nipples and tugging at them while pounding into her from behind. Slowly at first, a wet, tight journey in…a sloshing, terribly sexy sound when he withdrew and plunged back in. His balls slammed into her clit. "Come for me now."

That whispered order opened a floodgate of sensation, as though her body had accepted his mastery and was determined to accede to his every demand. She bit down on the pillow, determined not to make a sound. As she came, she clamped down on his cock with her vaginal muscles, loving the congested feeling in her pussy, the sense of being filled, the hot spurts of his climax against her womb and the sharp bite of his teeth on the back of her neck enhancing hers.

He collapsed on top of her, his weight welcome…reassuring. She felt him fiddle with the cuffs, felt it when they gave way, heard them clank when they hit the bedside table. He rolled to his side, taking her with him, holding her close. The sounds of them breathing, the shared warmth of their naked bodies…the thump-thump of his heartbeat against her back reminded her this was Mark. Her husband, father of their four children. The familiar man she'd loved forever.

Yet a new, exciting lover, too. A classic Master in the making.

* * * * *

Mark hadn't relished spending most of his first day off in months having his body hair ripped out, but it actually felt good when the aesthetician spread warm wax over his arms, legs and back, and the sting when she ripped off the strips and tweezed away a few stray hairs wasn't nearly as bad as he'd imagined. He couldn't say that about his chest hair or pubes, though. It took several painful yanks to get rid of the denser mat of hair growth there.

The sensation of total smoothness was worth it, though, as the Club Rio Brava hostess had assured him it would be. Showering off the wax residue, he stroked his hairless crotch, intrigued by how much being bare intensified sensations. He liked it even more when another technician laid him out on a massage table and rubbed down every inch of him, privates included, with mildly fragrant warmed coconut oil. He noticed she paid special attention to his scars, massaging them gently.

"This must have hurt terribly."

It had, not only physically but emotionally. He'd been sixteen, anxious to expose his developing muscles and athletic prowess on a surfboard, until that horrible day when he ran into an oncoming car coming home. They'd had to get him out of his dad's old Ford with the Jaws of Life, and he'd spent the next six months in the hospital or rehabilitation facilities. "It was a long time ago. I'm okay there now." He was, physically, other than that standing in one place for a long time still made him limp and have occasional bouts of shooting pain as a result of nerves that hadn't completely healed. Emotionally, his marriage to Lynn and his fame as a surgeon had pretty much wiped out the sense of inadequacy that had plagued him.

She made one more pass over his denuded crotch. "Mmmm. Nice package. Your slave will appreciate our handiwork when she goes down on you. I'm finished with you now. Lie back and rest until it's time for the barber."

Mark had never given a lot of thought to his package as she called it. It was there, it worked and he'd never been one to fix something that wasn't broken. It amazed him when he glanced down at himself that his cock looked appreciably bigger without that thatch of pubic hair. His bare balls looked soft, almost satiny, and his whole body glowed from the oil. He'd known Lynn would like him smooth down there, but he hadn't realized before he did it that he'd get turned on, too, by the clean way he looked now.

Idly he stroked his slick, smooth penis, enjoying the sounds of running water and the mild, almost undetectable smell of coconuts. The thin sheets on the massage table caressed his newly hairless body. Soon the aroma of coconuts took Mark out of the present, to a beach with swaying coconut palms and bikini-clad beauties showering him with attention. His own personal fantasy, one he'd never dared act out because of his scars. Maybe someday he would. After all, he was a Master. And the main bikini babe would be his wife, front and center, on her knees applying the oil to his eager cock.

"Master M. Time for your haircut." A booming voice brought Mark out of the pleasant dream he'd been enjoying.

Sitting up, he wrapped one of the sheets around his midsection.

"Come with me."

Mark took a seat in a barbershop chair and sized up his barber in the mirror.

He was a big, buff man whose closely shaven head had a polished sheen. "I see you had a body wax job. Want to go naked here, too?" he asked as he was brushing out Mark's damp curls.

"I don't think so." From his observations yesterday, Mark surmised that shaved was the hairstyle of choice for many of the male Dominants and a lot of female subs. But the chrome-dome look wasn't for him, not as long as his dark hair hadn't started to recede or get prematurely gray. "How about something shorter, like that?" he asked, gesturing toward a picture of a man with a short but conventional cut—longish on top, with a fade that was pretty extreme, at least for him. He figured the shaved hairline would give him a taste of the purported sensual benefits of being bald, but none of the stigma some in the vanilla world might attach to a shaved head. Not even Eli shaved his head, and he certainly was hard-core.

"If you want. Sooner or later you're gonna go all the way, though."

Mark laughed. "Maybe. Not today, though. Could you get on with it? My slave should be ready for me soon." He hadn't made a haircut appointment for Lynn, knowing she had her own favorite stylist at an upscale salon not far from home.

"Sure." The barber picked up a pair of clippers and dug into Mark's tangle of wet curls. Quicker than his stylist had ever done it, his hair was tamed and he was ready to go. For a long time he sat in the members' lounge, enjoying a coffee and the different textures of his shirt, jeans, boxers—even his soft cotton socks—against his naked skin. Different, but he liked the heightened sensations so much he might opt for laser removal later to avoid the hassle of frequent wax jobs.

Lynn would be through soon, he thought, imagining how erotic the most casual contact of skin on naked skin would feel. Idly, he stroked his thigh, found himself growing aroused as he imagined his sex slave running the tips of her fingernails all over his body, sliding her soft hands over his groin. He could hardly wait for her to experience the erotic brush of their completely hairless bodies when they made love.

* * * * *

Lynn sighed. How decadent could she be, taking a whole day to ready herself for her Master? In the two hours she'd been in the spa at Club Rio Brava, she'd been waxed neck to toe, massaged with fragrant coconut oil, cleansed internally, cunt and asshole, with warm, fragrant water that had something in it that made her incredibly aroused. Her technician was huge, at least six foot six with strong hands to work the kinks out of her muscles. What had surprised her was that he was totally hairless and clad in nothing but a sheer white G-string, a gold slave collar and thick silver nipple rings joined by a gold chain.

He reminded her of Mr. Clean, with his shaved, polished head and bright blue eyes. As he sorted through an assortment of jewel-toned glass bottles on a shelf, it struck Lynn that Mark would be in the adjoining spa, most likely being catered to by similarly attired women. Were they confining their services to the same sort of grooming she was enjoying?

The green monster caught her up for a minute before she lay back and relaxed. If her Master wanted to play with the help, she wouldn't object. Her goal was to make him happy, and if that was what it took…

She ogled her masseuse, found herself wondering how it would feel to cradle his head while he rubbed some of a musky, vaguely floral scent into her outer labia and breasts. "It's called Aphrodisia, for damn good reason. I promise, it will make your Master go wild for you," the masseuse told her with a grin. "I always say, apply it where it will do the most good."

He went back to kneading her thighs, his touch impersonal. Curious, she glanced at his crotch. Mark would have been heavily aroused by now if he'd been doing this to her.

"I'd be hard as stone if I were straight," he told her, never missing a beat with his talented hands. "I'm glad I'm not, because my Master would make me pay."

"Oh. I'm sorry, I didn't mean to be impolite." She sounded different to herself, knowing it was the tongue ring that had altered the cadence of her speech.

"No offense taken. You're obviously new to the club scene. Pretty soon you'll learn not to get shocked at all you see. We celebrate every sort of sexual pleasure, every sensual adventure through pain." He thumped her one more time then stood back and gave her the once-over. "I'm finished here. Your Master will certainly be pleased."

Lynn stood in front of a floor-to-ceiling mirror. The reflection staring back at her wasn't a forty-year-old surgeon's wife and mother of his children. They'd transformed her into this ravishing, sensual creature with a hairless body gleaming from the oil, surrounded by the arousing scent her gay masseuse had rubbed into all her erogenous zones. Instead of being loose around her shoulders, her hair had been pulled back severely and secured on top of her head. She'd protested the style would age her, but she was wrong. It drew attention to her features. Maybe even pulled her facial skin a little tauter than it had been.

Her makeup was minimal except for her lips and around her eyes. "Your Master told us they'll be your only features that anyone but him will see," the artist told her when he applied heavy eyeliner, shimmery silver eye shadow and glossy scarlet lip color that matched her nails. "I like your tongue ring."

"Thank you." She'd been practicing talking without opening her mouth or sticking her tongue out and thought she'd learned pretty well. Her distress at being discovered faded when she realized her makeup artist had insisted she open her lips so he could apply the color.

Was Mark finished yet? Lynn slipped on a see-through robe—no point in dressing when she was only going to change into whatever he'd bought her to wear in the club. Eager, her pussy juices already dampening her crotch, she picked up her phone and called him, and when she stepped out of the spa, he was there, a shopping bag in hand. His mouth dropped open when he looked at her. "Hurry. Go to the women's dressing room and put these on while I change. An attendant will bring you to me. I can hardly wait to play with you." He dropped a hard kiss on her lips, his hands straying to give her breasts a light squeeze. "Hurry. I've been waiting an hour for you, but it's worth it. You look ravishing, my darling slave."

Chapter Four

ꟗ

Lynn had never felt so sexy. So aware of her own femininity. A scarlet velvet corset cinched in her waist, showcased bare breasts and rouged nipples to be offered up for her Master's pleasure. Though she wasn't sure about walking in the black stiletto heels and black sheer thigh-high stockings, she had to admit they and the tightly cinched corset framed her pale, shaved pussy nicely. Her clit poked out, swollen with erotic anticipation, vulnerable to the onslaught of her Master's teeth and tongue.

"Master M wishes you gagged and masked for your scene." The dressing room attendant who'd laced her into the corset held up a ball gag and a thin, scarlet silk hood that looked almost transparent. "Open your mouth and stick out your tongue." When Lynn did, she felt a cock-shaped gag slide past her lips, heard the click of metal buckles that held it in place. "Good slave. Now bend your head and I'll lace you into the mask."

Silky, cool fabric molded to her face, obscured it but for two slits for her nostrils and a hole that left her mouth free. Light showed vaguely through the material, not enough that she could actually see, yet enough to cast the room in a rosy glow and keep her from losing her equilibrium.

The attendant finished lacing on the mask then stood back. "There. It's a perfect fit," she said as she made one final adjustment to the fabric beneath Lynn's chin.

In one way Lynn liked the sense of isolation, but a frisson of fear shot through her when she realized she'd surrendered her powers of speech and sight. Had Mark gone too far? It didn't matter. She trusted him. The gag felt like a cock, not

Mark's because it was too small when she explored it with her tongue. She found having it secured in her mouth erotic, almost as though its purpose was to stretch her to take his huge, rigid cock and suck him off the way she hadn't done during the week since he'd pierced her. The strap around her head secured the gag, and she found the pressure of it against her occipital bone surprisingly arousing.

Deprived of sight and speech, she concentrated on the sounds of soft, sensual music—reeds and woodwinds with a rhythmic background of muted percussion instruments. The music surrounded her, haunting and provocative, incredibly erotic though subtle, as though it waited to burst out into full harmony at a Master's order. It carried her, transformed her, took her from the remnants of her routine everyday world into a place in her head. That place was vaguely frightening, intensely arousing, charged with sensual excitement.

"I will take you to the private dungeon your Master has chosen. Others will see you as we go through the hallway, but after that you will be alone with him."

Lynn hesitated when the woman gripped her elbow. Her breasts were bare. The nipples tingled, as much from anticipation as from the aphrodisiac the masseuse had painted there. She imagined they looked hard as jewels—rouged jewels. Her bare ass got goose bumps in the cool air, reminding her she was naked below the corset and above the stockings. Totally naked, stripped to the skin for her Master's pleasure.

She wanted this, needed it. She'd practically begged Mark to join the BDSM club and bring her here. So why did every heavy footfall that punctuated the sharp clatter of her six-inch heels on the tiled floor make her want to run and hide? She held her head high, tried not to imagine strangers ogling her slick, bare pussy.

What in God's name had she been thinking?

And why was she nearly panicking when every cell in her body told her she wanted this? Wanted to please her Master beyond the confines of their bedroom walls, no holds barred.

Maggie did this, too. Surely she did, though she hadn't mentioned the exhibitionism Lynn was learning quickly made up a huge part of the foreplay here…the anticipation…the fear that had her in its grip. It didn't help that she couldn't see or speak. She jumped when she heard a door open then close again with a solid *thunk*. A very male-sounding intake of breath told her she was no longer alone with her attendant.

* * * * *

His woman. This delectable creature was his wife. His slave to do with as he saw fit, do anything to assure her pleasure. Mark grasped her waist, so tiny laced as it was into the corset that he could span it with both hands. The fabric felt smooth, sensual under his fingers as he lifted her, nipped at one rouged, swollen nipple and then the other. Lynn tasted like coconuts and something more, a strange yet not unpleasant aroma that heated his lips and tongue. He'd never gotten so hard, so fast.

When he lowered her, he did it slowly, savoring every brush of her incredibly soft, warm skin against his own. If he'd known not having body hair would feel so damn good he'd have gotten rid of his years ago. And hers. Her heartbeat was rapid, a little ragged, as if she was afraid even though her arousal was evident by the unique aura he'd known for so long. Now he found another element, the musky, erotic scent of coconuts and something much stronger, the stuff called Aphrodisia he'd chosen at the spa for them to use on Lynn. When he slipped a hand between her legs and palmed her damp, swollen labia he had all the evidence he needed that she was as hot as he was. Backing her up against the fucking swing in the center of the chamber, he positioned her then lifted her up.

"This is a fucking swing. Relax, baby, and I'll get you into it so I can take care of this needy cunt of yours." He turned the volume down on the music, savored the silence, her little moan when he stroked her naked pussy then squeezed her swollen clit. "I'm going to strap you in now."

He'd never been so hard. His cock felt like it would burst. Checking twice to be sure the straps would hold, he secured her face down on the swing. God but she looked hot, her rounded buttocks flaring below the tight corset, her pussy pale and naked between the corset and those dusky thigh-high stockings. He could hardly wait to eat her…fuck her…ream her tight little ass with his aching cock.

"My God but you're fucking beautiful." He spread her legs and stepped between them, securing her ankles and thighs to the swing as shown in the pictures the dungeon master had provided. Rubbing his cock along her slick, swollen slit was pure pleasure, but restraining himself from plunging it into her creamy cunt was agony.

She moaned behind the gag, as though she wanted more. Wanted him.

Instead he stepped back and worked a large gel vibrator into her cunt. Its slow, persistent vibrations seemed to enhance the sounds of music…the cadence of his breathing and hers, deliberate, a little strained. God but Lynn wanted to come. The cool air on her pussy lips should have calmed her, but instead it made her hotter. She sensed that her guide had left and that it was only her Master who was looking at her.

Seeing the submissive she'd become, not the beloved wife and mother she'd always been. Her cunt clenched, its juices flooding her slit. A drop slid down her thigh, stopped sliding when it reached the top of her stocking.

"Welcome to my dungeon, my precious slave." His voice, mellow, distinctive…seductive now, was unmistakable. She'd recognize it anywhere.

His breath tickled the back of her neck when he bent and licked her there. He wore a mask, too, she could tell from its cool smoothness above the prickly rasp of his late-afternoon stubble. The distinctive smell of new leather filled her nostrils, invaded her mask. It would be black, she imagined, picturing him in her mind in the leather chaps and vest she remembered from a sex-toy website.

He drew one of her hands to his clean-shaven groin. "Oh yeah. That feels so fucking good. Go ahead. I think I'll make it your job to keep me smooth. Yourself, too." When she obeyed, curling her fingers around his fully aroused shaft, he groaned. She fondled his satin-smooth sac, cupped it, loved feeling his heavy balls shift against her fingers. Her mouth watered to take him in her mouth, feel his hard, satiny cock that felt like satin over steel. If only he'd release her mouth, let her run her tongue over him…

She groaned.

"You like this, don't you? Like being my sex slave."

"Mmmff." She couldn't suck him so she sucked the gag, pretending she had him in her mouth, her cunt. She tested her restraints, found them as strong as she'd imagined. Helpless. She was helpless to his every whim, and knowing that got her even more desperate for him to fill her.

From the way she arched her back, from her fast, shallow breathing, from the lubrication that gushed from around the vibrator in her cunt and made her swollen pussy glisten, he knew it. She loved it. Loved having him possess her this way.

The knowledge gave him a heady feeling. She was wetter, hotter than he'd ever seen her. He pinched her clit, a rock-hard nub silently begging for his attention. The swollen folds of her smooth, wet pussy seemed to clutch his fingers when he turned up the speed of the vibrator.

"These need some attention, don't they?" With his free hand he caressed her breasts, pinching and tugging at the taut nipples. "Let's try these." He clamped first one nipple and then the other, watching with satisfaction when she started to squirm as much as her bonds would allow.

"Your ass is twitching, baby." Beckoned by her plump, pink ass cheeks, he bent and bit her there. "Tonight I'm going to take this hole, and you'll love it."

She mumbled something—probably an entreaty, but whether to proceed or stop he couldn't tell. "I'm putting on a condom…lubricating it…lubricating you. God but you're tight here. I've been thinking about fucking you in the ass ever since you showed me that butt plug." Slowly, he rotated his sheathed cock head around her puckered, well-lubricated anus. "Feel me? I'm about to burst, I want you so much."

The vibrator in her cunt buzzed as he stepped back and inserted first one, then two lubed fingers beyond her anal sphincter, a sucking sound punctuating the silence when he withdrew them.

"Steady now. I'm going to fuck you. Relax for me. Your pretty ass is already warm and damp."

She squirmed against him, almost as if she was begging him to proceed. He pressed against her anus, slowly. Deliberately. No way did he want to hurt her, but this was something she wanted, even if she hadn't put her desire into words. When her anal sphincter began to give, he worked his way in, taking her fully, more fully than he'd ever done before.

This wasn't about kinky sex. It wasn't about experimenting. The hood and gag, the restraints, the new sensations of smooth skin against skin, they were all props. The BDSM lifestyle whether in Club Rio Brava or in their bedroom at home was all about her submission, his control. About what he could do to pleasure her, keep their relationship fresh after it had almost fizzled. The toys were a small part of it, Mark realized. "Shake your head if you want me to stop."

Those nipple clamps had to be hurting her. He made a mental note to pierce her nipples so she could enjoy the stimulation without pain. His cock stretched her anus so tight that it hurt him, too. He slowed his thrusts, cradled her firm breasts in each hand, moving his fingers around the base of each nipple to ease the pain. "Relax, baby. This may hurt a little, but the pleasure will make up for it." The gentle way he moved on her reminded him of their first time together, when she'd cried out when he ruptured her hymen. "Easy now. This must feel a lot like losing your virginity all over again."

Hardly. That hadn't hurt like this, or else time had dulled her memory. Still, she didn't want him to stop. Gradually the splitting sensation subsided. She felt full. Highly aroused, between his slow fucking of her ass and the vibrator humming in her cunt. He had her completely vulnerable, controlled, helpless to resist the spasms that started in deep inside her and radiated outward. She loved the feel of his taut abs rippling against her back, the sound of his labored breathing. Familiar smells of sex filtered through her mask, and when she concentrated on all the feelings he evoked in her, the pain began to subside, replaced by…

A feeling of being totally possessed, swept away with every slow, deep thrust into her ass, the slick and very erotic sensations where his sweat and hers mingled with coconut oil and made the contact feel weightless. She'd never felt sexier, more loved. Or so totally free to relinquish control, take all her Master offered and enjoy it without guilt or restraint.

She floated in a world of his creation, a world where the only thing that counted was touching him, consuming him the way he'd consumed her. As if he knew she'd reached a flash point, he thrust harder, faster, tugging at her clamped nipples. She couldn't hold back the flood of ecstasy that rolled over her like waves breaking on an ocean, his own climax heightening hers. She wondered after he'd released the nipple clamps how even that enhanced her pleasure and created a final burst of erotic sensation along with the brief, blinding pain.

Long moments later he pulled out of her and removed the vibrator, then bent and nipped her left ass cheek, more a caress than a punishment. "I'm discarding the condom now. Did you know, last night when I joined the club I saw two Doms pleasuring one sub. Would you like that?"

No! Although she found the thought strangely arousing as well as shocking.

"Think about it. Next time we'll try the public room. Maybe… Right now I'm about to stand you against the wall and fuck your hot, wet cunt." He unfastened the straps that held her to the swing, but her liberation was short-lived, for he stood her up, her back against a velvet padded wall, and clamped some sort of metal devices around her waist and thighs. She hung, suspended off the ground, legs spread. "This time I'm leaving your hands free."

Scorched by his body heat when he approached, she reached out to touch him. His heart thumped in his smooth, muscular chest, its beat accelerating, seemingly in time with the crescendo of percussion flowing into her ears. His small nipples hardened instantly when she brushed her knuckles across them. "Mmmf." If only he'd remove the gag, let her say all she was thinking.

He stepped between her legs, his cock obviously erect again as he slid its broad, satiny head easily into her weeping cunt. "You're still hot, too. I like that." For a moment she'd thought he'd take her ass again. But he didn't, not that she would have been distressed if he had, now that he'd given her the profound pleasure of total surrender, serving her Master's every need.

He didn't, though. In one decisive thrust he filled her cunt. His cleanly depilated scrotum rested in her wet slit, the heavy testicles shifting deliciously against her as he pumped slowly in and out. Unable to move with him, she tightened her inner muscles, milking him, loving the way he sank into her so deep, the slick slide of his cock when he pulled back then thrust deeper still.

When she slid her hands up his sweaty back and ground her exposed breasts into his chest, he moaned. This total smoothness was so erotic, so sensually arousing she hoped he'd want to keep them both that way. Oh God. She needed for him to take her breasts, suckle her.

Apparently he heard her silent plea because he dipped his head, took an aching nipple in his mouth. She cupped the back of his head just below his hairline, realized it was as smooth as his body. She found the sweet spot that always drove him crazy, stroked it, so different yet as arousing for her as ever. More so, for this wasn't the Mark of her everyday life but the Master of her wildest fantasies.

She couldn't hold back any longer, had to take the release that built with every thrust. The slapping sound of his balls on her bare pussy, the slide of his cock in her wet, swollen cunt…the feel of his bare skin abrading her own, satin over steely muscles… God, she'd never come quite this hard before.

"Fuck. I'm coming. Oh God yes. Squeeze my cock. That's my good slave." His hot seed spurted into her womb, setting off more waves of ecstasy that took her breath away.

The aftermath was as sweet as their lovemaking was intense. While Lynn trembled from the force of her climax, Mark held her in his arms, whispered his jumbled thoughts of satisfaction, sex and a love deeper and more abiding than he'd expressed for years. When they got up he locked her brand-new collar around her neck and snapped the leash in place.

Lynn liked the feeling of the thick band of leather, the reminder on the leash dangling from it that she was Master M's slave, his to do with her as he chose. She liked it a lot.

* * * * *

As she walked out of the dressing room much later, her hair slicked up on top of her head to display her Master's collar properly, she saw it for what it was, a token of possession and eternal love. A promise that he'd protect her, love her with gentle Domination as long as they lived. She was happier having this simple collar than she would have been if he'd bought her a diamond-studded necklace like many of her friends wore.

As she'd been instructed, Lynn took the leash in her hand, held her head high and walked to the exit door where she placed the end of the leash in her Master's beloved hand. She wouldn't wear it at home, of course, other than in the privacy of their bedroom. But she liked it. Liked wearing the symbol of her complete surrender.

"Welcome to the world of BDSM, my darling slave."

Chapter Five

The following spring

ꟗ

Mark's forty-sixth birthday was tonight, and Lynn checked out the decorations for his surprise party she was hosting at home for his colleagues and a few family friends. Except for a very few, they were all as vanilla as could be.

What would they think if they knew? As she bent over to arrange a flower in the centerpiece, she brushed her pierced nipples with one forearm, loving the feel of the dangling jewelry that swayed when she moved and kept her in a barely controlled state of arousal while she looked to all the world like a typical suburban wife and mom. They made her so—so aware of her body, of the sensations that coursed through her. She wished she'd taken the plunge years earlier.

What had pleased her the most was Mark's new piercing—a Prince Albert he got during the holidays after he started feeling "undressed" beside most of the Doms who played in the public torture chamber at the club. The titanium curved barbell made his big cock feel even better, and she loved the look of the thick jewelry that went into his flesh through the opening for his urethra and came out on the bottom side of the thick, purplish cock head.

Who'd have believed Mark, her mild-mannered and considerate husband for sixteen years now, a surgeon almost as renowned as his senior partner, had fully embraced the BDSM lifestyle they'd once only wanted to experiment with? Both of them now loved taking sexual pleasure to the limit, experiencing acts they'd once thought were done only behind locked bedroom doors, not in private clubs where membership was as prestigious as the best country club in town.

Mark had even taken the plunge and embraced total hairlessness a month or so ago. She loved how his clean-shaven scalp felt against her fingertips, liked the rasp of two days' hair growth against the razor when she re-shaved him and the slick smoothness of his scalp when she massaged it with coconut oil. It had surprised her to see he was just as handsome and sexy bald as he'd been with his wavy dark brown hair. Maybe someday she'd take the plunge, too, at least for long enough to experience feelings Mark had quickly embraced. Even though she hadn't quite talked herself into it, she'd invested in two very good hand-tied wigs made of virgin human hair the color of her own and fitted to wear over a shaved or clipped head. One was in her locker at the club, the other in its case on an upper shelf in her closet here. If she got the urge, she'd be prepared. If he liked the tattoos she'd just gotten…well, maybe she'd follow her Master's bold example.

Tonight, after the main party, she and Mark would get together for the first time at the club with Eli, Maggie and two other couples Eli had invited, all of whom embraced the BDSM lifestyle. They'd have dinner here first, complete with a huge cheesecake made from Mark's mother's recipe. Then their vanilla friends would go home, and those very special guests would join them at Club Rio Brava. Lynn could barely wait. She hoped he'd like her present, the one she dared not show him in vanilla company.

* * * * *

"What is this present you won't tell me about?" Mark lifted Lynn's long silk caftan, found out quickly that was all she had on. "I can hardly wait to rub my five o'clock shadow against your silky pussy." He splayed his hand over her mound, tested her smoothness. "I didn't believe you could get any softer here, but you are." Keeping his hand on her, he turned his attention back to the road.

This was going to be the party to fulfill a Dom's kinkiest fantasies. One best held at Club Rio Brava, with only the four of their good friends who also happened to be into kinky sex. Eli and Maggie, along with Tom and Selina Latimer, had planned it. They'd wanted to invite Trace and Elle to join them, but Mark had vetoed that idea. Lynn loved her brother and knew he and Elle lived the BDSM lifestyle, too, but Mark figured there was no way she'd want her baby brother present in Club Rio Brava when she was stripped down and subbing for him. Maggie told him Eli had invited another couple neither he nor Lynn knew to fill in for the show they'd planned—apparently a scene that required six players.

* * * * *

When they got to the club, Mark went to the men's dressing room and Lynn to the one set aside for female subs. She stripped, braided her hair into a tight ponytail on top of her head and massaged Aphrodisia into her nipples. Dabbing more of the stuff on her fingertips, she rubbed it into the back of her neck where Mark liked to suck, and anointed her already swollen sex. Imagining what he'd do to her, she stood for a minute just savoring the heat and anticipation it sent coursing through her body.

Sometimes getting into her costume took a lot of cursing—or a lot of help. Tonight wasn't one of those nights. She'd opted to go naked but for her collar and leash, the stiletto heels and a leather half mask with holes for her eyes and one hole on top for her tightly braided blonde ponytail to fit through. It ended high on the back of her head, leaving her raised hairline bare, her mouth and chin free. Her only other decorations were the tattoos, one on her left ass cheek that said, "Property of Mark...Master M", on a placard bordered with a tiny, intricate pattern of red roses and leaves. The other, the one she hadn't been able to resist, was a closed pale-pink rosebud just above her natural hairline on the back of her neck. Its pastel green stem and leaves curved down her back until the stem disappeared into the crack of her ass. A pathway for her Master to follow, she'd thought while the tattoo artist worked his magic.

She hoped Mark would like the way she'd had to get the back of her neck shaved for the tattoo—and that he'd want to keep it smooth for a while so he could nip it and the rose to his heart's content. Reaching behind her, she realized that below the back of her tightly laced mask she was totally smooth—as smooth there as the rest of her body, now that she'd had laser treatments to take care of her body hair permanently. Her cunt clenched, needy and greedy for her Master's touch.

Like a good slave, she went down on all fours and crawled into the hallway, leaving the other women to finish getting ready for the show. Her job was to find her Master and blow his mind before the show started. When she crawled through the door of private chamber number nine, he was already there, and he took her breath away.

"Come here, slave." Lynn recognized his deep, soothing voice immediately, even though the leather mask he wore muted the words. When she rose at his command, she realized he was wearing not his usual leather crotchless pants but a G-string that framed his cock and balls but hid nothing. So, when no amount of protesting that he shouldn't worry about his scarred leg had worked, their embracing a hardcore BDSM lifestyle had. Lynn smiled, glad he'd finally realized what she'd known all along. With or without those marks of courage, Mark Blackstone was one hell of a man, a Master without equal, at least in her eyes.

When he stood and used the leash she'd placed in his hand to direct her head to his crotch, she went back down on her knees, cupped both hands around his swollen ball sac. "Service me tonight on my birthday," he said, tenderness in his voice as he lowered her head until his cock slipped into her open mouth. "I'm not hiding the scars anymore, from anybody. I'm no Texan aristocrat, no rancher. And I'm no longer a poor kid trying to prove I'm as rough and tough as any of my classmates, the way I was when I got stupid and nearly ripped off my leg."

"I'm glad, Master," she murmured against his hot, hard flesh as she used her tongue ring to make the barbell vibrate in his PA. "You're my Master. I worship every square inch of your gorgeous body, and that's what counts. If you look down at my back, you'll find your birthday presents."

His touch was almost reverent when he bent and traced the letters on her ass cheek with a finger. "No man could ask for a better gift." He lowered his head, nibbled at the tattoo then raised his head. "And what's this, my beautiful slave?" With his tongue he traced around the uppermost leaf on the stem then shifted her around so he had a good view of the pale pink rosebud, right up to where the tight petals disappeared under her mask. He touched her there where the tattoo artist had shaved off a little of her hair so he could trace and ink the rose. Breathing harshly, as if maintaining control was almost impossible, Mark seemed speechless. "Did you…" He grabbed her ponytail, gave it a tentative pull. "No, I can see you didn't."

If she had would it have made him happy? Angry? She had no clue. "Not yet, but if you want to see me as bald as you, feel free. You're my Master…my only Master. I'm sure it would feel as good to me as it does to you when I tidy up your scalp. After all, you're good to your slave. I'm certain you'd let me wear wigs in public so none of our vanilla friends would know." Lowering her head, she took him in her mouth again, sucked his cock while she rubbed her tongue ring up and down his shaft.

He caught her by her braid, drew her face up to his lips. "An arousing little secret between us, you think? What if I wanted you to go out in the main dungeon bald, put you in the stocks and make you suck me off so I could rub my come into your pretty scalp the way that Dom did to Snake Woman last weekend?"

"You are my Master. I do as you command."

God but he loved her. And it aroused him beyond belief to know she wanted them to sample every possible sensual, sexual pleasure. But now the show was about to start. Directing Lynn's mouth to his cock again, he sat back, eager to share with her what was going on to enhance their pleasure while he lightly rubbed the rose tattoo. His present, so much more valuable than the new gold and onyx studs and cufflinks she and the kids had given him at home.

"Eli's demonstrating how to use the cat on Selina. Looks as though she likes it, a lot. All the other women are doing what you're doing to me, only not nearly as effectively." His cock swelled against the back of her throat, distracting him when she swallowed his cock head and clamped her pretty lips around his shaft. "God, but that feels good. You give the best head..." Concentrating once more on the scene in front of them, he continued telling Lynn what she was missing. "I wouldn't dare use one of those on your beautiful ass, but I imagine you must know pretty well how to wield a whip, being brought up on the ranch and all. I bet Trace uses one on Elle. Now Tom's trying it. He looks pretty competent for a city boy.

"Would you like me to learn to do that, so I can flay your hide when you're naughty?" Mark lifted Lynn, guided her hips down on his lap, finding her hot, wet cunt and sliding his cock inside. "I think you would. My God but you feel good. You get off watching, don't you?" He lifted her then slammed her back down, hard. "Would my little slave like for me to tan her ass the way Tom's doing to Selina now?"

"If you wish. But I'd rather have you shave me, Master. That wouldn't hurt anything but my pride. And I wouldn't mind that because it would remind me I live to please you." When he slid his hands down her body, stopping to tug at her nipple rings and squeeze her breasts, she let out a moan.

Air swirled around them, redolent with the musky smells of sex. If he hadn't been concentrating on the way his own slave was caressing him with her strong inner muscles, he'd have wanted to join the fuckfest their friends were enjoying up on stage. In a circle, Eli was very carefully fucking Maggie's very pregnant pussy while Selina reamed his ass with a vibrating dildo. Tom had his cock up Selina's ass while a woman he didn't know used a dildo on her. Another man finished the circle by fucking the woman while the man bent over and finger-fucked Maggie's mouth. Soon they separated then resumed sucking and fucking, the slaves being controlled not by any device but by their masters' wills.

As each couple drifted off by themselves, Mark concentrated on his own slave, the sensual tattoo he imagined having embellished with another, smaller rose beside the original one, this one on his order, visible only to him and fellow members of Club Rio Brava… only while she kept her head clipped or shaved for his pleasure. Once he ordered her to grow out her hair, those tattoos would become their secrets. No one else's. He reached onto the floor, lifted a razor-sharp knife the club had apparently supplied as part of the preparations for his party. Before he could change his mind, he laid it between her mask and her tight braid.

"You're sure you want this, my love?" As much as it aroused him to imagine taking her hair, he wouldn't do it unless…

"Yes, Master. But only if it pleases you."

With one decisive slice he severed the braid and tucked it under the front of her collar.

His cock swelled even harder inside her pussy. Blood rushed to his groin so fast that he felt dizzy. His balls tightened. "I'll finish this at home," he said as he flooded Lynn with his seed. "You may come now, my darling slave."

That was an afterthought, because Mark had completely forgotten they'd been playing with having him control her orgasms. When he said it, though, she tightened her cunt around his still-spasming flesh and flooded them both with the sticky miracle of mating. Becoming not two but one.

The End

Also by Ann Jacobs

A Gift of Gold
A Mutual Favor
Another Love
Awakenings
Black Gold: Dallas Heat
Black Gold: Entrapped
Black Gold: Firestorm
Black Gold: Forever Enslaved
Black Gold: Love Slave
Colors of Love
Colors of Magic
D'Argent Honor 1: Vampire Justice
D'Argent Honor 2: Eternally His
D'Argent Honor 3: Eternal Surrender
D'Argent Honor 4: Eternal Victory
D'Argent Honor 5: Eternal Triangle
Dark Side of the Moon
Enchained (*anthology*)
Eye of the Storm
Gates of Hell
Haunted
Heart of the West: Hitched
Heart of the West: Lassoed
Heart of the West: Roped
Her Very Special Robot
Lawyers In Love: Bittersweet Homecoming
Lawyers In Love: Gettin' It On

Lawyers In Love: In His Own Defense

Lords of Pleasure: He Calls Her Jasmine

Love Magic

Out of Bounds

Tip of the Iceberg

Topaz Dream

Wrong Place, Wrong Time?

Zayed's Gift

About the Author

ꟹ

Ann Jacobs is a sucker for lusty Alpha heroes and happy endings, which makes Ellora's Cave an ideal publisher for her work. Romantica®, to her, is the perfect combination of sex, sensuality, deep emotional involvement and lifelong commitment—the elusive fantasy women often dream about but seldom achieve.

First published in 1996, Jacobs has sold over forty books and novellas, some of which have earned awards including the Passionate Plume (best novella, 2006), the Desert Rose (best hot and spicy romance, 2004) and More Than Magic (best erotic romance, 2004). She has been a double finalist in separate categories of the EPPIES and From the Heart RWA Chapter's contest. Three of her books have been translated and sold in several European countries.

A CPA and former hospital financial manager, Jacobs now writes full-time, with the help of Mr. Blue, the family cat who sometimes likes to perch on the back of her desk chair and lend his sage advice. He sometimes even contributes a few random letters when he decides he wants to try out the keyboard. She loves to hear from readers, and to put faces with names at signings and conventions.

Ann welcomes comments from readers. You can find her website and email address on her author bio page at www.ellorascave.com.

Tell Us What You Think

We appreciate hearing reader opinions about our books. You can email us at Comments@EllorasCave.com.

Why an electronic book?

We live in the Information Age—an exciting time in the history of human civilization, in which technology rules supreme and continues to progress in leaps and bounds every minute of every day. For a multitude of reasons, more and more avid literary fans are opting to purchase e-books instead of paper books. The question from those not yet initiated into the world of electronic reading is simply: *Why?*

1. ***Price.*** An electronic title at Ellora's Cave Publishing and Cerridwen Press runs anywhere from 40% to 75% less than the cover price of the exact same title in paperback format. Why? Basic mathematics and cost. It is less expensive to publish an e-book (no paper and printing, no warehousing and shipping) than it is to publish a paperback, so the savings are passed along to the consumer.
2. ***Space.*** Running out of room in your house for your books? That is one worry you will never have with electronic books. For a low one-time cost, you can purchase a handheld device specifically designed for e-reading. Many e-readers have large, convenient screens for viewing. Better yet, hundreds of titles can be stored within your new library—on a single microchip. There are a variety of e-readers from different manufacturers. You can also read e-books on your PC or laptop computer. (Please note that Ellora's Cave does not endorse any specific brands.

You can check our websites at www.ellorascave.com or www.cerridwenpress.com for information we make available to new consumers.)

3. ***Mobility***. Because your new e-library consists of only a microchip within a small, easily transportable e-reader, your entire cache of books can be taken with you wherever you go.
4. ***Personal Viewing Preferences.*** Are the words you are currently reading too small? Too large? Too... ANNOYING? Paperback books cannot be modified according to personal preferences, but e-books can.
5. ***Instant Gratification.*** Is it the middle of the night and all the bookstores near you are closed? Are you tired of waiting days, sometimes weeks, for bookstores to ship the novels you bought? Ellora's Cave Publishing sells instantaneous downloads twenty-four hours a day, seven days a week, every day of the year. Our webstore is never closed. Our e-book delivery system is 100% automated, meaning your order is filled as soon as you pay for it.

Those are a few of the top reasons why electronic books are replacing paperbacks for many avid readers.

As always, Ellora's Cave and Cerridwen Press welcome your questions and comments. We invite you to email us at Comments@ellorascave.com or write to us directly at Ellora's Cave Publishing Inc., 1056 Home Avenue, Akron, OH 44310-3502.

ELLORA'S CAVE
ROMANTICA PUBLISHING

1234780R00169

Made in the USA
San Bernardino, CA
02 December 2012